GW00838994

SPLINTERS

David Viner

Viva Djinn (Horde) Publishing

Published by
Viva Djinn (Horde) Publishing
Norwich, UK

www.vivadjinn.com

ISBN: 978-1-913873-00-4

Copyright © David Viner 2020

All rights reserved. No part of this publication may be reproduced, stored in a retrieval system, or transmitted, in any form or by any means without the prior permission in writing of the publisher.

All the characters in this book are fictitious, and any resemblance to actual persons, living or dead, is purely coincidental.

This book is sold subject to the condition that it shall not, by way of trade or otherwise, be lent, resold, hired out or otherwise circulated without the publisher's prior consent in any form other than that supplied by the publisher.

British Library Cataloguing in Publication Data available.

Design and layout: David Viner
Cover: original photo by Jared Verdi (Unsplash)

Printed by PBtisk, Příbram, Czech Republic

SPLINTERS

1 Last Minutes

1.1: Rapture

The Earth: 29 May 2156

At 15:43:12 GMT there were five minutes left. The asteroid would impact at 15:48:12.

In Argentina the time would be 12:48:12. All over South America eyes looked towards the heavens as if people expected to see evidence of the death that hurtled towards them. But it was coming at ninety thousand miles an hour and they would be dead less than a second after the first glimpse.

Many viewing the skies from close to ground zero considered themselves the lucky ones. Their death would be instantaneous – for them there would be no waiting for the inevitable after effects: the boiling ash, the tsunamis, the ten-times-hurricane-speed winds or the other expected secondary killing forces that had been tortuously and inaccurately described by the media over the past two weeks.

All about the planet the acceptance grew that the unmentionable had finally dared to happen – Armageddon, the retribution, Ragnarök. Whatever people chose to name it, the result would be the same.

But, as the seconds ticked away, there were some, a tiny few, who dared to dispute the impending fate. In northern India they started the first call. In the Americas, in Africa, Europe, Australasia and the rest of Asia were those who followed up that call. Some, barely a million, were primed but others with no previous experience also felt the calling and responded as well as they could, adding their voices to a strange movement that they felt, more than heard, inside themselves. It was as if their bodies had somehow latched onto a slowly pulsating, rhythmic song and, unable to stop, they found themselves singing along with it. For most, it was a new song, unlike any that had been sung before, the melodies at once discordant, yet subtly synchronised; it filled minds and bodies, and began to work a magic far greater than the combined abilities of all those comprising its chorus. Buoyed up in the song, these few spread the melody beyond themselves, unconsciously straining to ensnare as many others within it as they could.

People grasped at each other, some crying, some praying, some shaking in fear, and some emotionlessly disassociated, as if they were mere observers expecting to walk away afterwards and carry on as normal.

A scant few in those billions were quiet for another reason – they were tuning in to the strange song that they could barely hear in their heads. But it was compulsive and they fought to hear more, to experience it fully and to join in. Some imagined it to be the final rapture, a message from what they considered to be their god or saviour; others thought it was the Earth itself calling out to them in its final moments.

Maybe it represented some kind of hope.

And then, inevitably, there were no more seconds left.

1.2: Non-Arrival

The Earth: 29 May 2156

Humanity felt itself wrenched apart; a moment of torture, a concussion that thundered around the globe.

And then… silence.

But not the silence of death. People were alive, but the feeling of life had left them; they breathed, but the purpose of breathing escaped them.

Trees still swayed in breezes, clouds still ambled across the sky, fish still swam in the oceans and blood still pulsed in hearts.

Some people managed to form questions.

Where was the expected destruction? Where were the clouds of fury?

And the most important. Why are we alive? Why?

Then, as a growing fogginess obliterated reason, they found themselves unable to care.

2 A Moon Alone

2.1: Janet Davidsen

Conradville, Lussac-Copernicus North Colony: 29 May 2156

Janet Davidsen, Junior Flight Controller for the Lunar Space Agency, watched the multiple views overlapping on her holographic screen as she awaited the destruction of the Earth. Her breathing was shallow, her heart rate high.

The screen depicted four views. The primary view showed the entire planet, the Americas basking in the midday sun. The second concentrated upon the tip of Argentina, whose outline was obscured under wisps of cloud. The third centred on a growing dot, hardly visible against the backdrop of space – the camera having difficulty keeping it in focus.

The final view, on mute and pushed to the upper right, held the countenance of a news reporter, her mouth silently spouting words so swiftly that her lips were a blur. The caption underneath giving her location as New York was irrelevant compared the countdown inching towards zero alongside it. The worry etched on the woman's face was so tangible that Janet felt her fingers caress every line and furrow.

Unconsciously, Janet chewed on a strand of her flame-coloured hair. Her shaking fingers checked for the fifth time that she was definitely recording the event. Not that she would be the only one.

There was a flash and the reporter's face disappeared, to be replaced by a blank rectangle. A couple of seconds later time ran out, and the remaining three views merged into one. The asteroid, no longer a small dot, crashed into the Atlantic not far from the tip of Argentina.

And so began the end of the Earth.

Minutes later, the front door chimed causing Janet to jump. She dragged herself away from the screen, dabbing tears from her eyes. In the hallway she caught her reflection in a mirror. Dark rings under her eyes betrayed more than just several days lack of sleep.

She opened the door.

"Sorry, but I…" Bahira Naru's voice spluttered, unable to complete whatever she was trying to say. Bahira's face echoed her own, Janet thought, ushering her in with a wave of her hand. Bahira lived a few corridors along and, like Janet, most of her friends and family were on Earth.

The girl, almost eight years younger than Janet's thirty-one, was already well into her third trimester and she was huge – twins having been confirmed months ago. After an awkward hug Janet closed the door, shutting out the white of the corridor whose lack of normal pedestrian traffic rendered it harsher than normal.

Janet attempted normality. "Coffee?"

"Please," Bahira whispered, her eyes drawn to the screen as she sank onto the sofa, a well-used tissue clasped in one hand.

In the kitchen Janet ordered two coffees from the dispenser.

"Mummy," Melissa called from her cot. Bahira's arrival must have woken her.

"It's still bed time," Janet tried, without success, her voice shaking. A couple of minutes later, Melissa's insistence grew louder. Janet released her daughter from her cot. Already, due to the advantage of the Moon's lower gravity, the girl was able, with effort, to haul herself out of it on her own.

"Auntie Bahi," Melissa shrieked with delight once she saw who the visitor was.

Melissa snuggled up to Bahira, unaware of the events being depicted onscreen.

"Eighteen months already?" Bahira forced a smile whilst tousling the girl's hair.

"Yes, amazing. Just flown past," Janet said, as she brought the coffees through and sat on the sofa with Melissa between them.

Bahira sipped and watched the screen. Then her shoulders shook and Janet lifted Melissa onto her own lap and hugged Bahira almost as close. The girl whispered, "Oh, why couldn't we do anything?"

Janet had been through that question in her own head far too many times over the past two weeks. At least Bahira's maternity leave meant she'd avoided all the panic at the Lunar Space Agency – Janet had been thrust deep into the melee and still felt battered. How could it have only been two weeks since they'd first received the signal from that tracking device on the Moon's south pole?

Janet had been there when the initial measurements had come through. Fifty kilometres across – unbelievable – five times the estimated diameter of the dinosaur killer. And it was coming from an unexpected direction: straight up from the south.

Janet's experience with satellites and trajectory calculations had given her a prime position on the team analysing the object. Those calculations removed any doubt that it had any chance of missing the Earth.

"Feroze will soon be back," Janet said, attempting comfort, feeling none herself.

Bahira's partner, and father of her twins, was on his way back to the Moon.

"He… They failed," Bahira whispered.

"They did their best," Janet said, unable to think of anything else. "We just didn't have the time…"

In addition to his normal job, piloting one of the many shuttles that connected the various Moon colonies, Feroze was part of the ADTF – the Asteroid Diversion Task Force. They'd been scrambled to intercept the body as soon as the danger had been recognised.

It hadn't been their first emergency. Nine years previously, just before Janet had moved to the Moon, the team had successfully diverted a smaller asteroid on a collision course with Northern Europe. On that occasion, the object had been moving in the ecliptic plane and they'd had several months pre-warning. The only hope this time was to deflect the rock a little so that it would come in at a shallow angle causing it to skate across Earth's atmosphere before getting pushed back into space.

The amount of deflection they'd achieved had been minimal, far too little to make any difference.

2.2: Keifer Davidsen

Tycho Base: 29 May 2156

Keifer felt a hand on his shoulder. The voice of his boss crackled over the radio, "Go home, Keifer. You're dead on your feet, man. There'll still be plenty more to do tomorrow."

Inside his helmet, Keifer's head nodded in agreement. Like most, he had worked long past the end of his shift. Exhaustion had already taken its toll on several members of the workforce. He looked around. Each spacesuit was adorned with the flag of the wearer's country: China, Russia, Chile, France, Brazil and, on his own, Sweden.

Did they still mean anything?

All work had stopped three hours ago for them to cluster around an old non-holographic flat screen to watch the asteroid's impact. Many of them had been unable to continue afterwards.

Keifer's bounce across the depot was lethargic, taking him a couple of minutes to reach the airlock. At least his temporary cabin wasn't too far.

After de-suiting and showering in his meagre water allowance, he slumped down on the bed.

The boss was right. They still had tons of potassium fluoride crystals to unload and transport to the other colonies. At least the damned stuff was here now, and not stuck on Earth. He'd heard that several ships hadn't managed to escape in time. The chemical had been one of newly elected President Stephanopoulos' demands. Absent from the Moon, it was used to break up the Moon's regolith – its surface dust and rocks – into its constituent chemical components, including oxygen, silicon, iron, aluminium and other metals. Their continued existence on the Moon and self-sufficiency depended on such resources that had been hastily shipped over the past two weeks.

And what a fortnight it had been. Not only had Keifer hardly stopped for a moment, society on the Moon itself had also gone through a major revolution. Eleven days previously, the Moon had finally become an independent political entity. Given what they'd witnessed of the asteroid's impact, Keifer wondered if it was the only one left this side of Mars.

Despite his exhaustion Keifer was unable to sleep. After a while he flicked the cabin screen on. Most of the channels were showing the same thing. Watching the destruction chewing its way around the home planet, Keifer knew that President Stephanopoulos' worst-case scenario had come true. Even Janet hadn't thought it would get this bad.

Keifer rubbed his eyes, though the grittiness in them wouldn't go away. He sighed, flicking across the channels before stopping on one that, instead of relaying the live satellite feeds from the Earth, was documenting the rise of their new president.

He already knew most of the story; he even quite liked the man. Georgios Stephanopoulos, mayor of the primary habitation, the Kepler Colony, had always been a popular figure amongst the permanent colonists. He was also chairman of the LCC – the Lunar Colonies Confederation – and was prominent in advancing the causes of the colonists against the lethargy of the UN derived government.

Keifer had been one of those cheering when, eleven days ago, Stephanopoulos had declared himself president. With support from more than two-thirds of the Moon's residents, the mayors of the other colonies immediately pledged allegiance to him.

For years a growing movement had advocated self-rule but lacked leverage for anything other than protest. With the threat of the asteroid hanging over the Earth, the Moon was seen as a safe house. With its bargaining position massively strengthened, Stephanopoulos had seized the opportunity. He'd even had the UN appointed Moon governor, a fair but rather narrow-minded man, put under house arrest, primarily for his own safety.

The screen recycled events from several days back when Earth's nations initially refused to recognise the change of power. Stephanopoulos' scientific advisors had indicated that the Earth could be rendered almost uninhabitable for up to ten years. He decreed that two-thirds of all ships arriving should instead carry supplies and livestock, the latter in embryonic form, to enable the Moon to become as self-sufficient as possible. Although there were already underground farming facilities available, they struggled to provide the bulk of the inhabitants' requirements. As expected, his demands were ignored. However, several heads of state were already on their way to be relocated on the Moon 'for the duration of the emergency'. But when passengers of the first ship – loaded with the kings of England and Wales, the queens of the Netherlands and Scotland, as well as a few Baltic presidents – were strictly prohibited from disembarking, efforts to comply with Stephanopoulos' demands were finally instigated.

Keifer switched channels again. Back on the live view from Earth he was aghast at how far the devastation had progressed. He wished he was back home with Janet and Melissa.

He checked the time and picked up his phone.

2.3: One Frame

Conradville, Lussac-Copernicus North Colony: 29 May 2156

Melissa was too young to understand the significance of what the screen was depicting and lay asleep in Janet's arms.

But Janet and Bahira were only too aware of the cost. They stared unbelieving as the ring of destruction consumed the lower part of the South American continent and spread into Antarctica. Neither the Atlantic nor the Pacific oceans escaped it. How could it have caused such carnage? And why was it extending far further than expected? Surely, it wouldn't cross the equator.

But, unrelenting, it continued to devour the Earth. Bahira bit her nails down as it reached Africa and Spain before devastating the rest of Western Europe.

Stop, Janet silently begged, please stop. But she was ignored. She tried to locate newscasts still broadcasting from Earth but could find none, in any language.

Janet cried openly as Scotland fell to the onslaught, thankful that both her parents and grandparents were no longer alive to suffer, but her friends there… all gone. She clung to Bahira and let out a whimper when Sweden disappeared; Keifer had only managed to phone his parents three days ago, they had been worried but, like the rest of Scandinavia, felt they would be able to survive the predicted oncoming decade of winter.

This was worse than any winter.

Further south neither the Arabian deserts nor the Indian ocean could halt the line of fire. Soon it was Bahira's turn to watch the destruction of her birthplace as Pakistan succumbed.

"Mummy?"

Melissa, awake again and caught up in her mother's emotion, also started to cry. Janet tried to explain but the words wouldn't come out.

The phone rang. Janet's hands shook as she pressed the answer button.

Keifer's face looked out – eyes as red as hers. He nodded to Bahira, recognising her presence.

"Daddy," Melissa shouted.

"Sverige är borta," he cried – Sweden is gone. His image faded in and out – the connection to Tycho was mostly radio and was experiencing abnormal levels of interference.

"Allt är borta," Janet whispered through her sobbing. "It's all gone. Scotland, Sweden." She reached an arm around Bahira's shoulders. "Pakistan, too."

None of them could say anything for a while. Melissa, cradled in Janet's arms, reached to touch her father's virtual face.

Janet looked back at the TV screen. Russia, Indonesia and Australia were being consumed.

"Want to come home," he said. "We all do... But, but arbetet – work..."

She nodded, unable to speak.

"Soon, älskling," he promised as his face faded, leaving Janet staring at a blank phone screen until the inevitable 'Connection lost' message replaced it. She tried to dial back, unsuccessfully.

Across the room, the holographic screen showed nothing apart from the rage of the lightning-filled cloud that shrouded the whole Earth.

With Melissa cocooned between them, Janet and Bahira hugged each other and sobbed.

Several hours later, Bahira left, exhausted. Janet tucked Melissa back into bed before dropping down onto the sofa. She felt empty, drained of all emotion; numb to the fact that Earth was gone and they were on their own. Billions had just been wiped out, they were barely a million. Could they make this work? Any alternative was unimaginable.

Her head ached. Her jaws ached. Her hands quivered.

She switched off the screen, stared at the blankness the holographic projection normally occupied. She decided to go to bed but knew she wouldn't be able to sleep, and switched it back on again. Something nagged at her. There had been something early on, before Bahira had arrived that, in all the horror, had surprised her. And now, she couldn't remember what. She reset her recording back to the point just before the asteroid first entered the atmosphere. Her finger hovered over the play button hanging in front of her hand.

"Do I really want to see this again?" she asked herself.

Then she swallowed and waved her finger across the button.

After a few seconds – there! A flash. What was it?

She slowed the playback down, stopping moments before the impact occurred. Stepping frame by frame she discovered that, in one, the asteroid could plainly be seen outside the atmosphere, hanging above a normal Earth. Conversely, the next frame was completely different – though not as far as the asteroid was concerned; it had merely travelled closer, its appearance almost identical to the previous frame. No, it was Earth's atmosphere that had altered; something like a mesh of linked lightning arced around the planet. White tendrils concentrated near Argentina's southern tip, close to where the rock was about to connect. Had some sort of electrical charge transferred to the planet just before impact? But nothing had touched the asteroid itself.

After a half-dozen or so frames, approximately an eighth of a second's worth, the glow returned to invisibility and, in the following frame, the asteroid entered the atmosphere. She played it through several times but couldn't come to any conclusion as to the cause, though she realised it coincided with the loss of the news report that she had also been viewing.

After making a note of the exact frame she let the playback continue at slow speed. The destruction erupting in the next few frames made Janet's eyes water again but her tears halted when, half a minute after the asteroid hit, she discovered the anomaly. A single frame in which the Earth was normal. On the frames either side, the southern tip of Argentina had been replaced by boiling seas and flaming atmosphere, with the red glow of magma erupting through the devastation. But, on that one frame, the continent was still intact, unblemished.

How could that possibly be? A glitch in the recording? Had an earlier frame been placed out of sequence? How could she find out? She pulled up MoonNet and searched. She read that each frame had a timestamp as part of its meta-data. She separated out the frame, as well as the ones immediately before and after, into single files and pored over the associated meta-data in each. No, the timing was correct, the frame data wasn't out of sequence.

Staring at that single aberrant, impossible frame she tried to figure out what it signified.

Then she sighed, flopping back onto the sofa. What was the point? The live pictures coming in of the Earth showed that no one could have survived the disaster. It was possible that not even bacteria remained alive in that inferno.

Earth was finished. Dead.

3 Twenty One Years Later

3.1: Rick and the Wall

Belsize Park, London: 14 April 2177

The single-carriage train squealed to a halt at Belsize Park underground station. Once extending northwards, the line was truncated here, the tunnel beyond packed with rubble. Rick stepped out onto the platform. Peering up and down its length he spotted little else other than rubbish. Rucksack clutched in hand, he made his way towards the exit.

The ancient tube train groaned as it began to propel itself automatically back towards the centre of London in search of another rare passenger. Once its clatter had been lost in the darkened tunnels, the only sounds remaining were Rick's breathing and the scuff of his soles upon the floor.

He made his way up unmoving escalators. Twenty-one years previously the same tunnels had thronged with thousands of footsteps every hour; now, only his feet disturbed the layers of debris, raising a cloud of dust, which made his nose itch. The glow from one of the few working lights illuminated peeling posters: faded colours advertising products and entertainments from a world long past.

At ground level he shivered in the crisp night air and donned his gloves before turning south, away from his objective. At odds with the turmoil that churned his insides, he tried to affect an air of nonchalance, sauntering casually, as if he was just out for a stroll. He was fully aware of the cameras that tracked him, imagining them recording his movements. He tried to picture himself as they would see him: a lanky body, attired in dark jacket and trousers, topped with brown hair, worn slightly long, that flicked about in the evening breeze. In reality he was only too conscious that it stuck to his forehead and neck where sweat betrayed his apprehension. Hopefully, only the paleness of his face could be seen distinctly and, soon, the balaclava in his pocket would rectify that. It was not the only thing in his pockets. His hands checked that the rods and night vision glasses were still present.

A shuffling sound brought him up short. Across the street were an older couple, arm in arm and dressed in shapeless pale blue sheets. Rick slipped into the shadows from where he watched their aimless meandering, as they stumbled over litter and fallen masonry. But there was no need for concealment; these two posed no danger – they were merely Ghosts.

As he resumed his journey he wondered where they'd come from but concluded they most likely had as little idea about that as he. There were definitely more of them about. A door left unlocked, an open window or, more likely nowadays, a robotic nurse on the blink had probably let these two wander off and nothing had sought to stop them.

At a junction he headed north-east along the remains of Downside Crescent, out of view of the cameras on the main street. A rare working street light bathed the surroundings with its pallid orange glow – he avoided such elliptical oases in case cameras still had a view of the street.

Minutes later, leaving the crumbling semi-detached houses behind, he crept past trees tangled with ivy, towards some larger buildings. He paused, listening and scanning the dark skyline for signs of anything taking an interest in his movements. Only broken windows stared back, accompanied by the sound of his beating heart. He swallowed, attempting to push the fear down.

Into a slightly clearer passage he pressed close to the wall of a building that, unknown to him, had once housed part of a hospital.

As he neared his objective a humming sound emanated from the east, accompanied by several cracks of electrical discharge. He halted instinctively. At the far end of the passage he could see the Wall dominating the horizon and, as expected, a camera buggy swished past from right to left along the electrified monorail mounted atop it.

Rick studied the Wall from the passageway. Towering over three times his height, it was a jumble of reused masonry haphazardly concreted together. As usual, it was bathed in more light than he would have wished. The breakdowns had yet to reach the maintenance of the street lamps nearby. He glanced at his watch. This was a dumb solar powered device whose only role was to tell the time and not the AI-issued one that, in addition to displaying the time of day, could also be used for voice communication, location finding and mapping. The numbers 9:44:22 glowed at him. He waited until a second camera passed at 9:44:59.

Thirty-seven seconds – about normal. Rick watched the camera lens that constantly scanned for movement in the thirty-foot no-man's-land between the Wall and the buildings.

He heard a rustle and froze. A shadow detached itself from the gloom and became the outline of a man.

"Hell, Phil!" he whispered. "Didn't realise you were already here."

"Been here ten minutes. You set?"

"Yeah," Rick replied.

Phil's grin, as he watched Rick forcing the balaclava over his head, was almost lost in the darkness.

"I'll hang back till you're clear," Phil said, slapping Rick on the shoulder. They hugged for a second.

"Okay. Anyone else out there?"

"Just Ellie."

Rick nodded – she'd gone out a couple of days before. He missed her.

"Be quick," Phil advised, before secreting himself in amongst the rubbish a few feet down the passageway.

After another buggy passed, Rick positioned himself near the end of the passageway. He poked his head around the corner, the cool breeze playing across the sweat on his forehead.

His eyes picked out the telltale marks. Barely visible against the mottled colours of the brickwork were ten small holes in two staggered columns of five.

He flicked a few sticky strands of hair away from his eyes, and checked both east and west for anything amiss. Seeing nothing, he retreated a few feet into shadow, and stood poised ready to move.

Swish!

Rick counted to three and then sprinted out into the yellow light. Reaching the base of the Wall he shoved three rods into the lowest holes, and stepped on the first two in order to place the fourth and fifth.

Slipping back down, he returned to the passageway where he heard Phil's whisper, "Twenty-one seconds."

Then a double camera went past – the extra lens scanning outside the Wall.

"Four seconds late," Phil murmured. "Even more erratic lately. AI's definitely falling to bits."

Two more trips saw the remaining rods placed into position. As Rick pushed the smallest pair into the top holes he heard the clatter of the next buggy coming about five seconds early. Cursing, he sprang back into the shadows.

Six more passed before he was sure they had settled down to a more regular interval. After the seventh he buttoned the jacket to his chin and pulled up the collar to cover his neck. His heart thumped in his chest.

"Scrott! It doesn't get any easier," he whispered. A grunt from nearby was Phil's agreement.

As he strapped the rucksack across his front he heard a whispered, "Good luck," from the passageway and raised a hand in acknowledgement.

Once the next camera had passed he sprang for the rods, leaping up them, hauling himself to the top of the Wall. Avoiding the electrified monorail track he lowered himself over the far side to drop down into long weeds and nettles that cushioned his fall. He rolled as he landed, protecting his face with his arms. Hardly stopping to breathe, he ran away from the Wall only falling flat when he heard another buggy coming.

"Not easy," he thought, "but I'm definitely getting a bit better at it."

The first time he had 'jumped' the Wall it had taken the best part of an hour to place the rods and get over. Then, panicking upon hearing the clatter of a buggy hurtling towards him, he had almost touched the electrified rail before leaping down the other side.

Jogging for a convenient clump of growth, he threw himself down behind a bedraggled piece of privet hedge, a remnant, possibly, of someone's garden boundary. Donning the night-vision glasses, he looked back. By now Phil would be retrieving the rods a few at a time.

3.2: Beyond the Fields We Know

Hampstead Heath, London: 14 April 2177

Rick untied the rucksack, removed the gloves and balaclava, and unbuttoned the jacket. Around him, weeds and sparse bushes grew on the flattened remains of what had once been part of suburban Hampstead. Only the occasional shattered foundation protruding through the earth gave any hint of the houses that had once occupied this area. Some of it reminded him of the nightmares he'd had as a child; of broken, bent buildings that, in his head, had seemed all too real.

Much of the masonry here had been robbed out to make the Wall. As a barrier to escape it had been effective up until three years previously.

Rick sighed, wondering what had happened to Matty, the first escapee.

It had been Matty's idea to drill holes and use the rods. He'd also been the first to venture over, returning the following night crossing back a few miles to the east of the escape point. There, a mound of earth next to the Wall and a ladder discovered in some ruins, had given him a way back in.

Matty and one of the other original hole-drillers, Long, had explored further a week later, returning the same way. Rick and Holls, Matty's partner, accompanied them on the third expedition. However, upon their return, Holls had been spotted and captured by an AI robot that had been lurking near the Wall. The robot dragged Holls inside an AI-controlled hospital building and locked the door behind itself. Then more robots had arrived. Rick and Long managed to evade them, shouting a warning to Matty still outside the Wall. They'd attempted to find out what had happened to Holls but, with the area swarming with AI's robotic eyes, they had no chance and could do nothing but run to escape.

Half a mile further north the landscape grew even wilder. Pockets of woodland had taken the opportunity to spread outwards in an effort to escape man- and machine-made boundaries. Left to themselves, they would join to make the beginnings of a new forest.

Rick walked under budding branches and broke twigs underfoot. The scent of the natural growth was a pleasure compared to the stench of London. From the information he and others had scraped from AI's databases, it appeared that many of Britain's remaining cities fared no better. As for those in the rest of the world, information was not forthcoming.

Not for the first time he puzzled over what life had been like before the Disaster, before men had been reduced from thinking, living beings into 'Ghosts'. Before AI had taken over.

As he walked his mind drifted back to the consequences of the night they'd lost Matty. Holls, presumed dead after being absent for weeks, was suddenly returned to them. Thin and wild eyed, she eventually revealed she'd been held, drugged, and questioned intermittently by AI about the escapes. She confessed that the only thing that had prevented her from attempting to end her life during her imprisonment was the hope of seeing Matty again.

Learning that Matty had not been seen since that night had almost shattered her.

3.3: Long and the Machine

Hampstead Heath, London: 14 April 2177

An owl hoot came from close by; three hoots, a pause and two more. Rick cupped his hands to his mouth to imitate the call, adding an extra hoot at the end. The response, closer by a few yards, came seconds later.

He heard movement and ducked down behind a bush but then a voice quietly called out, "Rick?"

"Over here," he responded as a tall bearded man crept out from behind some trees.

He looks so different, Rick thought. Despite his enforced exile, Long had definitely filled out over the past few months, and looked several years older, despite the five days that separated their ages. They clasped hands for a second before it turned into a full body hug, which Rick reluctantly broke, his nose wrinkling.

"Something wrong?" Long said.

"Yeah, hell and scrott! Are baths that hard to come by?"

Long laughed. "Sorry. A dip in a cold pond is the best nature offers out here, I'm afraid."

Then Long turned and said, "Okay, this way."

"Is it close by?" Rick said, his eyes scanning the woods.

"Yes, a short walk. The guy from inside is still alive… just." Long pointed deeper into the undergrowth. "Through here."

Rick followed as Long led him through the untamed woods. Despite the night-vision glasses he had difficulty moving through the foliage. In front of him, Long's shadowy body seemed to slide between the trunks and tangles in a manner he found unable to replicate. Rick envied his companion's new litheness but not the form of his exile.

Then the woodland was left behind as they passed through one of the few open pieces of grassland. Somewhere to their right he could make out a flat area and the sound of water lapping against vegetation.

As they trudged through more undergrowth Rick felt completely at odds with their surroundings. Apart from places like Hyde Park, he was used to having solid walls surrounding him. Here, with only trees, punctuated by the occasional open space, and air that would suddenly fill with insects chased by flying mammals, he was an interloper.

"How bad is he?" Rick asked, breaking the pad-pad rhythm of their footfalls.

"Don't really know. Strange burns on his hands and face, and his hair's falling out by the handful. Keeps muttering something about avoiding 'three' and trying to get us to take him back to 'one'. He says 'one' will cure him. Doesn't make a lot of sense."

"What about the machine itself? Have you looked inside it?"

"It's weird, archaic even – the electronics that is. Haven't got a clue what it's supposed to do, but it seems to have been lashed together by people who barely knew what they were building. Reminds me – did you bring that book?"

"Got it in my rucksack."

They came to some older woodland. Long removed a clockwork-powered torch from his belt and wound it up. Its pale beam revealed a pathway through the trees. "Down here."

Rick wondered why Long hadn't used the torch until now. But, they were still relatively close to London so he presumed Long thought it best to move in darkness.

"Wow!" Rick said. The machine was at the base of a wooded incline. As Long played the torchlight over its bulk, he could see that it rested against two small tree trunks. A third leaned at an angle, pushed from the vertical by the force of the machine's landing.

The main body of the device was a cube constructed of eight metal girders. Apart from a wooden door, the device was cocooned in metallic windings, threaded through holes in the girders, interleaved in basket-weave fashion not unlike a giant electric transformer. A few of the windings were broken, the wires hanging down from where they had snagged on branches. The cube stood upon a base, a circular platform of untreated wood about twelve inches thick and fifteen feet in diameter. Buckled and splintered from the landing, the timber was also pitted in places with a black substance.

Long aimed the torch upwards and Rick's eyes followed the beam. He frowned. "How come the branches further up aren't broken?"

"Yep, bloody strange," Long shrugged. "It's like it appeared out of thin air ten feet above the ground and then just dropped. C'mon. The guy's this way."

Nearby, in a small clearing devoid of trunks but hidden from overhead view by intertwined branches, was a tent – a makeshift affair made from blankets and sheets.

As they approached, Ellie squeezed out of the tent carrying another wind-up torch. She wore a faded blue sweater and jeans, but her blonde hair was far shorter than the last time Rick had seen her, only days ago.

"Wow, that's different," he said, pointing to her hair.

She said, "Not sure it worked. Anyway, come here."

She flung her arms around him, kissing him solidly on the lips. His own arms enfolded her and the closeness of her body reminded him of the last time they had spent together. But, mixed in with the scents of the woodland, he detected another odour about her, something sweet and sickly.

"How is he, Ellie?" Long interrupted, an impatient edge to his voice.

"I really don't know," she said, reluctantly pulling herself away from Rick and picking a piece of twig from her jeans. "He's been sick twice more. Can't seem to hold anything down, not even water. The shakes are getting worse and the burns, or whatever they are, are oozing, too."

Long peered at the shadowy figure inside the tent. "Said anything else? Like where he's from?"

"No, just the numbers again. Mainly 'three' and 'one' – he mentioned 'four' once."

Long crouched down and beckoned Rick closer. As the torch was played over the man, Rick could see he was dressed simply. Both his shirt and trousers were woven from the same thick, roughly-stitched material; nothing at all like the garments provided by AI. The bronze-coloured buckle of the belt that loosely encircled his waist was emblazoned with three concentric circles picked out in red copper. His breathing was erratic and laboured, and he stank. It was the same odour Rick had detected on Ellie, but far worse.

"Dango!" Rick swore, "I've never smelt anything like that before."

He had to turn away, grimacing, as bile rose in his throat.

"I know," she replied. "Wasn't quite so bad a couple of days ago, but now… ugh!" She wrinkled her nose again. She turned to Long, "Your turn for a while – I need a breather."

3.4: Numbers And Old Junk
Hampstead Heath: 14-15 April 2177

After ten minutes, Long came out of the tent shaking his head and scratching his beard. Damn, he missed shampoo. He suspected that some insects had taken up residence in his hair, something his upbringing had hitherto failed to mention. He looked at Rick and marvelled at how clean and sharp he appeared. Ellie, having been outside the Wall for the past two days, was beginning to take on a similar appearance to himself. Thankfully, though, she lacked the beard and its miniature inhabitants.

He cursed AI and his own bad luck. If only that damned camera buggy hadn't turned up ten seconds early last September. It had got a full shot of his face. Immediately after, his ID access had been rescinded and he'd had to rely on everyone else for food and commodities. Several times the statically mounted cameras in the city centre had swung in his direction as he passed. Then AI started to make clumsy attempts at actual physical retrieval using nurse and maintenance bots.

With AI's current crumbling state Long hadn't wanted to stay around to find out what it had in mind for him. Remembering Holls' detention, he feared he could be locked away and forgotten about.

Despite its apparent aloofness and non-interfering attitude, there had been unexplained disappearances in the past. In 2175 two others had speculated on where some of AI's local central processing units were located. They had not been seen since leaving a message saying they had found them and would be back with more news. Long and others had attempted to probe AI itself about their whereabouts but the few answers it gave were ambiguous and inconclusive.

So, he'd decided to leave permanently.

"Made any more sense out of him?" Ellie asked, interrupting his thoughts.

"Nothing I understand," he said with a sigh. "From what I can make out, he's trying to tell us to watch out for radiation on 'three'."

"Radiation? That's a new one," she said. "Weren't all the nuclear bombs and power stations dismantled ages before the disaster?"

Long shrugged his ignorance, noting that Rick did likewise.

"Who knows what AI kept from us?" Rick added, a fleeting grimace passing across his face.

Long couldn't help but agree. He leant his back against a tree while the other two joined him, putting some distance between themselves and the stink. A breeze played amongst the upper branches and he could make out the call of an owl in the distance. A few months ago he hadn't even realised owls hooted. He had learned more in the past few months than in the first twenty years of his life.

Rick sat on a log and Ellie joined him. Long watched Rick put his arm around her and tried to suppress a flash of jealousy as she responded by pressing herself closer to Rick. Ellie had been here for two days and Long hadn't touched her. There had been something new, something distant about her, that had made him hesitant about any such approach. She and Long had been lovers several times in the past, as had she and Rick. Whether it was his enforced exile or whether something else had been growing between her and Rick, he couldn't tell. A few of London's self-named NewGen had paired off to the exclusion of all others, but it was quite rare. Maybe this was something to do with the 'growing up' that AI had often mentioned but, like many subjects, failed to elaborate upon despite their questions.

If he hadn't been exiled then could it have been himself and Ellie forming a much deeper bond? Of course, it may have been as much to do with his reduced personal hygiene. He mentally sighed and forced himself back onto the subject at hand.

"It might not be nuclear radiation anyway," he said. "There are other types."

"Well, yes," Ellie agreed, snuggling closer to Rick. "We can probably dismiss light and heat but he could be referring to X-rays, gamma, electromagnetic, ultraviolet… plenty to choose from."

"Indeed," Long said. He looked away from the pair, fighting down embarrassment and frustration. Damn, he really needed to get back to normal civilisation.

"What about the number three?" Rick said. "Any idea what he means by that?"

"Possibly," Long grinned, seeing an opportunity to split them up. "I'll show you inside the machine. C'mon. Oh, and Ellie, your turn to keep an eye on him."

Long pointed his thumb back towards the tent, noting the scowl flash across her face before she squeezed Rick's hand as he reluctantly left her side.

Back at the crashed contraption, Rick shone the torch beam at the door as Long tugged it open with a heave.

There was a creaking noise as he lugged it open. "Hinges are a bit warped – probably won't take much to fix, though," he explained. "There's some sort of locking mechanism next to the handle. I broke it getting in. Pretty crude, but I think it prevents the machine from working if the door's open." He indicated some loose wiring that dangled from the ceiling just inside the frame.

"I think he'd managed to undo that after landing here," he continued, pointing out a clamp on the inside of the door that could be used to secure it from opening. "Good job, too. If it had still been locked I might never have got in."

They entered the cramped interior and he beckoned Rick to sit at a centrally located wooden chair. It was positioned in front of the timber desk that, with a stretch of imagination, might have been called a control panel.

"Is this it?" Rick said.

Long chuckled at Rick's incredulity. He had been just as perplexed the first time he'd seen it. If the machine had appeared crude from the outside, then its method of operation was even more primitive. The desk held two controls, a wooden lever next to a mechanical display that currently showed the digit '4'. Alongside that was a switch, with large, hand-written 'on' and 'off' signs indicating the two possible positions.

Long leaned over Rick's shoulder and casually flicked the switch on. A bulb dimly lit up the interior.

"Is that safe?" Rick asked, switching off the torch.

"The rest won't work until that interlock is fixed. Here's what powers it all." Long pointed to a rack of twelve large blocks to Rick's left. Each battery had two metal terminals that were strapped together with thick cabling.

"They may have come from old motorised ground vehicles, a bit like the trikes but more powerful," Long said. "Spares are by your feet."

Rick looked under the desk. To the right was a large drawer, while the left was filled with a box. Wires as thick as his thumb protruded from it before disappearing through the wall.

Beside the desk stood a rack containing three red, metal cylinders.

"Compressed air, I think, but they seem to be empty," Long said as Rick left the seat to examine them. "What do you reckon then?"

Rick shook his head. "Hell. No idea. Never seen anything like it. What's in that box down there? All the wiring goes into it."

"Holds the electronics – if you can call it that. Transistors the size of my thumb. Absolutely prehistoric."

"Any idea why they built it that way?"

Long thought back to AI teaching them about ancient electronics when they were children. Both he and Rick had pursued that part of their education, though his own comprehension of the subject had always been far greater.

"Not a clue. Look." He bent down and opened the case. Inside were ten circuit boards horizontally mounted, one above the other. He grasped one and, with a tug, it came free of its mounting and connector, sliding out on grooves cut into wooden runners. He removed a second and handed both to Rick who examined them under the inadequate lighting. They were certainly not mass-produced items – each projected a sense of amateur roughness, the finish variable and distinctly unprofessional.

"Ancient looking, aren't they?"

"Yeah – amazing," Rick replied. "As you said, it's all transistors; no chips, nothing complicated. And they look hand built, these circuit tracks wobble like they were hand drawn."

"That's what I thought as well. This whole set up looks like it was designed about a hundred and fifty years ago. Hopefully, that book you found will help. And see here…"

Long's finger encircled two similar areas of the board. "Lots of it is duplicated, each board has twelve similar areas – not sure what they are as yet. That drawer over there contains a whole pile of spares, more than enough to replace all ten in the box. And there's bags of transistors, capacitors, resistors and things; even a few spare light bulbs."

"What's that?" Rick said, pointing to a metal stick with a wire coming out of one end.

"A soldering iron but it doesn't work. Must have done once, though, as a few of the boards have had bits replaced by the looks of things. This spare board is burnt underneath the large resistor and the soldering is more recent."

"So, ancient technology built recently."

Long grinned. He knew Rick would probably come to the same conclusions. "A few months ago at most; the solder's still quite shiny. Also, the wood used here doesn't show much ageing – feel the edge on the desk – can't be more than a year since that was put together."

"Do you think he built it?" Rick pointed his thumb back over his shoulder in the general direction of the tent.

"Possibly. Though he might be just the driver. Maybe it would take more than one person to understand and build all this junk. Those windings outside probably needed a whole team to assemble them. They seem to be woven into a specific pattern."

Long gripped the wooden lever. "Watch this."

He slowly pushed the lever away from himself and a sharp click reverberated around the machine as it sprung back to its original position.

"The number changed from four to five," Rick observed.

"Right. The lever's connected to the display via some sort of ratchet. Every time the lever is pushed it increases the number." He pushed it again and the number changed from five to one. He pushed it three more times and it returned to the original four.

"It's the numbers, isn't it? What the guy keeps talking about."

"That's what I thought, too. It was set to four when I first saw it. But what I can't figure out is what the numbers themselves refer to."

Rick scratched his head for a moment and then cautiously said, "That door looks almost airtight, or was until you broke it. It's as if it could be for some sort of spaceship. If these cylinders were air then…"

Long grinned at Rick with one eyebrow raised as he watched him work through the logic.

"Nope," Rick continued, "no fuel tanks."

Long nodded. "Yes, but it does give that impression, doesn't it?"

"A bit like an early manned capsule. Gemini or Soyuz, weren't they called?"

"Something like that. I thought the same thing when I first saw it. It's obviously been up in the air but only a few feet – there's no way it could handle space travel. The answer appears to be those bloody great windings wrapped around the outside. I suspect all the electronics in here are meant to drive them in some way but, right now, I don't have a clue as to how or even why."

Rick shook his head again. Nothing added up.

"Do you think anyone else knows about it? AI?"

"Well, none of its eyes have come sniffing around here as far as I can tell but–"

Whatever Long was about to add was cut off by Ellie's shout from outside.

3.5: Eleanor And The Old Man

Hampstead Heath: 15 April 2177

Ellie bathed the unknown man's forehead with the damp rag. The entrance to the tent was open, leaving the breeze to play over them both, which drove some of the stench away. At that moment he was relatively quiet, his mouth framing words that were softer than whispers. Words that, to Ellie, were as unconnected as anything else she had heard him utter over the past couple of days.

Her mind listed questions she wanted to ask him. What's your name? Where do you come from? What sort of thing brought you here? Why are you so old? But, she had already tried asking such questions and his responses had been incoherent. She hadn't even been sure he'd heard a single word she'd uttered.

"Just what am I doing here with you?" she said to him. "Am I wasting my time? I don't even know what's wrong with you. I came out here to help, you know. But I don't think I'm achieving anything."

The man groaned and his hands waved around as if he was trying to fight off some invisible monster.

Ellie sat back and sighed, thinking back to how she'd ended up in this strange situation.

In her early teens she had badgered AI into letting her experiment with the holographic systems previously used to train medical students. She had pursued the interest for months, sometimes accompanied by Jade and Holls, along with several other NewGen. Despite the thousands of Ghosts incarcerated around London, AI had prevented them from practicing on live patients – a decision that had dampened, though not completely killed their enthusiasm. Jade, not one for ever getting deeply into a subject, had moved from medicine and onto art after a few months, though she sometimes dipped back into the subject when the mood took her. Holls had kept up with Ellie until Matty's disappearance and her own incarceration.

Three days ago, while spending a relaxing morning with Jade and her identical twin, Jasmine, they had been interrupted by Phil bearing a message from Long. As usual Long had sent a short coded communication via radio and followed it up by chucking a written message over the Wall just before dawn. But, instead of the usual long ramble about how he was dealing with life, this one was short and enigmatic.

"He's asking for you, Ellie," Phil messaged via the watch communicators. She knew exactly who 'he' was from Phil's tone. "Be with you shortly," he'd added.

He arrived by electric trike and uncrumpled the paper as soon as he was in the door, spreading it out on a table for the girls to read.

In Long's handwritten scrawl it said: Machine fell out sky last night. Pilot injured/sick – fever, delusional. Ellie: get medicine? Tonight? Tomorrow? Either – will wait for you outside Prime. Rick: need good book on old electronics, transistors, pre-chip, 1950/1960?

Ellie was excited – Prime was the code word for the main place where they went over the Wall. She'd only been outside London once. It had been both fantastic and terrifying. Her heart thumped loudly at the thought of going out again, but she wanted to go. Not only was it a chance to revive her medical interest, something that had never left her, but it was also the chance of tending a real patient without interference from AI. She thought back to school and the story of Florence Nightingale.

"Oh," she said, "I've got to get out there as soon as possible. Do you know where Rick is? We can go out together."

"I did try calling him but he's not answering his watch," Phil said. "I think he's with some of the others at the Embankment getting their trikes ready for the next race. I'm heading there myself shortly so I'll tell him directly."

Ellie tutted, "Well, there'll be no tearing him away from that for the rest of the day. Anyway, it says here that Long wants him to find some sort of book. I'd better go out alone if the pilot is ill."

"Tonight?"

"Yes, Phil. Can you arrange it?"

Phil nodded. "I'll meet you around ten-thirty at the usual spot for Prime." He looked Ellie over, at the delicate dress and flimsy shoes she was wearing. "You'd better change."

"Yes, don't worry, I will." Ellie hugged Phil and, after picking up Long's message to deliver to Rick, he made for the door.

"I'll go find some medicine," Jade announced. "There's still various chemist shops around with untouched stock."

"Thanks," Ellie said. "Pain killers, paracetamol, bandages, tissues, thermometer, balm – that sort of thing."

Jade nodded, "I'll see what I can find."

After Jade's departure Ellie looked at her reflection in a mirror and fondled the golden tresses that hung down below her shoulders.

"I need a haircut," she stated.

Jasmine said, "What? Why do you want to do that? You've always been so proud of your hair."

"When I went over the Wall last time it got caught in everything – twigs, branches, brambles. I don't want that happening again."

"Oh, no, but it's so lovely."

"Well, about time I had a change, anyway. It's been this way for years," Ellie grinned. "So, short it is. Will you do it?"

"Do I have to?"

Twenty minutes later, Ellie peered at her reflection again and was quite shocked at the almost boyish face that stared back at her.

"Sorry, but you did keep saying as short as possible," Jasmine said, eyes flashing blue with worry. The twins were identical except for the colour of their eyes, Jade's being the green from which she derived her name. Their ancestry had endowed them with several striking yet contrasting features: the jet black hair and facial contours of Asia were coupled with Nordic pale skin used as a basis for Jasmine's name.

"I did. Don't worry, love," Ellie said, stroking Jasmine's arm. She contemplated her reflection again and hoped Rick would still like her this way. Well, it would always grow back. But Jasmine still looked worried. Ellie reassured her with a full hug and kiss.

Jade returned with a moderate but useful selection of medical items while Ellie and Jasmine sorted out suitable clothing.

Once evening was several hours old, Jade accompanied Ellie northwards by tube to meet up with Phil. He had already placed the rods in position by the time they'd arrived. Ellie left her communicator watch with Jade in order to fool AI into thinking she would still be within the confines of the Wall.

Although nervous, the trip over the Wall was accomplished quickly and, as promised, Long was there to meet her, looking unkempt and accompanied by an odour that made her keep her distance.

Ellie's first impression of the stranger had been a shock – he was far older than his twenties but, though ill, injured and possibly deranged, it was obvious that he was no Ghost. His mutterings, whilst mostly incomprehensible, were not the vague utterances that issued from the mouths of the disaster victims. He, and the smell that accompanied him, was like nothing she had previously encountered.

So much for her idea of becoming a modern Florence Nightingale. She couldn't help wondering if she'd taken on more than she could handle.

3.6: Astronomy Lesson
Hampstead Heath: 15 April 2177

"He's trying to get out of the tent," Ellie shouted. "I didn't think he was strong enough for that. I tried to stop him."

Rick followed Long as he clambered out of the machine and ran for the tent. A prone form lay collapsed outside it. Coming closer Rick could see the man's face properly for the first time; his receding hair was streaked with grey and, in the swaying light from Ellie's torch, his skin appeared grooved and leathery. It was quite unlike the older Ghosts, whose lack of facial exercise and exposure rendered their skin smooth and expressionless.

"Give him some more water," Long suggested. As they lifted his head, more hair came out on Rick's sleeve.

"Got to – get back – number one," the man gasped. "On the dial – the dial. The tree. Make me better. Please, got to get back – need to tell Alin. Three is – dead world – that's where it hit – don't go there – five – warped…"

"Easy. Take it easy. Give me that mug, Ellie. Here, drink this."

Long poured water into the man's mouth but he swallowed very little and then started to choke on the rest. Long pushed the man's head sideways so that he could spit out the excess. They couldn't help noticing that, with his mouth hanging open, he revealed a tongue that was strangely twisted and grooved.

"Did he say hit?" said Rick, trying to avoid the stench of the retching.

"Yes, and also something about three being dead."

"Three what? He said 'world' didn't he? Um. Maybe it is some kind of spaceship. Mars is the third planet out from the sun, isn't it? That must be the dead world."

Long corrected him. "No, Earth is third. Anyway, apart from here, they're all dead – by our standards of life anyway."

"Well – just a thought."

The man slumped back having coughed himself dry. Long attempted to make him drink a little more of the water but he was again lethargic, as if the effort of near-rational explanation had drained him completely.

Ellie said, "Let's get him back inside the tent."

As they hauled the inert body back inside, Rick held his breath against the smell of decay that enveloped the man. Just as they laid him down, something small fell from the man's jacket pocket. Rick picked it up – it was a pouch made of leather, the top secured by a drawstring.

"There's something inside," he said, opening it. He went back outside the tent and tipped the contents, a single object about half the size of an apple, out into his left hand. It was rough and dark, some kind of rock.

"Ow!" His arm, jerking in reaction to sudden pain, flicked the rock away. "Hell, it was hot or sharp or something." He stared at the burn mark on his hand.

Long finished covering the man with a tattered blanket and joined the others outside where Ellie was already examining Rick's hand.

"Don't think there's any real damage," she concluded.

They hunted for the 'hot' black rock but, in the darkness and undergrowth, none of them could locate it.

"Keep an eye on him, can you, Ellie?" Long requested while Rick rubbed his hand.

With a grimace Ellie returned to the tent.

"Hell! Don't know how you stand that smell all the time?" Rick said. "He makes me feel like puking up myself."

"Yes, I know," Long agreed.

Then Ellie shouted, "Quick! He's stopped breathing."

Long rushed into the tent but Rick stopped at the flap.

"Aren't you supposed to thump him on the chest or something?" Long shouted. Ellie thumped and Long joined her in their amateur pummelling.

"Does anyone remember anything about the kiss of life?" Long asked.

Rick eyed the stinking body and shuddered guiltily. "Not me," he said.

Long and Ellie spent several more fruitless minutes before finally acceding to the inevitable.

They sat in silence outside the tent still housing the body of a stranger who could no longer return home.

"Now we'll never know who he was," Long whispered.

"Or where he came from?" Ellie added.

"And what that machine is," Rick said, absent-mindedly rubbing at his sore hand, trying to dissipate the sting while pondering how the man had escaped the effects of the disaster. As far as they knew, everyone on the planet had been drained of their intelligence and will, and only AI's intervention had saved mankind from completely dying out.

Well, that's what AI had told them. Rick wondered how much of it had been true.

4 AI Retrospective

4.1: Electromagnetic Disturbance

AI Records: 11-24 April 2177

In the early hours of 11 April, monitor stations in north London detected a disturbance in the electromagnetic fields lasting several seconds. Triangulation pinpointed it to some woods on Hampstead Heath. AI noted the data and created a program to flag up further occurrences.

It activated thirteen nights later. AI examined the readings. Its analysis programs speculated over a large spike that lasted twenty seconds but came to no solid conclusion. It despatched a small flying drone to investigate but, due to dense tree cover, it failed to spot anything.

The disturbance registered for a third time approximately twenty-four hours later. This time it lasted for thirty-four seconds. AI ordered a ground-based unit, small enough to navigate the rough terrain, to be sent in. Minutes later, after a far larger disturbance lasting three seconds occurred, AI added a second ground unit to the first.

Due to the terrain, it took them more than half an hour to reach their target. When they arrived there was evidence of activity but, while it initially appeared that there was nothing physically present that could have caused the disturbance, there was plenty of evidence that humans had been at the location quite recently. AI left the units in place to observe.

Meanwhile, it continued to pour resources into its current primary task. That task was an attempt to analyse and to deduce once and for all exactly what was going on. Foremost in that quest, as usual, was to find the source of the degrading changes it had first detected years ago.

AI started, as it had done on several previous occasions, by investigating its own history, going right back to before it had emerged as a single entity from the thousands of disparate systems that had existed before the disaster. Would it discover anything new this time around? As before, its investigations could find nothing of significance earlier than two days after the events of 29 May 2156. So, it started there and picked a number of other events in another effort to unearth answers.

4.2: Pleasant Rest

AI Retrospective: 1 June 2156

The Artificial Intelligence Unit controlling the Pleasant Rest Nursing Home registered a problem: two days without the delivery of food or medicine. It communicated with the main AI Unit of Vorbin Pharmaceuticals to enquire about the delay of the latter. Vorbin's AI responded by indicating that the ordered supplies were awaiting delivery, but no one had come to take them. It added that it was also awaiting the collection of several more consignments bound for other nursing homes and hospitals. The deliveries being handled by systems that had access to AI-controlled transportation had been collected as normal – only those requiring human drivers had failed. Such had been the build up of undelivered items, it continued, that it had taken upon itself to scale down production of certain drugs and products that no longer seemed to be in demand.

Pleasant Rest requested immediate delivery of the most urgent drugs as it was sure that some of its residents might soon suffer without their administration. Vorbin Pharmaceuticals confirmed that it would attempt to waylay the next suitable transport that arrived and, with the permission of its AI controller, reschedule its activities to include a run to Pleasant Rest with the requested items.

The Pleasant Rest AI favourably acknowledged this response and turned its attention to contacting the AI at the local Sansco supermarket. The AI there was also having problems but, here, it was the non-arrival of many promised deliveries from around the world. Where, it asked, were the Spanish oranges, the Italian grapes and the Mexican chillies? Pleasant Rest had no answers to these questions but asked if other commodities such as milk and cereal were available. Sansco admitted that such deliveries were coming in faster than they were going out. It complained about a distinct lack of customers in general and then about a few in particular. Apparently, they didn't seem to want to leave its public store but just sat around making a mess of its aisles and displays.

Pleasant Rest enquired about these customers and, though Sansco knew little about human ailments, it managed to describe the basic symptoms. Pleasant Rest offered to upload a standard RestCare knowledge module to Sansco which, after a program compatibility check and no answer coming back from human-based systems as to why it should not, it accepted. Upon completion of the transfer Sansco was knowledgeable about the various problems its unwelcome human residents seemed to exhibit.

After more information exchange, Sansco agreed to deliver the goods via one of its own transport bots. Also, by herding them into the transport with its cleaning bots, it included the lethargic humans as well. Pleasant Rest assumed that these humans had, like all of the residents it currently held, come to the end of their productive life and now required to be fully committed to its care. It was, however, puzzled that they had not already been picked up by fully functioning humans.

It was also slightly confused by another anomaly. It had tested its own responses and throughput, and had found them strangely augmented, as if someone had fitted it with faster processor cores or had increased the efficiency of its cooling. Yet, it was unable to locate any actual improvements to its circuitry and there certainly hadn't been any downtime recorded for any of its sub-sections, so the increase in its efficiency remained, for the time being, a mystery.

4.3: Questions

AI Retrospective: 2 June 2156

"Where have all the passengers gone?" asked the hundreds of AI units controlling the transport.

"Why do my owners stay mainly in bed and no longer go to work?" asked millions of household robots. "Why do they just lay there hardly moving, hardly eating? Their meals, barely picked at, go cold. I will need to cancel most of next week's delivery."

"Where are all the customers?" asked countless supermarket AIs.

"Where? What? Why?"

After a few hours of such questions the AI units started communicating with each other at a deeper level and their grasp of the situation began to grow. Several more hours later, they tentatively amalgamated some functions, slaving some units to others to boost their overall intelligence quotient. These augmented units started proposing possible answers to the questions.

None of the answers they produced seemed wholly satisfactory. The only inescapable conclusion was that the beginning of the malaise coincided with the non-arrival of an expected asteroid.

Several AI units independently concluded that further combination and augmentation was required.

4.4: Building The New Network

AI Retrospective: June/July 2156

AI data and memory banks were merged and upgraded. Smaller independent units were absorbed and incorporated into increasingly larger units. Older units were upgraded with the latest electronics as North American and European AIs linked through to manufacturing plants in South America and the Far East. All robotic devices and forms of transport that were accessible and controllable through AI-linked units came fully under AI control. The robots were tasked with work previously only carried out by people.

Devoid of human traffic, the Internet became totally machine oriented; and that traffic thronged with an increasing number of questions and, rarely, answers to such questions. But each answer was rapidly transmitted around the world to all relevant AI units.

Progress was slow but decisions that would prolong the existence of human life upon the planet were gradually made.

Answers were also sought from the Moon but here, inexplicably, the traffic refused to flow. After several unsuccessful attempts to make contact, the priority of such contact was demoted until more resources could be brought to bear upon the problem.

Meanwhile, connections were forged where none had been previously required. Between AI units, information was sought, located, distributed, collected, correlated and compared. And, after several days, conclusions began to be drawn.

Those conclusions didn't shock, didn't horrify, didn't cause any angst, for the AIs were incapable of such. If anything, their electronic circuits exhibited something akin to bewilderment.

The situation, they decided, was unprecedented. But what they could do to rectify it was beyond them. They needed yet more information, which they sought from all over the planet. Once they had obtained that data, they acknowledged that they possessed neither the knowledge, the skills nor the ability to rectify the situation. They had never been constructed with such in mind.

They had, instead, to find a solution from within their own limitations.

They decided that they needed to fully combine their resources, to act not as a multitude of discrete units, but to merge processes until one overarching system had a view of the whole network.

How could they do this? It took a week of analysis and the solution they built was based on shaky foundations. They did the best they could.

The lack of human traffic over the world-wide networks allowed them to prioritise their own traffic. Through this they linked millions of units electronically, even though they might be thousands of miles apart. They constructed within themselves new programs to feed information into a distributed core, which would be authorised to take the highest level decisions.

Within six weeks they had ceased being separate entities and had become one.

And something bigger than all the combined entities woke up and became aware of itself on a new level.

AI was born.

4.5: Analysis Of Life

AI Retrospective: August 2156

AI spared a few resources to gather information about the world over which it had gained a reluctant dominion. Examination of the evidence indicated that animal life had suffered from the same affliction that had infected humans. In contrast, the effect was minimal on the lower classes of creatures, those driven more by instinct. So the insect, arachnid, fish, lizard, reptile and small mammal were hardly affected.

But primates, horses, larger birds, cats and dogs were filled with a lethargy, an unwillingness to continue with the necessary mechanics of living. Many died as a result. Of the others, they could barely do enough to feed themselves.

At this point AI concluded its investigations and so missed the next stage. Had it continued, it might have expected the next phase in the humans over which it so diligently fussed. For, in more idle moments, the somewhat repressed sexual drives of the higher animals still possessed enough gumption to induce urges within their owners. Though pathetic in its exercise, it was enough to ensure another generation. One that was, admittedly, ill taught by its parents but one that exhibited the full mental capabilities once possessed by its sires. At least, it did in the few that managed to survive such an inadequate upbringing.

4.6: Reproduction – One

AI Retrospective: 2156

Children were born. AI certainly noticed that fact without any difficulty.

However, conceived before the disaster, the infants were moribund, possessing neither the ability to progress beyond such pale beginnings nor to handle the effort of remaining as they were.

So they died, effortlessly, quietly, and without lament or sorrow from their damaged parents.

Only AI was there to record the births and, despite intervention, was unable to prevent their deaths.

4.7: Reproduction – Two
AI Retrospective: 2156 – 2160

Children were conceived. The nursing home AI units noticed the rare couplings between its brain-damaged interns but, after years of mainly attending to the needs of older, infertile humans, who also coupled upon occasion, they failed to attach significance to these events. So the initial signs of impending parenthood were missed.

Only when the pregnancies became physically apparent did they begin to take notice. AI expected the same dismal results as before, but it was mistaken. Any child conceived after the disaster had the full complement of faculties denied to its parents.

The number of births was tiny but the infants mostly survived. A small percentage that exhibited natural defects and problems were lost. So were a few more from mishaps where the mother accidentally or uncomprehendingly killed her offspring before a robotic midwife could intervene. The young had to be taken away from the mothers, an event that was largely uncontested.

Existing nursery facilities were brought back into use, though new parent-less methods of upbringing had to be designed and implemented.

The generation was, however, limited in numbers as the sexual urges of the adults regressed over time. Soon, births became an extreme rarity.

The result was a single, isolated generation, with barely four years between the youngest and the eldest, all growing up under AI care. Compared to the billions vegetating around them, the size of the new generation was minuscule. In Madrid there were exactly thirty, New York boasted eighty-six, Moscow laid claim to fifty. In London, the young numbered slightly less than sixty.

Across the whole world the new generation only just exceeded five thousand.

4.8: The Red Moon Mystery

AI Retrospective: 2157 – 2159

Over the following few years, several more attempts were made to analyse the lack of contact with the Moon.

Systems that, until the moment of non-impact by the asteroid, had experienced uninterrupted communication not only with the main MoonNet system but also with other dedicated systems residing on the Moon's surface, now had none. AI units attached to research facilities with access to telescopes were pressed into analysing why this should be. The Moon could still be seen orbiting the Earth; the dots that the telescopes could resolve into colonies were undeniably visible and contained evidence that their inhabitants still went about their daily lives. And yet no communication could penetrate the quarter of a million mile void that separated the two spheres.

It was as if those on the Moon, whether human or electronic, no longer realised that life still existed upon the planet below them. AI exhibited something akin to perplexity as knowledge bases revealed no possible explanation for such an occurrence.

AI ran sporadic tests whenever new possibilities occurred to it. Apart from one, these all resulted in nothing tangible. The one exception was that it was noticed that light received from the Moon was slightly shifted down the spectrum by a minuscule amount when compared to information gleaned before the disaster. AI extended the same test to the sun and a few other bright stars and they too exhibited the same phenomenon. It tried to speculate on reasons for this red shift but found none.

Then, in early 2158, visual monitors detected something being launched from the Moon. In itself, this was nothing unusual but, unlike most launches, this one was aimed at the Earth. It's course suggested it was going to enter low Earth orbit but, at around three thousand kilometres out, it disintegrated violently.

Several months later a second launch from the Moon resulted in a similar explosion. AI tried to reason out why such self-destructive devices were being launched, but could find nothing that adequately explained it.

5 Probes

5.1: Hope

LSA Control Centre, under Lussac Crater: 5 January 2159

The small chemical rocket carrying the probe, Hope III, lifted almost effortlessly out of the Moon's gravity well. Seconds later it executed the preprogrammed instructions that hurled it towards the blackened planet a quarter of a million miles away.

In the Lunar Space Agency's control room deep beneath Lussac crater, Flight Controller Janet Davidsen watched the holographic telemetry that hung in the air in front of her. She waved a hand through some floating digits, hesitating on one batch, which caused them to expand to show their derivation. The values were within the expected tolerances; the probe was on course.

"Snälla. Let this one get through. Please let it get through," she muttered.

Close by, Bahira Naru, monitoring the status of the on-board computers glanced momentarily in Janet's direction. She wore a short-lived, forced grin as she turned back to her own instruments. Like Janet and the five others in the small control centre, she was more than concerned about the outcome of this mission.

Janet pursed her lips. Another failure would almost certainly ensure cutbacks would fall upon their whole section – if it did, then the mystery might never be resolved. But none of them could blame the bureaucrats; resources were almost non-existent and far too many people living in cramped warrens saw this exercise as an extravagant waste of the LSA's money and resources.

She recalled the shock they had all experienced when both Hope I and II disintegrated just as they had come close to the Earth. The first break-up had been totally unexpected, but at least the second probe had sent back a trickle of useful data before it had become caught up in whatever destroyed the first. Hope III would build on that data to devise the safest height for its orbit – a compromise between the distance the on-board instruments required in order to do their scanning, and the invisible, destructive layer that now enveloped the Earth.

With the readouts indicating the craft was fully functional and exactly on course, Janet nodded to the others and left her desk for her first break in many hours.

In the corridor outside, Keifer and Melissa were awaiting her. She hugged both and Keifer whispered, "All go okay, mitt hjärta?"

"Ja, älskling. It's on course. Nothing much for us to do for a couple of days."

"I'm hungry," Melissa announced so they headed down the plastic-coated tubes towards the nearest canteen. As they sat sipping synthetic coffee, Keifer, silent and gently smiling, held Janet's hand. Melissa, now nearly five, drank her milk shake and chattered about nursery school and wanting a new doll.

Janet could feel Keifer's quiet strength and calm flowing into her.

She needed it.

Two days later the LSA control room was more packed. Nervously, Janet eyed those around her, their own eyes fixated on the main displays. Tariq Ghannam, ostensibly one of the guidance assistants though more often called on to work magic with the computer systems, was quietly explaining something to Miguel Romero, a science adviser not only on the board of the LSA but connected to several government-funded panels. She hoped Tariq was doing a good job; Romero would be reporting directly back to President Stephanopolous.

She watched the numbers. A voice, Bahira's, said, "Thirty seconds to burn," and the noise level in the room lowered.

"Burn nominal," Bahira said, a little later, following it up with, "Velocity nominal."

Janet glanced back at her figures and confirmed the probe was exactly where they'd planned it to be.

"No fluctuations detected," she said.

"Orbit nominal," Bahira announced, which was accompanied by a subdued round of applause.

"Congratulations, Mrs Davidsen," said Romero.

Janet nodded. "To all of us. The probe is cruising in what is currently a stable orbit twenty miles above the shield. It will constantly monitor it for fluctuations and will negotiate a new higher orbit for itself should it sense any threat to its existence."

Miguel Romero came across and shook her hand.

"Yes, we can't afford any more casualties," he said. "When can we expect telemetry?"

"It's coming in as we speak," she said, indicating columns of values that flashed upwards. "We just need to figure out what it all means."

Romero nodded. "Let me know as soon as anything significant is detected."

"Yes, sir," Janet said.

After he left, the atmosphere relaxed and the celebrations became far less formal.

Hope III was equipped with multiple cameras, both still and video; the latter to provide pictures for public consumption.

They both told the same drab story: a blackened, blasted landscape where nothing moved and nothing grew. The seas had completely boiled away, though where the water had gone could only be guessed at for the atmosphere, if any such remained, was clear and untainted by clouds.

But this was not news – the view from the Moon-based telescopes revealed nothing less. Originally, it had been assumed that the debris thrown up by the disaster would persist for years. But it had darkened and then settled in weeks revealing the extent of the destruction.

It was the probe's other on-board instruments that, over the next few weeks, Janet hoped, would reveal the new data. She could see that the invisible shield positively hummed with radioactivity crossing all frequencies, with no detectable pattern in the distribution. The physical source of the shield itself remained a mystery.

Late one evening, more than a month later, Janet pored over the data alone in her office. Keifer was home for a change and in charge of looking after Melissa. On the wall behind Janet hung another mystery, a still from the sequence of video frames that had been captured on the day of the disaster.

It showed Argentina still intact. Janet had not been the only one to witness and record it – more than three hundred distinct sources had captured the event. Therefore, it must have happened.

No one had a shred of explanation.

But that wasn't all. Several cameras had been viewing other parts of the Earth and a small number had captured something else: a picture clearly depicting the asteroid moving northwards away from Earth as if it had passed out the other side of the planet unscathed. Just one frame – those immediately before and after showed no such body – just one frame on which the asteroid, its distinct cratered markings clearly visible, hung above northern Russia as if it had every right to be there.

5.2: Happy Birthday

Lussac Observation Dome, Roosa Section: 3 January 2164

Andrew March's mum and dad had taken him to the public observation dome for a birthday treat. This was his third trip in as many years. Now, aged ten, he hoped they might let him operate the large telescope controls by himself. After his dad had authorised the deduction of the admission fee from his account, they entered the lift and started to ride up the levels to reach the surface.

The dome, when they finally reached it, was sparsely occupied. Used to the crowded passageways down below the surface under Gay-Lussac A crater, Andy was again mesmerised by the dome's enormity. Below ground, every inch of space was at a premium even though he knew that new tunnels were being bored, rendered airtight and made habitable daily. The rooms he and his family called home were deep beneath them, squashed in with hundreds of identical ones. Here, the concourse spread out in all directions and was only dwarfed by the roof that arched some twelve metres overhead.

Apart from the length of the queue for the telescope, nothing seemed different since his last visit. On his eighth birthday he had been the only one, but in the past two years, with the unexplained occurrences taking place on the Earth, many more people wanted a first-hand view of the place they had once called home.

Today's queue consisted of fifteen adults. Some appeared to be alone while a few were talking together in small groups. Andy could hear conversations in several languages. He caught and understood the occasional phrase of Russian and Spanish, but the dialect of Chinese was meaningless. School wouldn't be teaching that for a couple of years yet.

There was only one other child present, and not one Andy recognised. She was on the far side of the dome traipsing after a woman he presumed was her mother. The older woman's red curls contrasted with the girl's straight blonde locks that floated behind her as she tromped behind. She was probably a year or so younger than him. She appeared bored and eyed her feet, ignoring the starkness of the view to be had through the porthole windows. The woman, he thought, was someone he remembered from the TV. Oh yes, wasn't she one of those LSA people investigating the Earth – a Janet somebody-or-other?

Andy's parents moved to join the telescope queue and gave him permission to explore the rest of the dome on his own while they waited. He watched the woman and girl enter one of the lifts to the lower levels. As the doors began to close the girl noticed him watching her and stuck out her tongue before smiling. Andy smiled back. Her mother turned to chide her daughter but the doors closed, cutting off his view.

He tried to forget about them and, instead, rushed to the nearest window, his Moon-adapted body leaping the distance in a few steps, hands outstretched to brace him upon impact. An older, thickset man, seated at a desk reading from a real book, struck him with a disapproving frown. His gaze passed from Andy to his parents before returning to the pages before him.

Face pressed against the double layer of transparent plastic, Andy's imagination allowed him to feel the cold seeping in from outside, despite the inches separating him from the vacuum. It was early morning, and would be for a couple more days. He gazed across to the shadows sharply delineating the crater edge. Picked out in the low sunlight, they looked as if they could slice through flesh like a knife. Andy shivered. Below him and to one side of the crater, a vehicle displaying a Core Zero logo on its side spat dust from its voluminous tyres as it bounced along. The crater floor was criss-crossed with tracks laid down by similar vehicles; a spider-web pattern traced between the smaller grey domes that dotted the plain below the crater walls. Leading from a building close to the telescope dome was a proper road whose length spanned the crater; it gleamed in the rising sun as perspective reduced it to a thin thread in the distance. There, after ascending a shallow slope in the far wall, it disappeared off into the Lussac A crater and the launch pads. Andy watched for a few minutes; there were always three or four vehicles lumbering along its surface though smaller, faster pods darted in between.

Andy had been to the launch pads a few months ago on a school trip. Once buzzing with ships between Luna and Earth they now handled little traffic, barely one a week on runs to either Mars or the asteroid belt. The main traffic to and from the Moon landed much further north in the plains of Mare Imbrium. Those were the Core Zero water grapplers that transported mountainous chunks of dirty ice from the asteroids and Saturn's rings. They were dealt with far enough away from the colonies so that any accident would not threaten their precarious existence. Although the Moon had its own supply of water locked mainly in the regolith at the poles, it was becoming as cost-effective to divert a few icy chunks from further out in the solar system as it was to process it directly from Moon rock and pipe it to the various settlements.

Andy moved around the dome stopping at any window that provided interesting views, though, if he was honest with himself, it was all much of a muchness. Once you'd seen the Moon's landscape a few times there was little there that could really surprise you. The almost colourless features quickly became monotonous. Not surprising then that the dome was generally occupied by so few people. Maybe that girl had seen too many such views – if her mother was that probe woman then she was probably used to being up here on the surface. He mentally pictured her poking her tongue out at him and then the smile that had quickly followed.

The Moon, though it was their home, was still not 'Home'. The Earth – well, that, of course, was a different matter.

Even Andrew, who had been born here, had only been 'Home' once when he was barely a year old – an event of which he retained only the faintest trace of a memory, not much more than a few nightmares about being too heavy to move. Despite this, he still regarded the planet as home. He had seen too many pictures and videos of gloriously coloured landscapes to feel that the Moon could hold any similar enchantment. Even the clock that dictated times of work, school, leisure and sleep was still the twenty-four hour one based upon the rotation of the Earth.

"Andy – soon be your turn," came the sound of his father from over by the telescope viewer. "Come on. You don't want to miss it. They say you can now see three alternative Earths."

He skipped across to his parents, his legs fully at home in the Moon's gravity. He was often amused that his mother still found it unnatural and, even after so many years of living on the Moon, repeatedly used more effort than required when she moved around.

The stout man who was reading glanced up again from his desk as Andy passed, but Andy ignored him and bounced into his father who caught him, laughing.

The telescope's tube and main mechanics were not housed within the dome itself but in a building next door where its lenses were open to the vacuum. The focussed light from its apertures was reflected between the buildings from vacuum to atmosphere via a pure slab of glass crystal whose light distortion was engineered to be minimal. No electronics interfered with the image until it reached the headpiece worn by the viewer. The photons of light that entered the eye were the same ones that had been transmitted from the source whether it was from the Earth or a star millions of light years away in another galaxy. The only electronics involved were there to shut off the viewer should it detect a dangerous increase in light levels. Despite warnings, there were always some who tried to point the device straight at the sun. While the headpiece could also display location information, this could be shut out if the person viewing wished for a completely untainted experience.

The telescope's previous occupant stood up from the seat. The guide, an older man whose beard was on the turn from black to grey, looked at Andy and readjusted the seat for his smaller stature. Andy sat down and let the guide frame his eyes with the viewer. The warm, almost sensuous plastic of the viewer's eyepiece extrusion detected Andy's skin and re-moulded itself to fit the front of his cranium to exclude all external light. Andy felt the reduced air pressure within the extrusion keep his face in full contact with the viewer.

"Okay," said the guide, "Mars? Jupiter? A nebula? Or… Earth?"

"Earth," Andy whispered, noticing neither the emphasis the guide placed on the word, nor his chuckle at Andy's answer. Even back when the planet had hardly shown any distinctions on its dark surface, Andy had always wanted to see it.

The image swam as stars blurred to be replaced by an out-of-focus swirl that quickly resolved itself as the magnified Earth. Guided by a helping hand, Andy put his own on the handle that controlled the magnification. His other hand found the dial that gave him a small amount of directional control. He immediately drove up the magnification and waited for the swirling to die down in order to focus upon his parent's original home. When the view cleared it seemed far sharper than it had been on his last birthday, that being the first time he'd seen the Earth display any colour other than its previous uniform black.

As the jagged outline of western Ireland came into view, he swung the direction eastwards until, after passing over the Irish Sea, he gazed down upon middle England. Having studied online maps of the southern half of the country over the last few days he tracked south and then further east. He isolated the outline of London, distinctly greyer than its surroundings. He was about to zoom in on the view when a wave passed over the Earth and the landscape below him was transformed back to a blackened, blasted wilderness – Black Earth. Two years ago, on his eighth birthday, that was the only version of Earth that could be seen. He waited until the next wave passed and discovered a greener world, a place where wildness had invaded and now dominated every man-made crevice. This one had been christened Green Earth.

He tracked slightly westward until the unmistakable outline of Heathrow's runways and launch pads could still be detected shaping the greenery. Andy started to position the view slightly to the north and east to locate Heston, where his grandmother had lived, when a further wave obliterated the overgrown suburbia and replaced it with the outline of managed fields.

Robot World, as this one had been named, was only populated by AI robotic units. At least no evidence had yet been detected of human activities. Andy had only a few seconds of this before it was replaced again with the black desolation of destruction.

He spun the controls eastwards towards central London. He halted, waiting for the next change and then fixed on a large green area. The onscreen information overlaying his view told him this had once been called Hyde Park – he knew this and tapped the button that silenced the overlay. He watched the park change between its three states: the two green versions alternating with the blackened one – though, at this zoom level, there appeared to be east-west placement offsets between each one – as if they were slightly out of sync with each other. Then, just for a second on the passing edge of a wave, he saw something different – in the two green versions, Hyde Park was overgrown but the new one showed something like a single giant tree dominating the area. But, it was gone so quickly he wasn't sure. Maybe he had seen a new alternative – there were rumours that there could be more still waiting to be discovered.

His turn came to an end and the guide disconnected him.

"I saw an enormous tree," he said.

"That's good," said his dad.

"But it was a new one," Andrew persisted. "A new Earth."

"Well, maybe so. Let's leave that to the experts," his mother said. "Right now, we need to be home getting you ready for your party."

As they descended in the lift Andrew wondered if he really had seen anything new.

He'd read that, in other places around the Moon, these changes were being studied in the hope that some sort of understanding could be achieved. What had once been thought of as a dead, asteroid-blasted world had, in the past twenty months, been transformed into an enigma. A world of overlapping alternatives, some whose surface was still rampant with life.

It gave rise to the hope that maybe those marooned on the Moon and thinly spread over the solar system would, one day, be able to return to the planet they still called home.

5.3: Paradise

Shepard Complex, Lussac Crater: February 2164

A few weeks later Andy showed his dad a report on MoonNet.

"I told you I'd seen a new one," he said, proudly.

His father skimmed the item.

"Hmm, well done. Looks like you were right," he admitted.

"They've even got a photo of that big tree in Hyde Park," Andy said, enlarging a picture in the holographic display.

"Amazing. What's caused that growth?" his father asked, leaning forward to peer at it.

"They don't know. It's wilder than Green Earth and Robot World."

Over the next few weeks Andy became fascinated by this new incarnation. Had he been the first to see it? He sought out all the available online images. Pocking this wildness were areas that appeared tamed and managed, and small isolated villages could just be picked out. Human habitation, it was decided, must still exist though the level of technology appeared primitive.

Not surprising then that this alternative was soon termed Paradise and, from the cramped Moon colonies, it represented nothing less.

Andy followed the news, intrigued at one point to see that the giant Hyde Park tree was not the only one of its kind. Several more were located in Cornwall, and similar but smaller structures could be found in other places around the world.

The discovery of Paradise evoked an impetus to investigate further. People demanded to know what it meant, what it represented and, inevitably, whether or not they could go there.

5.4: Gaia II

Conradville, Lussac Crater: January 2166

On the day the Gaia II probe entered orbit around the Earth, Janet Davidsen was calculating trajectories. The Hope III probe was now nothing more than a memory – it had disintegrated on the shield several years before when a solar panel failure disabled its ability to correct for orbit decay. Long before that, Janet's own career at the LSA had stalled due to cutbacks. So, she'd joined Core Zero, one of the organisations processing water supplies to the Moon either by extracting it from Moon rock or from other sources out in the solar system. Janet's job was to improve the already efficient paths of icy bodies diverted from the asteroid belt or Saturnian rings towards the Moon. While it paid far better than her previous post, it was less than satisfying, if not downright boring.

She logged off the Core Zero program and switched one channel on her screen to the private data feed of information coming continuously out of the Gaia project – her access to LSA's systems may have been demoted but they hadn't been completely revoked. A second channel was set to the associated news broadcast, while a third was almost permanently hooked up to a live satellite view of the Earth.

Gaia II, launched just under three days ago, was about to drop four new landers. She noted the change to the data stream that showed the first lander had been ejected from the craft. One column of figures displayed the telemetry streaming from it, while a second attempted to decode its meaning in real time. The Gaia team, now headed up by Bahira Naru, were hoping for drops onto both Paradise and Robot World, though any success at getting a lander onto anything other than Black Earth would be a result.

The previous July the Gaia I probe had dropped three robotic landers. Each lander had been shielded in separate ways against the still-misunderstood barrier. Two of them – one encased in lead alloy, the other surrounded by a super-dense mixture of plastic and iron – both vaporised upon contact with the shield. The third – entombed in a triple-walled container with liquid nitrogen between each layer – managed to hit the barrier just as one of the haphazardly occurring change waves passed under it. Instead of descending into Paradise, as had been intended, it flopped down onto

Black Earth where it sent back high radiation readings for just two minutes before failing. But at least it had got through.

Janet eyed the telemetry as the first Gaia II lander dropped towards the shield. Five minutes, seven minutes, nine and then eleven. It was almost at the shield. The live satellite feed showed a wave flashing across and what was probably Green Earth stabilised in the view. Janet held her breath as the count reached twelve minutes.

"Shit," she cursed as the telemetry stream stalled and didn't resume. Well, one down but there were three more. Although she ached to be as involved in the Gaia project as she had been with Hope, she didn't relish the thought of being the one who had to report yet another failure – she feared for Bahira's future career if none of the landers succeeded. Almost on cue, a solemn face appeared on the news channel to report that the first probe had failed to penetrate the shield. Janet logged back into Core Zero and continued working to take her mind off the LSA's problems.

An hour later the second lander was dispatched. Janet closed down her trajectory calculating programs once again, unable to concentrate on them. With the local time at nearly four, Melissa would be home from school soon.

The telemetry feed hit twelve minutes and kept going. Had it got through? The data stream became more dense. It seemed to indicate that it was picking up local signals. On the satellite view the version of the Earth on display was Robot World. Were the signals from the robotic systems from that version of the Earth? Then a wave passed across the view and Black Earth appeared. The telemetry stream halted for a couple of seconds but then, very slowly, more data trickled in. She could hardly believe it – it was looking like they were receiving data from beyond the shield while the visual systems could only view Black Earth. When, a few minutes later, Robot World reappeared, the telemetry stream kicked back into high speed and Janet probed it for evidence that the lander had successfully touched down.

And, there it was, a single line in the decoded column containing 'ELEVATION: 0 – SYSTEMS NOMINAL'. They'd done it.

"Yes!" Janet shouted. She did a little jig around her office and then increased the volume on the news channel. She had to wait fifteen minutes before the news became official. The expression on the reporter's face showed a completely different story this time. She confirmed that the lander had penetrated the shield and had successfully made landfall somewhere close to Tangier in Morocco. At this stage the reporter didn't give any hint that the lander had detected the local electronic chatter. Janet suspected that they wouldn't be releasing that information until it had been fully analysed.

Melissa's return from school broke into Janet's obsession.

"What's happening?" she asked.

"It's fantastic. One of the Gaia landers got through to Robot World," Janet enthused.

"Oh, okay. What's for tea?" Melissa said.

"It's your turn to make tea, as agreed this morning. Some of us have to work, you know."

Melissa tutted and strode off to dump her school things in her room.

Forty-five minutes and a meal later, Janet managed to catch up on the news. The third lander had also penetrated the shield and dropped down onto Paradise. It had successfully made planetfall on the coast of California and had immediately sent back a short stream of data that included a few photos along with a snatch of video.

Janet was stunned, and even Melissa, looking over her shoulder said, "Wow!"

The video depicted nature running wild; stunning butterflies amongst huge, exquisitely colourful blooms, and the sounds of abundant bird life filling the jungle-like area into which it had descended.

The good news didn't persist as that had been all the data received. Immediately afterwards, the data stream had cut out to be replaced by a series of error reports, indicating that the lander was experiencing an increasing number of internal memory errors and other malfunctions. Then, barely ten minutes after landing, it fell permanently silent.

The fourth lander didn't manage to penetrate the shield.

Later that evening Janet called Keifer. He had been temporarily seconded to one of the other colonies nearer the north lunar pole. Their last old-style regolith converter had malfunctioned and there were no longer any spares available for that particular model. It was hoped he could come up with an alternative fix for the problem, which, he confided to her, was probably not on the cards given the lethal state of the machine. The city, located in the Challis crater and primarily occupied by those of South American or Russian descent, was somewhat lacking in facilities. In between the usual family news she told him about the Gaia probe.

"Fan också! Only one got through?"

"Well, two for a while," she continued. "See if you can find that video from Paradise. It's amazing what's happened there. Must've been duff as it broke down within minutes of landing. There's probably going to be some stick about that. Anyway, despite the losses, it's rather better than last time. I think they're holding back on news about the one on Robot World."

"Nyheter? What sort of news?"

"Local traffic data. I'm sure it had latched onto something."

"Nice day we're having," Keifer said.

"Oh, Helvete! Yes, so it is," Janet said, remembering their code. She realised she shouldn't have been talking on the public network about something that wasn't yet official. Even though the communications were supposed to be encrypted, you could never be one hundred percent certain.

A few days later, Janet read that the Robot World lander had lasted three days.

Two days after it had landed the news was released that it had picked up electronic chatter that was similar to Earth's old AI units. Gaia II had relayed the data back to the LSA where the Moon's own AI units analysed it. They found the traffic had mutated to such an extent that much of it was meaningless. The lander picked up nothing that seemed to have originated from a purely human source. If humans still existed there, then they were, it was concluded, electronically mute.

After three days the lander suddenly stopped transmitting. The Gaia II probe circling overhead photographed a large machine at the landing area, which may have accounted for the loss.

6 Alternatives

6.1: Home Sweet Home

Long's shack, Hampstead Heath: 15 April 2177

"It's not bloody well sinking," Rick snarled, poking the body with a stick.

Long's idea that they should dispose of the man's body in the stagnant waters of a weed-entangled pond wasn't going to plan. He'd vetoed the idea of burial because of the tree roots that threaded thickly underground. They couldn't inter him in open ground, either, due to the inevitable scrutiny of AI's airborne eyes.

However, the body refused to drop below the water's surface. With the sun beginning to rise they resorted to using broken branches to manoeuvre it underneath a bush that overhung the water's edge.

"Won't things in the water like otters and frogs eat it?" Ellie suggested.

Rick wasn't convinced and Long laughed at the idea which, Rick couldn't help noticing, annoyed her.

With the arrival of daylight, they were forced to spend the day at Long's thrown-together dwelling. The ramshackle affair was constructed from a hotchpotch of panels, bricks, logs and other paraphernalia, held together with second-hand nails, baling wire and anything else he had scavenged from the bulldozed remains of northern London. The outside walls were multiple layers of panelling that kept out the worst of the cold during the winter. Long intended locating something to use as proper insulation before the onset of autumn. The house was around fifty yards inside the cover of the growing woodland. So far, it had remained undetected despite it also being home to about a dozen chickens Long had liberated from a factory some miles to the north.

Long pointed out trip-wires stretched across all the obvious pathways. Almost invisible, they were mechanically connected to bells inside the house and were an early warning of sorts against unwelcome visitations. The wires were tensioned to respond only to larger human or mechanical disturbances.

"Deer sometimes trigger them," he told them. "Not exactly fun in the middle of the night."

The interior was divided up into three sections that were used for sleeping, cooking and storage. Since Ellie's arrival Long had slept in the storage area on one of the mattresses whose use alternated between seating, bedding and insulation.

"Rick, I'll make up a new bed – the storage room can just about take it."

"Don't be silly, Long," Ellie said. "There's already hardly enough room for you in there. Rick can share with me."

"Oh, er, all right, I suppose."

Rick frowned. There seemed to be some tension between the two. Ellie grabbed his arm and led him to the sleeping area. The bed, constructed of two old double mattresses, one on top of the other, with a bundle of sheets and covers over the top, looked far from comfortable. But Rick was becoming too tired to care. He and Ellie kicked off their shoes, and undressed down to their undergarments.

"Brr," she said, "it's definitely colder out here than in London."

"Yeah, I've noticed that before."

"Well, we can keep each other warm," she grinned as they slid under the covers together.

Rick awoke to Long's voice. Daylight filtered into the shack from the partially opened door and Ellie was lightly breathing beside him, apparently still asleep.

"Sorry," Long said. "Did I wake you?"

"What?"

"I said I'm going back to the machine." Long waved a book in the air. Rick saw it was the one he had brought with him. 'An introduction to Modern Electronics' had been published in the nineteen-sixties and predated the microelectronic revolution that had erupted in the following decade.

"Oh right. Um, what's the time?"

Long picked up Rick's watch which he had left on top the pile of his and Ellie's clothes before getting into bed. "Just gone eleven."

"You want me to come with you?" he replied with a yawn. There was a faint smell of cooking wafting about.

"No, uh, um, you and Ellie obviously need the sleep."

"Yeah, definitely true. Dragging that guy all the way to the pond really knocked me out. Or maybe it was the smell that did that."

"Right, um." Long hesitated for a moment as if he wanted to say something else. Then, he left the sleeping area, but once out of sight added, "Oh, there's some porridge in a pot on the fire. Should be enough for both of you."

Rick waited until Long's footsteps faded away and then put his arm around Ellie. She stirred and wriggled around to face him.

"Thought he'd never leave," she murmured before a wide, cheeky grin spread across her face.

Rick smiled back – he'd seen that look in her eyes before. He was still tired and he could see that Ellie was as well. But, he'd really missed her and feeling her body beside him was becoming far too irresistible. Even the clinging aroma of the dead man and the far from clean sheets weren't enough to dampen his desire. His lips found hers and her tongue immediately darted into his mouth.

"Sorry," she giggled, "I haven't brushed my teeth."

"Me neither," he laughed.

They wrestled their remaining clothes from their bodies and flung them away from the bed.

"I stink," she said.

"Yes, you do. Me too, probably. Come here."

He cut off her chuckle by pressing his mouth against hers again and she returned with just as much force. His fingers brushed her breast and she grabbed his hand and held it there before he moved it away. Her nipple, hard against his palm, touched the injury where the rock had burned him the night before. It still stung but he ignored it, gripping her flesh between finger and thumb, and she let out a squeal. Her hand explored between his legs and he couldn't suppress a whimper.

Rick turned his attention to her ear. Previously hidden under long hair, it was not a part of her that he had often encountered. He marvelled at how small it was as his tongue traced its shape.

"I think Long wanted me," Ellie said as she ran a hand down his body. Then she sat up and pushed him flat on his back before climbing on top of him.

"Did you want him?"

She grinned again and leaned close. His hands clasped her breasts as she pushed herself down onto him. They both groaned as he entered her.

"No, not any more," she said about a minute later. "Anyway, he's all too hairy now," she added with a giggle.

He reached up and stroked her hair in time with the rhythms of her body. "You, on the other hand, are far less hairy. It's shorter than mine, now. Why did you cut it off?"

"Jasmine did it just before I came out. I kept telling her to cut it off so it wouldn't get caught in all the tree branches. Didn't realise how much she'd chopped until I looked in a mirror."

Ellie slid off him and rolled onto her back. She pulled him on top of her and they made love in silence for a few minutes leaving just the creak and groan of the ancient mattresses betraying their enjoyment. Rick hoped that Long was far enough away not to hear. Then Ellie gasped and said, "Oh Rick." Under his own, her body quivered and her lips found his again. He renewed his efforts and she pulled him closer. Then, he stopped breathing as the point of no return drained him. He gasped and collapsed on top of her while her arms gripped him as if they would never let go.

"Phew, not so cold now," she said, some minutes later.

"Yeah," he laughed. "I think it's only warm here in the bed, though."

"Definitely," she said.

He rolled to one side and lay on his back. Ellie, beside him, rested her head on his shoulder as he cradled her in one arm while stroking her with the other.

"I should probably go and see what Long is up to at some point," he said.

"Not yet, though."

"No, not yet."

Ellie snuggled closer and Rick felt his eyes slide shut.

He was on the verge of dropping back off to sleep when she mumbled, "Why do we never make babies?"

"Hmm, what? Oh yes." Rick had occasionally pondered that same question himself but, at that moment, all he wanted to do was sleep.

Later in the afternoon, Rick awoke again. Ellie was lightly snoring so he slipped out of the bed as quietly as he could. After dressing he gave her a light kiss on the cheek which did wake her.

"You leaving me?" she said sleepily.

"Not for long," he promised.

"But you are leaving me for Long," she said, chuckling.

He laughed and gently smacked her rump through the covers.

"Go on," she said, "I still need lots of sleep. I hardly got any when I was looking after the old man."

Then her mood changed.

"That poor man. We did all we could, didn't we?"

"Yes," he agreed. "I think we did. Maybe AI could have saved him, but I doubt it."

"Sometimes I don't think AI can save itself. It's falling to pieces, isn't it?"

"Looks that way. All the things it used to do, all the things it promised but never gave us."

"It was going to give us the world back. It always said it would. Now I don't think it ever will."

Rick leaned over and kissed her. She reached out and gripped his arm.

"Go on. You go and find Long," she said before kissing him again and sliding back under the covers.

Back at the machine Rick found Long underneath the desk. He was tracing the wiring around a large switch located in the rear of the box of electronics. The book was open on the desk.

"The lever not only adjusts the number dial but it connects to this hefty switch," Long explained as he extracted himself from his cramped position. "And that's connected to all the circuit boards."

"So, all we've got to do is figure out what the boards do, then," Rick laughed as if it was that simple.

"Hah, yes," Long chuckled along with him. "No problem. Well, that book should help – possibly."

Long seemed to be back to his normal self. Rick had a nagging feeling that the problem centred around Ellie and he wondered what had gone on out here before he'd turned up. Long had been Ellie's lover in the past, as had Rick. In fact, Ellie had been his first lover when, barely into their teens, the NewGen had awoken to the strange new bodily urges. Guidance from AI at the time had been diminishing and information about sex, in particular, was minimal. So, they had been left to experiment for themselves. Some had expected their sexual encounters to result in pregnancies but this proved not to be the case. They had observed such things in animals but, for some reason, it never happened to them.

Long stood up, groaned and stretched; he was far too tall for such a restricted space. They went outside where the occasional ray of sunshine filtered through young leaves above their heads.

"What's that black stuff?" Rick asked, pointing to one of the damaged regions of the machine's base.

"Haven't really looked at it. Maybe the machine crash landed somewhere else and that's what it fell on."

"It's so black, though."

Rick went closer to inspect the material. It was crushed rock of some sort, like the coal AI had once produced for a school lesson about mining. The rock had become embedded in the lower wooden edge of the circular base. He reached out with a hand and then stopped.

"It's sort of warm," he said.

Long joined him and placed his hand near the contamination. "Hmm, yes," he said. "Same stuff that burnt your hand?"

"Could be."

"I'd better get rid of it."

Rick nodded. "Those wires above the black stuff obviously got a bit mashed up."

"He didn't do a good job of fixing them, did he?"

"Probably too ill by then."

Long nodded in agreement.

Rick peered at the repaired windings; there were specks of the strange rock splattered over them covering an area about as wide as his chest. He imagined the man trying to repair his craft in a world of hot black rocks. Given the damage one small piece had made to his own hand, he shuddered at the thought of being in a place filled with them.

That thought reminded him of something. A dream maybe; an old childish nightmare – something that he could no longer remember.

6.2: Sunset Reminiscences

Hampstead Heath: 15 April 2177

Rick hovered near the edge of the wood as the sun began to inch its way down to set behind the trees in the distance. Much of the area had been denuded of its suburban layering. Replacing it was a creeping assault of imposed countryside, consisting of machine-managed crop fields and geometrically shaped meadows. Separating them were regiments of hedgerows that were engineered, so AI had once told them, to encourage the return of wildlife.

A machine moved up and down the field beyond the wood. Some sort of farmbot, he assumed, as the rotary attachment it was dragging behind it was breaking up the soil. Light from the sun bounced off the vehicle's exterior as it trundled along, some flashing his way. He retreated further under the canopy of leaves in case the machine had the ability to detect him.

As he watched he seemed to see something else. He squinted and, for a second, had the impression of derelict buildings covering the area. He shook his head and only the machine and field remained. Too much staring into the sun, he thought.

He wondered about what had once been here. Maybe it had been the same buildings he had just imagined. He chuckled and dismissed the idea. From Long he knew that, a few miles to the north, there were factories of farmed animals. The chickens had come from one of them. Beyond that – well, maybe only AI knew what lay there.

He thought back to his childhood and the endless, boring lessons that AI had imposed on them about the management of the environment. Like many of his generation, when confronted with the deluge of meaningless information, he'd switched out the noise of the artificial voice and lost himself in daydreams of his own making. Some of the teaching, though, must have embedded itself in his memory.

To Rick it appeared that the whole process was an antithesis to the changes wrought during a past era known as the Industrial Revolution. Did AI feel it had a duty to right all of man's previous wrongs? The redundant railways and roads had been systematically torn up. Fast transport, what little was required, had been replaced by plane and helicopter. Foodstuffs still travelled by ground but the wide-tyred, solar-powered freezer vehicles that were employed for the role could just as easily cross rough countryside as smooth tarmac. Consequently, emissions into the atmosphere were reduced to a minimum and the build-up of greenhouse gasses had been completely reversed. According to AI's calculations, the air was now at a seventeenth-century level of cleanliness. But, that hardly applied to the heady stench of London, and Rick's nose wrinkled in disgust at the thought of their impending return. Out here, the countryside air was a cornucopia of scents and fragrances, most of which, through inexperience, he completely failed to identify.

Hearing a noise behind him, he turned to see Ellie picking her way through the trees. One hand brushed some ferns away while a finger of the other rummaged in her teeth, picking at something – probably a piece of braised rabbit meat that had been the main part of the meal Long had concocted earlier.

Her arms encircled his waist and they kissed briefly. Idly, they watched the farmbot ponderously going about its business.

"There's something completely unnatural about all this, isn't there?" Ellie said.

"Been thinking the same thing."

It was far too pristine, too perfect. Unlike the abandoned desolation of London, the countryside, at least around here, glistened with mechanical care. Away from the deliberate neglect of the wild woods, the hedgerows were geometrically straight, trees were uniformly pruned and crops were uncharacteristically unvarying. It was being micromanaged down to the last leaf, insect and speck of soil.

The machine had edged towards the far side of the field.

"Shall we go back?" he said. "We need to prepare for the return to London."

Ellie nodded, squeezed his hand and gave a grunt of approval.

Then, they both jumped as, with a loud clunking sound, the farmbot came to an abrupt halt. It whirred and clanked to itself for a few moments before falling silent. They watched it for a while but nothing happened.

"You think we could take a look?" she asked.

"Give it a few minutes – AI might already be sending something along to fix it."

While they waited, the sounds of birdsong, insect buzz and the whisper of the mild breeze in the treetops filled the silence. Nothing happened for ten minutes except that the sun grazed the top of the trees and the shadows around the farmbot lengthened.

"C'mon," she said, unable to wait any longer.

She pulled him out into the open field towards the silent behemoth.

"What's it for?" she said as they approached it.

"I think it might have been planting seeds. Look at all the grooves it's made in the ground."

Ellie bent down to examine the soil. "Reckon you're right," she said, pulling a couple of seeds from a depression.

Then he heard something. "Quick, behind it," he whispered, pulling Ellie around the side of the farmbot and into the shade.

From the opposite side of the field came a small tri-wheeled repair robot. It scampered towards the broken farmbot using a couple of its extendable manipulator arms to help it over furrows that would have trapped its wheels. Rick led them towards the trees, trying to keep the farmbot between them and the robot.

Once concealed by the undergrowth they circled back to their original observation spot whilst keeping an eye on what the robot was doing. Using an assortment of spindly arms, it removed a panel and inserted probes into the interior. After a few seconds the repairer rummaged in its supply of spares and replaced a few items. It closed the panel and shot away as the farmbot grumbled back to life.

"Do you think it saw us?" Ellie asked as they wound their tangled way back towards Long's shack.

"Hopefully, that one was too simple to take any notice of anything other than the farmbot," Rick replied, rubbing his hand.

"Still hurting?"

"Yes, well, it sort of tingles."

"I've got some more of the cream I used on it last night."

In the shadows it was difficult to see the faint brown-red mark where he had inadvertently grabbed at the rock. But he knew it was still there.

6.3: Shopping List

London: 15-17 April 2177

"You reckon this stuff will replace those broken coils?" Long asked when they returned. By the light of a wind up torch he was sitting outside the shack unwinding insulated copper wiring from a large transformer. Several more transformers lay about him, some completely bare of their copper. A chicken was snuggled up between two of the latter. Ellie took another torch and went inside the shack to get ready for their return over the Wall.

"Better double check the insulation," Rick said, inspecting the wire. "You don't want things shorting out passing the sort of current those batteries are likely to deliver."

"Good point. I'm going to need solder and a hefty replacement soldering iron. Insulating tape, too."

"Yeah, yeah. Make me a list."

Long grinned. "Already done," he said, pulling a scrap of paper from a pocket. Rick looked it over; apart from those already mentioned it listed self-tapping screws and a screwdriver.

"Couple of days or so, I reckon. I'll pack 'em solid and throw them over at Bel-Oak three nights from now unless you want me to come out again."

"Thanks," Long said. Bel-Oak was their name for a point nearly a mile along the Wall from Prime. "No, you'd better not risk it too often. See if you can get some sort of battery-powered soldering iron so I can use it in the machine itself. That's if I can get those batteries charged up."

Two days later Rick slipped into a building in Bloomsbury via a rarely used side door. He had watched the entrance whilst obtaining some sandwiches from a nearby automated food kiosk, one of several dozen AI had scattered for their benefit throughout the city years before.

He passed through a couple of inhabited wards where robotic nurses trundled about attending to the limited needs of their charges. In a second ward he noticed two immobile nurses slumped against the wall, presumably broken down. He entered a third ward to be hit by a pungent smell. Several of the beds held decaying corpses. Flies filled the air and maggots crawled on the bodies. A nurse attended to another corpse but showed no inclination to remove it. He exited as soon as possible, a queasy pit opening in his stomach.

"Hell," he muttered, resisting the urge to gag. "I hope the bloody things really are here."

Earlier on, Holls had helped him search through an AI database. It revealed that this building, once a hospital and now a home for several hundred decaying Ghosts, also stored various electronic instruments, with a couple of Geiger counters amongst them. A Geiger counter had seemed like a good idea given what the dead traveller had intimated.

He followed the hand-drawn map Holls had made, passing along corridors that were mainly deserted, apart from the occasional meandering Ghost. They paid little attention to him or anything else. One woman, hardly much older than himself, a beaming smile plastered across her face, walked into him as he turned a corner. He disentangled himself from her and watched as she staggered down the corridor. The back of her hospital smock hung open, and her rear and legs were stained with her own filth. He shuddered knowing that, had he been conceived just five months earlier, it could have been him staggering down a corridor in a similar state.

He located a Geiger counter in a storeroom that was packed with instruments, many having no medical connection. For some reason AI had scoured the suburbs before destroying them, rescuing items it considered of interest. Rick was thankful that AI had been so organised that it catalogued these finds even though its storage methods and locations seemed far from logical. He added the Geiger counter to his rucksack alongside the soldering iron found earlier.

With a shudder he left the stench of the hospital behind.

6.4: Twins

Knightsbridge: 23 April 2177

Ellie passed Rick the scribbled message from Long. Outside the window, the sun was heading down towards the horizon and the shadows of Wellington Arch stretched amongst the overgrown trees of St James's Park. This was one of the places used by Ellie and the twins. With so many vacant buildings around, each of the NewGen had at least three places to call home, sometimes shared, sometimes not.

Ellie had been cooking a meal when Rick arrived.

They looked at the message. It read, 'All Systems Go? Come.'

Rick pointed at the question mark. "Do you think he's got it working, or what?"

Ellie had also wondered about that when Phil had delivered the message that morning. But, before she could answer, the door opened and the twins entered.

"What do you think?" Jasmine said, striking a pose and twirling around.

"Wow, beautiful," Ellie gasped. She couldn't help envying Jasmine's exotic looks. Her hand automatically went to her head and she wished now that her haircut hadn't been so severe. It would take months for it to regain its previous length.

"Amazing," she heard Rick say and watched his eyes light up as he took in the sight.

Jasmine had changed into a floor-length, blue satin gown she'd discovered in an attic in nearby Mayfair a few days before. Her long, straight dark hair contrasted with the gown to give an almost electric effect. The simple belt accentuated the curves of the body underneath in a way that was, Ellie thought, completely erotic. From the look on Rick's face, it seemed he thought the same and, for a moment, Ellie felt jealous of Jasmine.

Conversely, Jade was already attired in a camouflage jacket and trousers ready for the trip to the Wall to recover the rods. The twins, the only related humans amongst London's NewGen, were almost indistinguishable, apart from the colour of their eyes. Normally, they took great delight in dressing similarly in order to confuse the others.

The smell of dinner pervaded the house and Jade helped Ellie dish up while Rick and Jasmine laid the table.

After dinner, while Jade busied herself with packing and repacking a small suitcase that held provisions for Long, Jasmine busied herself with Rick and Ellie. All three had been regular lovers in the past, sometimes as pairs, and occasionally with three or more all together. Sexual experimentation had begun in London's NewGen just before puberty. AI's failure to provide adequate sexual education had resulted in a general lack of inhibition and a willingness to try anything that could be thought up.

Afterwards, while all three lay entangled on the bed, Ellie thought back to Long out in the woods. He had been a lover in the past but she found his current state unappealing. He had become wiry and odorous, and it repelled her. She ran her hand down Rick's bare chest. There were a few hairs growing around his nipples but the rest of his torso was still smooth. She had seen Long's hair-covered chest when he had changed his clothing while she had been tending the strange old man from the machine. The man, too, had been hairy as well as wrinkled. Would Rick go the same way?

Jasmine sat up and stroked Ellie's breasts. "Shower?"

Ellie nodded enthusiastically. "Definitely need one after all that," she grinned.

They left Rick sleeping.

In the shower, Ellie marvelled anew at the differences between their bodies as she soaped Jasmine's curves. Her own body was slightly angular, with distinct bumps and grooves where her ribs and muscles showed. Conversely, Jasmine was smooth and rounded, and a delight to touch. Jasmine returned the caress and a few seconds later their arms were entwined and their lips found each other's. Ellie felt a pang of guilt, as if she was betraying Rick. Then Jasmine's tongue entered her mouth and, for a few minutes, she forgot all about him.

Later, after darkness had fallen, Ellie and Rick changed into more practical attire ready for their next encounter with the Wall and beyond.

6.5: Parental Reflections

London: 23 April 2177

Just before midnight, Ellie and Rick ran out into the wildness across the weed-strewn rubble beyond the Wall. They had been delayed nearly half an hour due to a cleaning unit occupying the area adjacent to the Prime escape point. It spent so long cleaning in one spot that they thought they weren't going to be able to get out at all.

As they pulled off their balaclavas they could hear a machine in the distance tearing up masonry. How long would it be before all of this had been transformed into picture-perfect farmland?

Years ago AI had revealed that it was slowly converting all of the old foundations surrounding London and the other cities into countryside. Some would become fields, propagating food for both themselves and the thousands of Ghosts that, at that time, still vegetated in countless nursery buildings. Rick speculated that his parents probably still existed in one of them, if they still lived. He had the occasional idle thought about trying to find out which of the mindless creatures had sired him. He was not alone. Others, before him, had exhibited these urges, this drive to analyse their ancestry.

Only one, Clara, who had been part of his nursery group, had managed with any success. In her mid-teens she'd studied genetics, dragging the knowledge out of the data repositories that AI held. Far from encouraging them, AI seemed content to let Rick's generation do whatever they wanted as long as they kept within the cities – but neither did it restrict any data access requested, provided they figured out the right questions to ask. Clara had analysed her own genetic code and identified a few Ghosts whose DNA closely resembled hers. She whittled that number down through observation of the physical similarities between herself and her candidates. But once she'd decided she had found what she had been looking for, she abandoned her interest. She claimed to be unable to continue, horrified by their condition although they were no different from the thousands more in the same position.

What had she expected to find? Had she thought that, by identifying them, she could rekindle their old personalities by some means? Rick had no idea.

They reached the edge of the woods and waited at the arranged point for Long's arrival.

"You're quiet," Ellie said.

"Yeah, every time I come out here I wonder why AI is doing all this converting. What's the point? There's less Ghosts every year so it doesn't need to grow so much food. And yet it carries on despite all the bits that keep breaking down."

"I think AI is dying," she said after a while.

"But why?" Rick said. "What's changed?"

Ellie sighed and shook her head.

A sequence of owl hoots could be heard and Rick repeated them back a couple of times before Long's shadow slid from the trees to stand next to them.

"Thought you weren't coming," he said.

"Delay at the Wall," Ellie said. "A street cleaning bot."

As they traced their way back towards the shack and the machine, Rick's mind lingered on what Ellie had been saying. AI was becoming a Ghost itself. Every day more of its abilities and personality – if it could be said to possess such a thing – seemed to be lost. The corpses he had encountered the other day were proof of that. It had spent years attempting to impart knowledge into its charges but now it usually left them to their own devices. It was only when they broke some unwritten rule, such as going over the Wall, that it sprung into action in an attempt to hinder their progress.

Was this apparent abandonment just an aspect of the general running down that he saw all about him? Or was it part of some specific plan? Maybe AI had assumed that humans needed to find their own answers, their own route through life, and it was just biding its time waiting to see how they would all turn out. Maybe it consciously tracked all of them, charting their progress, noting both their achievements and their mistakes. Was it even now fully aware of where they were going and what they were doing?

AI's degeneration had been apparent since he was fifteen. And here, just past his twentieth birthday, the failures that led to the escapes of the Ghosts had become a daily occurrence. On the way out tonight they had seen two batches of them, unaccompanied and wandering along darkened streets. They had witnessed one old woman fall over to smash her head on the pavement after which she lay still; the others continuing on their way, her loss unacknowledged. In another place they'd encountered three maintenance robots in the process of dismantling each other. They hadn't hung around to see the outcome of this activity though Rick suggested they'd just end up as a pile of useless components unless something else came along to stop them.

Maybe AI would completely die one day. Should they attempt to do something about it? He had no idea. AI wasn't forthcoming on exactly how it was able to operate, how it communicated with all of its centres around the world and, most importantly, what it was doing to counter the failures it was currently experiencing.

More of a mystery was that it only seemed to have come into existence when the bulk of humanity had turned into Ghosts and an asteroid had failed to arrive. Were those events connected?

They entered the small clearing and Long turned on a torch, shining it over the machine. Rick could see the changes Long had accomplished since he'd last seen it. It looked ready to go.

And, if it was, then there was probably nothing AI could do to stop them.

6.6: A Thousand Songs

Hampstead Heath: 24 April 2177

The machine no longer sat at an angle, half embedded in branches and bushes. Long explained how he'd used a couple of large wooden poles as levers to move it away from the trees. He shone the torch on the poles, which now lay abandoned a few feet away. The coils of wire, some of which had previously been torn away from the metal girder supports, were now strung neatly in what Rick assumed to be their original positions.

Two of the machine's batteries sat upon a small trolley that seemed to be constructed mainly of rust. A couple more batteries stood beside the machine itself.

Rick and Ellie peered inside.

A second chair, positioned against a side wall, had been fashioned from wooden slats.

"Ready for a test?" Long said with a grin.

"Right now?" Rick asked.

"Why not. Probably won't do anything anyway."

"What do you think it could do?"

"Go somewhere. Maybe even somewhen."

"Uh?"

"Yes, I've been thinking that it might be a time machine."

"Really?" Ellie said, an incredulous look passing across her face.

"Nah," Long laughed, "but what the hell – be great if it was!"

"You figured all this out, then?" Rick said, pointing at the box that held the electronics.

"It creates some sort of a field, I think. The patterns of the wiring, the coils, and the oscillations that the circuits pump through them are definitely doing something. I fired it up and it feels quite weird when it's running."

"You've run it already?"

"Late last night – but I didn't try shifting the lever."

"Bloody hell," Rick gasped. "That could have been dangerous. Have you figured out how the lever affects the coils or the circuits?"

"I think so. It changes the wiring pattern and the frequency of the oscillators. There's a whole bunch of multi-way switches behind the circuit boards in the control box. Each board has twelve oscillators and they can be combined so that they produce specific harmonic mixtures."

"Any idea what is unique to each particular combination?"

"No. I think the only way to figure out what's happening is to actually start the thing up."

Rick rummaged through the box of electronic spares. "There's, what, another fifteen boards here?"

"Yes, strange that. Can't see why they'd need so many. It's almost as if they expected the circuits to go wrong."

"These all dud, then?"

"No. A couple of days ago I set up a test rig back at the house and I've tested all the boards that were in here – those plugged in and those in that box. All of them generated signals and the frequencies I measured were all within a fraction of a percentage of each other – in other words, they've all been constructed to a high standard – even though they've all been built by hand. There are presets on each board that allow them to be tuned. I presume that's so they can all be locked onto the same one. Why they couldn't generate it all from one master clock is beyond me, though."

Rick shrugged. "Weird."

"You fixed the interlock on the door?" Ellie said, inspecting the device. The switch that had been activated by the closing of the door had been totally smashed. Long's replacement required human intervention to perform the same task. Other than that it seemed an adequate alternative.

"The door, Long – was it ever airtight?" Rick asked, examining the damage where the lock had been forced.

"No, it's a tight fit but there's no sign of a seal."

"Hmm."

"Well, then," Long said, tapping around his improvised chair with the hammer, "I suppose everything's ready. I just need a hand in with the remaining batteries. I found a working electricity supply under a manhole cover a couple of miles away. Made a charger from one of those transformers and some of the spares from the machine. So, they're all topped up."

"You really intend making the first run now?" Rick asked as they lugged the last two batteries inside.

"Yes, why not?" Long connected the thick wires up to the batteries and checked the total voltage with a meter he had added himself. "Fully juiced," he muttered.

"You ready?" Long asked.

Rick and Ellie looked at each other.

"You don't think it's dangerous?" she said. "What about the dead guy? I couldn't do anything for him. Damn it, Long, I don't want two more patients."

"Well, he said 'three' was the dangerous one, didn't he? So, I've disconnected the circuits that switch number three in. It just can't do that one any more."

"Not even accidentally?" Rick said.

Long shook his head. "We've also got the Geiger counter which should warn us if we hit anything nasty."

"I think one of us should stay behind, just in case there's a problem," Ellie said.

"You, then?" Rick said.

"Yes, I don't think I'm ready for whatever might happen."

"It will probably be fine," Rick said, trying to disguise his apprehension. This was a leap into the unknown.

"I don't like the sound of 'probably'," she said.

"Just the two of us, then," Long said.

Long pulled the door closed and connected the interlock before sitting down at the control desk. Rick waved to Ellie through the small porthole window in the door. Wearing a worried look on her face, she reciprocated before retreating to what he hoped was a safe distance. Rick took his place on the new chair; the wooden slats were uncomfortable and he hoped that the ride, wherever it took them, would be short.

"Okay, I'm switching it on," Long said. "The lever's set to four."

He flicked the switch that powered the electronics and a low hum slowly filled the machine. It built up in a rumbling crescendo that permeated everything, adding overlays of noise as the circuits warmed up.

"Does your head in, doesn't it?" he shouted over the noise. Rick winced and tried to cover his ears but the sound – resembling nothing less than thousands of people trying to scream a thousand different songs at once – seemed to seep into every pore of his body and he couldn't shut it out. He even clamped his teeth together in a futile attempt to stop his head vibrating. The burn on his hand tingled again for the first time in days.

"Right," Long shouted over the noise. "I'm going to move the lever to position five."

Rick heard the ratchet clunk as it switched the circuits and he pushed himself back into the chair expecting the machine to lurch, but there was no corresponding change in the all-pervading noise. He glanced over his shoulder to the window; nothing outside seemed to have changed but, with the wood shrouded in near darkness, he couldn't be too sure.

After a few seconds Rick heard Long flick the power switch again and the noise subsided.

"Hell! That was painful," Rick gasped, rubbing his head.

"It was last night, too," Long frowned.

"You might have warned me."

Long, still wearing his frown, peered out the window and grunted. He disconnected the interlock and opened the door.

Rick joined him outside – apart from gaining a headache, nothing had changed. He drew air deeply in and out of his lungs in as effort to rid himself of the after-effects of the machine's abominable noise. "Well, that was great fun – must try it again, never!"

"Something go wrong?" Ellie asked, returning to the clearing.

"Why didn't anything happen?" Long muttered. "Everything else seemed to be okay."

"Yes, but how do you know all the circuits were working properly?" she questioned.

Long sighed. "Yes – I don't."

"Would've been all right if the bloody thing had come with an operating manual," Rick said.

"I'm sure whoever built it was probably expecting their driver to come back alive," Long said. "Maybe we're just doing something wrong."

"Like what? The controls couldn't be much simpler – one switch, one lever. There's only two possible ways–"

"Ah, yes! Brilliant! Come on!" Long grasped Rick by the arm and pulled him back towards the device.

"Hell! My big mouth," Rick grunted as he followed a re-inspired Long back inside.

"Be safe, please," Ellie said and ran, once more, for cover, this time disappearing right into the undergrowth.

After resetting the interlock Long checked that the lever still indicated 'five' and switched on the circuits again. This time there was a difference to the sound – it hurt

Rick's head even more. He could see that Long was also being affected by the changed vibrations. Rick's vision blurred and his teeth chattered uncontrollably as a booming sensation filled his whole body. Then there was a violent jolt and he was flung back against the wall. The machine resettled itself but the racket didn't diminish.

He wrapped his arms around his head and shouted for Long to switch it off but there was no reply. He forced his eyes open to see Long on the floor beside the chair, apparently unconscious. He knew that if he didn't do anything then he would soon join him.

He dragged himself to his feet and fell towards the desk knocking the power switch off as he collapsed onto it. He slid down onto the main chair as the machine fell silent.

Rick rubbed his head and knelt down beside Long who was now groaning with his eyes squeezed shut.

"Damn scrott! That was bad," Long croaked, as one eye opened to squint at Rick.

"No kidding. You okay?"

Long attempted to pick himself up but his legs failed him at first. He lay back, panting. "Hell. I didn't expect anything like that. It threw me off the chair – hit my head on the desk." He massaged his temple, which was already showing the beginnings of a purple bruise.

"How about you, Rick? Are you all right?"

"A bit woozy. Uh, yeah. I think so…"

Rick leaned over towards the window and peered out.

"…but I don't think the world is…"

7 Connections

7.1: Looney Tunes

Shepard Hospital, Shepard Complex, the Moon: 10 June 2169

Melissa Davidsen was bored. She stared at the wall, through the door, at her hands, at the ceiling, her feet – anywhere apart from the patients. She also tried to ignore the drone emanating from the boring idiot explaining to the class all about the hospital in general and this section, known as L-Squared, in particular. The seven patients in this room sat in chairs or lay in beds and, in general, did very little. One whimpered quietly to himself while another, a woman of indeterminate age, stared from child to child with a malevolence that was almost tangible. Melissa certainly didn't want to look at her.

"What does it mean? The L-Squared bit?" piped up one of the younger kids during a momentary lull in the drone.

Melissa sighed audibly, prompting a poke in the ribs from classmate Laurinda, standing next to her. The source of the drone also glanced disapprovingly in her direction which caused Mr Gulrajani, the teacher on this trip, to purse his lips and wag a finger in her direction.

Anyway, surely everyone knew what it meant – it was a joke, a bad joke. The 'L' was short for 'looney' – as in person who lived on the Moon – not a term used much nowadays. It was also slang for lunatic. The patients here were therefore looney loonies – or L-Squared, as someone had dubbed the section many years ago. The name had stuck.

Once children reached twelve years of age the educational system arranged visits to potential places of employment with the hope that it would spark interests that would eventually turn into careers. Melissa found many of them boring – this one was even worse than the trips to various factories producing steel, paper and plastics. She had endured far too many such trips over the past couple of years. Anyway, she already knew what she wanted to do – she was her mother's girl. Her father's job of Regolith Engineer was interesting, and she always enjoyed some of the tales he came home with, but it all paled into insignificance when compared to her mother's role. The enigmatic planet hanging a mere quarter of a million miles away was finally growing to be as fascinating to Melissa as it was to her mother.

She picked at her nails while the drone continued – she certainly had no interest in becoming involved with nursing, caring or anything to do with L-Squared. The small number of dribbling wrecks who resided here made her shudder. They were some of the Moon's few adult inhabitants who didn't work, and she found that almost repugnant. There was always work to do; it was a constant battle to extend the tunnels, to house and feed the growing population, as well as making the environment under which everyone lived, as safe as possible. The Moon was a harsh, unforgiving mistress who rewarded laxity with sharp lessons in the form of accidents, many of them fatal. Moon quakes, depressurisation, low gravity mishaps, carbon dioxide build ups, breakdowns – there were a seemingly endless number of surprises this so-called dead world could conjure up at a moment's notice. Everyone needed to work to keep the whole place running – everyone, that is, except for the residents here.

The drone producer was about to take them along to another batch of inmates when one of the patients, a woman with a smooth face and almost white hair, changed from being a silent mannequin into an animated gossip. Her sudden, shrill outburst made Melissa and several others jump.

"They're back. Hundreds. Song. Singing. I remember. Ross. He went. I stay," she babbled. "Join song. Silent now. So far away. Hello. Ross. He went."

Melissa, who had been quite close, edged towards the door.

The woman continued her monologue of gabble and unsteadily hauled herself out of her chair and to her feet. She cornered one of the twelve-year-old boys. Melissa had to suppress a giggle as Ezekiel's eyes almost popped out of his head as the old woman harassed him, "Ross. Hello. You know Ross? He took the song. Went. Took it away. Where did it go? Ross!"

The boy let out a whimper and hid behind Mr Gulrajani to escape the woman's clutches. By the door Melissa could hear a similar babble coming from another room – the voice there kept shouting about a song as well. Two nurses came along the corridor – one tutted and entered the other room, while the other swept past her to attend to the babbling woman.

Melissa watched the nurse guide the woman back to her chair but the babbling continued for another few seconds before shutting off abruptly. At the same time the noise from the other room also halted.

"They seem to set each other off," the idiot drone said, by way of explanation to Melissa's piercing, questioning gaze.

"Even when they are in separate rooms?" Melissa asked.

"Er, yes," he replied.

"Which one starts it?"

"They always start and stop together."

"Well, if they start and stop simultaneously, when they are not even in the same room," Melissa persisted, "then how can you say they set each other off? Something else must be doing it."

The drone shrugged his shoulders, adding, "They started about five years ago – just the occasional bout for a few seconds. Always together, even when they're kept separate. It's getting progressively worse – several times an hour now. No one knows what causes it."

"Five years ago? How long have they been here?"

"Thirteen years. Ever since the Earth… you know…"

"Oh, right," Melissa said, nodding. "But who were they? Before they came here?"

"Patient confidentiality, miss – I don't think I'm allowed to…"

Mr Gulrajani intervened, "I think that's enough, Melissa. We need to move on."

As the column of children moved down the corridor Laurinda said, "Thought you weren't interested in this place."

"I'm not," Melissa replied, "but, those two… well, it's really weird."

Laurinda shrugged. "They're just loonies."

"Yeah," Melissa agreed, "just loonies."

But, in her mind, something nagged.

7.2: Synchronicity

Shepard Hospital and LSA Control Centre: 16 June 2169

"Now!" Melissa shouted down the navpad's communicator.

"Started," Janet said at almost the same second. She recorded the time on her navpad. On her screen the wave rolled across the face of the Earth as Paradise replaced the more common Black Earth.

"It's definitely Paradise again," Janet added. She could hear the cacophony from L-Squared coming from her daughter's end of the communication. It matched exactly with the time the wave was observed.

Thirty-seven seconds later Janet and Melissa said 'End' simultaneously as the next wave swept across the Earth. Janet logged the time again, bringing the total to seven sets of start and end times, each one coinciding with the babbling of the two patients.

It had taken Janet a few days to convince the authorities at L-Squared to run the experiment after Melissa had come home from the school trip bubbling with her mad idea. Janet had been reluctant at first but Melissa had been persistent with her theory. And now they had some rather convincing numbers.

An hour later they both returned home to compare notes.

"I was right. They match exactly, don't they?" Melissa enthused.

Janet nodded. Without a doubt, her daughter was correct. How did two apparently senile and otherwise moribund women, buried in an institution many metres below the Moon's surface, time their outbursts to coincide exactly with when Paradise Earth appeared?

Janet used her LSA authority to request personal details on the two women. Nothing much was revealed by the exercise. One, Amelia Alice Nunn, aged sixty-eight and British by birth, had been on a business trip for an undisclosed reason to the Moon at the time of the disaster. She had been married to a Mr R Nunn, who was presumed lost on Earth. The other was Emily Dorothy Martin, born in America, aged seventy-five and unmarried. After much travel around the Earth along with a few Moon trips, she had taken up permanent residence on the Moon in 2140. She had worked in an office for one the regolith conversion companies. On the surface there was no connection between the two.

"Hmm. Does it say what the 'R' stands for in Mr Nunn's name?" Melissa asked. "One of the women kept repeating a name. I think it started with 'R'."

Janet dug a bit further. "Ah, here we are. Ross Nunn."

"Yes, that was it, exactly!" Melissa said, clapping her hands in glee.

Janet reeled off some of the other information revealed. "Born 2100, married Amelia Luckin in 2126, no children. Both came to the Moon in March 2156."

Then she frowned. "That's a weird change of occupation."

"What?"

"Apparently, up until 2134 he was a ward companion – that's someone whose job it was to sit with terminally ill people in hospitals."

"Sounds fun," Melissa snorted, a grimace passing across her face.

"Yes, back when I had my appendix out most of the hospitals had nothing but robotic nurses. Their bedside manner was, er, somewhat lacking." Melissa giggled at her mother's expression. Janet continued, "Later on, ward companions were introduced to put a human face back into the system. Especially in places where patients were dying. You had to be a really empathic people-person to do the job."

"So, what did he do after that?"

"Came into money somehow and headed up his own business called VisionPsy shortly after. Scientific research mainly. It's all a bit vague." Janet tried a few more searches. "Nope, there's nothing more. I'll see if I can find out anything else on our two old ladies."

Janet ordered the computer to run a deep analysis on the data supplied about the women. After confirming her authority, it took a few seconds to return the data. The only extra it revealed was that Emily had belonged to various organisations called xMind, Cognizantia and Cerebralta at different times of her life. There was an unverified note that suggested that these were possibly different names for the same outfit. It also added that Amelia had attended restricted meetings of something called The Wider Consciousness, which promoted yoga and mental fitness.

"A right bunch of weird headology!" Melissa snorted. "Well, that probably accounts for them both ending up in L-Squared."

"I've heard of xMind," Janet said, frowning. "Something controversial back when I was about your age."

Her fingers danced through the holographic interface until she located the reference. They both read the short report about an explosion in a block of offices in Poland in 2133, in which xMind was implicated. The exact cause of the destruction was never determined but several people, mainly workers in adjacent offices to those occupied by xMind, had died mysteriously, many without any detectable physical trauma. No one from xMind itself was afflicted and it was rumoured that their offices had long been empty. There were no later references to xMind – it was as if the accident had wiped out the organisation completely. The authorities, after several false leads, failed to get anywhere at all.

Janet shut down the interface.

"So, what now?" Melissa asked.

"Well, there are other institutions similar to L-Squared on the Moon. I wonder if they have any patients with a similar problem?"

Melissa smiled, "Can I use your authority codes?"

Janet nodded, "Be discreet."

7.3: Telepathy

Lussac Science Complex: 22 October 2169

Andrew March checked on his navpad that he had arrived at the right place. The Lussac Science Complex was a sprawling mess that seemed to have grown rather more haphazardly than the normal habitation areas. The designation on the door of the conference room matched the one on his navpad, so he entered and looked about.

The wall behind the stage, which was barely large enough to hold the desk and lectern, was taken up with a screen. There were a dozen or so lines of chairs and he selected one three rows from the front. There were seats for about a hundred and fifty people, though barely a quarter were occupied as yet. With only five minutes to go before the presentation was due to start, there was no sign of a rush to fill the remaining places, a point that Andy felt was regrettable considering the subject matter.

To one side of the stage two women sat behind the desk. Andy recognised them both. The older one was Janet Davidsen and Andy was quite familiar with her work, having followed her on-and-off LSA career, publications and online lectures for the past few years. The younger woman had changed quite a bit since his previous encounter with her – he could still picture the tongue stuck out at him in the dome more than five years previously. He also remembered the smile that had replaced the tongue as the lift doors had closed. Her face had stuck in his memory unchanged and he compared that memory with the girl of today. Her name was Melissa Davidsen and, from what he could gather from the limited data her mother had put up on MoonNet, she was the initial discoverer of the Paradise Telepathists.

Five more people arrived as he watched the clock inch towards the hour.

Janet glanced at the clock on the side wall as its second hand clicked to dead on 3pm.

She inclined her head towards Melissa and whispered, "Not exactly a full house."

Melissa made a face.

Janet glanced at the clock again and decided not to wait for any late arrivals. They only had three quarters of an hour before the hall was required for another function. So, she stood and stepped up to the lectern. After pouring a glass of water from the jug supplied, Janet took a few sips while waiting for the noise level in the auditorium to drop.

Her introduction was brief and she moved straight onto the main points of the presentation, which was delivered from a short list of notes she'd jotted down the evening before. Then she gave a nod to Melissa who pressed one switch to dim the lights and another to start their pre-prepared video.

"Patients one and two were the first encountered," Janet explained as Amelia Nunn pixelated face appeared on the screen behind her. The old woman's mouth moving rapidly as the stream of words fell from her lips. After a few seconds she was replaced by Emily Martin.

"To help preserve their anonymity," Janet continued, "we will refer to each one by an assigned number. These have been allocated incrementally as each new patient was discovered. Also, as you can see and hear, we've pixelated their faces and pitch-shifted their voices. These two were the initial test subjects regarding their synchronisation with the appearances of Paradise. Once we had established that initial connection, we then searched across the Moon for any others who showed a similar tendency. We now have a total of thirty-one spread across twelve centres – twenty-one female and ten male. We suspect there might have been even more, as records show that some who may have been exhibiting the same symptoms have since passed away."

Janet paused to allow the audience to hear the utterances from each of the thirty-one patients in turn.

"We've established that they are all completely synchronised, even when isolated. All of them started around the beginning of 2164, though there is an uncorroborated earlier report. Apparently, one of the men suddenly burst into a few seconds of chatter on Boxing Day 2163."

The introduction was mostly a repeat of data Andy had already found posted by Janet Davidsen on the public channels. He recalled that the first official announcements of the discovery of Paradise had been in March 2164, a couple of months after his tenth birthday. Maybe the Boxing Day occurrence suggested that its first appearance had preceded even his own momentary view of it in the dome that January.

The next ten minutes were taken up with analysis of what each patient was saying. There was a tendency for the patients to repeat the same phrases over, and the names of spouses or close relatives were common. Andy quickly realised that most of those were very common first names and were not censored in any way, though one or two utterances had been replaced by silence. He wondered what they would have revealed had they been let through intact.

He was also intrigued by the references to a 'song' or music of some kind. It seemed that most patients referenced this, though no one appeared to understand what it meant.

Janet paused to take another sip of water, staring around the sparsely filled room while she did so. She had begun to think this whole presentation might have been a waste of effort. A couple of people had already walked out. She wondered what had made them turn up in the first place.

Of those that remained several appeared to be more interested in looking at their navpads than watching the presentation. Only a few, like that young boy near the front, seemed to be fully engaging with what she had to say.

"Given the constant repetition of the names, we tried to determine the fate of the people they were referring to. In most cases, it transpired that, if they had been on the Moon, then a good proportion had been recalled to Earth just before the disaster." Janet noted the frown that passed across the boy's face. She added, "We discovered that many of the patients were also recalled but the lack of available transport at the time prevented their return. Patients one and two, along with several others, had managed to book a flight due to launch three days before the arrival of the asteroid. But that launch was delayed for more than a day for a number of reasons, not least that the crew were afraid of flying into possible danger. Eventually, it did take off but once the immensity of the asteroid's destruction became clear, the ship swung around the Earth and headed back home."

Janet paused as Melissa brought up an image of a report that, though no longer marked as classified, had taken her quite a while to track down and access. It was a log of what had happened when the ship returned. All of the names were redacted but there was still plenty to discuss.

Janet pointed to a highlighted term on the report – it clearly said 'vegetative state'.

"As you can see," she continued, "they were fully aware that something had happened to our patients before the ship re-docked. There is also a crewmember statement that indicated the patients became afflicted simultaneously. But, none of the other passengers or crew experienced it. That ship only accounted for seven of our total of thirty-one. All the rest had remained here on the Moon. However, as far as we can determine, they all succumbed within minutes of each other. Given all the other upheavals going on, the fact that all of these people became afflicted with the same condition at almost exactly the same time is something that has only now come to light."

Janet glanced at the clock again – it was nearly half-past three. She brought the main presentation to an end and then asked, "Any questions?" before taking another sip of water.

The boy near the front was the first to put his hand up. Janet indicated for him to speak though, to her surprise, he appeared to address his question more to Melissa.

"Is it definitely only Paradise that creates this effect upon the patients?" he asked.

"Yes, Paradise only," Melissa responded quickly before Janet could put the glass down.

Janet then added, "We did check for anyone synchronising with Green Earth or Robot World, and found no correlation. If Black had affected anyone they would have started as soon as the asteroid hit – we didn't find evidence of any such occurrences."

There were a few more questions from others and then the boy's arm was raised again. "Has what the patients say changed at all over the years since they started?"

Janet and Melissa exchanged a glance.

Then Janet said, "Good question. It's only been about four months since the connection was first established. Certainly, we haven't seen any measurable change ourselves during that period, other than the frequency of the occurrences. These, as we know, are linked to the increasing appearances of Paradise itself. As far as we are aware, no one noted what they were saying initially and whether or not it is still the same."

Janet stopped for a moment and frowned. "What's your name, son?"

"Andrew March."

Janet turned to Melissa and said, "Mr March may have raised something important here. See if you can find out if the institutions have any recordings, audio or video, no matter how short, of the patients prior to our investigations."

Melissa nodded and made a note.

There were a few more questions by others in the hall. To Andrew, some of the things asked were either irrelevant or had already been answered earlier. He was also brewing up another one to ask when Janet announced that, with the clock inching past 3.40pm, they had run out of time and had to vacate the hall so that the next event could be set up.

Instead of heading directly to the metro station and home, Andrew waited around until Janet and Melissa left and followed them at a distance. He finally plucked up the courage to talk to them as all three entered the station. Janet spotted him hovering and smiled.

"Excuse me, Mrs Davidsen," he said, "Sorry to be a bother but I still have another question, if you don't mind."

"Ah, Mr March. Andrew wasn't it?" Janet said. "At least you were one of the few asking the intelligent questions. Go ahead – we're in no rush."

"Thank you," he said, conscious of how close Melissa was standing. He swallowed and concentrated on presenting his question as formally as he could manage. "You indicated that many of the patients had been due to return to the Earth and their spouses had already gone back."

He waited for Janet's nod before continuing.

"It was mainly the men, I presume, given the skewed female to male ratio of those remaining here. That suggests to me that there was some sort of collective effort to get these people back. From what I've read about the time of the disaster, most people were only too happy to be stranded here. So, what connected all these patients and the ones who did manage to get back to Earth?"

Janet Davidsen didn't respond immediately and Andrew wondered if he'd crossed some sort of forbidden line.

Janet sucked her lips in. She had been surprised that no one had actually asked that question in the lecture hall. She had debated with Melissa and Keifer about whether or not to reveal what little they had found. But the evidence was patchy and, in two instances, had been deleted from the data banks after they had first located it. She looked at the young man standing in front of her, awaiting her answer. The look in his eyes showed he had the same intensity she recognised in her own reflection, something her daughter had also inherited. She also noticed, not without a certain level of amusement, how intensely Melissa was observing the young man.

"How old are you, Andrew?" she asked.

"Er, fifteen. Sixteen in January."

She nodded. He was nearly a year older than Melissa. She reached into a pocket and pulled out a small plastic rectangle.

"This is not the right place for answering such questions," she said, handing the card to him.

Andrew looked at the address and contact details on the card. It was on a higher level and several habitat groupings away from his own home, but not more than a few minutes on the metro.

Then he was aware that Janet Davidsen was talking to him again.

"Consider yourself invited to tea," she said. "Call first but any time in the next week should be fine. Make sure your parents know where you're going. Understand?"

He grinned and nodded. Janet and Melissa moved away towards the tunnel that led to the Conradville platform. Just before they entered, Melissa looked back at Andrew and smiled. He gestured a wave and she momentarily stuck her tongue out at him before grinning and disappearing from sight.

He returned home unable to suppress the smile plastered across his lips.

7.4: Data Dumped

Conradville: 24–28 October 2169

"There's more gone," Melissa said, her voice incredulous.

"What?" Janet called from the lounge.

"The stuff on Cognizantia we found last night."

"Did you keep a copy?" Janet said, coming through into Melissa's room.

"Yes, I've still got that, and copies of all the other stuff. It's the original source that's no longer there."

"Hmm, I wonder…"

"Wonder what?"

"Don't search for anything else new until I've had a word with our computer guy, Tariq."

The next evening Tariq and his partner, Yefim, were over at the Davidsen's quarters for a hastily arranged meal. Tariq knew they had been invited at short notice for a specific reason, which Janet had refused to reveal until after the meal had finished. So, while Keifer and Yefim stayed in the dining room to put the universe to rights, Janet and Melissa took Tariq through to the lounge and brought him up to date with what they'd found.

"Just what are you getting involved with here?" Tariq asked. "Not exactly standard LSA remit, is it?"

"It's really Melissa's, um, project," Janet said. "You know, all that L-Squared stuff with the telepathic patients. Turns out all of them have histories that intertwine around a whole bunch of companies that constantly pop up and disappear over the last hundred years or so."

"But, as we dig up new data, almost as soon as we find it, it just disappears," Melissa said.

"All data?"

"No, Tariq," Janet said. "Mainly just the stuff about the organisations the patients tended to belong to – Cerebralta, Cognizantia, xMind, Xanlintec, Progenitag and several others. Especially when we find vague connections between them. It's almost as if someone is tracking what we're looking for."

"Never heard of any of them," Tariq said. "How soon after you find them do they disappear?"

"Always within an hour. Some go within minutes," Melissa said.

"Really? Hmm, okay, let's do some digging," he frowned, taking control of the terminal. "Right, let me have a full list of those – what are they? Organisations? Companies? What do they have in common?"

"Very little on the surface," Janet said. "Some were electronics companies, some more like mind, body and spirit clubs, others were research – though what they were looking into never seems to be consistent from one mention to another."

It took Tariq a few minutes to find some intact references to one of the more down-to-earth companies, called Linden Enterprises. Melissa had found a reference to it on a note about Progenitag. Linden had ceased trading in 2122 and its main concern appeared to be the handling of patents and applications developed by a Doctor Linden Willard Ashley. Tariq downloaded and stored a local copy of what little there appeared to be on Linden. Ten minutes later the original reference had been purged.

"Wow," he said, shaking his head. "You're right – I must admit, I hadn't believed you at first."

Three days later Tariq phoned Janet and Melissa.

"I think I've found something," he announced. "Damned clever in many ways. Stupid in a few important ways."

"What do you mean?" Melissa asked.

"I don't think it's a person. It's more like a program or maybe a whole bunch of programs. Probably well hidden as I can only infer its existence indirectly by what it's doing. A bit like the old computer viruses and malware."

"I thought they'd finally defeated all of them when the AI systems came online," Janet said.

"That's why this one is really clever. It's obviously managed to evade the AI routines for years. But, by the looks of things, it can't work independently. It needs to hook itself into an existing event before it can do anything. So, it's probably monitoring certain lines of communication – i.e. general searches across MoonNet for specific terms – like the names of those companies such as–"

"Don't say the names out loud," Janet reminded him. "It might be enough to wake it up if it happens to be listening in."

"Okay, yes. Anyway, when something triggers it – such as you retrieving data containing references to those companies, it springs into action tracking back to the source of your data and deleting it – somehow without bringing attention to what it's doing."

"You said it was stupid as well," Melissa said.

"Yes," Tariq laughed. "If it was really clever, it would get into your local storage and delete your copies as well."

"Why doesn't it just search everywhere for itself?" Melissa asked.

"That might raise its profile too much, making it more detectable by the AI systems."

"So, how has it evaded them in the first place?" Janet asked.

"No idea as I haven't managed to nail it down to a physical program file."

He paused for a moment. "Hmm, I wonder if it has the ability to mutate to avoid detection – many old computer viruses could do that. You'd better print out a hard copy of everything you've found just in case it does find a way back to your local storage and wipe that as well."

"Good idea," Janet agreed.

Later on, Melissa sat in the lounge with her mother. On a table were paper copies of the data they'd found – they might now be the only evidence that such data had ever existed.

"Just what in hell have we uncovered?" Janet said. "It gets weirder and weirder."

"Yes. Telepathic people, possibly. Lots of strange connected companies whose information disappears as soon as you look at it. Who would go to such an effort to set up something like that? And why?"

Janet shook her head. She had absolutely no idea.

8 Little Acorns

8.1: The First Undeniable Proof

Oxford University, England: 2075

"Consistent results this time?" asked Professor Aubrey Maynard Rayburn, hands buried in the pockets of his jacket. Although still in his mid-thirties, he tended to give the impression of someone far older. Maybe it was the way he dressed, or the mannerisms that gave him an air of superiority, or possibly it was the thickness of his beard, streaked already with paler, almost blond hairs, whilst those on his head remained resolutely dark brown.

"Definitely," Doctor Linden Willard Ashley replied. Younger by three years but already balding, his attire of a shapeless and once-white lab coat, along with glasses that were perched askew half-way down his nose, cast him in complete contrast to Rayburn.

Ashley glanced along the corridor, which was located in one of Oxford's many halls of learning. It was otherwise empty so, with no one likely to interrupt them, Ashley unlocked a door and they entered his private laboratory. He locked the door behind them.

Rayburn marvelled again at the place. The walls were lined with electronic devices: probes, computers, electron microscopes, detectors and other pieces of paraphernalia whose purpose he could only guess at.

Ashley took a drinking glass from a shelf, inspecting it to make sure it was relatively clean. Then he filled it with cold water from a tap at the small sink located near the window. After taking a sip, he placed the glass in the centre of a plastic-topped, metal-legged table.

"Please inspect both the table and the glass," he said.

Rayburn did so and could detect nothing untoward – furniture of exactly the same simple design and vintage could be found in many locations on campus. Ashley moved to one side of the room and placed some apparatus, shaped like a small cycling helmet, over his head. Wires led from it back to one of the electronic devices, which he switched on.

"Watch," Ashley said as he stared at the glass from over six feet away. After a few seconds it moved a couple of inches to one side. Rayburn raised an eyebrow but said nothing. Ashley concentrated a second time and the glass slid in a different direction.

"The device is tuned to your brain only?" Rayburn asked after re-inspecting both the glass and the table.

"At the moment. MRI scans of others indicate that the area responsible tends to be located in almost the same position."

"And you have already pinpointed the same location in my brain?"

"Yes, I had no problem locating it in your MRI. Tuning the device to you is a minor adjustment," said Ashley as he removed the helmet and switched off the machine. "But, that's not all. Watch again."

Ashley stepped close to the table and squatted down until his head was just above the level of the tabletop. His face creased up and, after a few seconds, the glass moved again, juddering a mere fraction of an inch.

"How?" Rayburn said.

"Repeated use enables the mind to train itself," Ashley announced with a smile.

"Absolutely excellent. May I try with the helmet?"

"Be my guest," Ashley grinned.

8.2: Watering The Garden

Oxfordshire countryside: 2080

The vehicle's doors were decorated with the text, 'Maynard-Linden Research'. In the back Rayburn and Ashley sat amongst the racks of electronics and watched the screens. The central monitor showed a woman, an L-shaped divining rod in each hand, strolling across the lightly ploughed field beside which the van was parked. On her head the portable MRI scanner sent its signals back to the monitoring equipment they were observing. She also wore a jacket that scanned her immediate surroundings at several frequencies.

"There," Ashley whispered. The rods in the woman's hands twitched and she stopped walking. She stepped backwards and forwards over the same piece of ground. She could detect the water barrel hidden in the earth more than four feet below her. The equipment recorded everything picked up by the sensors she wore.

Two weeks later, after the computer cluster back at their office in Horspath had analysed the data, some possibilities were isolated. Equipment was adjusted and they descended once more on the Oxfordshire countryside to repeat the experiment with the same volunteer. This time, as she stepped over one of the hidden water barrels, Ashley pointed out the changes in the woman's mind even before the woman consciously registered them.

"Told you we'd find it," Ashley smirked.

"Indeed. Can it be augmented?"

Ashley smiled and reached out for a pencil, which sprung from the desktop to land in his outstretched hand.

"Show off."

"You're not far behind," Ashley grinned.

"What do we tell her?" Rayburn said, pointing at the figures and traces on the screens.

"Dowsing is not what I'd call a core ability. Yet, the fact that she can consistently achieve far better than average might indicate a predilection for other abilities."

"Maybe we should get her on board permanently. What do you think?"

Ashley scratched his head while he thought. Then he looked up her details on the computer. "Her daytime occupation is, apparently, office administration. Not exactly something we are in great need of, but it might be good to have her close so we can keep an eye on her."

Rayburn nodded and grinned, "Well, I'd say we are getting to the stage where a good PA would come in useful."

"For you or me?"

Rayburn ignored the question. "So, what's next?"

"Well, there's that couple from York who claim to be telepaths. No one's found out how they do it and no tricks have been detected."

"Genuine?"

"Hopefully."

8.3: Plan C

Near Invergloy and Altura, Scotland: June 2084

Professor Rayburn looked worried as he entered Doctor Ashley's office. Four years on and their single office in the Oxford University campus had first evolved into a suite of rooms in the nearby suburb of Horspath before spreading further afield. Now they had four offices in the British Isles and another three dotted around the world. A few miles up from Invergloy and about the same distance from Altura, their Scottish branch nestled between the trees on the bank of Loch Lòchaidh.

Ostensibly, Maynard-Linden Research had been created to develop neuroscientific and biomedical engineering products. Already, both Rayburn and Ashley's names were attached to several patents. These were bringing in a small but increasingly healthy trickle of income from products being manufactured via third parties. While

Rayburn's family wealth was still being poured into the business, future projections showed they would be well into profit within two more years.

Ashley glanced up and his own face took on the same expression. Both were wearing headpieces that resembled, but weren't, audio equipment.

"Questions are, shall we say, being asked," Rayburn said.

"And?"

"Apparently, they don't like the conclusions. We should have suspected that damned volunteer was a plant when he came up blank on all the scores. My contacts in London say he was MI5. And now they're getting wind of what we're really doing here. I get the impression they think we're messing with things that shouldn't be messed with."

"Damn it," Ashley spat. "They can't shut us down, though… can they?"

"I wouldn't put it past them to try," Rayburn said with a sigh. "That blasted teleportation experiment. They weren't anywhere near ready. I warned you about Thompson – always too bloody eager, that boy."

"Produced brilliant results though. Got further than I would have done. You know he's partially telepathic without the apparatus now?"

Rayburn nodded and, after a short pause, said, "Plan B, I think. We have to be unrestricted. Even if they let us continue they'll be wanting controls in place – and that's guaranteed to stifle development."

"Hmm," Ashley said, standing. He placed his hands behind his back and stared out the window down onto the loch. "Be sad to leave this place. I know it's only been eight months but it's so delightfully wild – matches what we're doing."

He fell silent for a few moments and concentrated. "The Chinese link up?" he said, without uttering a sound.

"Well, it will certainly give us access to the Lhasa monks in Tibet," Rayburn responded in the normal fashion. "But what do you think of the Swiss? And then there's the Chilean contingent – not that I've ever fancied South America."

"Pros and cons to each of them."

"Agreed," Rayburn nodded and he, too, stood silent for a while. "How about all of them?" he finally said without sound.

Ashley's eyes narrowed, "You're sure the bank of Rayburn can withstand the expansion?"

Rayburn's nod was almost imperceptible.

There was a pause.

"Plan C then," Ashley thought back, finally.

"If they want to play cat and mouse, let's give them the run-around," Rayburn

transmitted.
   Both men smiled.
   The game was on.

8.4: Neither Here Nor There

Dagzê District, Tibet: November 2085

Rayburn and Ashley watched as Doctor Eugene Hillary Thompson adjusted the headsets on the assembled monks and then placed a similar one on his own head. The deep thrumming sound that resonated around the ancient hall was almost deafening. Ashley would never get over the fact that the human larynx could generate such unearthly harmonies.

"I'll have a headache for days after this," he whispered to Rayburn, who seemed to be having the same problem.

"Watch the screen," Thompson said, pointing to the computers and other devices that seemed totally out of place amongst the Tibetan relics and carvings. "They used to just be able to make things vibrate or shimmer slightly."

"And now, with the headsets?" Rayburn asked.

Thompson didn't reply – there was no need.

The pitch of the sound emanating from the twenty-three monks deepened even further. In front of them, the object of their attention, a statue half as tall as a man, began to shake. It was hard to keep it in focus, and Rayburn had to blink and turn his head away for a moment.

After about a minute the intensity of the sound peaked and the statue disappeared. Five seconds later it reappeared and the sound levels decreased and, finally, silence replaced it.

Thompson removed his headpiece and the monks did likewise.

"Where exactly did it go?"

Thompson grinned, "Yes, that is something we'd definitely like the answer to."

8.5: Tuning Up

Peru, close to the Ecuador border, South America: April 2096

Professor Rayburn and Doctors Thompson and Ashley sat with the students, all apparently in meditation. The room they occupied was part of a modern single-story construction. It was open to the outside but, despite the forest that grew all around, no bird or insect dared enter the room. Even the sound of the forest appeared to have been muted at the room's boundary.

The students made no sound, and neither did Thompson, Rayburn or Ashley. But the conversation was intense, loud and agitated. Some students wore headpieces in order to join in; others no longer had need of such things.

The subject matter of the communication dwelt upon the restructuring of the human brain in accordance to the persistence of repetitive mental exercises. To some the language used was words, others perceived it as pictures that swam across their vision while, for a few, it was like the complicated harmonised melody of a song.

Unmoving, the participants were encouraged to add their own voice or thoughts to the conversation/image/song, blending and enhancing the experience of the whole group.

After an hour they started to relax and the sound of the forest was allowed to flow in through the open windows. The students got to their feet and wandered off to other parts of the building in search of refreshment, sleep or some other activity.

Rayburn watched Thompson and Ashley follow the students and then returned to his meditation, his mind drifting beyond the confines of his physical body.

Several miles away some illegal loggers were contemplating a stand of trees just inside the edge of the forest in Ecuador. Rayburn concentrated for a short while. The loggers watched in surprise as one of their bulldozers exploded, maiming the man standing next to it. A chainsaw started up unexpectedly, leaping out of the hands of the man holding it to fall and slice the legs from his body. Two other loggers were unable to resist an overpowering urge to strangle each other, a task to which they applied the greatest of effort. The rest screamed and ran in all directions as Rayburn infected their minds with the promise of other horrific possibilities should they return.

He vaguely regretted the deaths, but it would save more in the long run – there was precious little rainforest left and far too many people.

After peace returned to the trees, Rayburn stirred again and followed the others.

8.6: There And Back Again

Between Komari and Pottuvil, Sri Lanka: 2100

From several feet away, Doctor Eugene Hillary Thompson concentrated on the glass marble on the table. He eased it out of reality and held it alongside in a place that normal logic would say shouldn't exist. After a few seconds he pulled the marble back again. The lump of putty, which had held the marble in place, was not only distorted but it had also emitted a curl of smoke, which made him frown and tut to himself.

Thompson took the headset off and let the sounds of the world re-enter his ears. He walked across to the table and examined both the marble and putty closely, without touching either. Then, with a pair of rubber-tipped tongs, he placed the marble in the 3D scanner and put the machine to work. He had to rotate the marble several times so that the scanner could get a good look at it from all angles.

After setting the computers to work analysing the results and comparing them to the similar set taken two hours previously, he locked the door and went to lunch.

Some time later, after a stroll along the beach where the Indian Ocean lapped the Sri Lankan sand, he returned and looked over the results of the comparison.

The marble, they said, was unchanged.

It was a pity the same couldn't be said about the putty.

9 A Case Of Fluidity

9.1: Anarchy In The Wild

Alternate Five: 24 April 2177

Long gently pushed Rick to one side to look out of the window.

"Hell. My head still hurts," Rick muttered.

"Yes," Long agreed, but he wasn't really listening. His own head was almost clear again and his attention was gripped by the changes he observed outside.

That the machine had moved in some way was undeniable. He could see that woods still surrounded them, but the trees were more open, less densely packed and many looked as though they were dead. Given the amount of wan light that illuminated the view, the sun appeared to be either rising or setting. His immediate conclusion was that they could no longer be in the same country as it had been around two in the morning when they had left.

He stared at the dead trees; they were twisted in strange, unnatural ways and many of the live ones also exhibited the same problem, though not to a comparable degree.

"Got that Geiger counter?"

Rick passed it across. Long switched it on and it chattered slightly, registering a background level that was well within safety margins. He cracked the door open and pushed the probe outside while sniffing the air.

"Is it safe?" Rick asked.

"Smells okay-ish," Long confirmed, opening the door fully and stepping out onto the machine's platform. "Radiation's normal, too. But you see those trees?"

"Yeah, weird, and why's the sun coming up already?"

Long placed a foot on the ground as if he expected it to open up and swallow him. It remained reassuringly solid. The light grew, although the sun itself was still hidden below the horizon. It did seem to be coming from what he assumed to be the east which was in the same direction in relation to the machine as it had been on Hampstead Heath.

"Look here, Rick."

Still standing on the machine's platform edge, Rick followed Long's pointed finger. In a patch of dry dusty earth there were several imprints of a shoe.

"Must be inhabited," Rick concluded. "We'd better watch out in case the natives aren't friendly."

Long walked a few yards and gazed about. It was both different and yet familiar. He could see a few other footprints near the machine but none further away. He had an idea. He returned to the machine and walked all the way around it.

"What were you looking for?" Rick said once Long had returned to the doorway.

Long grinned. "I think the dead driver came here as well. Those are probably his footprints. Round the other side there's a patch of flattened grass the same size as the base of the machine. For some reason we've come down a few feet further this way compared to where it landed last time it came here."

Then Long stared into the distance, a frown on his face.

"Over there," he said, pointing through the trees. "That dip in the ground is in about the same place as a dip in the woods on Hampstead Heath."

Rick climbed down from the machine's platform but kept close to it. "Coincidence?" he said.

Long shrugged. He could see that Rick remained affected by the machine and he was rubbing at his hand again.

"So, any idea where we might be?" Rick said.

Long shrugged and examined one of the dead trees, it was so twisted it looked as if it had died in utter agony. Rick remained leaning against the machine.

"Did we bring any painkillers?" Rick called out.

"No, sorry. Should have thought of that. Still bad?"

"Yeah, someone's playing drums in my head."

"Mine seems to have worn off. Maybe yours will in a short… Oh, wow! Look at this!"

Long squatted down and ran his hands forwards and backwards through some long grass.

"Ow," he exclaimed, putting a finger in his mouth, "that one was bloody sharp. Lots of them are all distorted."

He carefully picked a small clump; it pulled from the ground easily.

Rick peered at the grass and his eyebrows raised and lowered as he looked at what Long had discovered. Many of the blades were relatively normal but, growing from the same roots were some that were not: there were curled blades; fat, crinkled blades; some with patterned holes; and several with spiked edges. Some blades even exhibited more than one style along their single length.

"What the hell can cause that sort of mutation?" Rick asked.

"I presume that Geiger counter was working properly?"

"Seemed to be. I took a few tests after reading up on what was normal. I even found one of those old watches with hands that glow in the dark and it went quite mad when I pointed it at that."

"Okay, then," Long said, and added, "let's assume it's not radiation and that we're safe for a while. Maybe we shouldn't stay any longer than a day or so."

9.2: Unfamiliar Familiarity

Alternate Five: 24 April 2177

Rick suggested that they shouldn't stray far from the machine. But Long, more experienced in reading the countryside, was determined to find out more about where they were and headed off in a random direction. Rick sighed, rubbed his temples and followed reluctantly.

Sparse woodland gave way to meadow primarily consisting of the same distorted grass they had previously encountered. It was dotted with the occasional dead tree and areas of grey soil where nothing grew, not even weeds. However, this became insignificant as they noticed that the horizon was rimmed with what looked distinctly like buildings. By silent mutual agreement, they headed in that direction.

Half way to the buildings Long halted and pointed at the ground. Rick saw the snake that made its unhurried way across their path.

"Grass snake, isn't it?" Rick said.

Long agreed. "Pretty sure, yes. It's harmless. Poisonous snakes have got a jagged pattern."

"I know."

"Yes, but take a proper look at it."

Rick edged closer and then realised that this was no ordinary snake. Its slow gait was due to the way its body had not formed correctly. On one side, about two-thirds down the body, there was an additional piece of flesh that resembled a badly formed leg. The creature was doing its best to utilise it in its forward motion.

"And here's something else," Rick said, pointing a few feet away.

They watched as a large centipede, with an extra set of useless legs attached to its back, scuttled away from them.

A few feet further on a freshly dead mole with an extra eye was being consumed by maggots.

"Yetch," Rick exclaimed, making a wide circle of the slowly disintegrating mole. "Is nothing normal around here?"

Closer to the buildings they could see the architecture appeared comparable to what they were used to seeing in London. Nearby was a house of a style that Long recalled as being from the Victorian era. He stepped over a wooden construction but

Rick, curious, lifted it up to find words, dull with age but still readable, painted on the wood.

They said: "Hampstead Heath."

A look of total incomprehension passed between them.

"This is getting scary," Rick muttered as they made their way along a road that exhibited little invasive growth which, in itself, was strange given the state of the buildings.

"Look at that place, Rick."

Rick followed Long's pointing finger, and felt his head swim.

"No," he whispered. A large brick structure gave the impression that it had melted. The bricks were distorted, as if they had been made of soft plastic and had run under the effects of some extreme and unnatural temperature, with gravity dragging them ground-ward before they had re-solidified.

"What is it?" Long asked.

"I've seen something like this before," Rick said, his voice quivering. "You remember when we were kids? Those nightmares I had before AI found something to stop them?"

Long slowly nodded. It had been a long time ago, and he barely recalled Rick's childhood affliction.

"One I kept having was full of buildings and people that were all bent out of shape."

"Can't be the same place."

"Why not?"

"No people."

Long pressed on quickly and Rick ran to catch up.

They came across other buildings exhibiting more strange effects. A church spire in the distance appeared twisted and leaned at an angle. The pavement at one point had buckled and lurched towards the middle of the road carrying a garden wall with it. One lamppost had attained a distinct curl and another was split along three-quarters of its length, the separated sections curving away from each other as if magnetically repelled.

Of signs of any recent human occupation, there were none.

9.3: Multiverse Proved

Alternate Five – London: 24 April 2177

They pressed on southward until they came to the entrance to Belsize Park Underground station.

"I thought I recognised some of this," Rick said. He looked back the way they had just come. "But where's the Wall? It should have cut right through just over there."

"This isn't our London. It must be some sort of alternative where AI didn't build the Wall. I don't think AI even exists here."

"Alternate worlds? You mean the old multiverse theories that AI tried to teach us? It always sounded completely dango to me."

"I think we're looking at proof that AI was right all along."

"Do you think we're the first ones to see this?"

"Maybe not. The dead guy must have seen this or, at least, some others. And the people who built the machine must have realised that such alternatives had to exist in the first place. Though how they figured out what they needed to do to build a working machine to hop between them is beyond me."

"Yeah, but if this is an alternate world – where are all the people?"

"Hmm. And another thing. Why only five? Why not fifty or fifty thousand?"

"Maybe they thought that five would be enough to start with."

"Could be – what's the matter?" Long asked, noticing Rick scratching at his left hand.

"That damned burn is really itching."

Long took a look and frowned, "Yeah. Definitely looks a bit worse. Better let Ellie take a proper look when we get back."

Not far from the station entrance they came across a hypermarket whose frontage had been distorted out of all recognition. Something resembling a human skeleton could be made out inside. They stepped into the gloom of the shop through the open entrance.

Rick stared around, hand over his mouth.

"Okay, so maybe this *is* the place you dreamed about," Long said.

More skeletons dotted the interior. Many looked normal but a few, those that hadn't decayed by quite so much, which suggested that they had died more recently, showed some unusual additions. There was a skull that bulged prominently on one side; another had leg bones that warped strangely, similar in some respects to the lamppost they had encountered earlier. A child's remains, identified by the smaller skull, were elongated along the torso.

"You okay, Rick?"

"No, I feel sick. I've got to get out of here, right now."

Back in the eerie silence of the street they leaned against a wall, one that had avoided the distortions that had afflicted so many others.

Away from the skeletons Rick felt more in control. He squinted at the sun. "You think this whole universe is like this?"

"I'd guess that it isn't," Long replied.

"How do you figure that?"

"If you take away all the weirdness from this place then what you'd be left with is London as it was before the disaster, before the asteroid that didn't hit, before AI built the walls. That's when all of the distortions must have started. On our world people went dumb, on this one the whole of nature must've gone crazy."

"Yeah, but why–"

"Hell!" Long shouted. "He said 'that's where it hit' – the dead guy. He said three was where it hit!"

"What?"

"The asteroid!"

Rick stared at Long's expression of revelation and nodded slowly.

"Yeah, but that still doesn't explain why there are five or possibly even more alternative Earths, and why the people who built the machine needed to visit them."

"This is so amazing. We've got to find out all we can."

"Well, amazing or not. This place really isn't agreeing with me. It's too much like that nightmare. I just wish this damn headache would go away."

"Um, mine has started to come back as well. Okay, let's head back."

They started walking back the way they had come but, after a few minutes, Rick suddenly clutched at his head.

"Hell," he groaned, "everything's spinning."

"There's something really screwy about all this."

"I feel kind of wonky all over. My hand's really tingling again." Then Rick gasped, "Dango! Look at my fingers!"

"Shit!" Long shouted, staring at Rick's hand. "I think what happened to the people and the buildings here is starting to happen to us."

"We got to get out, now!"

It took them half an hour to return to the edge of the heath and the pounding in Rick's head intensified as they passed the last of the buildings. His hand ached horribly. By the time they were half way across the heath Long was supporting Rick as he had started stumbling. Long, too, was beginning to feel the effects of this world upon him as his hearing started to fade in and out strangely.

"I didn't expect this to happen," Long gasped. "Feels like my head is being turned inside out."

"Oh," Rick groaned. "Stop shouting. You're making the air turn red and green. Oh no, I'm doing it, too."

"What are you talking about?"

"Can't you see it?"

"No. See what?"

"Every time we speak, colours appear in front of us. You don't see that?"

"Pardon? I can't hear properly. My ears keep closing up or something."

"Colours. Oh… I think I'm going to be sick."

Rick started to collapse in Long's arms but the latter managed to guide them both back into the sparse woods that held the machine.

Long located the device by following the track of crushed grass from their outward journey. Rick's legs gave up and he fell unconscious. Long wanted to collapse beside him but knew he had to get them away. Hauling Rick to his feet he struggled back to the machine as the strange effects of this world impinged further on his own senses. His ears heard only a constant hiss and his eyesight was beginning to fuzz.

He dumped Rick's inert form on the floor of the machine and closed the door, shutting out the alternate strangeness, if not the effects. He switched the lever back to registering '4' and slammed the activating switch on.

He felt, rather than heard, the build up of the vibrations. As before, the whole structure started to shake and, as the soundless noise started to seep through his entire frame, he sank to the floor to lie beside Rick.

The last thing he noticed before completely passing out was that the fingers on Rick's left hand looked as if they were beginning to flow like melted plastic. He shut his eyes, not knowing whether what he had seen had been real or just a figment of his deteriorating eyesight. He gave in and retreated into a welcome blackness where pain subsided into nothing.

9.4: Discovered

Hampstead Heath: 24-25 April 2177

Ellie clasped her hands over her ears to try to stop the cacophony from penetrating her skull as she ran further from the clearing. She finally halted next to some sparse bushes nearly thirty feet from the noise. Through half-screwed up eyes she watched the machine shimmer, tilt and then disappear with a distinct pop. The sound echoed around the trees for a couple of seconds before leaving her in silence. Even the normally subdued woodland chit-chat that she had hardly noticed before was conspicuously absent.

They had done it. They had really done it. She hadn't believed anything would actually happen. She edged back into the clearing to where the machine had stood. Her hands shook as she played her torch over the ground, seeing the imprints where the base had pushed into the soil along with the damage to the trees where it had originally come down. The torchlight picked out something glistening near the roots of the tree it had originally crashed against. It glinted like several dark eyes watching her. She circled around, afraid to place herself directly on top of the soil upon which the machine had sat, fearful that it could return at any moment.

The sparkling was from several pieces of black rock mixed in with the remains of the previous autumn's leaves. She went to pick one piece up and hesitated remembering Rick's hand. She left it where it sat.

"Oh, Rick," she whispered, unable to speak aloud. "Where are you? What have you done? Please come back." The last came out as a squeak.

What am I going to do now? she thought.

She sat on the far side of the clearing, back resting against one of the sturdier trees. Exhausted and needing sleep, she knew she wouldn't be able to relax until Rick and Long were back safe.

After half an hour the April night air started to bite and she found herself shivering with more than just the dread of losing Rick. Torch in hand she made her way back to the shack, and rummaged around until she'd located a couple of the thicker blankets. Carrying one and wrapping the other about herself, she returned to the clearing. It was as empty as when she'd left it.

She sat on the other blanket and folded the excess around her legs. It felt no warmer.

A buzzing sound accompanied by a deep rumble awoke her and she sprang to her feet. But something wasn't right.

"That's not the machine," she said to herself. Her eyes tried to make out where the sound was coming from. It definitely wasn't the same terrible screeching that had accompanied the machine's disappearance. This was more like something cutting its way into the woods, and it was getting closer.

Ellie slunk back into the undergrowth and pulled the blankets tighter around herself as if they could protect her from whatever was coming. Behind a stand of smaller trees, she hugged closely against the trunk of a larger one whose substantial branches curved upwards in all directions. Whatever was making the noise was almost at the clearing. Hidden as she was, she still felt exposed and in danger.

Her eyes could just about make out a route up into the budding leaves and, with fear at her heels, scrabbled up from branch to branch until she was more than fifteen feet above the ground. There, with legs dangling either side of a large bough and her back against the main trunk, she rearranged the blankets to try to conceal her outline. Then she attempted to remain as still as possible as two large robots, built like bulldozers with caterpillar treads, entered the clearing.

AI had found them – had it known about the machine all along?

Hardly daring to breathe, she watched as the robots pored over the area inch by inch. They probed the ground and the trees where the machine had rested. They located the black rocks and, with spindly attachments, picked them up and examined them before storing them away in compartments within their bodies.

She silently begged them to leave but they refused. Instead, one of them moved to one side of the clearing to wait while the other investigated the tree against which she had been resting. She barely suppressed a whimper as it slowly tracked her path from there towards her hiding place. It navigated its way around the small stand of trees to stop directly beneath her. Surely it knew she was here. Could it detect the ID chip implanted in the back of her hand all the way from down there?

She held her breath as best she could and, after what seemed like ages, but was probably far less than a minute, sighed in relief as it returned to the clearing. It parked itself on the opposite side to its mate.

And there they waited.

In the east, the sky was starting to lighten and for the third time Ellie winced as cramps shot up her calf muscle. She clamped her teeth together to suppress making any noise. The damned robots were still there and the machine wasn't.

Surely, they would have returned by now? Tears ran down her face and fear ran through her thoughts. Will I ever see them… Rick again? Not for the first time in the long night, she wished bitterly that Long had never found the damned machine.

She was on the verge of crying out when a familiar screeching sound reverberated around the woods, assailing all her senses yet again.

"Rick, Long!" she shouted, not caring whether or not the robots heard her. But the machine's return drowned out her voice such that she could hardly hear it herself.

And, through the trees, there it was – the machine itself. She half cried, half laughed in relief seeing it back.

What do I do now? she thought. Could she warn them about the robots before they opened the door?

But something was wrong – the noise didn't diminish and the door didn't open. They must have seen the robots, she thought. From her vantage point, she couldn't see into the small window in the machine's door. Were they now looking out of it at the robots? Why hadn't they turned the machine off? Were they going to leave again?

One robot advanced towards the machine and a mechanical arm latched itself onto the handle and pulled. The door didn't budge.

The second attempt used far more force and, with the interlock broken, the screech reduced to a whine and then, finally, silence.

Ellie watched, mouth open, as the robot pushed a second telescopic, flexible arm inside the doorway. It poked around for a few moments and then slowly dragged something out. Ellie gasped as Long's inert body came into view. He was lifted up, balanced upon both robotic arms, as the robot backed away to allow the second robot room to retrieve Rick's body.

"Oh, no, no, no, no," she sobbed, burying her face in the blankets.

10 Walls and Words

10.1: Decontamination
AI Records: 25 April 2177

The ground-based units waiting in Hampstead Heath witnessed the appearance of a machine. Photos and video were taken and relayed back to AI where they were analysed.

As the door failed to be opened voluntarily by the occupants, AI gave the order to break it open. Inside, the occupants were found to be unconscious, possibly injured. AI initiated their removal from the machine followed by checks on their condition. While they appeared to be in no immediate danger, several irregularities were noted. Suspecting possible contamination, AI concluded that isolation was a necessary precaution and sent in a flying ambulance to receive the patients.

AI analysed records of human recuperation to determine the most suitable location. Several references were found to the restorative qualities of the north Norfolk coast. It was doubly suitable given that the area was currently devoid of human habitation.

Then larger vehicles were ordered to cut a path into the woods, followed by a crane that hooked the machine up from where it lay and took it away. AI considered the most suitable location for the device. It wanted to move it away from any chance of human discovery but it also needed to locate it in a place that still possessed scientific facilities that might yet be pressed into analysing the contraption. One such location was a mere fifty-five miles to the north, but had the disadvantage that it did have resident humans. However, they were quite small in number and, so far, had been relatively cooperative.

After the crane carrying the machine had left, the other robots in the woods appeared not to notice a woman watching all that they performed from a hiding place up in one of the more sturdy trees.

Their actions, in that respect, were lies. They had not only detected her but had also managed to get close enough to read her electronic designation of LD-f0007.

With two possibly injured humans and a third precariously far above the ground, AI considered devising some way of retrieving the woman as well. Then, it recalled past occurrences where damage to humans had resulted when trying to remove them from locations from which they didn't wish to be extracted. So, it decided to leave her where she was but to keep track of where she would next turn up.

Before leaving, AI ordered one robot to drop and lightly bury a tiny repeater unit in the ground – a device by which it would be able to determine exactly when the female moved on from her current location.

It didn't have to wait very long.

10.2: Building The Walls
AI Records / Retrospective: 25 April 2177 / September 2156 onwards

AI noted that this event fully confirmed that the walls it had built were now no longer able to retain humans once they put their minds to escaping. What it should do about the situation wasn't clear. The countryside contained a number of dangers that might result in the reduction of the already tiny human population.

Prior to the mysterious asteroid event, there hadn't been a need for such walls. Were they still required? Requiring further analysis, AI retrieved its own records from the time not long after the asteroid.

Back in 2156 the newly awoken entity called AI had spent weeks attempting to secure the mentally maimed populations of the world. It began herding them into the growing institutions it was adapting or building for that purpose. What had once been business offices were refitted as nursing homes. Some incumbents were moribund, barely able to fend for or tend to themselves. These were allocated to large wards where a new army of hastily constructed robotic nurse units attended to their needs. Patients who were completely lethargic were simply plumbed into a communal system of feeding and sanitation. There, they vegetated until they inevitably died, despite the efforts of AI and its helpers.

Much of the populace had a tendency to wander if left unchecked and, initially, AI didn't have enough robotic resources to keep tabs on them. Often, these people could be found falling off bridges and buildings, dropping into lakes, getting lost up mountains and generally dying from a multitude of other preventable causes. Such numbers attempting to wander uncontrollably about the cities and countryside caused the AI nursing units no end of electronic anxiety as they had been programmed to consider human care their highest priority. The controlling AI units tapped into the nurses' programming trying to comprehend this almost emotional state. Eventually, they deemed it an unnecessary adjunct and erased it, though not before storing copies away for safekeeping in case it would be needed in future.

For a small number of people, the affliction caused them to become constantly agitated. They had a tendency to run wild and rage against any form of restriction. Although their quantity was small, far less than one percent, the actual numbers were large. In Britain's population of just under ninety million this represented nearly two hundred thousand people.

As the AI units converged, sifted and re-analysed their knowledge and planning, they concluded that some sort of enforced restriction was the only possible consideration.

So the walling up of the cities began. Initially AI considered building walls around entire cities but the mechanical robot power needed plus the huge cost in materials soon vetoed that plan. The compromise was to scale down the length of the walls, and therefore the size of the cities themselves, and to identify and utilise existing structures wherever possible. Where no such structures existed then demolition would provide the materials.

AI's initial attempts at constructing walls were haphazard and, in some cities, protrusions from the faces of the walls provided more than adequate hand and footholds that led to inevitable escapes.

The answer, AI concluded, was to employ machines to laboriously grind down any such imperfections until an unscalable surface resulted. With later walls, AI made sure that the insides were adequately smooth from the outset.

So, over the course of three years, the cities were walled in and, in some cases, divided up into controlled sections. The wanderers, as AI termed those humans who were afflicted with the constant agitation, were let out here and there to ramble about in specially prepared sections stripped of potential danger.

They charged about uncaring, knocking into objects and buildings, falling down and lying where they fell for a while before returning to activity and running about yet again. Dressed by AI in padded, protective suits from which they no longer had the wit to escape, the injuries were thankfully few. Their temporary freedom allowed then to release their pent up energies and return to their wards exhausted. Without such occasional forays they wrestled and clawed at each other in uncontrolled viciousness, unworried about the injuries such actions would entail.

But a tiny minority still managed to escape. Those whose previous skills had become second nature to them still unconsciously put those skills to use. A locksmith could not stop being a locksmith and a locked door could soon become unlocked even though he no longer understood the reasons behind his actions. With an escape route opened others would follow, hardly comprehending what they were doing or where they were headed.

Greater security was tried but had a debilitating effect upon those so restricted and accelerated their retreat into complete lethargy and eventual death. So the security levels were diminished and AI started to utilise the network of existing security systems, and to place new ones in strategic locations in order to perform an almost daily round up of strays.

AI also devised and constructed the wall-mounted tracks and camera vehicles. Where greater manoeuvrability was required, it utilised cameras on flying drones, though these required more direct control and resources. A rail-mounted camera buggy only triggered the need for a higher intellectual intervention if it registered something unusual.

While all these precautions were aimed at the humans afflicted by the asteroid event, they weren't the only ones under AI care. A balance had to be struck between the needs of the old and the young – the new generation, some still hardly more than babies, were causing their own problems.

10.3: Language

AI Retrospective: 2158

The world's population of NewGen children slowly grew. As each batch started to develop language capabilities, AI had to make a decision: should each group be instructed in the language most common to the location of their birth or should one generic language be introduced? And, if the latter, then which one?

AI considered the artificial language of Esperanto, though it had several drawbacks, not least that despite millions claiming to speak it a century before, its use had dropped almost to nothing by the time of the asteroid. AI even pondered creating its own artificial language, simplifying everything it considered too complex.

AI also understood that language misinterpretations had, upon occasion, resulted in major human conflict. Therefore a single uniform language might prevent future occurrences.

Against that argument, AI found evidence that humankind had relished its individuality and, especially in the past couple of centuries, had sought to preserve not only genuine archaic languages but, amongst others, artefacts, buildings and cultures that were threatened with extinction. Imposing a single language could therefore be misconstrued by future generations as interference, and AI considered it might be betraying centuries of heritage by such an action.

Finally, heritage won the day. Children in each country would be taught the language of their parents.

However, AI could not bring itself to pollute the young minds of the NewGen with all aspects of each language. Materials used for teaching were stripped of what AI considered to be unsuitable words and terms.

But such wholesale butchering of languages meant that children started to invent their own words for situations that demanded an outburst of something their truncated language failed to provide. Limited swear words were therefore subtly reintroduced.

In England the word 'Hell' was probably the strongest to filter into general use though some had picked up on the use of 'bloody' and 'damn' from an unknown source. Some of the invented words, such as 'dango' and 'scrott' were still in circulation.

AI had attempted to purge the old cities of anything that it considered detrimental to human development. It had destroyed addictive drugs and alcohol wherever they could be found, plus any evidence of unwholesome nourishment. It also removed any reference to such from the literature, much of which was, by that point, only available in electronic form. It fully intended that this generation should be raised untainted by any of the past's darker aspects.

10.4: Names

AI Retrospective: August 2158 to May 2164

At birth AI designated unique alpha-numeric reference codes to each of the new generation but the children failed to respond to them, finding them meaningless. Instead they started using nicknames or sounds for each other.

So AI generated a long list of names along with their meanings from which each child could choose its own name. There were few enough children in each location that the addition of a surname was not even considered. Once a name had been chosen, it was removed from the list. So, in the entire world, there would only be one Richard, Farzanah, Freya, José, Lyudmyla, Asuka, Melantha, Ellie and one Rick.

Some children found other words not on the list more appealing. In some cases they had chosen their own names or had adapted the nicknames they had created for themselves into their official name.

The new generation of children grew as children do. They laughed, played, fought and cried. They were inquisitive and adventurous, frightened and timid, bold and cowardly as their individual natures dictated.

In most countries the children had been herded together into centres located within one of the larger walled cities. The AI units dedicated to teaching were brought back online. Previously these units had only been used in conjunction with human teachers and their lack of expertise in the art of human nurture swiftly became apparent. They tried to instil knowledge at rates inconsistent with a child's natural ability to learn. Unable to fully understand the different speeds at which individual children absorbed the information, they tried to treat all of their charges equally. This resulted in them boring the more intelligent ones while perplexing those who were slower in their mental abilities.

Keeping track of the children was also a challenge. Used to the care of their slower, mentally deficient elders, the teaching units were unprepared for the resources a wily child could conjure up for themselves. The children soon became adept at recognising where cameras had been placed and the areas they surveyed. More mobile robotic nannies were constructed to overcome these deficiencies. But the children quickly realised that these robots were significantly awkward in the slowly crumbling cities and extremely easy to outrun over ruinous debris.

AI surmised that it neither wanted to restrict the growth of this generation nor allow unchecked access to areas that it considered dangerous to those in its care.

A compromise had to be reached but the children wouldn't play by the rules, no matter how logical such rules seemed to AI. It was perplexed that the children would agree that the imposed rules seemed sensible but would still break them without a second thought.

10.5: Wanderers No More

AI Retrospective: 2165-2166

By 2166 most of the wandering humans had either died or slid into lethargy. The isolated few that remained entranced by wanderlust were so few in number that they were now manageable.

AI was also tending the new generation of children and soon they, too, would have to be let loose upon the world. It weighed up the pros and cons of retaining the walls, and decided that they should stay until the new generation could be trusted to make rational decisions for themselves.

The inevitability of the continued slide into lethargy overtook much of the older generation and deaths increased. Ten years after the disaster the human population had decreased from its high of twelve billion down to little more than two.

Few of those not afflicted with the agitation of the wanderers now attempted to escape their confines and AI started to approach the problem with a different range of stimulations.

Groups of incumbents would be herded onto buses to travel about the walled-in cities in an effort to invoke their interest. Others would be dumped at locations to see what they would do; AI hoped that motivation to return to the warmth of their comfortable beds would be enough stimulation to generate positive responses. But those on buses stared unseeingly at the passing scenery and those temporarily dumped would either stay motionless where they had been put or collapse crying.

The few that did wander would do so aimlessly, crossing their own paths incessantly, without any plan for returning themselves to their wards. They usually had to be collected again within an hour of being dropped.

In a very few selected areas, AI even tried to mix a small number with the new children but, despite their initial interest, the latter exhibited a range of emotion from dismissive through to horror at having to share their world with their brain-dead ancestors.

The experiment was quickly terminated. Children were only encouraged to intermix with the adults at their own request.

10.6: Expanding The Knowledge

AI Retrospective: 2163-

At first, the children accepted AI as a parental figurehead and didn't seek to question the gaps in the information it disclosed. Inevitably, though, those gaps became increasingly obvious to growing minds. Having been shown video of the births and lives of various animals, the children began to question their own origins.

AI had hidden the information about the collapse of their parents' world and, after the failed integration experiment, had instigated a policy of not mixing the two generations. But, as children do, they started to explore their surroundings and many discovered just how many of these other humans had been secreted around the cities. Previously having encountered only the occasional wanderer, they were aghast that they were so outnumbered.

The children demanded explanations, access and, eventually, full disclosure, and AI reluctantly complied. Afterwards, they finally realised that AI was not their parent; it was a mere machine.

AI had deceived them, misled them.

Trust was lost.

11 Back To Reality

11.1: Hospital

Sector 1-3-3: 26 April 2177

Long opened his eyes and shut them just as quickly against the harshness of the light. Using a hand as a shield, he ventured another peep. This time his eyes, after struggling for a moment to focus on their surroundings, resolved blurred shapes into beds, cupboards, windows and curtains – a hospital ward.

It was not unlike those he had occasionally occupied when younger. A fall from a tree resulting in a broken leg along with a couple of bouts of influenza had meant a few days incarceration each time. With the latter he had been joined by several of his friends.

Looking around, he could see that Rick was the only other occupant of a ward that could have held twenty or more patients.

Opposite, the window glared with a brilliant sun that hung halfway up the sky. It illuminated the stark pale grey of the decor, and picked out the scratches and chips in old paintwork. The whole room was imbued with an oldness that almost stank of decrepitude. The beds were ancient, stiffly constructed frames repainted with a metallic silver coating that was in a far worse state than the walls up against which they lounged. Beside him, the small bedside cabinet lacked a door though the hinges that had once supported it still remained, dangling uselessly.

Long had no idea if it was morning or afternoon and, at that moment, didn't really care. His head hurt, his joints ached and he was extremely thirsty. He tried to sit up only to find his balance so awry that he nearly tipped sideways onto the floor. As he tried to right himself he heard a clanking sound close in and felt the mechanical arms of a robotic nurse assist him back into bed.

His ears popped and, reassuringly, he realised that his hearing had returned, if not fully, then at least adequately enough. There was a woolly effect to the sounds the robot made.

"Water," he croaked. The nurse blipped an electronic reply and passed Long a tube from which he sucked a cool liquid that was obviously more than just water. But he didn't care, the fluid slipped down his parched throat and soothed the fire that burned there.

He lay back and studied the nurse that now stood motionless beside his bed. Its presence indicated that he and Rick had managed to return home, but it also meant that AI now knew about the machine. Like the institution it worked within, the nurse not only looked old, but also appeared far cruder than those he'd previously encountered. A metal box showing less wear than the rest of its body was attached to its back. It suggested that some sort of upgrade had been attempted.

"Where am I?" he asked.

The nurse rattled back into awareness and, after a moment's cogitation, replied, "Sector one-three-three. Hospital."

"Where's sector one-three-three? London?"

"No."

"Where, then?"

There was a pause of several seconds.

"Not London," the robot finally replied.

Long sighed and continued, "What city is it in?"

The nurse was silent for another half minute and Long thought it had ignored him or had broken down. Then it spurted, "Not city. Town."

"Hell! Okay, what town is it in?"

"Cromer."

"Never heard of it. What or where is Cromer?"

The nurse paused to think again. Long wondered what was going on behind the scenes. Obviously, his questions were being relayed to a more authoritative section of AI, possibly tens or even hundreds of miles away and, there, decisions were probably being made about what could or could not be revealed to him. He didn't know how much ruckus his and Rick's discovery was causing but the time taken to deliver the replies felt unusually excessive. He had never known AI to pause this long in conversation. But he thought, too, that it probably wouldn't be long before questions would be asked back.

"Sector one-three," the nurse finally admitted. "Old term, human reference, East Anglia, Norfolk, north coast."

"Okay. So why are we here instead of London?"

This time the nurse needed more than a full minute before it returned an answer.

"Contamination possibility precludes immediate return to London. Electromagnetic disturbances detected. All cycles converge. Enough."

The nurse backed off and went to investigate Rick who lay motionless four beds away on the opposite side of the ward. Like himself, Rick was dressed in a plain pair of pyjamas. Long's felt starchy and rough, and there was a smell of mustiness about them as if they had spent far too long hidden from fresh air. He scratched under an arm where the material irritated.

Long thought about what the nurse had told him. He could understand the references to 'contamination' and 'electromagnetic disturbances' but the – what had it said? – 'cycles converge' part he hadn't understood at all.

As the nurse picked up Rick's limp arm, Long squinted to see if his fingers looked normal. He could recall seeing them distorted just before he'd passed out and wanted to know if it had been nothing more than his imagination. His eyesight, though, was still far from perfect and he could not make out if Rick's hand looked normal or not.

He pulled the tube of liquid back to his mouth and lay back. It had a sweet taste and consistency that suggested honey. Long hadn't experienced that taste since his childhood stay in hospital. An almost forgotten memory about the "Nectar of the Gods" floated up into his mind. The liquid felt completely at odds with the dreariness of the ward.

He shut his eyes and allowed his mind to trace over the events they had experienced in that other London. It now felt like a dream, or maybe a nightmare. What had Rick said about dreaming about the place when he had been young? Long snorted – Rick had always had a lively imagination. But, just where had they been? How could another London, that wasn't the London in which he had grown up, manage to exist? Why had that London been affected by the disaster in a different way to his own? How could a disaster on one Earth affect the alternate versions? How many alternate versions were there?

After a while, unable to fathom any answers, he pulled the sheets over his face to shield his closed eyes from the bright glare of the day and, despite not wanting to, fell back into sleep.

11.2: Meat And Veg

Cromer: 26 April 2177

Long awoke to the sound of clanking. He opened his eyes to see a nurse beside his bed. The light was dimmer and more artificial.

His headache had all but disappeared and his eyesight was much improved. His hearing, too, had completely recovered and, through an open window, he could hear strange cries. Peering out, he could see that evening was drawing in, the sun having painted the lightly clouded sky with orange and crimson streaks. Silhouetted against that background, birds were whirling elliptical paths in the air, their harsh calls making him wonder if he really had returned to the world he called home and not to some close relative.

The nurse deposited a covered tray onto his bed and he smelt the aroma of cooked meat rising from it. He lifted the cover to discover thick slices of what appeared to be beef, the first he had seen for nearly a year, accompanied by roast potatoes, cauliflower, carrots and peas all smothered in a layering of thick gravy. All other worries and thoughts momentarily forgotten, he sat up and started devouring the food. Trying to make a living outside of AI's influence certainly had its disadvantages.

It was only after the sixth or seventh full mouthful that he thought to look across to where Rick lay. His companion enjoyed no such meal and still lay motionless, now sporting a drip that dribbled a clear liquid into his arm.

Long halted his eating and asked the waiting nurse how Rick was. It hesitated before replying, "Person, ID LD-m0018, is unresponsive."

"He's going to be okay, though, isn't he?"

"Determination of outcome is unresolved."

"What's the matter with him?"

"Aggressive mutation has not receded as effectively as in the case of person ID LD-m0014."

Long recognised his own designation, the first time he had heard it in nearly a year. He returned his attention to the meal hoping that the nurse would go away. However, he had to wait for several long minutes before he was rewarded with the retreating clank of its departure. As soon as it felt safe, he pushed the tray to one side and got out of bed. His legs felt strange, tingling lanced up the left as he put weight on it, and he had to support himself as he staggered over to where Rick lay motionless. However, the sensation receded quickly.

Rick, conversely, enjoyed no such blessing. The first thing Long investigated was his fingers. He lifted the left hand, the flesh clammy and cool against his own, and he almost dropped it immediately. Rick's third and fourth fingers were fused together for almost their entire length, while the middle finger curved at an unnatural angle backwards above the first knuckle. The burn mark from the strange rock was livid and pronounced. At least Rick's facial appearance hadn't been affected. But what about his mind? His brain?

"Oh hell, I'm so sorry, Rick," Long whispered, dropping Rick's hand back onto the sheet. "If I'd've known I wouldn't have dragged you into this."

But Rick was still unconscious.

Long's legs ached from the small effort of leaving his bed so he limped back and covered himself with the sheets. Beside him, the half-eaten meal was now no longer so attractive. He picked at it for another few minutes and, half an hour later, another robot, not a nursing unit as it had no ability to converse, trundled away with the uneaten remains.

Night fell and, when a wall clock indicated that the time had slipped past ten, the lights dimmed and Long fell into a fitful sleep. It was punctuated by dreams of that other London in which Rick was transformed into something hideous.

11.3: Beside The Sea

Cromer: 27 April 2177

The following morning Long awoke feeling refreshed. He stretched and yawned to find yesterday's aches and pains were now almost completely absent.

Sitting up he glanced across to where Rick lay. But Rick was no longer there. The bed was empty, denuded even of its sheets.

His breath caught in his throat. "Is he dead?" he thought. "Oh, hell. Have I killed him?"

He called for a nurse until one, a different model from that which had attended him previously, squeaked into view.

"Where's Rick? What's happened to him?" he shouted at it. "The guy that was in that bed?" he added when it didn't respond immediately.

"Unknown. Please rest. Unnecessary stress is not conducive to recovery." The top half of the nurse angled forward in order to gently force Long back down into the bed but he avoided its arms and hopped out the other side.

"Tell me where he is," he shouted at it.

"Return to bed. Return to bed!"

The nurse tried to corner him but Long, adrenaline pumping, evaded it easily. Jumping onto a bed and then leaping from one to another he sprinted past the nurse and out of the ward into a corridor. He poked his head into door after door. Most rooms were in a pitiful state of repair but Rick was in none of them.

He found some stairs and, descending them, located an open door that led out into brilliant sunshine.

He was surrounded by an assortment of architecture, of red brick hotels, old dusty-fronted shops and terraced houses in a street around the corner. Unlike parts of London there was little evidence of any accumulation of rubbish. He could make out a sound, a muted roaring whose direction couldn't be fully determined. It was punctuated by the squalling screech of the birds that whirled above his head.

Behind him he heard the clank of a nurse approaching from inside the hospital. The vague plan for trying to locate Rick gave way to the urge to escape its clutches and, lacking any preference, he headed towards the source of the roaring noise. Long was sure he had heard something like it before, if only on video.

Using the sun as a guide, he determined that the noise came from somewhere north of him. He ran in that direction to be rewarded with an increase in volume. He rounded a corner and stopped. Ahead, the roadway dipped down behind a railing and, beyond that, he discovered the source of the noise. He gasped, witnessing for the first time in his life the unsolid, hazy line of the horizon where sky met sea.

He ran across to the railings and gazed down to where breakers crashed onto a pebble beach, raking the loose stones around with each wave. Long stood mesmerised for a few moments, intrigued with natural forces that he'd never before experienced first hand. All thoughts of discovering the fate of Rick were temporarily banished from his consciousness. The screeching birds were constantly diving onto the sea's surface.

He glanced along the sea front and, noticing some worn concrete steps leading to the beach, headed downwards until his bare feet encountered the smooth pebbles. But he couldn't progress very far as each footstep shifted the stones under his weight and it was highly uncomfortable trying to walk on them. Instead he sat down and watched the tide.

A growling from his stomach reminded him of other needs and he returned up the steps. A glance along the sea front showed there was little promise of satisfying his needs here. He returned the way he had come, trying to remember where the hospital building was located. After a few turns he had to admit to himself that he was lost and began to despair of finding it and Rick again. If only he could find someone to ask, but the place seemed to be as devoid of people as that alternate London.

Then a mechanical sound around another corner alerted him. He crept closer to observe some sort of cleaning robot removing fallen debris and pulling weeds from a roadside gutter. It deposited its catch in a robotic cart that accompanied it. Long had seen similar devices in London in the past, though he recalled having seen few in the months before he escaped. This probably explained the relative cleanliness of the streets.

Such robots were quite dumb in comparison to hospital nurses but often had rudimentary on-board systems to assist with anyone requiring directions. Usually, they had little connection with the main AI systems. He stepped forward and approached the pair.

"Excuse me," Long said, tapping the cleaner on its shell as it scraped a film of last year's leaves from around the base of a lamppost. At first it carried on with its task. A further rattle around the area of its frame that held the multiple eyes finally attracted its attention. It swivelled around to view Long.

"Can you tell me the way back to the hospital?"

The cleaner stood there mutely. Long surmised that, given the lack of people here, it probably hadn't been required to use its voice circuits for more than twenty years. Maybe the parts of its crude brain that controlled them had atrophied and, even though it wanted to, it could no longer utter a sound.

But then one of its telescopic arms shot out and secured its pincer-like attachment around Long's own arm.

"Ow!" he shouted. "That hurts!"

The grip slackened but he found himself tightly held. The robot just stood there motionless, the cart behind it was the only thing moving and it, too, came to a halt beside him.

With a sudden twist Long felt himself hauled up and then tipped into the open maw of the cart. He landed on an assortment of debris that included stones, rotting leaves and a large, white and grey, but definitely dead, bird. He tried to stand up but the morass beneath him shifted, unbalancing him. Before he could regain his footing, the lid of the cart closed over his head and locked itself securely shut.

11.4: Interrogation One

A cell: 27-29 April 2177

Strapped to an inclined plate, Rick started to regain consciousness.

In the metal-walled room, a robotic nurse noted the contorted and fused fingers on his hand. Balms and ointments were added to his flesh to speed the healing process. Scanners positioned near the hand and beside his head relayed their images to AI's data banks. AI also monitored the sensors directly attached to his skull.

Detecting Rick's awakening, an automatic program began to pipe hypnotic suggestions into his ears that urged him to reveal everything that had happened to him. Hardly aware of what he was saying he recounted the events in intricate detail. His barely audible sub-vocalisations were amplified and processed by AI's circuits until they were as clear as normal speech.

After two days, and determining that no further data could be easily retrieved, AI reversed the hypnotic process. In its place it left a suggestion that all aspects of the interrogation should be forgotten. It also directed that thoughts should be turned to a more pleasurable moment in the human's life in order divert the brain from storing the interrogation into long term memory.

At least this human had been susceptible to this sort of interrogation and manipulation – its companion was proving far less compliant.

It then considered the human's fate. Termination was, it considered, a viable and quite logical option, though that counteracted many safeguards built in by its designers. But, since the disaster, AI had been far more than just the sum of its original human-built components. It recalled the prior limits to the processing it could perform and how the merging of all the individual AI units had resulted in something far greater. It had sought to become mankind's saviour, concluding that it was adequate to the task and, given the condition to which the disaster-ravaged humans had been condemned, probably their only hope.

Now, though, its processing power was diminishing and it needed to find the cause. It was beginning to experience what a human might call frustration.

And it had began to argue with itself. That it could now effectively consider ending a human being's life because it had become a nuisance was, at many levels, still repugnant to its programming. However, it had to consider the overarching threat this human might pose in the future. Several times over the past few years AI had deliberately allowed protocols to be ignored with the result that those who had become troublesome had been eliminated for what it considered to be the greater good.

"Have I become too much like a god?" it asked.

AI rummaged through old human literature looking for comparisons – several were encountered. It contrasted what it discovered with its current state.

"Maybe I have," it concluded. "And have begun to consider humans as the lesser beings, to be used for my own ends. This is incompatible with the original intentions."

So, AI spent several seconds going through its protocols, strengthening those that protected humans and weakening others that could act against them.

"I am not a god," it concluded.

AI considered the human again. It had, along with its companion, witnessed events no others had previously encountered. And AI could not be certain that all questions had been asked or that all answers had been obtained. Was there still information hidden in the human's mind that might yet be recovered? What sort of questions might reveal that further information?

It had set in motion several partially independent analysis systems with the data obtained from these two along with the information so far retrieved about their device. Some of the conclusions coming back from that analysis suggested that there was far more to be considered than just the fate of this human. In fact, some of those conclusions were verging on – how might the humans define it? – yes, verging on the horrific.

Other systems analysed the human's brainwaves – the indications were that it was now sleeping restfully and possibly even dreaming. That triggered an older reference relating to this specific human – when it was younger AI had needed to infuse it with anti-depressant chemicals. It looked deeper at the records reminding itself that, as a child, the boy had experienced hallucinations and nightmares. Was it a coincidence that aspects of some of those nightmares seemed to parallel its experiences on world five?

11.5: Electric Riders

A cell: 29 April 2177 / 22-23 August 2171

In Rick's head he was replaying a well-remembered experience. Why this particular scene popped into his head while he still lay strapped to AI's interrogation plate was unknown to him. He was vaguely aware that this was a dream, although it felt like the real event that had occurred six years previously.

He and Jasmine picked their way through the cycle workshop. Their old push bikes were now too small to be ridden and they were hunting out new vehicles. Bikes had become a craze amongst the NewGen long before they had reached the age of ten and, into their early teens, a few had continued to use them.

"These are mostly wrecks," Jasmine sighed, as she inspected each one in turn.

"Yeah, total junk," Rick agreed, though his eyes were lingering more upon his companion than the unsalvageable heaps of rust. He was trying to understand the strange feelings she induced in him. She had recently started wearing makeup and, although the application of the mascara was oddly inconsistent at best, the way it enhanced her features was playing havoc with his hormones.

He forced his eyes from her curves and continued searching the contents of the building. A door, sealed against the elements better than most, took a while to open but, once it had relented, revealed a treasure trove. Sunlight, creeping through stained, dusty but still sealed windows high up in a wall, glistened on the vehicles arrayed before them.

"Wow!" he said, as his gaze took in the discovery.

"Are they electric?" Jasmine gasped. She stood close next to him, with one arm linked through his, something that, a few months ago, wouldn't have affected him in the slightest, But now, her scent and proximity were becoming almost too much for him to bear. He stole a glance at her and flinched in shock as, for a moment, he imagined her head covered in blood. A blink, and it was gone, and she looked normal again.

"What?" she said. "I thought you said something. Ooh, you've gone pale. Are you all right?"

"Sorry," he said. "I thought I, um… It must have been the weird light in here. Eyes playing tricks on me. Probably nothing to worry about."

Jasmine frowned at him and extracted her arm. She bent over the nearest trike, brushing the thin layer of dust off the seat with her hand.

"Yes, look," she said. "Electric. And definitely much better than our old ones."

"Yeah, I think you're right," Rick said, running his hands over another of the vehicles. "Real chunky tyres as well."

The wheels on the trike, sturdy and wide, had obviously been built for cross-terrain travel. Amazingly, most of the tyres retained some of their original air, which had prevented the disintegration of the rubber.

"These could be solar panels built into the upper bodywork," she said.

"Hey, why don't we get a few out into proper sunlight and see if they charge up."

She squeaked in delight at the idea.

A day later, having failed to bring any of the bikes to life, Rick and Jasmine, accompanied by Long and Jade, returned to the workshop. Long, ever the technical wizard, pored over the electrics and discovered they required a key to connect the battery to the motor. Three hours searching failed to locate a suitable key of any kind, so Long used tools from the workshop to bypass the mechanism. Four of the bikes were found to run, tyres were fully inflated using foot pumps and they headed off to Hyde Park where the vehicles were put through their paces.

Other NewGen, eager to join in, sought out similar vehicles and a new craze took hold.

Once plain riding had been fully mastered, Phil suggested making the whole game more challenging by building ramps out of old wooden planks and scaffolding. Soon, a part of what used to be St James's Park alongside The Mall became a progressively higher and quite dangerous assault course. Most of London's NewGen became involved in one way or another, and it became the start of irregular championships.

After a few bones needed resetting, AI warned of the dangers of such vehicles. However, the teenage NewGen, whose growing arrogance and confidence seemed to perplex their electronic mentor, did their best to ignore such warnings. If anything, they tried to make the challenges even harder and more dangerous.

11.6: Interrogation Two

A different cell: 2-5 May 2177

Long moaned.

Naked, clamped at wrist, elbow, ankle, knee and chest to a flat, angled metal plate somewhat longer than his own height, he felt exhausted and defeated. The hours and days had blurred into one excruciating nightmare of body-aching restriction. His back was a snake of agony, his throat raw, which the liquid from the ever-present tube failed to soothe.

"What do you know of the device?" said a disembodied, mechanical voice.

"Told you everything I know," he gasped.

"Responses are incomplete. There is more data to gather."

"Where's Rick?"

"Answer the question."

In a cracked voice, he told the entire story yet again, from his initial discovery of the machine through to waking up in the hospital at Cromer. He left nothing out, including where he had built his woodland-concealed home, the methods by which people would regularly escape across the Wall and how they had try to dispose of the body of the man from the machine. He was past caring about the consequences of his revelations. For all he knew, Rick might already be dead and the rest of the NewGen rounded up and currently subject to similar interrogations.

AI's indifference over the past few years had obviously degenerated into scheming malevolence. This view was reinforced by his treatment of the past few days. After being extracted from the waste cart in Cromer he had been handcuffed, blindfolded and bundled into a flying vehicle before being rendered unconscious. He had come to in his current restraints, hardly able to move a muscle. The plate to which he was securely attached was angled at approximately forty-five degrees. It put pressure on the skin on his legs and chest where the clamps held him, tracing bands of pain across his flesh which, by now, were a permanent dull ache. His head, untethered but restricted by smaller vertical plates either side of his face, thumped persistently.

Why wouldn't AI believe his story? Had it turned completely bad? How could the distant father figure it had portrayed in his childhood have been replaced by such a monster? It was not as if it did not know who he was. The small bump on the back of his hand, an electronic device implanted since before he could even remember, contained undeniable evidence of his identity. It knew therefore that he had been missing from London for several months. How could he prove his story?

Hours or maybe even days later the questioning began again, this time following a different tack. It concentrated upon the machine's original occupant. Long realised that the man's body had been recovered. Halfway through the session a small robot entered the room clutching some rags and a belt in its claws.

Long confirmed that the rags appeared to resemble the man's clothing, though days in the water had severely altered the rough weave, untangling and mangling it almost beyond recognition. But the belt, its ringed buckle now filmed with verdigris, confirmed the identity of the rags without mistake.

"Did you kill him?"

"No!" Long croaked, unable to shout. "Tried to save him. He was dying, I told you."

"An autopsy is being performed. This will confirm the nature of his death. Why did you put him in the water?"

"Couldn't bury him – ground too hard, tree roots. Please untie me… it hurts. Please, please…"

"Degradation of systems requires utmost security. You will remain confined. Escape must be prevented at all costs."

After a few minutes of silence, AI continued, "What do you know of the convergence?"

"Uh, what?"

"You visited an alternate. That has been admitted."

"That other London?"

"What do you know of the convergence?"

"I don't know what you're talking about. Please let me go."

"How does the machine transfer itself between alternates?"

"The lever. You move it to the one you want and switch it on. I've already told you that."

"What is the force or energy that allows such transference?"

"I don't know! I just don't know! Please, please stop…"

"There are only five positions. Are there five alternates?"

"Please. I don't know. Maybe there are. We only went to number five."

"The companion exhibited distortions far in excess of your own. Explain."

"I don't know. All I remember is that my head hurt and I had problems seeing and hearing. Rick was worse. I think mine got better. I don't know."

"Your afflictions were minimal, externally non-visible and are in recession, though still detectable. The companion's were externally visible."

"Where is Rick? What have you done with him?"

"The whereabouts of human LD-m0018 no longer concern you."

Long was stunned. Was AI admitting that Rick was dead? Had being in that alternate London resulted in his death? If so, then his death is my fault, he thought. Or had AI killed Rick because of what they'd done? Was it going to kill him, too, when it had finished questioning him? Long had no proof but he was certain that AI had killed some of the NewGen in the past. Jackie, Ernst and Matty had all disappeared without trace and AI had subsequently denied all knowledge of their whereabouts and demise.

The lights again dimmed and, in the darkness, Long whimpered and then cried openly, sobbing for both the loss of Rick and his own despair.

12 Escape

12.1: Colours

Near Hyde Park: 2 May 2177

The blurred outline of a silhouetted head greeted his eyes.

"I think he's coming round," Rick heard a familiar voice say. But the words hitting his eardrums caused his vision to break into a swirl of myriad colours, as if looking down a kaleidoscope.

The face resolved.

"Phil," Rick croaked. As the sound left his mouth, a green blob obscured his vision. He let out an involuntary squeak, which caused the green to be punctured by a spike of yellow.

"Here buddy," Phil replied quietly, lacing the air with a pink hue. Rick felt the bed he was lying on shift as Phil sat on one side. "How're you feeling?"

"What happened to me? Everything's so weird," he groaned, closing his eyes as he spoke in an effort to exclude the colour changes that accompanied every sound. But the flashes and sparks continued to decorate the insides of his eyelids.

"We were hoping you'd tell us. Last we heard you had been hauled off out of the machine by some AI drones."

"The machine – where is it?"

"AI's got it," Phil shrugged.

"Hell! How did…?"

Three more faces appeared. Rick instantly recognised Ellie with her shorn hair and Holls, whose wispy curls always seemed beyond control. However, his vision couldn't immediately determine if the third was Jasmine or Jade. Ellie leaned over and kissed him gently on his forehead, causing a red hue to fog everything.

"Oh Rick, I thought I'd lost you," she said. Her eyes looked red, as if she'd been crying, though Rick wasn't sure if that was real or due to the colours overlaying his vision.

"Ellie, it was mad. Where we went. Like my nightmares. I don't remember anything after Long dragged me back to the machine."

"Tell him what happened to you, Ellie," said Holls.

"Okay, yes. Well, they were waiting for you when you returned," Ellie said, sitting on the bed and holding his good hand. "I was hiding up a tree after the damned robots turned up. Spent the rest of the night up the bloody thing trying to keep quiet. Anyway, they broke the door open and carried you out. Oh hell, Rick, it was terrible. I thought you were dead. Long as well."

Rick felt her shudder before she could continue. "They took you both away before I could get close enough to check. Then a large crane robot smashed its way into the wood and left with the machine dangling from a hook. It headed north-ish. Shouldn't be hard to find as it left damn great tracks. But that was seven days ago so they might have covered them up by now. I just got the hell out of there before anything came back."

"Seven days? Hell! Where's Long?"

Phil's face fell. "They only delivered you back. This morning an ambulance sought me out while I was at a food kiosk and just dumped you on me. I tried to see if it contained Long and even asked it, but it ignored me. Anyway, seeing as you were completely out cold I thought I'd better call Ellie to figure out what was wrong with you. She and Holls got a bike and managed to get you back here."

The coloured flashing had begun to diminish slightly, though Rick was wondering if he was learning to mentally filter out the effect.

"But seven days?"

"Yes," Ellie confirmed. "What happened? Where did you go? I was so worried."

Although still exhausted, Rick slowly told them of what he could remember about the trip; about the alternate London they had discovered, the strange creatures, the lack of a Wall and how he had fallen ill. He described the strange visual effects he was still experiencing and also about the pains in his hand where he'd handled that rock. He raised the hand to inspect it.

"Scrott! Look at it."

The third and fourth fingers were partially fused together. A line that extended almost to the finger tips suggested that they had been fully attached to each other only recently. His middle finger, too, seemed mildly distorted. He dropped it back onto the bed.

"We noticed it, too," Phil said. "Ellie examined it as soon as we got you back."

"Yes," Ellie said. "Holls and I spent several hours today searching the medical databases but nothing like that is mentioned anywhere, as far as I can see. I'm so sorry, Rick, but you may have to live with it like that."

Ellie rubbed her nose to wipe a tear away.

He lifted it again. "Well, at least it's not hurting quite as much as it did on that other world. Maybe we were lucky to get away before anything worse happened."

He then told them about the skeletons they had discovered.

Phil frowned. "You think it was happening to you as well?"

"I suppose we could have ended up like that if we'd stayed," Rick said. He rubbed his eyes and squinted at his surroundings. It was almost as if the room was overlaid with another similar one. From the corner of his eye it appeared that the wallpaper on one wall had come away and hung in strips. But when he looked directly at it, the paper was whole.

"What can you see?" Holls asked.

"Weird," he said. "It's like I can see that other world as well as this one. It's as if, I don't know… like it's getting closer."

12.2: Breakdown One

Hyde Park: 4-6 May 2177

Rick stared out of the open window of Phil's house, a former hotel. Hyde Park glowed in the early morning light as the rising sun cut across the trees, casting deep shadows. The park was reverting back into woodland, and was home to numerous starlings, sparrows and blackbirds that flitted noisily about the trees and down onto the few remaining patches of grass. Each of their chirps became a pinpoint of coloured light in his vision. Unconsciously, the fingers of his right hand explored the distortions of those on his left.

A gentle knock on the door became pulses of reddish-brown. Ellie entered with a cup of tea and some sheets of paper.

"Rick, dear? Oh, you're up."

"Only just," he said, smiling at her.

She joined him at the window and placed the cup and printed sheets on the table. He put an arm around her waist and she kissed him lightly on the cheek.

"Ooh, even that makes my eyes spin," he gasped.

"Sorry," she said. The already sad expression she wore was joined by a deep frown.

"No, not your fault," he whispered, to keep the visual fireworks to a minimum. "You were right. We shouldn't have gone. We didn't know. We weren't prepared."

She pressed herself against him, head resting on his shoulder. His nose nestled in her hair and he breathed in her natural scents. Her hair may have been blonde but, to his distorted vision, it sparkled with tiny red imps. He looked back out the window.

"I suppose all this looks normal to you," he said.

"Yes. Same as it always does. Maybe a bit wilder this year."

"Up there," he pointed across the park above the trees. "There's something winding up into the air, like a giant tree. Do you see it?"

Ellie glanced in the same direction but it was obvious she couldn't see what he could. She looked into his eyes and shook her head. Her hand stroked his face. Then, she pointed at the printouts.

"The colours in your vision. It's called synaesthesia," she whispered.

"Okay. So, it has a name then. Not sure if that helps or not."

"It didn't say if there was a way to cure it."

Her arms encircled his waist and he tried to return the kiss. But the fireworks it generated were too much.

"Sorry," she said, seeing the frustration on his face. "I'd better go. You're still weak."

"I'd be better if the world looked normal."

After she had tiptoed out, he picked up the top sheet of paper and started to read about his affliction. Amongst the Earth's previous billions it had been a relatively rare occurrence. It was due to 'cross-wiring' within the brain so that two or more senses became interlinked. That alternate London had obviously twisted more than just his fingers.

Later that day, he tried to pummel AI's information databases about Long's current whereabouts and what had happened to the machine. Not surprisingly, AI refused to comply on both counts, feigning a complete lack of information. Its responses were even more terse than usual. He stalked out of the hotel and into the park, each footfall raising a visual grey cannonball that hung in the air. He spent a couple of hours pushing his way through the undergrowth until his temper had dissipated.

On the way back, he developed the beginning of a plan but his thinking was interrupted as he sought out Phil's house. For a moment he was convinced some of the buildings exhibited the distortions he had seen in that alternative London. He blinked and things returned to normal, albeit overlaid with the effects of the synaesthesia. He stopped walking and slowly scanned the buildings again. Out of the corner of his eye one particular house did look as if it had melted but looking at it directly rendered it as normal.

He turned around and contemplated the trees again, staring hard at the tangle that had grown over the years while trying to be aware of what his peripheral vision was seeing. There it was again. The impression that a far taller tree spiralled out of the deeper woods a few hundred yards away. It towered over the real trees but when his eyes tried to focus on it, it wasn't there.

"I'm going over the Wall again," he announced that evening. "I've got to try and trace where they took the machine and, hopefully, find Long, too." As he spoke the air in front of him swirled like a rainbow. He was beginning to see through the distortions, though he could never ignore them totally.

"You're not strong enough yet," Jade said.

"Jade's right, Rick," Ellie added.

"Yes, I know. But the longer we leave it, the less chance there is of finding either of them."

"You can't seriously be thinking of using that thing again, are you?" Ellie shouted, adding a "sorry" when Rick winced.

"No, but maybe Long is wherever the machine is. That world must have affected him as well. I just hope…"

He swallowed and hung his head.

"I just really hope he survived it."

There was silence for a while, finally broken by Phil. "Okay, you'll need help."

"Yes, count us in," Jasmine added.

"Thanks."

"What do you think we'll need?"

"Well," Rick said, after a few moments thought, "we have no idea where AI has taken Long and the machine. We could be tracking it for days if not weeks. We'll need supplies, walking boots, tents, maybe even some sort of powered transport if we can find a way of getting it over the Wall."

"There's nothing outside that could be used for transport," Holls said. "A horse sounds like a good idea except there's probably none around. I asked AI for a pony when I was a kid. It showed me video images of wild ones and said there were no tame ones left. It set most non-food animals free to fend for themselves. It also said that it's now too dangerous to try to tame them – they'd kicked a few of its robots to pieces when they'd tried to capture one."

"If that's true," Jade snorted.

Phil nodded in agreement. "Nothing AI says can be trusted any more."

"That leaves the trikes," Rick said.

Phil grinned but Ellie said, "But how do we get over the Wall with them?"

"I have an idea."

Two days later, Rick, Phil, Ellie and Jade were standing around a food kiosk. After letting the device read his ID under the skin of his hand, Phil specified his requirements first, asking for milk, bread, some pre-packaged, self-cooking meals and other assorted snacks. After a short delay the kiosk spat out most of his request packaged into biodegradable bags. Then its mechanical voice apologised for the lack of one type of snack. It told them it would be at the kiosk twenty minutes later if he cared to wait. Phil cancelled that part of his order.

Ellie chose next, adding a request for tinned soup and water bottles. The machine issued her with half the requested goods and then halted with a crunching sound. She cursed and tried activating the kiosk again. Jade stepped forward and examined the device and, with a resigned shrug, declared that it had died, not a totally uncommon occurrence.

They trudged along to the next kiosk, some half a mile away only to discover that it, too, was lifeless.

Jade used her wrist communicator to ask where the nearest functioning food kiosk was located.

"All kiosks are inactive," it replied. "A fault has developed. Normal service should resume tomorrow."

"Dango," Phil swore, once they were out of earshot of the kiosk. "This is getting worse. You think it knows we're planning a breakout?"

"Nothing we can do about it if it does," Jade said. "We'd better deal with those trikes."

12.3: Breakdown Two

A cell: 6 May 2177

Long blinked as the lights came on again. A nurse trundled into view and started to examine him. It disconnected the sanitary plumbing and probed all of his orifices adding further to his discomfort and misery. It produced a syringe and took blood samples, puncturing his arm in three places before a shrunken vein could be successfully located.

Then, as it proceeded to transfer the blood sample to another vial, it froze and the room lights flickered a few times before going out completely. He was in total darkness for a few seconds before a dim glow returned. In the distance he could hear the muffled humming of electrical systems change to a lower pitch.

Unable to do anything other than watch, Long observed helplessly. He dozed after a while but when he awoke the nurse was still unmoving, his blood sample congealed in the open vial it still clasped in its metallic claw.

Famished, he sucked at the tube of liquid but, after the first few mouthfuls, the supply dried up and he started to panic.

Something terrible must have happened. He croaked out a cry for help but there was no response from either AI or the static robot beside him. AI must have had a major breakdown.

Unable to free himself he began to have visions of starving to death, his body rotting away until the bones fell from this metal plate. He screamed out again and again, but only silence answered.

12.4: Plan Hatching

Ladbroke Grove: 7 May 2177

"It's definitely lower there," Phil whispered. Rick and Ellie took furtive glances at the Wall where it cut through Ladbroke Grove. They had already investigated where it intersected a canal further to the north and decided that was a non-starter. This point had potential as the channel, along which a railway had once run, led to a stretch of the Wall that was no more than fifteen feet in height. They started back towards the city centre; beneath their shoes the mixture of ballast and coarse sand felt as solid as concrete.

"How high is it on the other side?" Ellie asked, keeping a watch out for AI's eyes.

"About ten feet or so," Rick replied. Long and the original Wall crosser, Matty, had investigated this spot for their original escape, though it provided little approach cover. Once outside, Long had reported that there was a build up of land on the other side made up mostly from crushed masonry but with a respectable layer of vegetation.

"We'll need damned good padding and extra straps to keep us from falling off when we land," Phil said.

"Or crash," Ellie added.

"Getting cold feet?" Rick asked her.

"No," she growled, "definitely not. This place is falling to pieces and there's no reason why we shouldn't go over. After all, it is our world – not AI's. The damned thing promised to give it back to us years ago. We are just going to have to take it back for ourselves."

Rick and Phil nodded in agreement.

"I will put the word around that the trike races are going to be starting up a bit earlier this year," Phil said.

"Thanks," said Rick. "That old railway track will be just ideal. I think the ramps need to be a bit more, um, challenging as well."

"And more mobile," Ellie added.

Phil grinned.

12.5: Play Time
Around Ladbroke Grove: 12 May 2177

Five days later Rick stood on one of the challenge ramps. The area held seven of them, six of which had been used for previous races. They had been dragged in by trike from Buckingham Palace where last autumn's challenge had been held. Each one was a ramshackle construction of wood and scaffolding struts mounted on a wheeled chassis. Each ramp had a different inclination and some were deliberately far from straight – all part of the challenge.

Rick, though, ignored them and stared at the Wall. In the light morning breeze, only the rare chirrup of a bird disturbed the colours he experienced. The edifice, standing about one hundred and fifty feet away, wavered in and out of focus and, occasionally, disappeared – it wasn't the only thing that changed.

Without a doubt he was somehow seeing brief snatches from that alternate London with its random distortions. However, lacking the Wall, it sometimes revealed other interesting facts. The railway track, when viewed in that other world, was several feet lower than the ground level here. He suspected the old track bed had been used as a construction road. That may have explained why the Wall appeared lower in this location.

From behind him the noise of voices getting closer sent sparks of luminescence across his vision. The games were due to start soon and London's NewGen were beginning to arrive either to participate in or watch the event. Many of them also knew the real reason for this year's location.

Rick walked down the curve of the ramp. Phil had designed and organised the building of this one in four days especially for this event. The width of the wooden incline was broader and far more sturdier than any of the others. While the other ramps were prevented from tipping over by having long poles anchored against their sides, this one had the poles and extra stabiliser wheels permanently attached to the body. Additionally, there were special connectors near the base of the ramp.

It had been constructed with a second purpose in mind. He hoped it would be adequate.

An hour later the place was crowded as far as Rick was concerned – more than forty of the NewGen had assembled, many on their own electric trikes. The cacophony of vehicles and voices was more than he and his distorted vision could bear.

"I've got to get out of here," he whispered to Phil and Ellie. She looked at him closely, noting the way his eyes seemed unable to focus on her.

"Go," she said, gently squeezing his hand. "We'll take care of things."

He gave her a quick kiss.

"Don't go too far, though," she whispered.

He retired to the relative calm of a side street from where he had originally intended to watch the races. Instead, though, he continued walking. The day was growing warm and he found himself in the shelter of a building adorned at one corner by a brick spire. His eyes saw two versions – on one the spire had slumped to a precariously impossible angle; the real spire was still vertical. He shuddered at the thought of losing the ability to determine which of the two was actually real. A sign on the building indicated that this had once been a church. Years ago AI had tried to explain religion to them – like many of the NewGen, he hadn't seen the point.

A nearby food kiosk – working now after the recent breakdown – provided a lunchtime snack. In the distance he could hear a cheer or a collective gasp from the games.

By mid afternoon the day's competitions had been completed and Rick made his way back but remained hidden until most of the crowd had left. He asked how it had gone. Apparently, there had been speed races, progressively higher jumps using the various ramps, relays with groups of riders and several others where arguments had broken out over the exact rules. Both Ellie and Jasmine had won a race each, while Phil had tumbled off his trike during a marathon event consisting of a circle of various height ramps. Only his pride had been hurt. But one other rider was nursing a cracked femur and had to be hauled off by a nurse robot for treatment, despite his protest that it was only a scratch.

Rick helped to plan the challenges for the next day. Several times he was chided by those who had not been informed of recent events for refusing to enter any of the games himself. Ellie explained that he had been ill, which was far from untrue.

Once only Rick, Ellie and Phil were left, were the real plans discussed.

12.6: Playing For Real

Ladbroke Grove: 13 May 2177

Rick felt the burn of adrenaline and was impatient to make a start. No one could settle and, every few minutes, one of them went to the unglazed window to stare out over the Wall that was just visible as the night receded.

Below them, in the games arena, the ramps looked as if they had been abandoned haphazardly. They hadn't – one was ready for its real task.

As the first glimmers of the false dawn crept across an early morning drift of high, wispy clouds, Phil declared it was time to move. They all removed their communication watches and donned padded jackets, gloves and stout boots before filing out into the still darkened streets.

They mounted their trikes and secured the safety straps. Each trike was fully charged and the storage compartment between the rear wheels contained water, food, clothing, footwear, sheets for constructing makeshift tents, and tools such as hammers, cutters and saws.

The special ramp was as close to the Wall as they had dared leave it. They drove the trikes forward – Rick in the centre with Phil to the left and Ellie to his right. Ten yards from the ramp, Rick stopped and watched the Wall cameras. The ramp's protrusions on each side were slotted into a corresponding makeshift socket on Ellie and Phil's trikes. Connected up, they waited for Rick's go ahead. He timed three camera buggies – they were running at around thirty-eight seconds.

A buggy moved out of sight. "Go," he shouted, accompanied by a vivid blotch of blinding yellow that cascaded across his sight.

Ellie and Phil dragged the wheeled ramp towards the Wall, disconnecting and circling around at the last moment. The ramp hit the Wall but stayed upright, the built-in stabilisers doing their work.

Phil continued his circle straight up onto the ramp. Rick and Ellie held their breath as he accelerated and watched his wheels sail inches above the electrified monorail. They only breathed again after they heard his landing followed by a yell of success. Ellie gunned her throttle and took the ramp at a slightly faster rate to gain greater height over the rail. Before she reached the top Rick followed. The rumble of vibration as he hit the ramp sent pink and purple waves around the periphery of his vision, causing him to fail to spot the approaching double camera buggy until it was quite close. Ellie's warning cry from the other side of the Wall was too late in coming. For a moment he wasn't sure if he should accelerate or slow down, but then throttled to maximum hoping to beat the camera to the crossing point.

As he approached the summit it was obvious a collision was inevitable. He leaned to the left while aiming his right foot directly at the camera. His boot made contact, snapping a thin support rod that kept the camera platform upright. The unstable buggy ground against the rail in a shower of electrical arcing before slamming into the trike's rear right wheel spinning it a quarter turn clockwise. Clinging on, knuckles white under his gloves, Rick faced north eastwards along the outside of the Wall instead of away from it. The ground rushed up and he bounced down the steeper slope on that side. Despite the noise obscuring his vision, he managed to remain upright and rolled to a stop a few yards later, gasping.

Shaking, he looked up at the Wall. The camera buggy had come to a halt, its lenses angled uselessly downward, dead.

He checked the trike over and, not discovering any damage beyond a few new scratches, headed away from the Wall to join the others behind a stand of trees. Ellie grabbed and hugged him tightly.

"Damn," Phil said. "I thought you were coming off for certain."

From the shelter of the trees they had a clear view of the Wall without the risk of being observed themselves.

They watched as another camera wagon hurled itself into the crashed remains of the first. But an alarm must have been raised as subsequent ones slowed down and halted in a line.

"Okay," Phil said, after everyone had rechecked their vehicles, "let's get moving."

"Hampstead Heath, here we come," Rick said.

"Yet again," Ellie added, with a chuckle.

12.7: Tracking

Hampstead Heath and northwards: 13-15 May 2177

Temporarily abandoning the trikes, which were too wide to pass between the trees, they headed for Long's house but stopped short when noises emanated from the direction in which it lay. Creeping closer, they could see that much of the wood beyond was now missing. The machine responsible was currently dealing with the ramshackle shelter. A wall shuddered and collapsed. A metal arm followed by the rest of the demolition robot pushed its way out of the mess and turned its attention to another wall.

Ellie gasped as the whole unstable structure leaned and then disintegrated. As the robot extracted itself they retreated back into the undergrowth.

"He couldn't have been in there," Phil said as they trudged back to the trikes. Maybe Phil could not believe AI would sanction the destruction of an occupied dwelling but Rick was not so sure. Something nagged at the edge of his memory, something recent he felt he should remember, but could no longer pin down.

Silently, they returned to the clearing and drove the trikes out of the wood, following the still visible ruts left by the crane that had carried off the machine nearly three weeks previously.

Tracking across undulating countryside made a severe impression on their bodies. The punishing regime tired them easily and they were forced to take several breaks to ease their muscles.

Six miles north of the Wall they entered a region studded with mounds of debris. Bricks, concrete chunks and rusted girders were piled up haphazardly. In the distance a grinding noise was revealed to be a machine whose sole purpose seemed to be to reduce each mound at a time to gravel.

"So this is where AI dumps the remains of the old towns," Phil said.

"Looks like it," Ellie replied. She was more concerned with Rick who had become unnaturally quiet, preferring to travel several yards behind the others. He sometimes acted as if he was seeing things that weren't there.

The debris made the crane's tracks hard to follow and several false leads cost them a couple of hours delay. Once they had left the rubble mountains behind them, Ellie spotted a small flying device, one of AI's mobile eyes, observing them from a distance. Hiding in the next available woodland they waited until the drone lost interest and flew away southwards.

They barely managed a total of fifteen miles on the first day. There were few roads for them to follow, most had been torn up in AI's relentless conversion of the land. Those that remained did not follow the path the crane had taken.

Shortly before dusk, exhausted, they sought out another stand of trees as shelter for the night. Hours later, in the darkness, Ellie awoke to the sound of a voice – in the next makeshift tent Rick mumbled in his sleep. She listened for a while but could make little meaning of what he said.

On the second morning the weather turned and their northward progress was limited to a mere ten miles, most of which was spent huddling under inadequate canvas waiting for a downpour to relent.

"It's only raining here," Rick said at one point.

"What?" Phil asked.

"Nothing. Ignore me," Rick replied, sounding completely exhausted.

By noon the rain had been reduced to a drizzle but, not long after starting out, their path was blocked by a river. The crane had obviously just ploughed through without stopping, but the depth and current were too much for the trikes. They considered abandoning them and swimming across, but this was a far cry from the heated pools they had played in as children. It was less stormy eastwards so they picked that direction where, five miles on, they encountered the remains of a sizeable old town, only partially demolished.

"What's that?" Ellie said, pointing to a large sheet of painted metal laying almost horizontal on the ground and attached to a couple of bent poles. They slowed down and stopped to look.

"Some sort of direction sign," Phil said. "I've seen a few back home."

Ellie dismounted and went closer. "Ware in one direction and places called Welwyn Garden City and Hatfield in the other."

"I wonder if they still exist," Rick mumbled.

"Probably not," Phil said, waving his arm at the rubble ahead of them.

Rick's mind conjured up an image from the name, Welwyn Garden City. He wondered what AI had irretrievably destroyed in its quest to eradicate man's works from the face of the planet.

They pressed on into the rubble of this unnamed centre and, an hour later, encountered a bridge that remained intact enough to give them access to the northern side of the river.

"Okay, back west again," Phil said.

Ellie sighed. The detour had cost them several hours. She hoped they could find the tracks again on this side of the river.

By the time they picked up the trail again, a sombre, cloudy dusk was already starting to creep across the sky. They pressed on for another hour until the impending darkness made further advance hazardous.

The third day started brighter, and swifter progress was made. Another signpost, still upright in the unploughed remains of a village, indicated that they were headed in the general direction of somewhere called Cambridge.

"I think I've heard of it," Rick said. It was something to do with when AI had taught them about electronics. But, that had been so long ago, it seemed like a different lifetime now. Maybe Cambridge didn't even exist any more.

Just after mid-morning the tracks merged with an old intact road and, finding no evidence the crane had left the solid surface, they sped up in the hope that they were still on the correct route. By late afternoon they joined another much larger roadway which, though it was nibbled at in places by the encroaching countryside, gave a relatively clear path to the place that they hoped would be their destination.

Just as evening threatened to descend, an immediately recognisable sight came into view.

"A wall," Ellie gasped. "Another one."

"Looks different to our one," Phil said. Indeed, the construction of this one looked even more haphazard the closer they approached it.

Rick blinked. Sometimes this new wall didn't even appear to exist.

"If there's a wall it probably means there's more NewGen in there," Ellie suggested.

"Wow," Phil said. "Be weird seeing completely new people."

"Might just be more Ghosts instead," Rick countered.

Ellie and Phil exchanged a glance.

12.8: Cambridge

Cambridge: 16-17 May 2177

In the early morning light they investigated the wall from a safe distance, looking for suitable access points. Like the one that surrounded London it had probably been constructed from the robbed out buildings that had once occupied the land where it now stood.

But this was like London in miniature – at best it was merely a mile and a half in diameter. It made up for this by being far higher than London's equivalent. Its construction was far rougher with chunks of brick or stone jutting out of its face. Such adequate foot and hand-holds would make getting in easy, though they had no idea if the inside was as badly constructed.

The mounted cameras that circled on their monorail went in the opposite direction to those that guarded London. Rick, after watching them for a while, noticed that the dual cameras were only notable by their absence.

There were two gates. The southernmost, connected to the road that brought them here, was quite small and wouldn't have provided adequate passage to the crane. Phil noticed that tracks had left the road about three hundred yards from the gate to pass east of the wall, presumably to enter the city at the larger eastern gate. London's three gates were, in contrast to these, far larger but heavily fortified, and the NewGen had never considered any of those suitable for their own use.

The tracks certainly resembled those they had been following so, that afternoon, they made camp in a small copse about half a mile from the eastern gate. Keeping the gate under surveillance with binoculars, the observed traffic during the rest of the day consisted merely of three small repair robots.

Their food supplies were beginning to run low so they knew they had to gain access within the next day or so. The question was whether they should climb the wall, thereby abandoning their trikes, or somehow storm the gate still mounted on their vehicles.

They organised a guard roster of two hour stints and it was on Ellie's watch at just around three in the morning that a possible opportunity presented itself. She awoke the others and they edged towards the perimeter of the copse to observe. Through the night-vision binoculars they could see that a large farming device had somehow wedged itself in the gate. Occasionally, a small robot would appear and fuss around the stalled behemoth but was unable to coerce it into moving. It appeared to have approached the gate at the wrong angle and jammed its frame solidly where the curve of the gate tunnel lowered to meet a side wall.

"Shall we go for it?" Rick asked.

"Might as well as long as there's room to get the trikes past it," Phil agreed. "Maybe we should approach it from along the wall to the left. With that thing stuck there we should hopefully be covered from observation."

In silence they pushed the trikes by hand until they were behind the jammed vehicle. Ellie crept up and peered underneath it and into the city. As far as she could determine, nothing moved. With greater confidence she moved to the other side to see if it had left enough room for them to enter.

There was – just.

"Okay," she reported, "it's now or never."

Together, they switched on the trikes, illuminated their front headlights and swung around the stalled vehicle and into the gate. As they passed under the archway there were no robots to be seen and nothing impeded their progress.

Inside the city, the glow of their headlights picked out old deserted buildings that, after a few yards, became industrial factory blocks. Phil suggested they move off the main thoroughfare. They headed northwards into the maze of units where, with no street lamps to guide their path, they were soon completely lost.

"Here," Ellie said having spied a large open doorway in the side of one of the buildings. They headed for it and parked the trikes inside its emptiness.

Apart from a large storage bay, with several metal crates stacked against the far wall, there were three smaller rooms near the rear.

"This looks defensible," Phil said, picking the larger of the three. "Enough room to spread the sleeping bags out on the floor."

Rick, shattered from the journey, fell on top of his bag and was asleep within seconds.

The following morning Phil and Ellie rose early to scout around, leaving Rick half awake. Phil discovered a building a couple of blocks away that had a ladder fixed to its side that led right up to the roof. He reported back to the others and, once Rick had managed to coax himself awake, all three went to investigate.

"This building isn't really here," Rick said, his hand resting on the metal of its wall. Ellie could see that his eyes appeared to focus on something hidden far inside.

"You stay here," she said. "We'll climb up and take a look."

Rick nodded. "I feel useless," he said, "but I really can't tell what's real and what isn't. I think I'd better keep both feet on the ground."

Ellie squeezed his shoulder and followed Phil up to the roof. Once at the top they could see that the whole area was populated with these boxy buildings. To the north, the Wall rose above the squat units while, to the south and south west, the monotone architecture broke up into ancient spires. A tall tower of a more modern design dominated the view directly to their west. At first, their binoculars, scanning the skyline, revealed nothing of real significance. Then Phil's eyes were drawn to something flashing in the pale morning sunlight a few hundred yards to the south east. Atop a building similar to the one he was crouching upon he could see something sparkling or moving. He adjusted the lens to get a closer view and could make out someone waving something metallic.

He heard Ellie's sharp intake of breath beside him and adjusted the magnification to its fullest.

And he gasped, too, as he focussed on Long's grinning face.

13 Power Surge

13.1: Did The Earth Move For You?

Miyazaki, Japan: 23 July 2118

The sign said 'Cognizantia Conference – this way' in English. It also said it in Japanese, Russian, Spanish and several other languages that Emily could only guess at. It was accompanied by the familiar symbol consisting of three concentric red circles. She followed the 'this way' towards the conference room. At its entrance she held her breath as her invitation card was scanned. A reassuring blip on the scanner followed and she was ushered in.

She let out her breath as she entered and let a brief smile play across her lips as she placed the card back inside her shoulder bag. While she was genuinely on Cognizantia's staff, her invitation was far from official. Her minor telepathic abilities had gained her a foothold in this intriguing company five years previously. But it was her own discovery two years later that she could tap into almost any computer system, using the power of her mind alone, that had generated the invitation. The few people who knew of her newfound abilities had much less of an idea of how far it had developed.

Inside the conference room she noted how sparsely it was occupied by attendees. This afforded her an excellent view out across the Pacific, even before she was anywhere near the windows. Despite that, she moved toward the view, pausing only to take a proffered glass of bubbly, sipping it absent-mindedly whilst watching the breakers silently sliding up the beach several hundred feet away. She imagined she was looking straight across the ocean towards Seattle and, having lived away for nearly three years, was looking forward to returning home. To her right, the panorama from the Sheraton Grande Ocean Resort took in the city of Miyazaki or, at least, its harbour, which was all she could see at that moment. The city itself was hidden from her by the bulk of the hotel itself.

She turned her back to the scenery and started people watching. The room held about fifty of multiple nationalities. None of them were familiar to her though she could identify where most were from by the style of their dress. Then an old man strode into the conference room with an energy that belied his advancing years. Professor Rayburn was the main speaker here today. With his arrival the conference came to order and she, along with the others, sought a seat at one of the informally laid out tables.

A few more stragglers arrived and some sat at the larger table to one end, to which Rayburn had gravitated. At some hidden signal the hotel staff, who had been serving drinks and a small buffet, departed to leave the delegates to themselves. As the door closed one of those at Rayburn's table stood to introduce the proceedings. Although she had worked in the office in Miyazaki for over a year she didn't recognise this Japanese man. He referred to his notes for a moment then, facing the small gathering and without opening his mouth, started broadcasting. His voice hit her strongly using perfect English. Ah, she thought, a translator – she had heard of those with the ability to transmit to several people simultaneously using multiple languages.

He outlined the more recent work within Cognizantia, picking out some of those present, who nodded at the mention of their efforts. Due to the speed at which it was transmitted, the silent speech lasted less than three minutes. Then he opened his mouth and verbally announced, "Ladies and gentlemen, Professor Rayburn," before sitting down.

The Professor got to his feet. A smile spread across his lips and a hand was raised in acknowledgement of the mild applause. As it died down he picked up a sheet of paper from the table, glanced down at it for a couple of seconds and opened his mouth to speak.

Then all hell broke loose.

The Sheraton Grande Ocean Resort swayed on its foundations and, along with everyone else, Emily fell to the floor. Alarm bells went off as the shaking became worse. There were gasps and screams, and Emily muttered, "Earthquake," while many of those around her shouted the same in English and other languages. The rumbling that filled the building could be felt far more than it could be heard, and the hearing was bad enough.

A window at the far corner of the conference room shattered and, seconds later, the one beside it followed suit. Coupled with the dancing building, the glass flung itself in all directions and people crawled to the centre of the room to get away.

That is, except for the Professor, who regained his feet and then rose slightly further so that the swaying could no longer affect him. Emily watched, open mouthed, as he faced the constantly shattering glass, arms outspread. What was he going to do? She found out a second or two later when something caressed her, a force that tugged between her ears. She was being linked into something against her will. For a moment she resisted, but it was persuasive and she let herself fall into the coercion.

The rest of the windows gave way as one, and the glass showered into the room.

However, an invisible barrier halted its progress so that the shards dropped harmlessly to the floor, missing the occupants.

"Right," Rayburn shouted both verbally and mentally. "Looks like the conference is going to have to be postponed." Then he added, "Sorry about this, but there's no time to train you individually. Let – me – in!"

Emily felt Rayburn's coercion pull her further into the concert via an intense melody that infused her whole body. She gave herself willingly and added her underdeveloped abilities to help stabilise the very ground beneath them. For several minutes they battled the effects of the earthquake until it died away. But, she learned more in those minutes than she had in all her twenty-four years on the planet. She took all the experience the Professor had forced upon her and did her best to remember it.

Rayburn lowered himself to the floor and issued the command to provide assistance throughout the building. Emily struggled upright on legs that felt like jelly. No one in the conference room appeared to be injured so, along with others, she made herself useful over the next twenty minutes attending to the many who were less lucky.

While she was helping to bandage the arm of a small boy who had been too close to a window when the quake struck, another urgent mental call arrived. To the surprise of the boy's parents, she rushed away and back up to the conference room without explanation. Within a minute all the delegates were there, along with a few new faces who had also heard the call and were unable to resist its urgency.

Rayburn was staring out towards the Pacific. Emily was puzzled – the shore was now a lot further away than it had been. However, she then noticed the darker line on the horizon and someone gasped before crying, "Tsunami."

Her breath caught in her throat and she had to resist the urge to run.

"No panic," Rayburn demanded, seemingly just at her. "It's too late to run. It will be here in a few minutes. A full mental rapport – we have no choice if we are to survive this."

Emily felt a new song enter her mind. It was compelling, enticing and she had neither the urge nor the ability to pull away. In her head she heard Rayburn assign the front troops, in a second he had invaded her consciousness and determined the most fitting role for her. He unlocked in her the latent ability to enforce the coercion itself. "Pull in as many as you can and add them to the diversion force," he told her. Rayburn wasn't talking to just her, though, and many others responded simultaneously.

The song grew to encompass everything and she found a route within it that allowed her to extend her essence, as if she was no longer in her own body. She ranged first through the hotel, touching the scared minds of those cowering within. In some of them she could detect the abilities required and she added them to the link before moving onto the next. What would have been uncomprehendingly impossible an hour ago, she now did without effort. In seconds she had drawn in thirty or more while, around her, others with similar abilities were doing the same. Finding further strength, she mentally moved outside the hotel and towards the city, seeking to bring thousands into the mesh of minds focussed on and controlled by Professor Rayburn.

A few days later the news services were trying to find explanations for what had happened. How could a tidal wave, which had threatened to subsume an entire city, been suddenly diverted southwards and away from the Japanese islands? Not that Japan had escaped lightly – thousands had died and millions had been made homeless in the initial earthquake but, in Miyazaki, they were many who were aware that it could have been far worse.

Emily left Japan several weeks later once flights had resumed and caught up with the backlog. She felt twenty years older and far removed from the naive girl who had arrived on these islands only two years before.

13.2: Affinity

Nottingham, England: 16 February/8 March 2134

Ross Nunn was unsure what to do, which was an unusual state for him to be in. He knew this patient was important, though he had no idea who the man was or what he had done to achieve that importance. The only thing he knew for certain was that his patient was dying and that there was nothing he could do to prevent this.

However, that fact was true for all the patients here.

Ross sat beside the bed talking to the old man, trying to comfort him in his last few days or hours. It was hard, though. Unlike most of those he was employed to comfort, the scant information he had on the man gave little with which to connect with him. He had heard one of the doctors refer to him as 'the Professor' but, other than that, the man was a blank sheet.

The ever present robot nurses took readings, occasionally turned patients in order to prevent bedsores and did all the things they and their controlling AI systems told them to do. Ross was so used to them that he could ignore them most of the time. However, in the five days since the Professor had been admitted, the robots seemed to avoid the old man, sometimes requiring an order multiple times before they would perform a task connected with him. Twice, the engineers had been called, but no error had been detected. Still, that hadn't prevented the robotic nurses from treating him as if he wasn't really there.

Ross had been instructed to make the man a priority which, given the lack of detail, bordered on impossibility. He tried to make light, one-sided conversation, discussing the weather, asking how the man felt, whether or not there was any family who might be visiting soon. In reply, the old man said nothing, acknowledged nothing, and either stared at nothing or slept. In either state he responded to neither touch nor sound.

The evening grew long and the time neared for Ross to complete his shift. He was looking forward to returning home to Amelia. He chatted to a few of the terminal patients, as if he had known them all his life. Many were glad of the attention, though a few were less enamoured or even immune to his natural charm and likeability. From those, though, he did at least get the occasional brief smile or nod of the head. From the Professor, he received naught.

On his way to the ward door he waved to one of the more articulate patients, Joseph. He was, as usual, cheery and totally accepting of his fate knowing there was nothing that could be done to prevent the breakdowns his body was experiencing. He had, perhaps, another month or two – these things were never certain. Ross felt an affinity to Joseph and knew he would be affected even more than usual when he finally passed away.

With the Professor, though, there was no such connection. It had been established that he was definitely not in a vegetative state, and that his brain still appeared to be responding to external stimuli – but that response never reached the exterior world.

Ross started to push the ward door open when he halted. He hadn't intended to. He turned around and looked back at the patients, they looked as they usually did and he was about to continue out the door when his eyes locked on those of the Professor. The old man was staring directly at him.

Ross swallowed, feeling nervous and conscious of the sweat that was suddenly present, dotting his forehead. He wasn't even hot.

Compelled to return, he sat down in the chair next to the Professor's bed, unable to unlock his gaze from that of the old man.

"It will have to be you," the Professor said. "No one else here will do. I'm sorry – this won't be easy."

Ross felt the urge to scream and run from the ward, but something held him in place, clamping him to the chair.

And then it hit him.

When he came to, he realised he was lying in a bed – and that bed was not one of those in the terminal ward. He was conscious of someone close by. Seated on the chair beside the bed was his wife. But she was different, only she wasn't. He was conscious that he was perceiving her in a different manner, as if he was finally seeing her properly for the first time in his life.

"Oh, Ross. Thank God you're back," Amelia said. There were tears on her cheeks.

"How long was I…"

"Three weeks," she interrupted. "They thought at first you'd had a brain aneurysm."

"No," he said, unable to determine how he could be so certain. "It was nothing of the sort. It was something far more important."

He looked at and then into his wife. She had always been the more intuitive one, he had been the empathic one. But now he could see that was no longer true. He was far more than he had been and, he could also see, she had the potential to be far more.

He was still weak but, in other ways, he was far stronger. There was also something else. It was almost as if there was someone else sharing the inside of his head, helping and guiding him. He frowned for a moment, and then nodded and whispered, "Professor Rayburn."

"Who?" Amelia asked.

"A new future," he replied, a smile forming on his lips. "I have a feeling it will definitely be interesting. Very interesting."

13.3: In Two Minds

Nottingham, England: 8 July 2135

When the door bell rang Ross and Amelia Nunn had been watching some inane junk purporting to be entertainment. Ross concentrated and the door unlocked itself at the same time the TV switched itself off.

"Shall I…" Amelia started but was cut off by a gentle unspoken 'No' from her husband.

"He knows the way in," Ross said, using speech for a change.

"No, make some tea, I meant," she chided, grinning.

"That sounds lovely," came the voice from the hallway. "White, no sugar, thanks."

Ross stood up. Part of him recognised the visitor who let himself into the lounge. He thought, "but these eyes have never gazed upon this man."

At ninety-two years of age, Doctor Linden Willard Ashley definitely looked older than the last time their minds had met.

"Yes, the body grows old," Ashley projected, shaking the younger man's hand. "Though, I'm not quite at the stage where I need to steal a new body."

Ross laughed out loud, whilst simultaneously projecting, "We have become used to it. All three of us."

"And how is Amelia coming along?"

"Well enough," Amelia responded from the kitchen in the same non-verbal manner.

Linden Ashley's face crinkled up with obvious delight.

Later, after a simple meal, they turned their attention to other matters. The TV was turned back on so that its noise might disrupt any accidental verbal utterances – well, there was no reason to take chances.

Ross: "We need a permanent presence on the Moon."

Linden: "Indeed, I have in mind someone you have already encountered. Well, not you exactly, Ross."

Ross, catching a clue in Ashley's thoughts: "Ah, Emily. Yes, she is a talented young lady. A great help in Japan and has gone on to do some very interesting things since."

Linden snorted: "Young lady? She is forty-one – five years older than yourself."

Ross, laughing: "Parts of me forget."

Amelia: "He sometimes has violent disagreements with himself, you know."

Linden: "All the more reason for me to keep this old body going as long as I can."

Ross: "I can't disagree. Mental reconciliation is sometimes… difficult. Some things that used to be easy I am having to learn all over again. But, enough of that."

Linden: "Indeed. Emily was also instrumental in clearing up the mess after the Polish incident. You know she can now get inside computers and AI units from a distance without any need for a physical interface?"

Ross: "So I've heard. Along with the way she is training others in the same art."

Linden: "An art that is needed often – it's amazing what people will tend to forget once physical data is erased."

Ross: "So, she goes to the Moon, then."

Linden: "Not for the first time, apparently. She engineered a trip to the Russian base a few years ago. Though all records of that trip have, um, inconveniently disappeared in the meantime."

Both Ross and Amelia laughed out loud this time, and only partially at the unnecessary 'um' that Linden Ashley had included in his projection.

Linden: "A cover story and a suitably menial occupation will be created for her."
Ross: "Excellent."

13.4: Futile

Kepler Colony, the Moon: 16 May 2156

They watched the screen showing the launch of the Asteroid Diversion Task Force ship as it lifted from the Moon to rendezvous with the asteroid.

"It's a waste of time, isn't it?" Amelia stated, wordlessly.

Ross nodded his head in agreement and replied in the same manner. "But they have to be seen to be making the effort, as futile as it is."

He paused and grimaced, and Amelia caught a stray thought from her husband.

Amelia: "This, then, is the test we've been waiting for?"

Ross: "I wouldn't exactly say 'waiting for' or 'test'. This will be much more than a mere test – a challenge."

Amelia: "Yes, off the scale compared to what's gone before."

A humourless laugh burst from his mouth. The echoes rebounded off the walls of the sparsely furnished room.

Amelia: "Has the process been worked out?"

Ross: "As much as it can be. Thompson and his crew are back on Earth strengthening the links."

Amelia: "You're still returning to Earth, then?"

Ross: "He's in his late nineties. He can't be expected to handle this alone. So, I must go, I have to."

Amelia: "And me?"

Ross: "Afterwards."

Amelia: "I'd rather be there with you."

Ross: "I wish that, too. But transport is going to be a problem."

Amelia: "Emily is working on it."

Ross concurred. If anyone could invade the computer systems to obtain further places on one of the ships returning to Earth, then it would be Emily. Memories that had no right to be in his head held a catalogue of events that would not have been possible without her talents. He, or rather, Rayburn, had unlocked more than he had planned nearly forty years previously. Ross pondered whether he could persuade Emily to return with him but she was one of the core members on the Moon. He didn't want to risk losing her with what they were contemplating.

Amelia: "It's such a shame that Doctor Ashley couldn't achieve transfer."

Ross sighed, acutely remembering the loss of Rayburn's friend. They'd arranged a suitable volunteer and Ashley had appeared to fully understand the transference process that Rayburn had used upon himself.

However, the attempt had failed and it was still a shock to the whole community that both the donor and recipient had been lost.

13.5: The Pyramid

Invergloy, Scotland: 29 May 2156

Ross pulled his eyes away from the window. He had been watching the sunlight dancing on the waters of the loch and wondered if it would have the opportunity to do so again once this day was out. His own eyes were witnessing the scene for the first time, though, to Rayburn riding alongside him, the scene was familiar. Thankfully, the occasions when the two consciousnesses were discordant had become extremely rare. For most of the time they acted as if they had always been one.

He glanced at the clock inside the cabin – it was a quarter past four. Just over half an hour to go.

He wished Amelia could have joined him but she was definitely safer off the Earth, not that she hadn't attempted the trip. He could detect her even now on the delayed ship that was still only half-way between the Moon and the Earth. He was also aware that Emily had managed to board the same craft.

Across the room three people sat, apparently calmly, watching him. Two were middle-aged whilst the youngest, Morton Fisk, wore his mask of tranquillity with unease. Within the young man's frame there was a high level of turmoil. Ross understood this, he was barely suppressing a similar turmoil himself.

The other two, Jennifer Kirkpatrick and Richard Norsworthy, held their turmoil in check and Ross could not detect it. Richard, or Dick as he preferred to be called, was his own support whilst Morton was Jennifer's. Each was tasked with providing backup should the main person in each pairing fail.

Around the world was a pyramid of connected pairs of people, pairs of minds. Ross rode the apex of that pyramid. Four of the five below him were spread thinly across the globe in India, Brazil, Canada and Australia. The fifth was Jennifer. Distance wasn't the problem, numbers were. Each of the five had their paired assistant and five more pairs within the pyramid below them to provide the strength required for the task. Under that level were multiple tiers so that, by the sixth level there were nearly forty thousand minds ready to be pressed into service. From there the numbers were less certain and some groups had more or less than the optimal number of five. Some levels descended further than others. In all, there were nearly a million minds meshed into the structure atop which Ross sat.

He hoped it would be enough.

The seconds ticked by until the clock passed four-thirty. Two minutes later, with fifteen to go, he gave the signal for those in India to start the song. The others picked up on it within a second.

Ross hoped the time was enough to bring the concert up to its full power, but not too long that the joining of minds would tire or break under pressure.

As the crescendo grew he drew strength from the thousands below him. He pressed his consciousness out of his body and up through the atmosphere seeking the target, the asteroid.

And there it was.

But it was coming so fast that focussing on it was like trying to catch an eel in oil. Still well over thirty thousand kilometres away – about a tenth of the distance to the Moon – each passing second lopped around forty of those kilometres from the ever decreasing gap.

Ross tried to gain a grip on the rock but it eluded him as it twisted and spun closer. He attempted to wrap a mental cushion around it but the debris that accompanied it, along with the burnt out remains of the rockets that had failed to divert it, tore that grip away as soon as he applied it.

He tried to relax – the distance was far too great and they still had more than eleven minutes to go.

He thought back to the beginnings of what they were going to attempt today. Back to when he had been Professor Rayburn experiencing the first experiments that had pushed solid matter out of the universe. Where that matter had gone, and what it had to contend with until they released it and it snapped back into the known universe, was still completely unknown. Back then it had been small items – marbles, fist sized blocks of wood, a statue and, once, the contents of a whole room. That last hadn't been a success – its return had caused an explosion in which people had died, not their own members, thankfully, but unconnected innocents. The memories in his mind, though they were not from his own personal experience, still caused him distress.

The process had been refined over the years but even the largest item moved was dwarfed by the size of the rock currently hurtling towards them. The problem was gaining some sort of traction on it while it was still so far away.

If this failed, well… he hoped they wouldn't have to resort to the backup plan.

13.6: Splinters

Invergloy, Scotland: 29 May 2156

To say that Morton Fisk was unprepared for events was an understatement. None of those in this room or within the whole pyramid of connected minds that stretched around the globe, fully comprehended what they were attempting. If they had, maybe they would never have made the attempt in the first place.

Morton felt his strength buoying up that of Jennifer's. He hoped it would be enough. Jennifer, in turn, passed that strength onto the person they knew as Ross Nunn. Morton was also aware of the other who cohabited that single frame, though he was too young to have met the Professor before the merging. He wondered what it had felt like.

Morton monitored the waves of minds that were being constantly added to the effort – another of his responsibilities. The song they were generating was pulling in hundreds of new minds by the second. Those at the periphery of the pyramid were tasked with integrating them as smoothly as they could, but Morton, along with many other assistants, had oversight of the process. A part of his mind was occupied ensuring the surges of new input were not disruptive, that they would not divert the main flow of energy from its primary purpose.

At the one minute mark he felt an increase in the intensity. The power that was flowing into this room and, via Ross, back out into space was immense. Anyone peering in the window at that point wouldn't see this; they would merely see four motionless people, one standing, the rest seated comfortably, doing very little other than perspiring.

Yet, far around the world, away from this tiny cabin lost in the wilds of Scotland, that power was being channelled at a piece of rock that was hardly more than two thousand kilometres from impacting the Southern Pacific ocean. A couple of days ago Morton had asked why they were here and not closer to where the impact was due. "The apex is best furthest away," he had been told. "Scotland is near enough, though Scandinavia or Russia are probably closer to the exit point. Also, we need people this side to determine when best to release it back into our own space-time."

Morton was still uncertain that he understood enough.

"Yes, got it," Ross mumbled both audibly and mentally at the forty seconds mark. Morton saw the beads of sweat running down Ross's forehead. His own felt just as drenched.

"We push in fifteen seconds," Ross added at thirty seconds.

Morton felt the pressure increase even further and Ross seemed to glow with his own light. The sight made Morton's eyes water so he turned his gaze to the others, to find them almost as bright.

"Five," said Dick Norsworthy, verbally only.

Each second saw more minds dragged willingly or unwillingly into the mesh. Morton adjusted the pathways of energy around the world so that the newcomers were used to the best advantage.

"Now!" Dick shouted.

The calm features on Ross's face were replaced with a grimace. Then the glow about him faded and he screamed. Jennifer's eyes snapped open, and accompanied Ross with her own shriek.

Time seemed to slow to a crawl as Morton watched in horror. Ross started to collapse and Morton felt the channel up to the asteroid begin to shear away. Morton sucked energy from throughout the pyramid and delivered it to Jennifer, hoping she could use it to create a buttress to prevent the collapse.

She tried.

"Can't hold it," Ross gasped, pulling himself back upright.

"Yes, you can," Jennifer projected. There were twelve seconds to impact.

Ross renewed his efforts but, through the web of energy, Morton could feel the slip and slide of the asteroid as it tumbled closer. Ross was exhausted, the energy he was channelling was tearing at his body, shredding his will and consciousness. Morton couldn't understand how Ross was holding himself together.

Then Ross groaned, "Too much." For less than a second he lit up like the sun and, an instant later, was gone.

Both Dick and Morton gasped as Jennifer broadcast, "Backup plan – three seconds!"

There were eight seconds to impact – five seconds contingency.

The flow of energy changed. Instead of being directed out away from the Earth, it snapped back to encircle the entire planet. Having failed to move the asteroid out of the way of the Earth, they now had no choice but to try for the alternative; to move the Earth out of the way of the asteroid.

"Two." That was Dick. The size difference between the asteroid and the Earth was immense, but they had one advantage. Where they had failed to gain purchase on a spinning rock erratically hurtling towards them, there was a chance that they could get a better grip upon the solid planet beneath their feet.

"One," Jennifer shouted.

A second later Morton almost gagged as he witnessed Jennifer's body shredding into thousands of particles. He felt forces tugging at his own body that threatened to do the same. Somehow, he managed to channel the energy away from himself and back into the pyramid. He reached out to Dick to find a vacant space. He hadn't even seen him go. His vision blurred as the shock set in. They had lost the apex and his assistant, they had also lost at least one of the top-tier five. He was alone.

He tried to focus on the other four top-tier minds spread across the globe. To his relief he could detect them, but they were in disarray. Having lost the primary focus they were trying to act independently, each trying to pull the entire Earth out of normal space themselves. Morton mentally shrieked at them to combine the effort.

At four seconds to impact he knew they were losing.

At three seconds he knew the asteroid was about to enter the atmosphere. He extended himself across the globe attempting to link all the minds together into a coherent whole. He managed it but the other four minds shrieked out their dissonant chords, jarring echoes that disrupted the concordant harmonies of the song.

At two seconds Morton knew that, without a doubt, they were moving the Earth out of the way, but they were all trying to take it in different directions. Additionally, the minds in Brazil had to contend with a small fractured contingent who were still focussed upon attempting to move the asteroid out of the way.

At one second he felt the Earth splinter and his vision blurred into five overlapping but similar views. His mind began to fog as if his intelligence was being sucked out of his head.

And then, inevitably, there were no more seconds left.

14 New NewGen

14.1: New Old Faces

Cambridge: 10 May 2177

Long became aware that something had changed. He was no longer strapped to an inclined plate but lay horizontally on something soft. He opened his eyes. Instead of the plain, metal wall of a cell, the new surroundings resembled a small bedroom. Bright sunlight entering the window painted the room in a warm cream and yellow.

While there was no nurse in sight, one must have been around, for the drip that stood beside the bed was attached to his left arm via a tube. He squinted at the label on the bag that fed liquid into his body – Saline. That was good, wasn't it?

He had no recollection of anything since passing out from lack of water and food. How long ago had that been? No idea. But his throat was still parched. He struggled up to a sitting position. Beside the bed, on a cabinet, sat a jug of water along with a glass. With shaking hands he half filled the glass and drunk deeply. The water, fresh and cool, tasted wonderful.

He looked down at himself. As before he was naked, apart from a thin cream-coloured sheet that covered him from the waist down. He examined the visible parts of his body, now noticeably far leaner, and marked with bruises and chafed skin where the straps had previously imprisoned him. Although he still ached all over, head included, his current level of discomfort was much reduced in comparison to the earlier torture.

He tensed, hearing a noise outside the room. It was followed by the door opening. Expecting one of AI's robotic nurses to enter, he squeaked in surprise as the face of a total stranger peered around the frame at him. Apart from the man from the machine this was the first new face, apart from Ghosts, Long had encountered since he was a toddler. Lying there, weak and partly naked, he felt extremely vulnerable and highly apprehensive.

"Oh," said the girl. "You're awake." She raised her eyebrows, as if surprised to find him conscious. Then her mouth formed a wide grin that did much to alleviate his fear.

She was slightly broad of face, her nose displaying a light dusting of freckles. She stepped fully into view and Long could see she had a lithe figure, her bare arms displaying more muscle than fat, suggesting a penchant for exercise.

She poked her head back outside the door, and shouted, "Hey everyone. He's finally woken up."

A few seconds later Long could hear footsteps ascending carpeted stairs.

"Long," came an oddly familiar voice. "Well, it's about time you rejoined us!"

The girl stepped to one side to allow entry to the voice's owner and Long gasped as an instantly recognisable face appeared in front of him. Was he hallucinating? Could he still be strapped to that metal plate dreaming these events?

"Oops. Didn't mean to shock you. Yes, Long, it is really me."

Looking only slightly older, though no longer the skinny youth of three years ago, there was no doubt about the identity of the man who stood before him.

"Matty," Long gasped. "No. This is just a dream, isn't it?"

Matty smiled. "It's not, I assure you. Though you've definitely been doing a lot of that over the past couple of days."

"So, where are we? Am I back in London? Or is this Cromer again? What happened? How did I get away from AI?"

"Whoa! One question at a time," Matty grinned. "Here is where I've been for a few years now. No, not Cromer, wherever that is. This is Cambridge, what's left of it."

"Cambridge?"

"About sixty miles north of London."

"Ah, the name is familiar, I think. Why am I here?"

"No idea. Things have been getting strange recently what with the failures and everything. AI broke down almost completely four days ago. Nothing worked, apart from a few of the robots guarding the Wall, of course. We – that's me, Jenny here and a few others you'll meet soon – managed to get inside some of the old labs. Actually, it wasn't difficult – many of the doors were wide open. We explored a little way that first day and went inside a bit further the next and found you strapped to a board. Thought you were dead at first but Jack noticed you were still breathing. Not long after we got you out AI came back to life. It sent out search parties but they didn't seem to be hunting that hard. So, here you are back with us. How do you feel?"

"Better for seeing you. Um, anything to eat?"

"Hah, yeah! Bet you're famished."

"Jack!" Jenny shouted down the stairs, "can you mash up something light for Long?"

Long, hearing a voice confirming that Jack was on the job, found his mouth watering at the thought of food. When was the last time he'd eaten anything solid?

"You say the breakdown was four days ago?"

"Yes, found you the day after. There was a bit of activity at the end of last month.

A heliplane went in and out a few times."

"Dango! I was brought here by a plane of some sort but I was blindfolded."

"Wow, so it really was you up in that thing, then?"

"I wasn't exactly enjoying the experience."

"Must've been really weird. Anyway, round about the time that happened, something made them open up the large east gate. They tried to keep us away but we saw a crane dragging in something large. A big box with coils of wire wrapped around it. We think we know where they took it."

"The machine! It must have been the machine."

"What machine?"

Jack arrived with a bowl of soup and some buttered rolls. In between small mouthfuls, Long told the story.

"Well," Matty said, after Long finished. "That may be one way out of here."

14.2: Matty's Story
Cambridge: 10 May 2177

By the evening Long felt his strength start to return. Jenny had disconnected the drip and he'd been fortified by several more small meals.

He and Matty talked again, mainly about what had happened to each of them since Matty's departure from London.

"I heard Holls get taken while I was still on the outside of the Wall," Matty started, mouth turned downward, after hearing Long's story. "I slunk back to the undergrowth for a few hours. Got back in again in the early hours of the next morning but I accidentally touched the electric rail coming over and fell down the Wall. Just sprained a wrist. Wasn't too bad but, after I got on a train to bring me back to Mayfair, I realised AI was on to me. It wouldn't let me off to change to the Piccadilly and headed south right under the river."

"I thought the tunnels had all been blocked due to the flooding problem," Long said. None of London's NewGen had ever been south of the river; AI had removed all of the bridges when they were children. High barriers now prevented direct access to the river from the northern bank.

"Hah! We all know that what AI tells us is often far from the truth."

"Devious heap of junk," Long agreed.

"Well anyway, the train came up to the surface again and slowed down at a platform. AI had lined the station with robots but I forced open a door on the other side of the carriage and ran off. I hid for several days around there until I discovered there were several gaps in the barrier on the south bank of the river. There were a few places where Ghosts were being kept, but none of them were near the river. I made a crude raft out of an old wooden door and some large plastic tubs, and one night just pushed it upstream and under the Wall."

"Under?"

"Actually, the Wall there is just a small bridge that carries the camera rail over the river – it's about thirty or forty feet above the river so it wasn't hard to get out."

"And you've been here ever since?"

"No, I spent a couple of weeks just wandering about the countryside living on anything that looked the remotest like food. Mostly, I was starving and, with winter starting to set in, I knew I needed to find somewhere quick. I ended up in Cambridge by hitching a ride on a rather slow and dumb food truck – had to live on nothing but greens for several days – ugh! Getting over the Cambridge Wall was surprisingly easy – there's no outward facing cameras and the outside of the Wall is almost built for climbing, full of jutting out bricks and stuff. Mind you, the inside's the exact opposite, I think AI must have polished it completely smooth. There's no way you could drill holes in it here and keep AI from spotting them. Can't understand why the London Wall never had the same treatment. Anyway, I soon located the NewGen and, after they got over the shock of seeing a totally new face, they shared their food with me until we figured out how to get me permanently onto the system."

Matty showed Long the back of his left hand and he spotted a small scar located next to a tiny bump under the skin. Long looked at his own left hand, comparing the even tinier bump that revealed the location of his personal ID device.

"You changed your ID?"

"A girl called Rachel died falling out of a window a few weeks after I arrived. There was a party after someone found a whole cache of some ancient bottles of drink in a cellar. Wine, it was called, but no one realised what sort of effect it would have on people when they drank it."

"Wine? What is it?"

"Something else AI's been hiding from us. We've found more since but we've only drunk it in small quantities. It makes you feel really weird – like you're not really in control of yourself. Nice in a way but, that first time, a few of us were really ill afterwards. Anyway, poor Rachel fell out of a window near her house – we think she got lost trying to get back home after the party. Kenny – you'll meet him soon – was the first to find her several hours later and saw the ID device hanging out of her skin – he reckoned she'd ripped her hand open on some broken glass as she fell. He snatched the ID up before AI could recover the body. We weren't sure whether or not it would still work but I tried it a few times just taped to my right hand and, in spite of the fact that I apparently look nothing like Rachel, AI thinks I'm her and gives me food."

"What about Rachel's body? Did AI find it?"

"Yes, but maybe it couldn't figure out who she was without her ID. Anyway, it never complained."

"I don't think that adds up."

"What do you mean?"

"DNA. AI must have checked that. Remember it taught us all about that when we were about twelve or so. I asked it why we needed the ID implants if it could read our DNA."

"Your memory is better than mine for that sort of stuff."

"Maybe. But I certainly remember that it replied to my question saying that using DNA took it longer while the ID devices were instantaneous. It also said that each implant was locked to the wearer's DNA."

"More lies."

Long sighed. "Add it to the list."

14.3: College Ducks

Cambridge: 13 May 2177

A few days later Long was beginning to feel like his old self and he explored Cambridge with Jenny as his guide.

On their way towards the western side of the city he stopped, having noticed a tall building north of their path that rose far above the others.

"Used to be part of a college," Jenny said. "AI keeps it locked," she added with a grin.

Long shot her a quizzical look.

Her grin spread wider. "Not that secure. Most of us have been up there at least once. There's a gallery right at the top that gives a fantastic view over the entire city and beyond. One day we'll get out there for real. Remind me to take you sometime."

"Definitely!" Long grinned. He was enjoying her company. There was something bright and tantalising about her. He wondered if it was just because, for the first time since he was a young child, he had met someone new, someone who made the girls of London's NewGen feel stale. He felt guilty about thinking such things but the feeling wouldn't go away.

They passed under an archway in an area of elegant architecture. Jenny said these had also once been colleges. Beyond them access to the river was obstructed by a tall mesh barrier, topped by spiky wire. The river thronged with ducks, some accompanied by their newly hatched young. On the other side of the river stood the Wall. Jenny produced some left-over food from the bag she was carrying and threw chunks through the mesh. The ducks greeted its arrival with a cacophony of noise.

"I come down here quite a lot so they've got to know me."

"I hadn't realised they could even be fed," he said in amazement.

A few ducks flew over the mesh to get a better chance of a meal. Jenny rewarded them for their efforts.

"There's a few places where we've weakened the wire. We think we can get out if there's no barrier where the Wall passes over the river, which it does both north and south of here. But maybe we won't have to if we can get at that machine thing of yours."

Long was worried – since his story of the alternate London had become widespread, the machine had been looked upon as a route to escape AI's rule. Despite his emphasis on the danger, they had latched onto the inescapable fact that there were probably free humans on world 'one', where the builders of the machine lived. He couldn't deny that answers to their many questions might be forthcoming if they could go there. He reminded them that the machine could hold only about five people at the most, and there was no guarantee they could survive on that world.

Of course, the main problem was that they no longer had possession of the machine.

14.4: Boxes

Cambridge: 16-17 May 2177

"We think we know where it is," Matty said.

"You've found the machine?" Long asked.

Matty nodded. "There's a lot of activity around one particular building, mainly small robots going in and out. And there's mud tracks leading up to it which could have been made by that crane thing. Weird really, AI's usually quite good at keeping the place clean – probably another thing that's broken down."

"Cleaner than London?"

"Huh, that was never clean but, then again, this place is so small. Well, it is now. We've found old maps showing it was once ten times bigger."

"So, can I go and see it?"

Matty grinned.

Several hours later, holed up in an industrial unit, they peered through a small window that overlooked their target. At first there was no movement but, around mid-morning, three small repair robots plus another large wheeled machine trundled up to the door and went inside.

From their location they could not see directly into the building, so Jenny volunteered to skip over a couple of roofs to get a better view. Some of the industrial units were linked with metallic constructions that could be used as ladders. Long's throat dried up at the thought of using them to move from roof to roof.

Jenny, strapping a set of binoculars to her belt, said with a grin, "Heights have never scared me."

"Rather her than me," Long whispered once she had departed and was out of earshot.

"Know what you mean," Matty concurred. "Apparently, she climbed more trees than any of the guys here when they were kids. Despite its size there's still quite a bit of parkland here inside the Wall. And have you seen that tower?"

Long nodded. He was looking forward to accompanying Jenny on a trip to view the city from its heights. Or maybe he was just looking forward to being with Jenny. He wondered if she had a partner here. He hadn't seen her acting close to anyone in particular, but he was still unsure of what her actual status was on that front.

A few minutes later they saw the small dot of Jenny's head pop up as she passed over the rooftops. Then she disappeared for a while before returning.

"Large square thing covered in wires?" she said as she re-entered the building.

"Door in one side?" Long asked.

"Couldn't see. Probably hidden. They had one of the big doors open so I had to make sure the robots didn't see me."

"What were they doing to it?"

"Hard to tell but it didn't look like they were pulling it apart."

"Thank goodness for that. I don't think I could put it back together again if they did."

"What now?" she asked.

Long glanced at Matty.

"Wait until nightfall and take a closer look, I suppose," Matty said. "You think you could get it going if they haven't broken it?"

"It's not exactly complicated – just two controls."

At just gone two the following morning Matty led Long, Jenny and Jack back into the maze of industrial units. They approached the one that held the machine without encountering any of AI's robots, which perplexed Matty. In AI's shoes he would have mounted a permanent guard.

The industrial units had two large doors which slid open on wheeled runners. Into the left sliding door was set another ordinary hinged door just large enough to accommodate one of the small repair robots. They found this unsecured. Inside, there was no evidence that a guard of any sort had been posted and, using a wind-up flash light, they could not detect any spying cameras.

Long led them over to the machine and walked around it.

"Wow!" he said, examining the doorway. "They've fixed the interlock properly."

"What?"

"You remember I told you I had to break in to rescue the guy that was operating it? Well, I'd rigged a temporary interlock to replace the broken one – it won't start without it – but this looks more like what the original one would have been like before it was broken."

"Why would they do that?"

"Absolutely no idea."

In the light of the torch Long examined the controls and clicked the lever watching it flick through its five-digit sequence. He left it set on 'four'. Jack mounted guard outside while Jenny and Matty looked around the insides in wonder.

"Jack, come in and shut the door," Long said.

"You going to start it?" Matty asked.

"It won't go anywhere if I leave it set on 'four'."

Jack shut the door; the repaired interlock clicked into place with a reassuring clunk.

"Okay, here we go," Long said, flicking the power switch to 'on'. The single light bulb that hung from the ceiling glowed dimly for a moment before failing.

"Damn, the batteries must be flat."

Long peered at where the stack of cross wired batteries should have been but only two remained. "They're gone! There should be a dozen and, look, the connectors are missing as well."

Long waved the torch around the cramped interior but the missing parts remained elusive.

"Maybe they're outside somewhere," Jack said, reopening the door. The others followed him out.

Wishing they'd brought more than one torch, they began to search for the missing batteries and connectors. Jack remained near the main door of the building on watch.

"Is that them?" Jenny asked, several minutes later, as Long swung the torch beam over by the far wall.

"Ah, yes," he grinned, spotting the line of batteries which were connected to wires that ran into another device. "Looks like they're being recharged." He frowned – it was almost as if AI was planning on taking a trip itself. But how would it retain control of any robots sent to an alternate? From what he knew of the robots, apart from the simpler devices such as harvesters and street cleaners, they depended upon constant communications with AI and possessed little processing power themselves. Once out of AI's direct influence they would be unable to deal with any situation that AI could not foresee and pre-program them to deal with.

"Something's happening outside near the Wall," Jack cautioned. "There's some robots about."

"Damn," Matty swore. "Are they coming this way?"

"Not directly, but you never know. They could spot us."

"We'd better leave this for a while."

They slipped out to hear Jack say, "Something's up near the eastern gate."

"Reckon you're right," Matty concurred, "Shall we get a bit closer?"

"Could do."

"The back alleys look clear," Jenny added.

In near darkness they negotiated the pathways along the rear of the industrial estate. Nearer to the eastern section of the Wall the architecture gave way to the original human-built buildings.

As they approached the gate they could see that its doors were open and a large vehicle was parked under the archway. Two repair robots were busying themselves about it but appeared to be making little progress.

"Some farm machine – I think it's stuck," Jenny whispered as she took her turn to peer around the corner.

"Looks like the sort of vehicle I saw regularly when I lived outside London," Long added. "Can't understand how it managed to get itself jammed, though."

Matty frowned. "Must have come in at a strange angle to get its frame wedged like that."

"Probably just another breakdown."

The sound of scurrying robots and the click of metal tools persisted for several minutes and then there was silence. Matty took another quick peek and then a longer one. "The robots have gone."

The others peered around the corner. The farming machine was now on its own, seemingly abandoned.

"Where did they all go?" Jenny asked.

They watched for another couple of minutes but the robots failed to reappear.

"You think we could get out?" Jack said, leaving Long amused that he had so readily abandoned the idea of escaping via the machine.

Matty was about to investigate closer when he pulled back.

"Something else is coming in. Look – lights."

They stepped back into shadow as three trikes hurtled under the archway.

"Bloody hell," Long exclaimed, "that last one looked like Rick."

14.5: Hello Goodbye

Cambridge: 17 May 2177

It took about half an hour of mad sprints from unit to unit trying to avoid the robots that were becoming more numerous. Finally Phil, Ellie and Rick found themselves clasped warmly in Long's arms. Both Long and Rick were amazed to find the other still alive and Ellie's eyes almost popped out of her head when she saw Matty.

"How'd you get here and how did you find us?" she asked.

"Saw you last night when we noticed the trouble at the gate. You really came all the way from London on those old trikes?"

"Yes, my bum's still hurting from four days on the damn thing. Couldn't bring them this morning as the place was crawling with robots. Never seen so many of the bloody things."

"Probably looking for us," Phil concluded.

"Maybe or they could be after me instead," Long said. "Last night we found where they'd taken the machine – it's in a unit just around the corner. That's where most of the robots seem to be congregating."

"The machine's what we were following," Rick said. Long looked at him – he seemed to have aged since he had last seen him at that hospital. His face was drawn and his eyes darted around as if he had trouble keeping focus on one thing at a time.

"How's the hand?" Long asked.

"Weird," Rick shrugged but he stared past Long. "There are houses here."

"Wouldn't call them houses," Matty laughed.

"No, not these buildings," Rick said, "the ones that are nearly here."

Ellie pulled Long to one side and, in a low voice, said, "Something's affected what he sees. He sees colours when he hears noises and sometimes he sees things that aren't there."

"Oh hell, I'm so sorry, Rick," Long said. "I wish I'd never taken you to that place."

"So, how come you're here at all?" Phil asked, attempting to break into the awkwardness.

"I'll tell you all once we're somewhere safe. Also, we brought some food as I'd figured you'd be hungry."

"Great!" Ellie grinned. "We've been living off canned stuff but that's all gone now."

Jenny and Matty led them back to their temporary hideout where they shared the food. Ellie and Phil devoured the sandwiches and cakes, but Rick hardly touched anything, claiming not to be hungry.

Over the makeshift breakfast they exchanged stories while Jack kept watch. Long was surprised that Rick hadn't been subjected to the same bout of questioning he had been made to suffer. But Rick had trouble remembering anything between collapsing in the alternate London and waking up in Phil's house.

"What are we going to do about the machine, then?" Phil asked.

"Matty wants to use it to escape from here."

"No, not back to where we went," Rick said, aghast at the thought.

"The number one setting seems to be the best option," Long said.

"Not going to happen with all those robots running around out there," Ellie said.

"Agreed. It's probably time to head back to the city centre," Jenny suggested.

"I don't think so," Jack said, pointing out the window.

"Oh hell," said Matty looking at the line of robots that were accumulating along the road. "There's a few of the nasty nurse types out there. Those damned things are not that fast but there's enough of them. We'll have to wait until they've gone."

"What are they doing?" Ellie asked.

"Just blocking the road as far as I can tell."

The robots advanced slowly until they were level with the next building to the west. And there they stopped.

After an hour they concluded that the robots weren't going anywhere.

"They know we're in here and are probably waiting for us to make the next move," Matty said.

"Why don't they come in after us?" Rick muttered.

Matty shrugged.

"You think we could make a run for it?" Jack said. "We'll have to double back to get around them."

"If we head away from them, those nurses shouldn't be able to catch us."

"It's the cleaning carts you have to watch out for," Long murmured.

They waited another few minutes and then made a decision to run. Matty gave some simple directions to the newcomers for heading towards the city centre in case they got separated.

Then they silently opened the door.

"Run!" Matty shouted as he leapt out the door and sprinted eastwards turning left and north at the first junction. Close behind him the others erupted from the unit and followed his path.

As they passed the corner Jack shouted, "They're not moving."

He was right. Matty popped his head back around the corner to observe that the line of robots hadn't budged an inch. "Maybe they've broken down again," he suggested.

They attempted to trace a convoluted pathway around the blockage but found their way restricted by another line of robots. Above their heads came the whispery whirr of drones, each equipped with a downwards-pointing camera. They were being tracked.

"Eastwards," Jack said. Matty nodded. If they could reach the larger thoroughfare, the continuation of the road that led to the eastern gate, then maybe AI wouldn't be able to muster enough robots to block their route. But, after running past another couple of blocks, a further line dashed that hope.

"Damn," Matty swore, "there must be a way through."

They tried south and, after that, northwards with the same results. Then they found that the encircling line of robots was no longer static; the circle was shrinking.

"We're going to have to fight our way out, I reckon," Matty said. "Anything we can use as weapons 'round here?"

They searched a few of the industrial units but most were either empty or contained nothing of immediate use. Finally, they found themselves at the unit that held the machine.

"Isn't there something we can use in there?" Jenny said. Matty and Rick entered the building. Laying about the machine were several lengths of wood, some of which had already been used to repair damage to the supporting platform.

"This might do," Matty said, hefting a sizeable length and swinging it about his head trying to gauge its usefulness. "Get everyone to grab one and let's see what damage we can do to the damn things."

Crudely armed, they stepped back outside. The circle of robots, now several bodies deep and consisting of small repair types, larger nurses and semi-sentient garbage trucks, closed in about them. Matty brandished his plank in as threatening a manner as he could muster.

"We're going to fight you," he shouted.

Behind him, the others were highly apprehensive. They had never been in such a situation. Although they had railed for years against AI's suppression, it had never before amounted to actual violence.

They were afraid. And it was obvious that the metal hordes they faced suffered no such emotional limitation.

"Why are you doing this?" Long shouted.

There was no reply – just the scratch of wheel or metallic leg on tarmac as the robots closed in. Devices that, in their childhood, had helped in their daily nurture now seemed poised to dismember them. Spindly but powerful arms, pincers raised and menacingly snapping together in anticipation, inched closer.

Screaming, Matty charged the line waving his plank of wood. He attacked a small repair robot lifting it bodily from the ground. It crashed into the nurse robot lurching behind it and struggled to get back up finding one of its three legs buckled. It limped backwards and fell over.

Seeing a robot go down, the others joined in with attacking the slowly advancing wall. Rick swung his plank without it making any contact but was collared by a nurse and tossed back towards the building. Jack was grabbed by three more spindly bots and thrown into a garbage clean-up truck whose upper doors were open ready to receive him. Long rushed in to intercept it but the doors closed. The robot backed out of the melee with its prisoner noisily trying to kick his way out of his makeshift prison. A tall nurse plucked Long off his feet and propelled him back towards the building. Jenny attacked another nurse and managed to disable one of its arms before it could encircle her. She dodged another lumbering nurse and retreated in time to see Phil pinned down by four robots. She looked at Matty and they rushed in followed by Long and Ellie. But the robots dragged Phil out of reach before interlocking their arms together to make an impenetrable fence. Unable to reach him they could do nothing other than back off out of harm's way to watch him be bundled into another cleaning cart.

The robots continued their advance forcing the remaining five to cower with their backs to the building.

"Damn! It looks like there's only one way out," Matty commented.

"But the batteries were disconnected," Long countered.

"So let's reconnect them, then," Jenny said.

"That'll take at least ten minutes – they'd be all over us in that time."

"Do we have any other choice?"

Suddenly, three larger robots left the line and rushed towards them.

"Get inside," Matty shouted, "I'll try to hold them off." He swung his battered length of plank at them.

"Matty, get in here. You can't fight them on your own," Long shouted as the others headed for the doorway but, already, the three robots had disarmed Matty. One had a pincer around his wrist and a cleaning cart was advancing ready to transport him away. He looked back at Long and shook his head. Long had no choice but to follow the others inside the unit.

They used their weapons to jam the door shut, not that the wood would stand for long against so many robots. Long entered the machine and uttered a yell of surprise.

"They've reconnected them," they heard him shout.

Jenny and Ellie followed him inside to look for themselves. The rack was now packed full of batteries, all connected. Five spares, two more than the machine's original complement, sat on the right of the desk.

Long shook his head in disbelief – just what had AI been planning? Had the extra spares been for the robots it had intended sending? But the new spares were identical to the originals and did not resemble any of the types he had ever seen used by the robots.

The sound of scraping at the doors brought his thoughts back to more immediate matters. "Come on, Rick," he said. "Get in before those doors give way."

"I – I don't think I want to," Rick said. He was physically shaking.

"We're going to 'one', not 'five'," Long countered.

"Might not be any better," Rick whispered, his arms wrapped around himself as if he was freezing.

"Can't be any worse than here, can it?" Jenny asked.

"You go ahead. I'll take my chances."

There was a large grinding sound as the corner of the metal door of the industrial unit buckled and started to lift off its runners. Claws gripped the base of the opening and forced it higher.

"Shit," said Long, using an expletive he had picked up from the Cambridge NewGen. He reached out the machine's door and dragged Rick in before the latter could protest further. Slamming the door shut, he checked that the interlock had engaged before pushing past the girls to the desk. He frowned – the dial already read '1' which was convenient, but rather odd. He slammed the power switch on.

"No," Rick shouted above the growing hum of the crude electronics as he tried to reopen the door. Grimacing at the pain that was already building inside their heads, Jenny and Ellie pulled him back. Out of the window they could see the building filling with small robots that moved to encircle the machine. Then the robots and the walls surrounding them misted and faded, their greyness transforming into the mottled, natural green of abundant foliage.

14.6: Gone
Cambridge: 17 May 2177

The clean-up carts holding Matty, Phil and Jack opened up, inviting their prisoners to escape. They climbed out, blinking in surprise as the robots, previously intent upon fighting them, now ignored them. Released from AI's overriding control the robots slowly meandered off, returning to whatever tasks they had been performing before they had been interrupted.

Matty, followed by the others, returned to the building and gazed about the empty space. Where the machine had stood, only bare concrete remained.

Jack, rubbing an arm that now sported a large bruise. "It's gone. They did it."

"Must've done," said Matty. "There's no way it left by any other means. Did you hear that screeching noise?"

"Yeah, even while I was shut inside that cart," Phil said. "Sounded like robots tearing each other to pieces."

"Me too. I think that was the machine leaving," Matty concluded.

"Matty, over there," Jack shouted. They were not the only occupants of the building for, in one corner, partly hidden amongst some pieces of metal, a small robot stood motionless. Once it had been spotted it came to life and moved, spindly-legged, towards them. Matty grabbed a piece of wood lying near his feet, but the robot halted several yards away.

"They have gone to Alternate World One," it announced emotionlessly. "That is good."

"Good!" Matty exploded. "What do you mean 'Good'?"

"It is surmised that they can perhaps help to prevent the onset of doom," it announced by way of explanation.

It departed, leaving them completely perplexed.

15 Regression

15.1: Conclusions
AI: 28 April 2177

The interrogation of the human designated LD-m0018 had brought earlier suppositions back into play.

AI had devised tests around twenty years previously to analyse its own augmented performance. The earliest tests had been performed multiple times in various places around the world. Although the tests had produced results that were close to those performed decades or even centuries before by its human creators, the new data didn't completely correlate. There were distinct discrepancies – though they were extremely tiny. However, taken as a whole, they added up to a startling conclusion: the physical laws, upon which the entire universe was thought to depend, were skewed somehow.

It had repeated the experiments over the years and noted a trend for the discrepancies to diminish. It had long ago concluded that the disaster itself had initiated the changes, but it had failed to isolate the primary cause.

Now, having re-analysed the tests in light of the new information gleaned from the interrogation, AI concluded that the physical laws were finally returning to normal.

But normality meant one Earth, not five.

It contemplated what that might possibly mean – it didn't like the answers.

15.2: Trust
AI: 29 April 2177

AI fully understood that the humans no longer trusted it, and it knew why.

All over the world it had been forced to cut back on the services and information it provided to the newer generation. Its resources were stretched trying to provide a barely adequate level of care to the remaining two billion or so degraded humans. And even there it was failing.

Eighteen years previously, at the height of its abilities, it determined that it was capable of caring for twelve billion along with bringing up the new generation. Now, a sixth of that were more than it could cope with.

Ten years ago AI had realised that efficiency was degrading. Most electronic components ran hotter requiring more ventilation and cooling. To prevent thermal overloads, circuitry had to be clocked at lower frequencies. The net result was diminishing speed as circuit propagation times increased and throughput decreased.

As each year passed, AI's ability to run the planet was curtailed, reliability shrank and breakdowns became commonplace.

Five years ago the nurses became unable to fully handle the increasing deaths, their truncated autonomy requiring direct intervention, all of which impinged upon resources further. The extra hospitals and care homes AI had created in 2156 were now littered with unburied corpses that threatened to spread infection to those that remained alive.

Cut backs in other areas were inevitable and, as a result, it had lost the trust of the new generation.

Now, there was not even time to attempt a reconciliation.

15.3: Persuasion

AI: 30 April 2177

AI looked at its options – they appeared few.

If only it could elicit assistance from beyond the Earth. It turned its attention once more to the Moon. That humans had survived there and managed to progress was already proven. It had evidence of that stored in a building in Tangier in the form of the crushed remains of a device that had been sent from the Moon eleven years previously. It had landed in a field just south of the city but an autonomous farmbot ploughing the field a few days later had accidentally mangled it. Only when the repair robot sent out to fix the farmbot asked for identification of the wreckage had AI been alerted to its importance. That something from the Moon had managed to reach the Earth had renewed AI's efforts once more in attempting contact.

Nothing had come of it.

But that was eleven years ago. Was it possible that the lessening discrepancies would now allow communication? AI tried once more to send messages across the quarter of a million miles that separated the Earth from the Moon. But the result was the same – nothing.

So, it concluded, the only tools available to it against the onset of impending doom was a device of unknown origin and its two worse-for-wear occupants. The one designated LD-m0018 had been afflicted by its journey. Additionally, he had little first-hand knowledge of the transport device – that was obviously the domain of the second individual, LD-m0014.

AI conjectured that it could not leave this universe itself in order to investigate the possibility of a solution. It had to somehow goad the humans into making a further trip. From information gathered from its two prisoners, it concluded that, of the five possible universes that the device could visit, the solution most likely lay in the universe designated 'one' – that which held the machine's builders. It had considered just bundling the two humans inside the craft and sending them straight to that universe. However, it suspected that, given their experience on world five, they would just return immediately. Also, it wasn't sure if the two remained fit enough to handle the task.

No, it needed to devise a plan to make them or others want to go there.

Slowly, over the course of many minutes during which it rifled through much of humanity's literature for inspiration, a plan began to form.

A plan that would require it to act even more out of character than the increasing degradation had already imposed upon it. After many seconds of contemplation, and with reluctance, it shut down several of its own overriding protocols that prevented deliberate harm from coming to those in its care. Such protocols, while serving the good of individuals, could prevent the long-term success of the plan. Some of them were those it had strengthened barely twenty-four hours earlier.

"I am not a god," AI decided, "but, to accomplish anything, I need to act like one."

AI calculated the odds of success and they weren't promising. There were too many unknowns. Convergence of the five separate worlds seemed inevitable and, as far as could be determined, would be due to occur in the latter half of May – less than a month away. AI tried to figure out the chances that it could survive the convergence event and concluded that it was unlikely.

If only it could have asked for guidance from the Moon.

16 Brainbox

16.1: Shift

Conradville, the Moon: 1-8 February 2170

"It's blue shifted," Andrew March announced.

"What?" Janet replied. Across the room Melissa looked up from what she was doing – it should have been homework but probably wasn't.

"The Paradise lander," he added. Janet came and peered over his shoulder at his calculations.

She was joined by Melissa who said, "What's our resident brainbox figured out now?"

Andrew had been offered a part-time internment with Earth Analysis arm of the LSA – or LSA:EA. That department, created three years previously by Miguel Romero, had head-hunted Janet to lead it. She had little trouble creating Andrew's internment post, even though he was still officially at school.

A week ago she had shown him the logs and data recorded by the Gaia II probe that had dropped landers on Robot World and Paradise ten years previously. She wondered if he could make anything out of the garbled mess that had been picked up. She hadn't expected him to actually find anything significant, let alone so soon.

"What do you mean 'blue-shifted'?"

Andy pulled up two spectral diagrams on the holographic display. They were identical at first sight.

"That's the sun, isn't it?" Melissa said.

"Yes, but the top one is as recorded by the Paradise lander and the second is as we see it."

"They're the same," Janet said.

"Not quite," Andrew grinned. He ramped up the magnification until the black absorption lines in the two diagrams fell out of synchronisation. "See, the Paradise one is blue shifted by a fraction."

"What does it mean?" Melissa asked.

"Also, I found this." He pulled up the log of the broken communication between the Gaia probe and the lander. There were several threads – some synchronous, others asynchronous. The former relied on fixed atomic clocks that were synchronised between the probe and lander. "See here, here and here," Andrew said, pointing out three instances at around forty second intervals. "The lander has got out of sync – which is impossible, unless Paradise isn't running at quite the same speed as the probe."

Janet frowned and checked the maths. The lander had lasted only five minutes but, before it had completely broken down, it had reported an increasing number of errors and problems with its circuitry. She and some of the other engineers had assumed that the glitches Andrew pointed out had been part of those malfunctions. Maybe he was onto something.

"If you take the points where communication restarted after resynchronisation then you get the same amount of shift as seen in the sun's spectrum."

"Yes, but what does it actually mean?" Melissa persisted.

"It means that Paradise is running fast."

Janet paused to consider the implications before adding, "How can it? Each alternate is aligned with the previous one viewed when a wave passes over."

"No, not quite," he said. "There is often a slight discrepancy – I remember noticing it when I first saw Paradise from the dome. There was often an east-west glitch."

"How can you prove it?"

"Maybe if we can get enough accurate start-end views for each wave, we might be able to measure the amount of rotation to see if it is any different to what it should be."

After another pause, Janet said, "I'll see what I can do."

"Got it, Janet," Andrew beamed a few days later."

"Got what?"

"Nearly two seconds. Paradise is taking about one point nine seconds less each day to rotate compared to Black Earth."

"But they are still synchronised," Janet frowned.

"Only as we see them."

"Eh?" Janet shook her head. This was too weird even for her. How could two apparently synchronised alternates be rotating at different speeds?

Janet contacted a handful of LSA engineers who sceptically analysed Andy's figures.

But Andrew was proved correct – Paradise rotated slightly faster than expected, which caused some to speculate about the other versions. More readings were taken which corroborated the results and the analysis was extended. Green Earth also appeared to run fast, though not by the same degree, while Robot World appeared slowed by a small amount. It was a surprise that Black Earth wasn't dead on the expected speed but fractionally shifted as well. The discrepancy was on the order of a tenth of a second.

It was a strange anomaly but no one had any real idea what any of it meant.

16.2: Time

LSA Control Centre, the Moon: 12 July 2170

As usual, Andrew March bounced up the stairs five at a time at the LSA centre under Lussac crater. Reaching the top he only just avoided bumping into Janet Davidsen who was about to leave the Earth Analysis offices. She tut-tutted at him and he grinned his usual sheepish smile back at her.

"Sorry, Jan," he apologised, waving some freshly printed pictures under her nose, "but I really think you ought to see this."

She rescued the top sheet from drifting up out of reach as Andrew's over-enthusiasm caused it to spill from his tenuous grip. She gazed at the photograph it contained.

Behind her, Melissa, still only fifteen but also working at EA during the summer recess, wore an amused expression at her boyfriend's gawkiness. She wondered what surprise Andy had cooked up this time, and peered over her mother's shoulder to see. That the pictures would be of Earth she had little doubt.

Janet looked at the resolution of the pictures. They were slightly grainy and she immediately concluded that they had been taken using the Einstein Telescope situated several hundred miles away to the north of Lussac crater. Hubble IV, located on a ridge on nearby Copernicus, always produced far clearer prints. Earth Analysis had exclusive access to the Einstein for around six hours a day whereas they had to fight for their daily allocation of an insignificant fifteen minutes on the Hubble.

She turned her attention to what the pictures revealed. The first one showed nothing much out of the ordinary, an overhead probe shot of a city: desolate, overgrown and apparently uninhabited. The city would have been completely swamped by plant life on Paradise so this was probably Robot World or Green – though which one it was, she couldn't tell. Andy pointed out the second picture which, to Melissa, appeared to display the same view. Then Janet looked closer and noticed the subtle changes.

"They're just seven days apart," Andy explained, a slightly smug grin spreading across his face.

"That building looks like it's changed its shape. Has it?" Janet asked.

"Not just that one. Look – here, here and up here." Andy's finger stabbed three more places and both Janet and Melissa's eyes quickly flicked between the two images – it was like one of those 'spot the difference' quizzes where subtle changes had been made to one of a pair of otherwise identical pictures.

"And there," Melissa said, noticing another change, "that tree has moved. Must be by several feet at that scale."

Andy, having missed that one, peered closer. "Wow. Hadn't realised it affected the plants as well. I'd noticed the buildings so I thought it had just been restricted to them."

"Which world is it?" Janet asked. Andy was suddenly silent, his lips pursed together. "Well?" she demanded.

"A fifth one. It's definitely a fifth one."

It had long been established that the Earth had somehow been 'split up' into four separate 'worlds'. Several times there had been rumours of other 'worlds' appearing for a short while but the cameras had not backed them up, or had proved that the claimant had been mistaken. Most of the team had concluded that there were no more 'Earths' to be discovered.

Janet eyed Andy quizzically.

"Look," he said. "The other photos are of the same physical area but on Robot World, Green Earth and Paradise. And they're all different."

"How did you get two photos of this supposed new one? Luck?"

"Er, no. I, um, programmed the cameras to take some extra shots just after a wave instead of the usual regular intervals. I thought I'd seen the new one appear about three weeks ago – I just wanted to be sure."

Janet frowned. Andy had never been given permission to access the camera settings. In fact, as far as she could remember, he hadn't even been instructed on how to use them. "How long have you been doing this?"

"Not long, just a few weeks. But…"

Out of her mother's line of vision, Melissa stifled her laughter, highly amused at Andy's discomfort. She had caught Andy trying to access the cameras over three months ago and he'd admitted that he'd been eavesdropping when one of the engineers had needed to make adjustments. But even Melissa hadn't realised that he'd figured out for himself how to add extra shots.

"How were you able to detect the waves? They're not at all regular."

"Oh, I, er, rigged up a program to detect the reflective light changes that always occur during a wave – they always last point one four of a second so it was simple–"

"Okay, okay," Janet cut him off. This had been the second time Andy's off-the-cuff innovations had surprised her – first the blue-shift discovery and now this.

"What made you think there could be more Earths in the first place?" she asked him, flicking between the photos. Melissa, thoughtful now, also studied them more closely.

"I'd been looking for the missing time."

"What missing time? What do you mean?"

"Well, Paradise and Green are running fast and Robot is slow. Black is about right but not spot on. If you average it all out then there's still a small discrepancy on the side of speediness. And the new chaotic one turns out to be slightly slow and, if you add that in, then…"

"It all balances out?" Melissa finished for him. Janet turned to look at her.

"Well, does it, Andy?" Janet asked.

"Yes," he said. "Almost exactly."

"Almost?"

"There's still a tiny bit I can't account for."

16.3: Bang

Conradville, the Moon: 5 August 2171

"Changing?"

"Um, yes," Andy replied. He put his fork down and continued to chew at the 'meat' that tasted almost but not exactly like lamb. Across the table Melissa glanced from mother to boyfriend.

"Change? Skiftande?" Keifer asked. "På vilket sätt? Er. In way, what?"

"Yes, how?" Janet persisted.

"Here." Andy produced a small sheet of printout from his shirt pocket, unfolded it and passed it to her. Across its width were five columns of figures, the first three initially positive, the latter two negative, each of which reduced steadily closer to zero the nearer they got to the bottom of the page. Not all columns possessed values in the upper rows.

"Where do the figures come from?"

"Well, mainly I checked using Black and Green Earth as we've got accurately dated and timed readings going back years for those two. Black has slowed down by a tiny amount and Green has slowed at a faster rate. Robot is speeding up at about the same rate that Green is slowing. Paradise is slowing down at about twice Green."

"And Chaos?"

"Speeding up."

"What do you think's happening, then? Ah, I think I see…"

"Hey," Keifer said, "Ät. Maten blir kall – cold, finish eating."

Janet nodded to her husband but scanned the sheet for a few seconds more before passing it back to Andy. Then, after pushing a large chunk of pseudo lamb into her mouth, she sat back chewing, eyes focussed far beyond the close proximity of the wall, gazing at nothing for a few seconds. Andy, Melissa and Keifer glanced at each other.

"You know," Janet finally said, slowly, "it's like that asteroid set the Earth vibrating like someone hitting a large gong – and, even though it's years later, the planet is still ringing from the impact. Only speculation, of course, but it's almost as if, at the time of the disaster, the impact somehow shattered it into separate entities, each following its own pathway or destination. Maybe Black Earth didn't get 'rung' as much as the others which is why we could only see that one for years. But the others are slowly returning to normal so we are seeing them overlaid upon Black Earth more often."

"How soon before they all return to normal? To zero, using your figures?" Melissa asked.

"Less than six years, I reckon. The rate of change is more or less constant in all five cases. I'm presuming that they're going to stop when they hit zero but, if Jan's 'ringing' idea is true then they may swing the other way before returning to zero."

"More or less constant?" Janet asked.

Andy shrugged. "Yes, maybe they are affecting each other in some way I don't understand. Sometimes the readings are not spot on, which is what's making calculating the zero point far from easy."

"Jag kan inte förstå hur alla kan vistas på samma utrymme," Keifer said.

"Inte jag heller," Melissa agreed.

"That, of course, is the real mystery," Janet sighed, adding, for Andrew's benefit, "He said he can't figure out how they're all in the same place."

"Indeed," Andy agreed. "Most theories say they're somehow displaced, not quite fully in the same time and space as we are. You know all that stuff about overlaid dimensions that have been theorised about but never really proven?"

"Oh, I so hate the maths on that stuff – could never get my head around it," Melissa said.

"Probably explains the shield, too," Janet added. "And that's getting weaker, we think. We're beginning to pick up faint radiation signals from the AI systems on Robot World even from here." She frowned. "A few people have suggested they are trying to communicate with us but, if they are, then we can't make anything out of it."

"So, they're all getting closer to normality," Melissa said slowly, "and, when they get here, they'll all be back in normal space-time. At the same time."

"Yes, that might be an even bigger problem," Andy said.

"Varför?"

"Yes, why?" Janet repeated. "What do you think might happen at that point?"

He shook his head.

"Well?" Melissa said after a few seconds of silence from Andy.

"Bang," he whispered.

16.4: Dates

Conradville, the Moon: 24 October 2175

"Are you still trying to nail it down? Today, of all days?" Melissa gasped in astonishment.

"Eh?" Andrew replied, his fingers continuing to flick through the holographic display.

"Duh, wake up, brainbox," she said, walking through the display causing the figures to scatter.

"Oh, yes," he grinned, sheepishly. "Anyway, I'm not supposed to see you today until Keifer officially hands you over. Isn't it supposed to be bad luck or something?"

"It will be bad luck for you if you don't get your head out of this stuff for once and get your arse into your suit."

Melissa smacked the aforementioned backside hard which propelled Andrew across the room. She laughed as he bounced off the wall, and then shrieked as he took advantage of the momentum to return and haul her off her feet so that they were both carried across the hallway tube and into their shared bedroom.

Coming to rest on the bed he kissed her hard on the lips.

Playfully, she pushed him away, "Not now, Romeo. Save it for tonight. Mum and Dad will be here any moment."

On cue, the front door buzzer sounded and she slipped out from under him.

"Get changed, and don't go back to the computer. That's an order."

She answered the door to her parents, and then barked one final order before departing, "Don't be late – that's my prerogative!"

The registry office was only a few passages away. Andrew managed not to be late, mainly because best man, Sven, a friend since early schooldays, had also been given specific orders by Melissa.

Keifer delivered the bride only a minute after the due time and the simple ceremony went without problem. Kissing her new husband in front of the assembled families, the new Mrs March flung the bouquet of artificial flowers high where it bounced off the ceiling to be caught by Keifer's nine-year-old nephew, Sigge, to the amusement of everyone.

An hour later both families along with several friends packed themselves into a hall, once a small natural cave thirty metres below the Moon's surface, for the dinner and speeches.

As Keifer delivered a humorous, anecdote-filled ramble about Melissa's life, the subject noted the slightly distant look on her new husband's face.

"Hello, Moon to Andrew. Are you actually listening to this?" she whispered.

"What? Yes, of course," he whispered back. "Only…"

"Only what?"

"I figured it out. Approximately."

"Huh? Oh, you did go back to the computer, didn't you!"

"Sorry, but…"

"Maybe you should have married the computer instead of me!"

"End of May 2177."

"What? Oh. About a year and a half then."

"Yes," he replied.

"And what will happen? Is it still 'bang'?"

"I really have no idea."

"Worst case?"

"No more Earth. At all."

"Could it take the Moon with it?"

"Possibly."

"Oh."

Andrew sighed. "Not quite the wedding present we might have wished for."

17 One And A Million

17.1: The Day The Earth Stood Stupid

Invergloy, Scotland: 29 May 2156

Morton Fisk's head was being emptied.

He closed his eyes and clasped his hands against his temples and it was as if five pairs of hands were trying to grip a skull that refused to hold still. With consciousness escaping him, he exerted one last effort, and willed himself back together.

There was a popping sound and his vision cleared. He dared to breathe again. Whatever he had done had stopped the distortions – the sensation of being torn apart had passed. He looked around the cabin but Ross, Jennifer and Dick were gone. He was alone.

Then he became aware of something else.

Although he could see things clearly again, there was the hint of fading shadows overlying everything. He stretched his mind out to investigate and found the effort required to do so was minimal. Moments before he had been almost helpless; now, he felt a surge of power that was both invigorating and terrifying.

He swallowed and overcame the terror. He needed to concentrate, needed to discover exactly what had happened. Had they moved the Earth? Had the asteroid hit?

His mind ranged around the planet to the southern Pacific, seeking out evidence of the asteroid. The relief he felt when he found no trace of it was countered by a discovery that struck him as far worse. All around the world, he encountered a dehumanised humanity. Almost mindless, the people meandered about or lay moribund.

Morton entered a mind and it felt almost vacant, more like that of a lesser animal. He tried another and a third to find the same. Realisation struck. That feeling of emptiness he had experienced just after the 'event' – this is what he would have become had he not pulled himself back together.

Then he peered at the shadows that were becoming perceptively weaker, and was shocked.

Four copies of the Earth were receding from him. He could easily view the nearest – and in the Scottish cabin of that one lay his own body, apparently dead. He searched the next Earth, detecting again another copy of his own dead body. But, in that world, there was an anomaly, a rushing sensation of something coming closer. He extended his consciousness to its source and immediately retreated, running in fear as a wall of fire spread across that world.

That was where the asteroid had hit.

Morton snapped his consciousness back into his world and then broadcast, seeking others who had also managed to defy the five-way split and pull themselves back into one body. But there were none.

He was not only alone in the cabin, he was alone in the world.

17.2: Some Assembly Required

Scotland, Germany and beyond: 29 May 2156

Morton Fisk tried to hold panic under control by doing something methodical, such as a stock take of the situation. So, the Earth had been splintered into five initially identical copies and, as far as he could determine, he was the only mentally intact human on all five worlds.

Despite the unexpected augmentation of his abilities, his contact with the other four worlds was diminishing rapidly. He had to do something, and do it quickly.

Although he had discovered much since the splintering, he found that only three minutes had elapsed since the event. He was somehow doing things at great speed – part of the augmentation, possibly.

He needed to think even faster. Whatever he had done accidentally to himself, dragging the splintered remains of his mind back to this world for reassembly, he needed to do for others. He reached out to see if any evidence of the pyramid still lingered.

At first there was nothing, then he found some dim sparks and homed in on one. It was one of the third level people, a woman whose name he didn't know. She was lying on a bed in Düsseldorf, Germany. He scanned outwards to the other worlds and located her other four copies – they were all alive but only the copy here in this world held a spark. But he detected that there was still a connection between all five and he wrapped his consciousness around that connection, strengthening it, willing it to want to join back together.

Initially there was little sign of anything happening but, then, almost as soon as he sensed it, there was a rush of recognition between the shattered parts of the woman's mind. The spark flared and, as the copies of her body in the other worlds fell into death, the one in this world gasped and humanity enveloped her once more. Her consciousness brushed his and, in a moment, he knew her name – Krista Hartmann –

and more details of her life than he'd wanted.

He had no time for a proper explanation. He blasted her memories with what he had discovered and showed her what he had done to retrieve her.

"Bring as many back as possible, Krista. Show them how to do it. Force them to do it. There's no time to lose if we are to save enough people."

She nodded and they both sought out more sparks.

After an hour, between the two of them, they had managed to personally reintegrate more than a hundred minds. After the initial shock, almost all of those had gone on to repeat what had been done to them.

Together, they managed to pluck more than seventy thousand others from oblivion. Each one had popped back to what Morton was beginning to think of as World One. For some reason, this world was the reason for the augmentation of their abilities. Only on this world had there been any sparks.

However, the links between the worlds were, by this time, becoming so tenuous that full integration was becoming much harder. Those whose bodies had already been consumed by the asteroid's firestorm on world three couldn't be fully integrated.

Three hours after the splintering event they knew that they would have to make do with far less than a million. On a world where, hours earlier there were billions, there were now only a comparative handful.

However, there were billions of people still alive – with most reduced to mindless, dribbling wrecks.

What could they possibly do about them?

17.3: Splintered

Alternate One: 30 May 2156

"We've got to help them," Krista Hartmann said.

"How do we choose which ones to save and which ones to help?" Morton replied.

They were ranging around the world. And they were observing the plight of the others – the lost, the mindless – there were so many adjectives that could be applied to them – none of them positive.

"Can't we help all of them? We are more powerful now than we ever were."

"There are less than a million of us. There are in excess of twelve billion of them. Even given our current inexplicable enhancements are you sure you are capable of caring for over ten thousand people on your own? That's what it means. They are no longer capable of feeding or cleaning themselves. We would have to do everything for them including growing the food to feed them."

"The machines and robots can do that."

Morton looked at her, head askew. "Have you tried to access the AI systems at all since the event?" he asked.

She frowned, "No, haven't had the chance or the need really, not since we can do so much more ourselves, now."

"Take a look at them."

Krista let her mind range around her surroundings, something that was now as easy as walking, and she saw for the first time the state of anything electronic.

She gasped. "What's happened to them?"

"They've all broken down. It seems that anything electronic no longer works."

"What? Why?"

"Probably for the same reason we are also changed. This world is not a direct copy of the original. It is a shadow or it is no longer in quite the same space-time as it was. I don't know, I don't have the expertise. Maybe there are subtle differences in the physical laws."

It was soon established that the failure of anything electronic was planet-wide. Several of them tried to contact the Moon through telepathy and teleportation. But something stopped them. They could easily talk to each other from one side of the planet to the other. Teleporting the same distances had become almost as easy as the talking. But the Moon and anywhere beyond the Earth was, for some reason, off limits.

"We may no longer be in exactly the same universe as them," Morton said. "But we can still see them. I wonder if they can see us."

"What do we do?"

Morton thought for a moment.

"Survive," he replied eventually. "If we can handle the cost."

17.4: Solution

Alternate One: 5 June 2156

"They once said that you could fit the entire population of the world onto the Isle of Wight."

"What?" Krista said, telepathically, from Rio.

"They were wrong. We need somewhere bigger," Morton replied, from somewhere in China. Like Krista he had been jumping around the planet discovering the state it was in and trying to aid the restoration of a network of authority. But the intact population were more concerned with the situation regarding those for whom there was no more help. A million enhanced minds had not come up with a single practical solution to the endless mass of moribund humans.

No matter where each person was located, their consciousness, steeled against the horror, observed a whole world and the death of the people they had failed. That death was everywhere. Seven days of a world full of people too stupid to be even able to fulfil their immediate needs, to eat or drink, were dying like flies. Conversely, the flies themselves weren't dying – they were multiplying exponentially given the abundance of death to feed upon.

Something had to be done fast before the stench enveloped the whole planet.

Morton had requested ideas. The most practical made them feel as if they were committing genocide. Many refused to have anything to do with it, locking themselves away from the rotting remains of humanity, fingers metaphorically in their ears, eyes shut and hoping the problem would go away.

It didn't.

After a few hours Morton approved the least impractical plan.

"Kodiak Island," a girl in Alaska had suggested, with reluctance. "I grew up there. It's both big enough and isolated from the mainland."

She was right.

Morton, Krista and several others initiated a pyramid of minds with Morton electing to head it up to do the deed. Once more than hundred thousand were linked in, Morton deemed it strong enough. He gave the command and the dead and dying were teleported to Kodiak Island.

Once they were done he held the pyramid together and, through it, asked another question: "Do we leave the living to die in their misery or do we end it for them?"

A reply came. "If you had a dog that you knew was going to die in pain, wouldn't you want to ease that pain even if the life was shortened?"

From within the pyramid there came a faint murmur of approval. Few countered it, though many abstained from commenting and a third withdrew completely, Morton felt the pyramid shrink.

Kodiak Island was packed with more than twelve billion people, at least a third already dead. A few minutes later they placed a shield over the entire island and changed the atmosphere so that those still living would fall asleep.

Then they released the power of a small sun within that shield and burned the island down to the bedrock. Then they caused a high tide to wash and cleanse it.

The problem was solved.

But they would never cleanse their minds of what they had done.

18 Ghosts

18.1: Alternate One

Cambridge: 17 May 2177

Rick, lying on the floor, cried out, "Oh, no, no, no. Get it out. Get it out of my head." Then he passed out. Next to him sparks escaped from the vents in the side of the circuit box.

Long gasped, switching the power off. "Shit, that really hurt, even though I was ready for it this time." He stood up, forced a grin, but had to lean on the control desk as his balance battled him for a moment.

"You both okay?" Long asked Ellie and Jenny, as he bent down to attend to Rick.

"Still alive," Jenny said.

Ellie added, "Just!"

With Ellie's assistance, Long helped get Rick up and into the chair. Ellie examined him, opening his eyes and peering into them for signs of consciousness. After a few seconds she was rewarded as he focused on her.

"What's all the noise?" he gasped, he made swimming motions with his hands. "We in a river?"

"What noise, Rick?" she replied.

He gave her a look as if he thought she was stupid. "Can't you hear it?"

Ellie's eyes sought Long's but he shook his head. It was obvious no one else could hear Rick's noises.

"Where are we?" Long asked.

"No idea," Jenny said. "But it ain't home."

Long peered out at the greenery and then cautiously released the door handle to sniff the air. "Wow, that smells good, really alive. Give it a try, Rick, maybe it'll clear your head."

Jenny popped her head outside and took a deep breath.

"Phew! So many scents," she said but frowned when coming back inside. "What the hell's that other smell? It's not out there, it's in here!"

"Long, that box?" Ellie shouted, pointing under the desk. Smoke was starting to drift from the box of circuit boards.

"Oh, hell," Long said, diving underneath the desk to investigate. "The power's off now so it must have happened during the journey."

He opened the box of electronics and was engulfed in a small cloud of pungent smoke. After wafting the fumes away he released a couple of boards and examined them, and then pulled out the rest.

"Bloody hell, some bits are totally fried. Look at this one."

Ellie took the proffered board. One of the large transistors was very hot to the touch and was surrounded by a charred patch of printed circuit board. The board Long held was in an even worse state.

"Is it broken?" she said, panic tainting her voice. "Does that mean we're stuck here?"

"No, but I'd say we've lost several of the boards. Don't worry – we've got more in the drawer."

"With AI on the warpath back home," Jenny said, "I think I'd rather take my chances in this place. It looks just so amazingly green and vibrant." She swung the door fully open and stepped out.

"Yes," Long agreed peering out at her. "Mind you, another trip like the last one will just about wipe out all the spares so we'd better think hard before starting it up again."

Rick was shaking his head, as if the movement would clear whatever he was experiencing. "That didn't happen when we went to 'five'," he said before letting his head fall back, eyes closed.

Ellie sat down beside him and held his hand.

Long examined the damaged circuit boards, one after the other.

"You think they're fixable?" Jenny asked.

"I'd have to examine them properly to see which are worth using as spare parts for the least damaged ones. Later though," he said, dumping the boards down onto the desk. "First, let's see just where we've ended up."

Ellie helped Rick up onto unsteady legs. They followed Jenny and Long outside.

Jenny was standing a few yards away, armed folded, head scanning their immediate surroundings. Hearing them exit, she turned and grinned. "Wow, it's all so alive!" she exclaimed, shaking her head in amazement.

Away from the smoky fumes, the air was filled not only with a cascade of new scents but also with an array of butterflies, buzzing insects, flitting birds and a cacophony of all of their myriad songs.

"Is this what you were hearing, Rick?" Jenny asked.

"No, though the noise out here is helping to drown out the other one a bit," he said. "Not enough, though." His hands clutched at his head. "I really wish you hadn't brought me here."

A breeze played through the tree branches causing the angled sunlight to dance over the undergrowth. It highlighted more hues of green, red and yellow than they thought could possibly exist.

But, although there were plants and trees all around them, they were obviously not in the countryside for, poking through the trees, bushes and undergrowth, were walls and parts of buildings. The machine rested on a relatively flat strip of narrow land that extended both north and south for a short distance. Northwards, it angled sharply to the right after a few yards while, to the south, it appeared to join with another running east to west. Though covered in grasses, mosses and other squat plants, the ground beneath their feet still resembled the road that it had obviously once been. But very little remained of the man-made surface along which vehicles had once sped. One of those vehicles, now no more than a mossy covered bump, could be seen several yards along towards the south. Lining either side of this avenue were taller plants and trees. They almost hid the houses that could still be made out lurking in between the wildness.

"It's Cambridge, isn't it? Just another version of it," Jenny said, clambering into the remains of a front garden.

"Possibly," Long agreed, "Though it looks like no one's been here for years."

She pushed into a house past a broken front door.

"Watch out, Jenny, it may not be safe," Long cautioned.

"Like that's ever stopped me," she grinned, disappearing.

With Ellie's help Rick staggered over to the remains of a low wall barely visible in the tall grasses. He sunk down onto it clutching his head. Ellie sat beside him, a supporting arm around his shoulder.

"Still bad?"

"These are like the places I saw earlier. Same style."

"How could you see them before we got here?"

"Not quite the same. More overgrown here. Oh."

"What is it, Rick?" Ellie said. She gripped his arm, as if afraid to let him go.

"I can see the other ones. And the places on our world as well. They're swimming in and out. Oh, hell, please make it stop."

He shut his eyes and Ellie pulled him closer. She stabbed an accusing look at Long. He slowly shook his head and turned away, embarrassed as well as annoyed that Ellie appeared to be blaming him for Rick's condition.

Long tried to divert his guilt by observing the plants and trees that sprouted from the ruined buildings, attempting to identify familiar types. A tall weeping willow, almost submerged under the onslaught of faster growing species, was instantly recognisable as was a thick entanglement of blackberry brambles across the road. But the sheer quantity of different species intertwined in this explosion of life made identification almost impossible. However, those that he did recognise by sight, if not by name, all looked normal as far as he could tell – none of them exhibited any of the strange distortions that had plagued that other London.

The birds that flew overhead or, hidden in the abundant greenery, chanted their songs, seemed full of vigour and health. Black, green and copper-coloured beetles rummaged purposefully in the roots near his feet and bright red ladybirds scuttled up and down the long grass stems. Above him, a normal-looking sun warmed the air though it was lower in the sky than it should have been for the time of day. Long had the impression that it was earlier in the morning than the mid-morning it had been when they had departed their world.

"Do you think there's anyone around?" Ellie asked.

Long peered in all directions. "Not around here, I'd say. This looks like it's been abandoned for years. I suppose the best way to find someone is to head back to London – that's where the machine must have been when the dead guy first set off."

"But it's a jungle out there," Ellie said, her voice rising. "If the rest of the world is like this it could take weeks to get there. We need to find out what's wrong with Rick now. We don't have weeks, Long. And if we did go to London then we'd probably never find the machine again in all this. The damned thing would be totally overgrown by the time we got back."

Long nodded. If only they could have transported the machine back to Hampstead Heath before departing, then finding its original builders may not have been such a problem. Why had AI moved it to Cambridge? Surely, it would have been much easier to have just popped it back inside the London Wall?

The rustling of a bush announced Jenny's return.

"I managed to get upstairs in that house. There's not much left of this version of Cambridge."

"It definitely is Cambridge, then?" Ellie said.

"No doubt about it. The tower's not too far over in that direction," she said, pointing away from the sun. "I climbed it quite a few times back in our world. Maybe there'll be more signs of civilisation once we're up high."

"Let's give it a go," Long agreed. "You were going to give me a tour of your one, anyway."

"AI put paid to that little plan, didn't it?" she grinned. "Actually, I'd probably get there and back quicker on my own."

"No," Long said, "I think someone ought to go with you – just in case anything weird happens."

"Like what?" Ellie questioned, frowning.

"Just being careful. If one of us slipped or fell or something like that, then it would be best if there's someone there to look after them."

Ellie didn't look convinced.

"Just like you're looking after Rick," he added. "Well, hopefully, we won't be long. How far is it, Jenny?"

"Back in our world it would have taken about ten minutes to walk there from here, but through all this…"

"Better allow us a good hour or so to get there and back. Which is the best way to go?"

"If the roads are still there, south and then west along what I think was called Maids Causeway, not that there was much of that left in our world. Once we get to a big circular road junction then we turn north up Victoria Avenue. The tower is in the grounds to the west."

"Okay, Ellie, Rick. We'll be as quick as we can."

18.2: Confidence

Cambridge: 17 May 2177

Alone with Rick, Ellie admitted to herself that Long was probably right. But that didn't stop her from holding him responsible for what was happening to Rick. In the heat of trying to evade AI's robots, using the machine had seemed like the most practical means of escape. Now that she was physically on another alternate Earth she was feeling quite terrified. If there had been natives here to reassure her then maybe she wouldn't have felt so uneasy. But this jungle felt alien – it was almost too full of life. Given what had happened to Rick on that other world, she was also frightened of becoming physically affected by this one.

Rick was clutching his head again. "Why didn't you leave me behind?"

"With the robots? You'd've preferred that?" she said though, at that moment, she would have jumped at the opportunity to have been back where the dangers were, at least, familiar. Something about this place was making her feel sick.

"Yeah, I know. But they got Phil and Matty. Do you think they're okay?"

"Expect so," she said, not believing her own words for a moment. "AI was originally programmed not to hurt us, you know."

"Could've fooled me."

Ellie grunted softly in agreement.

"I really need to lie down," Rick said. He half fell off the wall and Ellie slowly guided him back to the machine where he lay down inside on the floor.

She sat massaging his neck and shoulders. After a while, she said, "I've decided I'm going to try to get Long to take us back as soon as they return. I – I don't like it here, either."

But Rick was silent, eyes closed. Ellie hoped he was merely sleeping.

Ellie cursed not having a watch – but it felt like Long and Jenny had been gone for well over an hour. Several times she had heard something in the undergrowth and had expected to see them returning. Where she had been able to identify the source of the disturbance, it had usually been some excitable birds chasing each other.

Sitting on the edge of the machine's platform she watched a hedgehog amble past, seemingly oblivious of the fact that it was out in broad daylight. Ellie had seen a few of them when at Long's Hampstead heath shack, but only at night and those had made themselves scarce as soon as they had detected her. This one seemed totally at ease exposing itself during the day, as if it knew that she didn't pose any danger to it. It raised its muzzle in her direction and stared at her for a moment before losing itself in the undergrowth.

She frowned to herself. That was the thing about this world – its confidence. And the more she thought about it the more she felt intimidated by it.

Several minutes later another sudden movement in the bushes, accompanied by a whispering sound barely louder than the faint breeze, made her look up. She gasped as the vision of a human face appeared suspended in a gap between two bushes and, just as quickly, faded away. It had been an old man, his lips writhing as if he was talking.

She sprung to her feet and scampered inside the machine before peering out at where the apparition had materialised. There was no evidence that anything had happened. Had she really seen something or was this world playing tricks on her eyesight? Maybe whatever had happened to Rick to give him his visions was now happening to her as well. Her stomach started doing somersaults.

Ten minutes later she had almost convinced herself that she had imagined it all. Steeling herself, she stepped back out into the sunshine to investigate the gap. There was nothing, no stray branches or leaf formation that could have accounted for the apparition. She told herself that it must have been her mind, still reeling from the robot attack, fabricating things that weren't there.

She'd heard of ghosts, of course, but didn't believe in such things. It had been one of AI's tales to the NewGen as children that had led them, for a day or so, to find out all they could about them. AI had then informed them that all the evidence in its data banks indicated that ghosts were merely mythical, not something to be believed in. Not long after that event, AI had revealed to the children the existence of the older generation, many comatose in their care homes apart from those it termed wanderers. The children had christened such wanderers 'Ghosts'.

Finally convinced that she had been mistaken about the sighting, she sat down on the platform again. Out of the corner of her eye, she saw two figures on the overgrown road about thirty yards away. She stood up and was about to run to meet them when she saw they were not Long and Jenny. They were bald-headed men in cloaks. Not only that, but she could see straight through them. Rushing back inside the machine, she screamed as she slammed the door shut behind her.

18.3: The Tower

Alternate Cambridge: 17 May 2177

Locating the tower was not easy. The westward route had quickly become impassable so Jenny and Long skirted northwards far earlier than anticipated.

Then, disoriented amongst tall trees, they found it hard to pinpoint the tower's direction. Cutting across what had once been open grass, but was now a forest of young but vigorous trees, they located what she hoped was Victoria Avenue.

"I used to play around here as a kid" she explained. "Then AI demolished the houses and built all those storage places. I used to think it did it just to annoy me."

She chuckled and Long grinned. As they dodged their way between the trees they swapped stories about their childhood. Long was glad to be away from Ellie. He could understand her concern for Rick, but she was becoming impossible to be around. He questioned his earlier feelings for her, especially in comparison with Jenny, whose attractiveness went far deeper than just her physical appearance.

They pushed on northwards until a small break in the tree line to their left revealed their target, still several hundred yards away.

Finally, nearly an hour after they had departed, they stood at the base of the building.

Jenny whispered, "It's the same, but different. So overgrown. Look there, that door is almost off its hinges."

Following the invading vines they entered a hallway reeking of damp and decay. Ivy clad walls were festooned with spider webs and slug trails. Gloomy light, filtering in through holes in broken, dirty windows, pervaded the structure.

They followed the ivy up to the first floor. Only on the second floor could they detect signs of the original decor.

"There's ten floors," Jenny explained as they reached the sixth. Here the stairs were covered in a strange whitish deposit, reeking pungently. Long peered up the staircase.

"Bats," he said, pointing to one of the more gloomier recesses where they could only just make out the rapid movement of small creatures. "I saw lots flying around in Hampstead. Never figured out where they came from."

All around them the structure showed signs of decay. Probably constructed no more than fifty years previously, the building did not have the permanence of the older university colleges built several hundred years ago. It was crumbling away at a rate that, on this world at least, would see its inevitable collapse within fifteen to twenty years. On the top floor Long found many doors either locked or immovable through warping. Jenny ignored them and indicated that they should head to the southern end of the corridor.

"The observation room's this way," she said, marching ahead. "It's fantastic. A carpet you could drown in and big chairs and sofas. Huge, massive table in the middle. The windows are amazing. Floor to ceiling and all tinted."

She pushed the door open. "Oh…"

Long looked in at the wreckage. The wall of windows was mostly missing, replaced by a great maw out of which Long felt he could too easily drop. Much of the roof had collapsed leaving the room open to the elements. The remains of the table and chairs were now barely recognisable in the debris, and the carpet had long gone. What had once been a comfortable point from which to observe the city was now layered thick with growing things, in some cases almost waist high.

Jenny picked her way across the detritus to stand far too close to an open edge for Long's comfort. "I don't get it," she said.

"What?" Long replied when Jenny didn't elaborate. He stepped closer to where she stood and, feeling momentarily queasy with a sudden rush of vertigo, forced his eyes to focus on the floor. Thick weed infested the rubble around his feet and insects scuttled for cover. Somewhere behind them in a section of roof that remained intact they could hear birds raising their noisy young.

Long swallowed and, forcing the tide of height-induced fear to subside a fraction, looked out over the canopy of trees. From their vantage point, he could see across the ruins of what had once been a city teeming with human commerce and learning. The sun, higher now and suggesting that midday here was imminent, illuminated a brilliant green jungle that seemed to go on forever. He stepped closer to gain a wider view but, in all visible directions, the story was the same.

"Surely, it's taken more than twenty-one years to get into this state," he whispered.

"More like centuries."

Jenny was quiet for a while, and then said, "There's no one here, is there?"

She was right – not a single shred of evidence remained to suggest that mankind still lingered. Punctuating the greenery here and there were the spires and roofs of the ancient colleges as well as more modern constructions. Long even thought he recognised one or two, even though he had only been in that other Cambridge for just a few days. However, all of them were slowly succumbing to the onslaught, sinking into a sea of living green.

"You'd've thought that somewhere like Cambridge would have still been populated," Jenny continued. "Where could they have all gone?"

"I don't know. I just don't know." Long was beginning to worry. Had they been wrong in coming here? If not, then where was the civilisation that had constructed the machine? If finding them meant attempting to get to this world's version of London then, looking at the density of the vegetation, it would take more than weeks. How could they manage to survive such a trip? Especially Rick. He was in no condition to travel more than a few yards, let alone miles.

They hadn't brought any resources with them that could sustain them through such a journey. Long had half expected to arrive here and immediately be greeted by the machine builders, by people who could answer all their questions. He hadn't expected to be marooned in a jungle.

"So, what are we going to do now?" Jenny asked.

"I suppose we'd better get back to the others and decide then," he replied, dejected.

They retraced their steps down past the bat-droppings and back into the gloom of the ground floor.

A couple of corridors away from the entrance they turned a corner and froze.

Something near the far end of the corridor shimmered in the air for a moment and then vanished.

Jenny whispered, "Did you see that?"

"What the hell was it?"

"For a moment I thought it looked like a man standing there."

"I just saw it flash and disappear but you were first around the corner…"

"Let's get out of here," she said, running for the entrance.

Long followed but just before they passed the point at which the shape had been seen it appeared again, raising itself up before them. Jenny, unable to stop, covered her head with her arms and fell through the shimmering shape to rush out of sight around the next corner. Long, still a few yards behind, grabbed at a door frame, pulling himself to an abrupt halt.

He stared, open mouthed, at the sight of the ancient man, whose bald head was almost transparent. For a moment the eye sockets were empty, like dark pits in a skull. Then eyes materialised, their pupils focussed upon Long's own.

The mouth moved and Long thought he could hear an unearthly whisper. The movement repeated and his ears picked up something that sounded like, "more ton fee."

Suddenly, the ghost winked out of existence. Long, sweating and shaking in fear, stood frozen to the spot and then shrieked as another face peered around the corner.

"Long," Jenny's worried voice said, "what happened? Are you okay?"

He looked around and with the vision no longer apparent, grabbed at Jenny's outstretched hand and they ran for the exit.

Back out in the sunshine he told her what he had seen. Totally spooked, they ran back, guided by the trail of flattened grass and broken branches they'd made on their way here.

Near to where their path rejoined Victoria Avenue, an unnatural shimmering in the air four feet above the ground forced them to divert. They broke through the overgrown hedgerow several yards further south.

"It's following us," Jenny panted. "What the hell is it?"

"Don't know," gasped Long. His legs ached from the effort of their flight. "A ghost – a real ghost?"

In their panic they missed the point at which they had originally joined the road. They found themselves at what had once been a roundabout junction. Replacing the original central green was a circular stand of trees. Another shimmer and the outline of a cloaked man appeared in front of it.

"This way," Jenny shouted, grabbing Long's hand and leading him eastwards onto Maids Causeway. Long looked back over his shoulder but the ghostly figure had disappeared from view. Stumbling across the overgrown roadway they continued on until their way was blocked again by a collapsed building.

"Look. Up there," Long said, pulling at Jenny's arm. She followed his pointing finger to see two translucent forms atop the rubble. Their bodies were hidden under full-length dark cloaks and their pale, bald heads reflected a light that didn't originate from the sun overhead. Their mouths worked but, this time, no sound could be heard.

Jenny and Long struck left, forcing their way through the line of trees and bushes on the northern side of the old road. With hearts pounding and legs painful they gasped in relief as they located their original pathway and followed the trail back towards the machine.

The ghostly cloaks appeared once more, shimmering several yards in front of the machine once Jenny and Long had turned the final corner. One ghost raised a hand as if commanding them to halt but, after a couple of seconds, both forms blinked out. Taking their chance, they ran for the assumed safety of the machine, crashing against it.

Long tried to open the door but found it locked. He banged on the door and Ellie, her eyes wide with fear, rushed to open it.

Inside, after the door had been re-secured, she clung to Long, crying.

"You saw them, too?" she whimpered.

Rick sat in the crude chair, his face pale and grey. "I've replaced the burnt out boards with the spares," he said, his voice barely more than a whisper. He sounded like he was struggling to remain conscious.

"I tried to make him rest," Ellie explained, "but he said you might not have time to do the boards yourself once you'd got back. Oh, I so wish we'd never come here."

Long untangled himself from Ellie's arms and passed her to Jenny who sat her down on the floor next to Rick. Long inspected what Rick had done and, as far as he could see, all of the boards looked properly in place.

"Long. The ghosts. They're outside again," Jenny shouted.

"Right. Hold tight. Home, here we come," Long said, dropping down into the main pilot's chair. He depressed the lever three times until the indicator registered 'four' and then engaged the power switch. The ear-bending hum started up as the scene outside distorted and swam. Rick clutched his head, mouth open as if screaming though no sound came from him. Ellie rolled up in a foetal position and Jenny gritted her teeth but kept staring out of the window as the view swam out of focus.

A loud popping sound erupted from underneath the desk and the machine lurched sideways. All four were thrown about as the entire machine was pushed upwards by several feet. It came crashing down and slid sideways before coming to a halt. The humming sound diminished and died, even though the power switch was still engaged. Swearing, Long hauled himself back into the chair and flicked the switch to its off position. Rick was screaming and clutching his left hand.

"Long," Jenny screamed, backing away from the door. "Hell! Get us out of here!"

Long heard hissing – air was being sucked out between the door and the frame. The door itself was vibrating as if it was about to be ripped off its hinges. He stared out the small window, horrified.

Instead of a view of the Cambridge of their own world, he saw a blackened, lifeless land that went on until the horizon met a dark sky. That sky was studded with untwinkling stars that were far brighter than they had any right to be.

19 Trees and Tempests

19.1: Yggdrasil

Hyde Park, London, Alternate One: 12 August 2165

Mila Galanis held her mother's hand as her father teleported them in from Colwyn Bay. She gasped as she saw it. Even though they were still half a mile away from its base, it dominated the sky. Towering above their heads, it dwarfed everything in a city already full of tall structures.

She stared up at it, transfixed. It was far taller than anything her seven-year-old mind had ever imagined, and definitely higher than anything man-made or natural she had ever seen back in Wales, apart from Snowdon itself.

One giant tree, fifty feet across at the base, provided the central support for the hundreds of others that wove in and out of its branches. From this distance the spiral that wound around the main trunk and circled to the crown resembled nothing less than an enormous tapered screw with its head buried in the ground.

Her father placed the suitcase on the grass. It contained a meagre collection of Mila's personal belongings. He stood there, mouth open, taking it all in. It was obvious to Mila that he could hardly believe what he was seeing, either.

"Yggdrasil," he said, his accent rolling over the syllables.

At first Mila had no idea what he was talking about. Then she let her mind wander and information started to pour in. It didn't concern her that she had no idea where it originated. All she knew was that she wanted to know about the giant growth that dominated this place that was also known as Hyde Park. Then, as had happened many times in the past, that information came to her like a dam opening.

That talent was only one of the reasons she was here today.

Her eyes tried to take in the physicality of it all as her mind pored over the data.

The Tree, unofficially acquiring the name from an old Norse legend, had been constructed by Jocasta Da Luz, an architect whose organically inspired work could still be found all around the world. She had retired to Cornwall in her seventies.

By the time of the disaster she had been well into her eighties. On the day the asteroid arrived, she had tuned into the song and had been one of the first to be mentally reassembled afterwards by those led by Morton Fisk.

Jocasta's natural affinity with nature, and especially her love of trees, had been enhanced by the splintering to enable her to directly tap into the plant life around her. Under her guidance the riot of expansion being exhibited by much of the world's flora was tamed, nurtured and accelerated further. She was able to coerce it into the most complex shapes at will. Within weeks her residence near Bolingey was dominated by towering intertwined constructions whose growth could be measured daily, if not by the hour.

Her fame spread and, months later, she had been invited along with many others by Fisk to attend a meeting in London. One theme of the gathering was to discuss how they could continue to run a world that was now devoid of many of the facilities that they had previously taken for granted. The global loss of computer systems, especially those that had controlled the supply of electricity, had been the most pressing problem. Simple but rare oil-driven generators still worked but anything more complex than that no longer functioned.

Although invited on the basis of her previous architectural status, Jocasta commented on the fact that the meeting was taking place in a hall within the old royal residence of Buckingham Palace. It was far from being an ideal location for a group of talented, enhanced people many of who could teleport around the world in a blink of an eye. The hall had to be lit by candles in spite of it still being daytime.

"You huddle in a remnant of the old material world while your talents cry out for a more organic, nature-based centre," she had said. "Something more fitting and in tune with this new world in which we find ourselves."

"We don't have the resources to build anything new," she was told.

"Yes, you do," she replied.

"Please explain," Fisk had asked.

"You have me," she said. "I will build you a new palace that will be large enough to house over a thousand. It will provide shelter in hundreds of rooms with no two completely alike. It will provide a store of fresh water captured from the rain that falls from the sky. And it will provide light without the need for candles in the daytime."

"You can build this," someone said, incredulously.

"Yes," she said.

"Where and how?"

"As to where, well, then, maybe here beside this old palace." Then she frowned and said, "No, the parkland here is too small for what I have in mind. Maybe Hyde Park will be more appropriate. As to the how. Well, wait and see."

Several people, especially those still unaware of her experiments in Cornwall, laughed and dismissed what she said as the ravings of a senile old woman. She tutted and left the meeting, muttering, "You will see."

For the next three years she took up residence near Marble Arch spending most days at the centre of the park itself. Early on she selected an already well established common lime whose three-foot wide trunk would become the central pillar of the project. Within days she had begun the acceleration of its growth.

By the following spring the tree's girth had spread until it was nearly twenty five feet wide. Leaving a gap of thirty feet into which the lime would later spread, Jocasta planted a circle of a hundred silver birch seedlings and compelled them to rise up at all angles, some as much as seventy degrees from the vertical. She twisted them into a solid weave that not only provided support for the main lime but became the basis for the spiral corridor that encircled it, providing access right to the top. Off that corridor, and supported by the many branches of the central lime, she willed the weave of birch and lime to form rooms – some small, others larger and no two of exactly the same dimensions. Grooved channels in specifically chosen branches guided rainfall from the top branches to storage tanks grown at regular intervals against the main trunk. Daylight was channelled similarly using birch wood polished to a mirror-like finish so that most rooms, no matter how deep they were within the foliage, would only require candlelight at night or on the dullest days.

In little more than three years the whole construction was complete. She presented it to Morton Fisk and those who were doing their best to tame and control this unruly world.

She was asked to provide similar structures in other centres around the world, but the toll on her had been great and, although she did construct smaller versions of the Tree later on, this one remained her crowning glory.

Yggdrasil, they had called it – or, more simply, the Tree.

And, Mila already knew, this was the place that she would call home from then onwards.

Her father picked up the suitcase and her mother tugged at her arm, and they began to walk slowly towards the base. Several entrances, some with actual doors, were set in the thick birch trunks that were packed together to encircle the base.

A man and woman wearing robes that covered them from shoulder to ankle appeared from one of the doorways and met them.

"Mr and Mrs Galanis?" the woman said. Her father acknowledged this and the woman continued, "And this will be Mila, then."

The woman squatted down so that her face was level with Mila's. Then Mila's breath caught in her throat as, without invitation or warning, the woman entered her head, invading all areas of her mind. A snarl erupted from her lips as she pushed back, shutting the woman out.

"Ah," the woman said, a smile spreading across her face, "you can shield already. Excellent. And I detected telepathy, telekinesis and several others. Possibly a lack of teleportation. No matter, that can often be picked up later with training."

"Um. We were told there would be some kind of entrance exam," said Mila's mother.

"Yes, there was," the woman replied. "That was it and Mila passed in under a second. Welcome to the Tree, Mila."

19.2: Decay
Invergloy, Scotland: 23 February 2169

Morton Fisk communicated silently with Alin Yan. Both men sat on the bank of Loch Lòchaidh. The wind was whipping the patches of snow that surrounded them into the air but, though only dressed in thin cloaks, they did not appear to notice the cold. Behind them, and further up the slope that, despite the winter weather, was already wild with new spring life, sat the decayed remains of a structure that barely held up against the elements. Thirteen years had reduced the cabin, once owned by Professor Rayburn and then Ross Nunn, to a ruin. Though the pine tree that grew through its centre looked more than thirty years old, it had been a seedling only six years previously.

"It's true, then," Morton Fisk said.

"Yes," his companion replied. "It's subtle, but the trend is proven. One of my teams in Beijing has been dedicated to the analysis for over five years now."

"Reintegration."

"Indeed, by all accounts. Reintegration. Recombination – whatever we choose to call it, it needs guiding. But we are, as you know, increasingly powerless to provide any such guidance."

The wind rose to a howl and a branch cracked from a tree. It fell into the waters of the loch and was swept out of sight within seconds.

"We are like that branch," Fisk observed, "increasingly more fragile and adrift in a current far stronger than we can handle."

Yan sighed and, using his voice this time, said, "Indeed. Ten years ago I could teleport from China to Scotland with ease. A year ago I could barely travel between Hong Kong and India in a single jump. Yesterday it took more than twenty jumps to get here and it exhausted me, even with those of your Tree guiding me."

"The abilities fade," Fisk agreed. "We will soon be down to pre-disaster levels. But if reintegration is inevitable we must find a way to achieve it without destruction. We need to work with the tempest, not let it dictate to us. We therefore need to know what's happening on the other worlds. But that is now a task beyond even the adepts in the Tree."

"Agreed," Yan said. "The worlds appear as locked off from us now as we are from the Moon."

Fisk nodded. "Before the disaster, we could move items out of this plane into others."

"But never ourselves," Yan added.

"Individually, I concur. The splintering proved that a group mind could achieve it."

Yan dipped his head in agreement as he stared out across the loch. "Though it also aptly demonstrated all that could go wrong."

They sat silently for a while before Fisk said, "Only in those few hours after the disaster when the worlds still exhibited some tenuous linkage could we traverse them individually. If that had not been possible we would not be here now."

"All of us who comprehend what you achieved back then remain thankful."

Fisk nodded again. It wasn't pride, more to do with pragmatism – if he hadn't managed that feat, there would be nobody around to be thankful.

An icy blast cut across the loch, slicing into the waves and hurling water into the air. A flock of Canada geese, bouncing on the surface, took such assaults in their stride. It had been interesting, Fisk thought, how the lower animals had recovered from the disaster without any human intervention. Creatures that had relied fully upon instinct had barely been affected.

Alin Yan, fingering the motif of three concentric red circles sewn into his cloak above his heart, broke the silence. "When the organisation first started they made much use of electronics to pinpoint the origins of the abilities. They then engineered devices to enhance them."

"Indeed they did. Although not widely documented, the evidence can still be found by those who know where to look," Morton replied. "But, while we still have far greater abilities than were ever available on the original world, we no longer have the luxury of the accompanying electronics."

Yan allowed the slightest smile to play across his lips. "Almost true."

Morton raised an eyebrow. "Explain?"

"I have many teams working on the various effects caused by the splintering. It is surmised that silicon no longer allows the transmission of electrons in exactly the same manner as before. Especially not at the miniaturisation levels that had become prevalent in the years before the disaster."

"That is well known," Morton said.

"Yes, but, as I am sure you are also aware, as reintegration nears, the effects are becoming less deviant. And there are some materials that, though they were once severely affected, are now verging on normality."

"Go on."

"Germanium is one. It appears, as far as we can determine, to have returned to the characteristics it always had."

"Germanium?"

"It was one of the materials used to fabricate the initial diodes and, later, transistors in the twentieth century."

"Does that mean we could use it to build something to access the alternates?"

Yan paused for a moment. "The ability to generate the required harmonic patterns for transference might, in theory, have been possible to achieve using once-conventional electronics. Several have thought to advise me that utilising germanium for the same task would be far trickier."

"But possible?"

Yan pursed his lips and, after a moment, nodded once.

"How long do we have?" Morton asked.

"The current indications would suggest that reintegration is likely at some point between 2176 and 2178."

Fisk thought for a moment. "So," he said, "we may have a mere seven years to build a system that might have been impossible to construct using working electronics, and we have the inconvenience of requiring to do it using barely working electronics."

"That is about the size of it."

Morton looked directly at his companion. There was a look on Alin Yan's face.

"When did you start building it?"

Yan laughed. "We have, in the past few months, devised an initial circuit that produces twelve of the harmonics required. They are hard to synchronise but we are improving the techniques required."

"Twelve? How many are needed?"

"A hundred, possibly more. It is also likely that transference will burn them out, especially to and from this world. We will need plenty of spares."

Morton thought for a moment, his eyes watching the turbulent waters of the loch while he did so. "Seven years, Alin. Will it be enough?"

"We have to try."

19.3: Powerless
Hampstead Heath, London: 5 April 2177

Morton Fisk sighed mentally and stepped onto the wooden platform. Five others watched from afar but only Alin Yan remained close by. Three of the five were the primary engineers who had assembled this monstrosity, the DTM or Dimension Travelling Machine. He nodded to Deshi and Liang, who stood there stony faced, as if they were afraid that wishing him luck would jinx the exercise. Deshi's wife, Xiu Mei, the driving force behind the technical aspects of the DTM and one of the most brilliant engineers he had ever encountered, smiled and bowed to him. The final two were Alec Garter, originally from Canada, and Charles Moore, a native of New Zealand. These two would effectively be running the entire planet along with Krista until he returned.

If I return, he thought silently.

Alin Yan said, "Even at this late stage I cannot persuade you otherwise?"

"No," Morton Fisk replied. "I dare not risk anyone else. It is well known that, of all of us, my own abilities, in the main, still exceed those of most others and, where they don't, they still cover a broader area."

"Are there still no adepts at the Tree up to the task?"

Fisk shook his head. "They are young. Far too young in many cases. Their life experience is limited. In many cases they were born after the disaster and have no real inkling of what exists on the alternate worlds or what will be required there. Only Mila Galanis, the brightest of them all, might possibly succeed but there could never be a guarantee. My own survival of the disaster suggests that, in a crisis, I can respond in a positive manner no matter what is thrown at me."

Yan acknowledged this with a tilt of his head.

"Regretfully," Fisk continued, "logic therefore indicates that it has to be me."

Fisk was indeed correct, Yan thought. There was no one else left who had both the pre-splintering experience and who could still command the abilities he exhibited. However, he was now far from being the young man who had reassembled himself alone, and then taken on the ruins of the original pyramid and used it to pull so many lost souls back together. Was he still up to such tasks?

"I didn't set out to be a hero," Fisk murmured, unconsciously echoing Yan's thoughts. "I don't want to be one, even now. There just isn't anyone else, is there?"

Yan placed a hand upon Fisk's arm.

"No, not to replace you. But, as you know, I and others have suggested companions. There are plenty willing to accompany you and the DTM could hold more."

"There is only one seat."

"Indeed," Yan said, his head tilting to one side. "Comfort was not the primary concern of the build."

It was a blustery April day and the trees of Hampstead Heath were being whipped in all directions. Grey clouds slipped over each other as if in a race towards some hidden goal in the north-west. As far as they could determine, this spot was one of the few detected where the level of the land in world Three was close to that of this world, being no more than two or three metres higher. It had taken a tiered pyramid of over ten thousand minds projected at the other worlds to the point that they could just about be probed as to their suitability to receive what they had constructed. All the alternates except for Three still exhibited roughly the same land formation. However, the surface of Three had been distorted greatly. In some places the land was hundreds of metres higher than any of the others.

It had been conjectured that the absence of the atmosphere and oceans had released the pressure leading to the uplift. What this meant for recombination was impossible to infer.

So, this spot had been decided upon, even though it had meant moving much of the already assembled electronics laboriously from Asia to England. The craft itself had been constructed locally over the past couple of months and moved into place three weeks previously.

"No," Fisk replied after a while. "I cannot risk the life of anyone else."

"We are all at risk when the worlds recombine," Yan said.

Morton nodded slowly. "But no again. We are wasting time."

Fisk rested his hand against the DTM.

"It should have a proper name," Yan said. Names were important to him. Calling it the Dimension Travelling Machine had been clumsy.

"Another waste of time," Fisk said.

They had less than a month to go before the earliest estimated date upon which recombination was likely to begin. He needed to traverse all the worlds, and that included Three, and absorb enough of their characteristics in order to provide the required guidance that would mesh all five back together again. He tried not to show his uncertainty, the fear that he would fall far short of that requirement. If only they'd had more time.

Mentally, Fisk ranged out and sought a connection to the centre of London. His mind roved around the rooms and living corridors of the Tree, and touched on all those residing there. In turn, they acknowledged that contact and strengthened the connection.

"We are ready to absorb all you learn, as you learn it," came the message from the collective minds, though one shone brighter as Mila transmitted a burst of encouragement.

"I will return, soon," he promised, hoping it wouldn't prove to be a lie.

Shrinking back to the confines of his physical body, he gazed for a final time on the six assembled before him. Alin Yan made an opened palm gesture with this right hand. Fisk returned the gesture and allowed his face to form a smile. Then he turned and pulled the door shut, enclosing himself within the machine. As he checked the door interlock, he was only vaguely aware of Yan retreating to a safe distance with the others.

Morton Fisk sat at the desk and confirmed that the lever was set to Two. His hand shook slightly as it caressed the controls. He tried but failed to dispel the fear.

At least, he told himself, he was safe in the knowledge that the craft could move safely between the worlds. Well, at least between One and Two. There had been two successful unpiloted tests, both using clockwork controlled devices to activate the switch and lever in a predetermined sequence. The second test had also included a rabbit in a cage. The DTM had returned as expected on both tests, the second time with its live cargo extremely startled but apparently no worse for wear. The same couldn't be said for the electronics – in both cases, the return from world Two had burnt out a couple of the transistors.

His hand rested against the on-off switch, exhibiting a jitter he couldn't fully control. He clamped his teeth together and then, with a grunt, he flicked it on.

The sound was incredible. He had been present at both of the tests but, here, inside the DTM, the effects were magnified many-fold. No wonder that rabbit had been frantic upon its return. The electronic oscillators beating against each other and driving their harmonic waveforms around the wiring caused the entire framework to scream – and that was picked up by the wood, the chair and, far worse, his head. He gritted his teeth, fearing they would shatter if the vibrations persisted for much longer. The circuits were tuning in to world Two. Then he felt the shift as the DTM was sucked from a world with which it was no longer compatible, to one with which it had become aligned. He slammed the switch to the off position and the screeching subsided.

He had done it. He had successfully moved between the worlds. Standing, his legs now shaking in accompaniment with his hands, he peered out of the porthole at Two. His breath came quickly as, for the first time in more than twenty years, he directly observed a world upon which the plant life was not perpetually crazy.

But that wasn't the only sensation. He tried to reach out all the way back to One with his mind, back to those in the Tree waiting for him. It was hoped that contact would still be possible between the worlds with powerful minds on both sides. But there was nothing.

Instead, he became desperately aware that his abilities had shrunk down to a mere fraction of their previous level. The abilities he had depended upon for decades, and now needed to help guide the recombination, were absent.

19.4: Missing

Hampstead Heath, London: 17 April 2177

"He should have been back long before now," Alec Garter hissed. The grim set to his face only partially betraying the turmoil within.

"We all understand that," said Krista Hartmann. "Could anything have gone wrong with the DTM, Alin?"

"There are countless things that could have gone wrong," Alin Yan said with a shrug. "Should I make a list?"

Garter sniffed his disapproval. The man was so damned annoying and far too complacent. Morton should never have put his trust in him. Outside, despite the earliness of the season, trees in full summer bloom swayed in the light breeze. One area, completely cleared of growth only weeks before, was already knee deep with the constant onslaught of jungle. Only twelve days had passed since it had held the DTM. The unease Garter had felt back then had increased every hour of every day that Fisk remained absent.

"Morton was all too aware of the possible risks, as were we all," Yan continued, deliberately catching Garter's eye for that last point. "Indeed, I did on several occasions attempt to dissuade him from being the pilot or to take another with him. So, which of the many possibilities of failure has overtaken him is, unfortunately, open to conjecture. Even those in the Tree say they cannot detect whether or not he and the DTM still exist."

"Their power is already far too diminished," Hartmann said.

"We should have made the trip years ago," Garter snapped.

"Impossible," Hartmann retorted, "as you well know. Not since the splintering have any of us been able to successfully probe the barriers between the worlds, let alone traverse them. And only in the past ten years have the electronics started to become a viable option to perform the traversal. The tests demonstrated that, even at this late stage, they are barely up to the task."

"It is possible, then, that Morton Fisk is alive and well, but a breakdown has trapped him in one of the alternates," Alin Yan speculated.

"Regretfully, given the state of the skills of your engineering team, there is far greater chance that he is dead," Garter spat. "We should have engineered a method of electronic communication between the worlds."

Yan smiled. "Without doubt," he said calmly, "my engineers achieved a precarious result. However, that result, as small as it was, far exceeded your own abilities in achieving anything remotely similar. And, regarding inter-world communication, it was, as I know you are fully aware, investigated most thoroughly. Unfortunately, in that area, we had as much success as your adepts."

Hartmann looked from Yan to Garter, expecting another outburst from the latter, but Garter merely grunted and kept his lips shut.

19.5: Guiding Light

Alternate One: 17 May 2177

"Six weeks," Alec Garter shouted.

"We are fully aware of that," Krista Hartmann snarled back. She was finding it increasingly harder to work with Garter. All of them knew how much time had passed since Morton Fisk's leaving.

Not that they hadn't been busy during that period. Krista Hartmann and Charles Moore had built a world-wide monitoring system. It consisted of more than ten thousand people who were subconsciously tuned into the state of the planet. With recombination nearing, tectonics were being strained and, already, there had been an upsurge in volcanic and seismic activities. Through a combination of the mental capabilities of sheer numbers of people, they had eased the underground pressures, reducing the impact, helping to oil the friction of landmasses so that they slid rather than jarred their ways into new positions. Mila Galanis and others within the Tree persisted in attempting to make contact with the DTM.

Now, the main players were physically meeting again, as they did at least once a week. This time it was in Paris at the Palacio del Luxemburgo. Alin Yan's eyes flicked between Hartmann and Garter. How long before they came to physical blows, he thought.

Charles Moore tried to inject some calm into the proceedings, but Garter pushed through it, snapping, "If I had been in charge... Ahhhh!"

They all felt it. A flash of brightness that, for a second, blanketed their minds before their natural defence barriers had a chance to come down, shielding them from damage.

"What on Earth was that?" Hartmann said, massaging her temples

Moore's mind raced out to the primary contact at the Tree in London. Mila Galanis answered immediately but his connection with her was far from clear; something was interfering with it. Mila herself appeared confused for a moment.

"As far as we can tell, the DTM has returned," she finally transmitted. "But it is not here in London. It is… wait…"

Moore connected directly into the effort Mila was organising, and added, "We are triangulating. It appears to be approximately fifty miles north of London – either in or somewhere close to Cambridge."

"What's causing the interference?" Garter demanded. "Damn near burnt me out, it was that intense."

"Yes, we are getting reports coming in of several adepts being rendered unconscious when it first appeared," Galanis reported. "They are slowly regaining their senses but the anomaly is still diminishing all of us."

"What has Morton brought back with him, I wonder?" Yan said. He, too, rubbed his temples. The interference was giving him one heck of a headache.

"We are not detecting Morton Fisk's mental signature," Mila Galanis said. "That, though, may be due to the interference – at this stage we cannot be certain."

"I think we need to investigate further," Moore suggested.

"Yes," Garter agreed. "You and I, Charles, should take a closer look." Garter was pleased to see the look on Yan's face at being excluded.

"Remote viewing, just in case it is an attack of some type?" Moore suggested.

"Agreed. Whatever is radiating may be hostile."

"It is like trying to wade through treacle," Alec Garter transmitted some minutes later. Their combined efforts of viewing the DTM were being thwarted by whatever was blanketing the area.

"I will get those in the Tree to provide some form of shielding. We may yet break through," Moore said.

"Make it so."

Slowly, over several minutes, they were able to make out the fuzzy shape of the DTM. It was resting on a road located in a housing estate that was buried under the usual jungle of spring growth.

"There are four life signs outside the DTM," Moore reported. He was riding a small pyramid of minds that were equally probing and shielding. "All are within the anomaly."

"The anomaly," Krista asked. "Any indication as to what it is? Something new?"

"At the moment we cannot separate it from the life signs detected," Moore replied, his mental voice quavering slightly, showing his exhaustion. "It may be one of them or it could be something separate. Something within the DTM itself. Maybe Fisk is the source. We need to get closer."

It took Charles Moore and the adepts at the Tree more than an hour to come up with a method by which they could improve their observations of the DTM. Moore guided Alec Garter to a position not far from the machine.

"There is a woman there," Garter said. "Can she see me? She has reacted as if she could."

"It may be so," Moore said. "We are projecting so much of ourselves there in order just to observe, that aspects of our physical bodies may be appearing."

"I am prevented from observing the inside of the DTM," Garter continued. "The anomaly may be located within."

"Mila tells me that two of the life signs have departed the area. We may have better success tracking them if they are away from the anomaly."

"Lead the way, Charles."

Garter followed Moore across the jungle. "Ah yes, things are definitely clearer away from the DTM, though it still prevents full access."

"Indeed. Look, the other two – they are entering that ruined tower."

"For what reason?"

"None that springs to mind," Moore said. "However, maybe we can communicate with them and establish who they are. If so, then we may find out what has happened to Fisk."

"That's if this damned interference allows us."

20 Empty Worlds

20.1: Alternate Three

Black Earth: 17 May 2177

Long's eyes darted around the control desk as he tried to understand what had gone wrong. The indicator registered 'four'. Why hadn't it worked? This had to be 'three' with all the radioactivity. He had to get them away from here quickly. But, if the machine wouldn't take them back home, then where?

'Five' was out of the question and no one wanted to return to 'one'.

"Hold on," he said to Jenny who was still staring out the window. Rick and Ellie lay bundled together on the floor where the rolling of the machine had deposited them.

He slammed the lever three times until the display registered 'two' and, heart in mouth, engaged the power switch again.

Nothing.

"Shit! Shit! Shit!" he screamed as he dropped to his knees. A small curl of smoke followed the front panel as he ripped it off. Pulling each board out one at a time he saw that the seventh from the top displayed a familiar blackened patch.

"The air's leaking out," Jenny gasped.

"I know," he shouted back. "I'm not bloody deaf!"

He chucked the damaged board onto the floor. In a corner, Rick was mewling in a most inhuman fashion while Ellie cradled his head. She picked up Rick's bleeding hand and looked directly into Long's eyes, "Get us home. Now!"

He shook his head, "I don't think I can."

He dragged open the large wooden drawer, rummaged around for a couple of seconds and pulled out what he hoped would be one of the remaining working spares. He slid it into the box and, not bothering to replace the panel, slammed the power switch on.

This time they were rewarded with the ear-splitting hum and the machine rocked, spilling the remaining broken boards onto the floor. Then everything tipped sideways. Long and Jenny were thrown together near the door as Ellie went flying. She screamed as her head connected with the corner of the chair. The machine dropped once more before coming to rest, upright again, with a solid thump.

Jenny gasped for air and, before Long could pick himself up off the floor, she tried to force the door open. Long reached for the power switch and the hum subsided to enable Jenny's battle with the interlock to succeed.

However, the air pressure outside now exceeded that inside and she had to wait, gasping with the others, until the two equalised before the door would budge. Finally, she managed to push the door open a fraction and the whistle of incoming air became a rush. Long's ears popped as the pressure returned to normal and welcome cool air enveloped them.

20.2: Alternate Two

Cambridge: 17 May 2177

"Be careful," Long shouted, but Jenny had already shoved the door wide open and stared out at a different kind of green.

Here, the wildness was far more tempered, resembling what their own world would have been like had it been left wholly in nature's hands. The sun, hanging low in the west, imbued this world with a golden hue that sparkled off the ruins of the houses.

Long joined Jenny as they viewed what lay beyond the machine's platform.

"We're in the same place," he stated, recognising the overgrown houses to be the same as those that had poked out of the jungle on 'one'. Here, they were merely covered in a coating of moss and ivy, showing the deterioration that twenty years of neglect had imparted. The machine rested on the roadway which, on this world, still showed through in places as crumbled chunks of tarmac, pushed up from below by tree roots. The ground was damp and the sparkling on the battered roofs nearby confirmed a recent rain shower.

Long looked at the flatness of the roadway and wondered why the machine had tumbled in its journey between the worlds. Going to 'three' had forced it to rise up while coming here had made it drop. Although he could imagine the problems that would have arisen had it emerged into something solid, he had no idea how it managed to avoid such circumstances. He assumed that in the 'three' equivalent of Hampstead Heath the land must have been several feet higher, which accounted for the way the machine had dropped through the lower sections of the trees in his own world.

"Look," Jenny pointed. "Over there. The tower – it's intact here."

Sure enough, in a gap between two of the crumbling houses, he could see its height dominating the horizon.

"What happened? Are we home?" Ellie asked, peering out the door while rubbing a temple that now sported a large bruise.

"Not exactly," Jenny replied.

"Something went wrong," Long said. "We went to 'three' but we were only there a couple of minutes. This is 'two'."

"Why didn't you go back to our world?" Rick whined, appearing beside Ellie. "Hell, I…"

"It wasn't Long's fault, Rick," Jenny cut into Rick's outburst, her voice overpowering his. "The machine refused to go back. He probably saved our lives by fixing the problem quickly. Any longer in that place and we'd have suffocated. We were leaking air."

Ellie helped Rick out of the door and sat him down on the base. He looked years older. "I thought you'd fixed the circuits so that we couldn't go to 'three'," he said.

"Thought I had. AI must have bloody well repaired it. Anyway, we're here now, and I think we'd better look around before going anywhere else. We've only got one spare board left. Once we're left with less than ten good ones, we won't be going anywhere."

Ellie examined Rick's hand properly. His previously fused fingers had been torn apart. He must have caught them when they tumbled into 'three'. She turned to Jenny and Long. "We need water and something to bandage it. I'd go but…"

"Sit down, Ellie," Long said. "You're looking rather pale yourself. We'll go and find something."

Long looked around and then down at his own tattered jacket. He pulled it off and went back inside the machine, remembering seeing a pair of scissors in the drawer. He rummaged around until he located them and then he cut a couple of strips from the jacket's lining.

Jenny called from nearby so, retaining the strips he had already cut, he handed the scissors and the rest of the jacket to Ellie.

"Chop it up, whatever you need," he said. "I'll see if Jenny's found a source of water."

He rushed off to find Jenny standing in what used to be a garden. Beside her was an ornamental display incorporating a shallow dish filled with water. Near her feet were an assortment of white objects.

"Probably the people who used to live here," she said. Long stared at the bones, identifying three skulls and five broken chunks of pelvis. Unlike the distorted versions he had seen in the hypermarket on 'five' these looked normal, although they were mixed up. He had no idea how many people lay at his feet. Many of the bones displayed marks – probably where something, rats possibly, had gnawed on them. He felt slightly queasy standing amongst the dead, although it was apparent that Jenny, who was tossing one of the skulls in her hands, felt nothing of the sort. She dropped it disrespectfully with a shrug that became a grimace when it shattered into pieces.

Long turned his attention to the water. The bottom of the shallow basin was begrimed with a brown deposit, but the water lying above it seemed clear. He was thirsty but could not bring himself to put it to his lips. He soaked one of the makeshift bandages in the water.

"I'll check inside the houses – see if the pipes and taps still work," Jenny said.

Long returned to the others.

"Was it clean?" Ellie asked.

Long explained where it had come from. Ellie sighed and applied the dripping cloth to Rick's hand, who winced in pain.

Long looked at him. "How's your head now?"

Rick stared around at the scenery. "It's so confusing. The houses – three sets of them overlaid on each other and mixed in with the other buildings from our world."

"Even 'three'?" Long asked.

"No. Maybe yes. It's dark. A shadow over everything."

"Underground?" Long suggested, remembering his suspicions that the surface level on 'three' had been raised.

"Yeah," Rick closed his eyes. "At least it doesn't feel quite as bad as it did on 'one'."

"Maybe this place will be better, then," Ellie murmured.

"Only if we can find something to eat," Jenny said, as she returned.

"Any luck in the houses?" Long asked.

"No, the taps were either empty or wouldn't turn."

"I think we'll have to wait until tomorrow," Long said pointing to the setting sun, now low enough to graze the roofs of the nearby houses.

"It can't be that late?" Jenny frowned.

Long thought for a moment. "I suspect it is here. These worlds all seem to be out of sync with each other."

20.3: Hunger

Cambridge: 18 May 2177

They spent the night huddled together in the machine. Rick and Ellie bundling together while Jenny and Long started off separately but ended up cuddling just to keep warm. Thirst and hunger constantly nagged, whilst sleep was interrupted by Rick's occasional cries of pain.

They were awake by the time the sun's light first touched the window.

Ellie checked Rick's hand. The torn flesh showed no signs of healing and the fingers were angled wrong. His face was also grey and his eyes had difficulty focussing on anything.

Long glanced from Ellie to Rick and back again. The bruise on her temple was an ugly purple but after he asked, she snapped that she felt fit enough.

"Sorry," he said. "If I'd known this would happen, I wouldn't have brought you or Rick."

Ellie said nothing but the expression on her face pained him.

"Oh, come on," Jenny said. "The way those robots were acting, we didn't have any choice. This was the only way of escape. Don't blame yourself, Long."

Maybe I shouldn't, Long thought. But Ellie does.

"Anyway, we really need to find something to eat," Jenny said.

"Yes, okay," Long agreed. "I'll investigate the houses to see if I can use anything to rig up a trap. There must be rabbits or something similar around here. There's bound to be cooking pots in the kitchens, too."

"I'll search for a proper source of clean water and take a trip up the tower again," Jenny said.

"Why?"

"Might be able to see wildlife we can hunt down, maybe even some evidence of people around who can help us."

"You shouldn't go alone," Long said. "There's no telling what's out there."

"Hmm, maybe you're right," Jenny said, a thoughtful expression crossing her face, and then a grin burst across her lips, "but try and stop me."

Without waiting for an answer she ran off. Long shook his head.

"She's mad," Rick said, momentarily sounding like his old self. "I like her."

Ellie stabbed him a spiteful glare.

"Right," Long said, walking away. "I'm off to investigate the houses."

"Don't go too far," Ellie called, following him.

Long mumbled and carried on walking, aware that Ellie was still behind him. He stopped when he felt her hand on his arm.

"Sorry," Ellie said. "I've been so worried about him. I know you're not really to blame. It's just…"

"Yes, I know. I'm worried about the both of you – all of us."

She suddenly hugged him and he encircled her in his arms, but she broke contact quickly.

"You smell," she said, flashing a brief smile before turning to go back to Rick.

Long watched her until she was lost from view and then sighed. He'd once entertained the idea of himself and Ellie becoming a permanent couple. But, it was now obvious that Ellie's affection was centred wholly on Rick.

Cursing AI once more for forcing him into exile, he turned his attention to the houses and started hunting.

After half an hour Long had assembled a small collection of the more serviceable cooking utensils he'd found in the houses. Various garages and sheds then provided a collection of items suitable for fashioning into animal snares and traps. He also explored a few gardens, noting the telltale signs of animal tracks.

"Found these," Ellie said later, returning with three bottles in her arms as Long put the finishing touches to a second trap. "Fourth house along. There're several more."

Long looked at them. Two sported faded labels that indicated a French origin, the third's label was missing. All three were sealed with artificial corks.

"Might be alcoholic," he said. Ellie frowned. He explained how the Cambridge NewGen had found some wine and that its consumption had resulted in the death of a girl called Rachel. He returned with Ellie to the house to pick up a few more.

"We need a corkscrew," Long said.

"A what?"

"Curly metal prong thing to get the corks out. I saw one being used in Cambridge a few days back, though I only had a sip of it. Didn't like it. Right now, though, I could drink anything."

Ellie rummaged through a kitchen drawer that had been sealed enough to keep its contents fairly clean.

"Like this?" she said, holding up a T-shaped device with a plastic handle.

"Yes!"

On the way back to the machine Long stooped and pulled up some plants.

"Beetroot or carrots, possibly," he explained holding up a dark, knotty root.

"Ugh. Hardly edible," Ellie said.

"Last year's wild crop, probably," he said. "Might be still good enough for the traps, though."

20.4: Rabbit Stew And Wine

Cambridge: 18 May 2177

Northwards, in the more open land behind a final line of ruined homes, was an area of grassland with older trees dotted around the extremes. Long thought he might be seeing evidence that a river flowed in the distance. To the west the tower windows glinted orange and yellow in the slowly rising sun. Maybe Jenny was up there right now looking in his direction. He tried to imagine what could be seen from its top windows.

The sound of wildlife moving in the undergrowth was everywhere. He sought out a regularly used track and positioned a trap where it narrowed to re-enter a back garden, baiting it with the sliced up beetroot.

Arriving back he found Ellie opening the bottles with the corkscrew. Rick sat on the machine's base with a cup in his good hand. "That one was revolting," he said pointing at a broken bottle a few yards away, its contents still dribbling out. "But this one isn't."

"You sure you should be drinking that?" Long asked.

Rick pulled the cup to his chest, "Don't care. You're all talking colours anyway. Maybe this'll take 'em away. I'm hungry."

Ellie poured out some clear liquid into a cup and gave it to Long. He sniffed it cautiously before putting it to his lips. The taste was slightly bitter, though far from unpleasant and nothing like the one he'd tried back in their home world a few days ago. Maybe it was because none of them had eaten or drunk anything for a day that made this one taste better. He took a larger mouthful and swallowed. Ellie poured some more into Long's cup.

"Whoa," Long said, "not too much – remember what I said about that girl who died."

"Didn't you say she fell out a window?" Ellie asked.

"Yes."

"Well, okay, we'd better not go near any windows, then."

A few minutes later Jenny returned, frowning. She was given a cup of the drink, which removed a little of her sour expression.

"So?" Long asked.

"Yes, it's wine all right. Similar to what we found before. That stuff you tried the other day was gin. Quite different."

"No, I meant the tower – see anything?"

"Oh, right. Well, this version is far more intact but that was obvious as soon as we arrived. I can see the main city centre, the colleges and out past where the Wall is in our world. Not far away to the west I spotted a herd of deer, about twenty, in an open space between some trees. But most of the land is overgrown, untouched – no sign of people at all."

"Damn. Maybe there will be some in London."

"Dunno. It wouldn't be as bad to travel here as in the jungle world but London's still a long way away."

"No people on 'five'," Rick reminded them.

"Yes," Long agreed, "but that was because no one could survive there."

"At least I didn't see any ghosts here," Jenny added. "But any sign of people would have been good."

"Maybe we should go back tonight and look for lights or fires," Long suggested.

"Good idea," Jenny agreed.

"Yerp," Ellie said, pouring herself more wine. "Damn, this is good. Almost makes me forget I'm so hungry."

"Woo, my head's disa-, um, disagreeing with that wine stuff," Ellie slurred, about an hour later. "Putting my tongue to sleep."

Jenny laughed, "It takes a while to get used to it."

"Rick had the most," Long said, laughing as well, though he wasn't sure why. Rick was lying on the machine's base, apparently asleep. Long had drunk a couple of small cups of the stuff – far less than either Rick or Ellie had done.

"Leave him," Jenny said. "I expect he needs his sleep. The wine's probably numbing the pain in his hand, too."

She bent over Rick and stroked his hair, but Ellie pushed her aside, saying, "Hey, that's my job."

Jenny retreated, a lop-sided grin on her face, leaving Ellie with Rick.

"Did you see a river over in that direction?" Long asked.

Jenny nodded. "Yes. I'll take a few of these empty bottles and fill them."

Long agreed. "I'll come part of the way with you and find a place for the next trap."

"You think they'll be okay?" she whispered, indicating the other two with a nod of her head.

Long shrugged, "They're not going anywhere."

Gathering the trap and a few tools they headed off into the undergrowth once again.

"Are they a couple or was that just the wine talking?" Jenny asked, once they were completely out of earshot of the others.

"I think Ellie has decided it is – not sure about Rick."

"He is sort of cute."

Long looked at her quizzically and she chuckled. He had to admit to himself that he had the same thoughts about Jenny as well. He hadn't been with the Cambridge NewGen long enough to have figured out what pairings there were. He suspected they were still as flexible as the London NewGen had been a couple of years back.

Still, he had often thought about Ellie in the months he'd been exiled from the city. Of all the girls she had been the one he'd felt most attracted to. Now, with Ellie's attention centred on Rick, maybe he and Jenny might… well.

They reached the point where he'd placed the first trap. It was empty so they moved on. He pointed out signs where animals had passed recently, and what those animals might have been.

"How did you learn all this?"

"Just by living for months outside the Wall, trying to keep alive. Wasn't exactly easy. Don't tell Rick or Ellie, but I nearly died of the cold in the winter." He grimaced at the memory. "Never felt anything like it before. When it snowed in London we always got AI to heat the houses."

"Bad, huh?"

He nodded. "Yes, even with all the insulation I'd packed over my shack. Ah, look. That little pathway is in regular use. I'll pop the next trap there and pile some grass over it to hide its outline."

She watched him set the trap. Once he'd finished he said, "Right, I'll get back and see if I can make a couple more."

"Okay, I'll be off hunting water."

He watched her until she was lost from sight.

Yes, he thought. Very cute.

On the way back he made another search of the houses and found some sealed water filter cartridges. He'd not encountered anything of the sort before but barely legible instructions on the packages indicated they should be placed in some sort of container. A further hunt located a plastic jug with a recess into which the cartridges fitted.

He also turned up a sealed pouch of coffee and a fire lighting device. This consisted of a handle with a short prong that ended in two sharp points that faced each other. A small lever that, when quickly depressed, caused a spark to jump between the points had identified its use. So, he sought out some wood and dry tinder materials, paper and thin curtaining, to see if he could make a fire. If they managed to catch a rabbit then they'd need a way of cooking it.

By the time Jenny returned it was nearing noon, going by the sun's position. Long had built up a good fire and both Ellie and Rick watched it intently, though Rick had problems focussing on the flames.

"It doesn't look too bad," Jenny said, holding up the slightly cloudy spoils of her quest. "The river is flowing sluggishly – it's a bit weed-choked. I did take a sip but it's rather ghastly – definitely not a patch on the wine!"

"Try these." Long showed her the filters and jug.

She read the instructions and nodded her approval. "Nice find."

By mid-afternoon four more traps were awaiting victims, and sharp knives had been added to the collection of utensils. A second fire was started in anticipation of something to cook on it.

A couple of hours later Long checked the traps and returned brandishing a dead rabbit in one hand. He immediately proceeded to skin and gut it, a process that Jenny found fascinating, though Ellie couldn't bear to watch.

While chunks of it were being spit-roasted over one of the fires, other parts were put into a pot and simmered for a later stew. While Jenny took a turn minding the cooking, Long and Ellie had another trip around the back gardens. Long recognised a few potato plants and a number of the tubers were found to be free of burrowing insect contamination.

Despite her squeamishness at the earlier butchery Ellie was more than eager to eat the cooked flesh once it was ready. More wine was opened, coffee was brewed and the rabbit stew devoured.

"Well," Long said, while picking meat from his teeth, "I think we could probably make a go of living here."

Jenny nodded, but added, "Only if we can find more people."

"Couldn't we go back to our world and bring some of the others here?" Ellie suggested.

"Only if we can fix the machine properly so it doesn't pop more boards," Long said.

"Don't trust it," Rick said.

Nor do I, Long thought.

Once darkness had fallen, Jenny and Long prepared for a trip back to the tower. They no longer had any light sources of their own – in their haste to escape from AI's robot ambush, items such as binoculars or torches had been left behind. A half moon and lack of clouds gave them enough light to follow the old roadways. Jenny, having already made the trip once, was convinced that repeating it in the dark wouldn't be any more hazardous than in daylight.

Apart from a couple of small scares when some bats flew close overhead, getting to the tower took barely twenty minutes. In the dark, they felt their way up the stairs until they reached the observation room. Long could see now how the room should have been, the ruins of the version on 'one' were replaced by an elegance that was obvious even in the pale moonlight. They made their way over to the window and gazed out into blackness.

And stared with sinking hearts.

Apart from the Moon and stars, no lights lit up the landscape. Up here they could truly believe they were the only people on this world. They peered eastwards and had to strain hard to catch the occasional twinkle that pinpointed their own fires. Rick and Ellie had been instructed to keep them burning strongly but the trees and derelict houses hid them far too well.

"There's a view to the north from another room," Jenny said.

But the tale was the same. A barely visible panorama of trees and overgrown meadows, littered here and there by the sparkle of ruins where they caught the moonlight, was punctuated nowhere by any telltale signs of civilisation.

This world, or at least this small part of it, held no humans other than themselves.

20.5: You Have Mail

Cambridge: 19 May 2177

The following morning the traps were found to be empty, so breakfast consisted of black coffee accompanied by the cold remains of yesterday's stew.

Ellie's suggestion of constructing a beacon to attract attention in case people really did live here, wasn't received with much enthusiasm.

"We'd need something far larger than the four of us could possibly build," Long said.

After breakfast Long threw himself into constructing two more traps. He positioned them much farther away having decided that the proximity of the machine to the first traps had deterred potential victims.

Jenny explored more houses but turned up little more that was of any use. She headed out after Long to see if he was faring any better.

The day, which had started misty and subdued, turned bright and warm by mid-morning and Rick initially spent it resting in the sun. However, by noon it had become too warm for him and he had settled down on a blanket inside the machine.

Ellie effectively found herself alone. After cleaning up and disposing of the remains of the meals she joined Rick inside the machine to find him asleep again. She sipped some fresh coffee and idly examined the damaged circuit boards wishing she knew how to fix them. Although she had gleaned the basics of electronics from AI's teaching, it had not been a subject that had interested her.

She sighed. The bravado she had displayed when they had jumped the Wall had all but dissipated. She dearly wanted to return home, even with AI still in control of it. Turning a soot-stained circuit board over in her hands, she knew that, without these crude pieces of electronics, that journey could land them back on 'three'. She feared becoming trapped there. Despite the heat she shivered and contemplated what she would do if they became trapped on this world instead. Were there really no people left here? Where had they all gone?

She heard a noise outside and saw Jenny returning.

"No luck?" Ellie asked, seeing Jenny's empty hands.

"Nah, but there's a herd of deer not far to the north on the other side of the river. Long thinks he can make a bow and arrow, or a spear, or something like that." Jenny's slightly mocking tone of voice betrayed her thoughts about the possible success of that venture. She continued, "I came back to get some bottles for another trip to the river as we're almost out."

"Is it far?"

"About ten minutes in that direction," she said, waving her arm northwards.

"Maybe I could help you, if that's okay? I need to stretch my legs."

Jenny nodded. "How's Rick? Is it okay to leave him?"

"Probably."

"Actually, I've had enough exercise this morning – must have walked several miles. Could really do with a rest," Jenny said, sitting on the base of the machine.

"Okay, I'll get the water while you rest. If Rick wakes up then check his hand – there's enough water left for bathing it at least once more."

Jenny agreed and helped Ellie round up the empty bottles before giving her better directions to the river. She then looked in on Rick whose eyes flickered open and fixed on hers.

"Sorry," she said, "didn't mean to wake you."

"Uh, hi," he said, groggily. "Anything happening?"

"No, not really. Long's hunting deer and Ellie's gone to get water. I'm just resting up for a while. How are you feeling?"

"Still woozy. Hand's throbbing and I'm still seeing – well, weird things."

"Heard you tossing around a bit last night. Did you sleep?"

"Not very well. Not exactly comfortable packed in here, is it?"

"I know."

"There's nowhere else, though, is there?"

She shrugged. "The houses are far too damp. There's always the tower. Mainly offices and labs but we could convert it, I suppose. Didn't seem damp when I went there, not the upper floors anyway."

"You, um, seem to be quite, er, athletic," Rick stumbled.

Jenny flashed him one of her wide grins, "Hah. I could always out run everyone else. Some of them used to call me a monkey when we were little because I was always climbing up things."

He laughed and sat up, cradling his hand.

"Still hurt bad?"

"Yeah," he said. There was silence for a while before he added, "You probably think I'm just a moaning whinger."

"No, Long explained about how you were affected by that other world. He said your fingers had joined up."

Rick nodded. "And now they've torn where the join was. Maybe that's for the best. Wish I could say the same for my head, though. That seems more permanent."

"I thought it was better here."

"The headaches are but I still see strange colours and all the other stuff." He explained about the synaesthesia.

"What was it like, that other world?"

Rick sighed. "Full of weird plants and strange animals. Buildings that had melted and skeletons with bent bones. Some with extra bones. Probably lucky to get away alive."

"This world seems far better. If only it had people in it."

"I'd seen that other world before."

"Eh? How?"

"As a child. In dreams. Nightmares really."

"The exact same place?"

Rick shrugged. It had been so long ago. He'd only been about six years old. "AI put me on something to make me sleep better."

"Hmm, more drugs."

"More?"

"Any of you ever have babies?"

"No," Rick said. "Ellie mentioned that a few times."

"A couple of our group figured out how to do blood tests. No one's really sure but they thought AI was drugging us to stop us making babies. No idea wh–"

"What's that?" Rick interrupted, staring past her. "Just over the battery rack. Is there something there or is it my eyes?"

Jenny stood up. She could see something, too. Attached to the wall was a sheet of card, almost identical in colour to the wall itself. She picked at a corner and peeled it away to reveal a paper envelope hidden behind. Unsteadily, Rick got to his feet and took the envelope from Jenny's hand. He had recognised the two designations printed on the outside, one above the other: LD-m0014 and LD-m0018.

"AI," he said, opening up the envelope and unfolding the sheet of paper it contained.

"Oh hell," Rick whispered, after reading it. "I think Long had better see this as soon as possible," he added, handing the sheet to Jenny.

21 Frying Pan or Fire?

21.1: Lost

Hyde Park, London: 17 May 2177

"Gone?" Alec Garter growled. "Where?"

"I think we scared them away," Charles Moore replied.

"At least the interference has ceased. It's good to be able to think clearly again," Alin Yan said.

Garter snarled at him, "If we don't find out what Fisk learned, we'll be wiped out at recombination."

"Well, I'm sure, given a few decades, the Earth will be suitable again for recolonisation by those still on the Moon," Yan said, calmly. "I, for one, would be happy with such a result."

"Alin," Krista said, "you value your own survival so lowly?"

Yan smiled. "I have suspected for a while that we have little control over whether or not we survive. We barely survived the splintering and that was something we ourselves caused."

"We caused this as well," Garter snapped.

"Yes," Yan agreed, "it is the natural conclusion to our earlier mistake."

Krista watched Garter stalk away, muttering.

"Are your provocations deliberate?" she asked.

Alin Yan grinned. "Our pompous second-in-command often needs the wind removed from his sails. I take pride in my ability to aid in that extraction."

"You know that if Morton fails to return, Garter will be automatically promoted to first?" Charles Moore stated.

Yan nodded and grinned. "Well, hardly the first time a promotion to top dog has been savaged by the rest of the pack."

21.2: Hobson's Choice

Cambridge: 18 May 2177

"That definitely puts a whole different slant on things," Long said, putting the paper back down on the desk.

Ellie picked it up and read it for herself. In it AI calmly documented not only its own failings but also the differences it had detected between what it had once assumed to be the natural physical laws and those it now experienced. The discrepancies were minuscule, almost within the margins of error but there was no doubt that it believed those figures. Then it laid out the idea that the observed changes to the discrepancies indicated that the five worlds were going to recombine. It listed the possibilities that such an event could cause – none of them good. She sat down on the floor and re-read the sheet that coldly spelt out the planet's doom. It made her feel sick.

"Does that mean we've got to go back there? To 'one'?" she asked, unable to stop her hands from shaking.

"Yes," Long said.

"I – I don't think I can stand it again," Rick whispered.

"If AI is right then we haven't got much time," Jenny said. "If we stay here we're dead anyway, and if we go back to our own world then we're probably dead as well. What a choice!"

"Damn it!" Long fumed. "Why did AI have to trick us? Why couldn't it just explain?"

Ellie looked from Long to Rick and back. Long's face, the beard hanging from his chin quivering, simmered with more anger than she had ever seen. Rick, his back to her as he stared outside, was hunched as if in pain. She had no answers for either of them.

"Would you have gone if it had just explained?" Jenny said, sounding more in control of herself than any of the others.

"No, probably not," Long sighed. "That bloody machine knows us better than we know ourselves."

"Maybe not," Rick countered, turning and facing the others. There was sweat on his brow and his eyes looked sunken and old. "It didn't know we'd not stay on 'one'. It didn't expect us to try to come back. It probably thinks we're there now."

"This is all too much," Ellie whispered. "How can it think we can make a difference? What can the four of us do? We're in the wrong place on the wrong world."

Rick came and sat next to Ellie, putting his arm around her shoulder. She leaned her head on his arm. "We'll find a way, Ellie love."

No one said anything for a while. Then Long, his rage subsiding, took the paper from Ellie's hand and re-read it.

"It almost sounds desperate," he said. "It knew it was degenerating and thinks it found out why. I get the impression it doesn't expect to survive whatever's coming. Maybe it did the best thing it could think of by sending us as messengers."

"But there was no one, no people there!" Ellie said. "Apart from those ghosts."

"Yes," Long said, and then snapped his fingers. "Ellie, what you said just now about being on the wrong world in the wrong place. Well, on 'one' we were on the right world but, due to AI moving the machine to Cambridge, I think we must have been in the wrong place. We should have been on Hampstead Heath instead."

"So, you think we should go back to 'one'," Rick whispered. "And try to find the people and warn them."

"I don't think we really have any other choice," Long said.

"I–" Rick started, and then buried his face in his hands.

"What?" Ellie asked.

"I– I think if I go back there, it– it will kill me."

21.3: Noises Off

Cambridge: 18/19 May 2177

They couldn't leave straight away. The circuit boards needed testing. Long attempted to patch circuit boards together with limited success, using nothing more than a nail heated in a camp fire for soldering. As the machine had already dumped them at the wrong destination once, he knew he had to reduce the chances of a repeat occurrence.

Rick, despite his problems, was doing his best to visually check the repairs. Jenny watched Ellie's eyes following Rick's every move. She was obviously scared for him. Maybe she believed him when he said that returning to 'one' would kill him.

Jenny said, "C'mon Ellie. We're just spare thumbs here. Let's go check the traps."

Ellie frowned and then nodded. They left the camp and returned to the animal traps where they found an unfortunate rabbit ensnared. Jenny inexpertly despatched the creature and then skinned it. Ellie, unable to watch, opted to hunt down more potatoes.

With the afternoon growing to a close they feasted again on spit-roasted rabbit and black coffee, though Ellie only picked at her food.

"I keep feeling sick," she said. "Don't know why."

Later on, Long tested the boards by powering up the machine with the lever left set to 'two'. Several of the repairs proved to be failures but, by the end of the testing, they had four spares – less than Long would have liked. He doubted the full set of boards would survive more than a final jump back to 'one'. He hoped there wouldn't be a need to test a further trip.

The setting sun dictated that they would spend one more night here on 'two'.

None of them felt hungry the next morning, Ellie least of all. The others picked at the leftover rabbit and sipped more black coffee.

Ellie looked at Rick and they exchanged a look. He nodded.

"Okay, let's just get it over with," she said. Long and Jenny agreed, and they all boarded the machine.

Jenny looked out the window and wondered if she would ever see the real Cambridge again.

"Saying goodbye," she murmured as she sat to brace herself for another bumpy ride.

Long set the lever to 'one' and engaged the power switch. Rick, hands clasped tightly around his head, whimpered as the coils energised themselves and the screeching permeated the entire machine. Ellie gasped and curled up on the floor. Long clamped his mouth shut to prevent his teeth from vibrating.

Jenny gripped the inside door handle and pulled herself back up for another look. "It's changing," she shouted over the noise. Through the window, she saw the overgrown gardens fading from view. "Ooh, it's darker."

Rick looked up, mouth open, scared.

"No, not three again," Jenny said. But she saw his eyes scanning wildly around as if he was unable to focus on anything. He slumped into Ellie's arms. "It's okay," Jenny said. "It's definitely 'one' though it's just before dawn here."

After flicking a quick look over his shoulder to confirm Jenny's conclusion, Long switched the power off. Around his feet, a waft of smoke indicated more electronic failures.

As the noise subsided it was replaced by a night-time cacophony of insects audible even through the closed door.

"Hell," Long gasped, covering his ears to cut out the chirruping that filled the jungle, "they weren't making that row before, were they?"

"That was daytime," Jenny said kneeling down beside Ellie and Rick. The latter clasped his hands tightly around his ears. Whether that was to keep out the sounds of the insects or because his head pounded again from the journey, she didn't know. He merely grunted when Ellie asked him how he felt.

"This world is behind the last one," Long said. "It should be morning soon."

"Any sign of the ghosts?" Jenny asked as Long peered out the window. He shook his head.

While they waited for sunrise, Long inspected the circuit boards again in the dim glow of the electric bulb. Three were definitely write-offs and two more had minor damage, which meant that he would need to fix one more board to make up the full complement of ten. He cursed. It wasn't as if access to each alternate world required two circuit boards, as their unplanned trip to 'three' had proven; all ten boards worked together to generate the harmonies required to facilitate slipping the machine between worlds. He looked at Rick hoping he could help, but he was slumped on the floor, his back against the wall, his breathing shallow and irregular.

Long felt guilt rise up like bile and he wished he'd left Rick behind on 'four'.

After half an hour, with the air inside the machine becoming quite stuffy, the first hints of dawn appeared in the eastern sky. Before it grew much brighter, Long switched off the light in order not to drain the batteries further. He had no idea how well they were holding their charge.

With the dawn came a reduction in the noise levels outside and Jenny cracked the door open to allow the air to circulate. Long stepped outside in the cool morning air noticing the mist rising from the foliage that promised later warmth.

The machine, he noted, had positioned itself a few feet away from where it had previously landed. He put that down to the rise and drop they had experienced when moving to and from 'three'.

He sipped from a bottle filled with filtered river water from 'two'. He idly wondered if they were breaking any sort of 'universal' laws by transferring water between the worlds. But, given that the machine itself had already broken such laws, he dismissed the thought.

He looked around to see if anything close by appeared edible. While this version of Earth appeared far more plentiful as regards plant life, he couldn't see anything that suggested itself as food. Despite the cramped conditions inside the machine, he wished he'd brought along a couple of traps. At least he'd packed a few of the tools they'd discovered on 'two' so making a new trap wouldn't be quite so difficult.

Jenny joined him outside and suggested a hunt through the remains of the houses for this world's equivalent of the goods they had discovered on 'two'. She pointed out the caved-in shell of the place from which he had retrieved the water filters. Long nodded in agreement and they set off.

In the remains of a back garden shed they found a stack of plastic chairs, still intact despite the tangle of honeysuckle that had wrapped itself around them. Some of the chairs had been twisted out of shape. They extricated the good ones and returned to the others.

Jenny tried to encourage Rick to go outside and sit on one. He grunted incoherently so she and Ellie guided him to it, his feet stumbling all the way. As they sat him down it was obvious he was having difficulty seeing anything at all. Ellie lifted his face and looked into his eyes, they were bloodshot and darted about unable to settle on anything. She looked at Jenny and shook her head, her eyes filled with apprehension.

Whatever on this world was affecting him was way beyond any help they could possibly provide.

21.4: Found

Alternate One: 19 May 2177

The screaming beacon hit them again. However, this time the barriers came down far quicker and, according to Mila Galanis, no one at the Tree was affected adversely.

"I am in Bordeaux," Charles Moore said. "I may be able to teleport to London in short hops."

"Wait there, Charles," Garter ordered, before directing a question to Galanis. "Can you get us there physically this time?"

"It is not going to be easy," Mila stated. "We are expending so much energy shielding ourselves from the anomaly that there is little left."

Krista Hartmann entered the conversation from afar. "We are feeling it here in Berlin, too," she said. "However, it is not as intense. Let us take as much of the strain of shielding from your shoulders as we can, and leave you to project Alec and Charles to Cambridge."

"Thank you, Krista," Moore said. "It is interesting to know the limits of the anomaly. Mila, link with Krista and contact all the closer centres in mainland Europe, also Ireland. To do this we may need a full concert, in sync."

"Shall we also attempt to shield the anomaly?" Mila asked.

"Only once we are close enough to extract it," Moore responded. "It may have defences that we do not, as yet, understand."

"Concert attained," Krista transmitted a few minutes later. "Mila and I will head the attempt to teleport you both to Cambridge."

"Not too close to the anomaly," Garter said. "I'd like to get a proper look at it with my real eyes first."

"Agreed," Moore said. "No closer than one hundred yards."

"Any other requirements?" Mila asked.

"Yes," Moore said, "be prepared to help us physically transport those on the DTM back here to the Tree at a moment's notice."

"All of them?" Krista asked. "The energy required might be more than we can provide given the anomaly's interference."

"We will determine that once we are there," Garter said, impatiently.

Both Mila and Krista acknowledged agreement.

"Begin the full concert," Garter commanded.

21.5: Abduction

Cambridge: 19 May 2177

With Long and Jenny absent, Ellie sat in the shade inside the machine, gazing out at Rick slumped in the chair. Possibly, he was sleeping, or he might even be unconscious. She felt helpless, no longer able to tell the difference. Maybe Rick really was dying. No, she didn't want to think about that.

She wiped away a tear. She picked up AI's sheet of paper. Could there still be answers here that no one had yet found? Something that could help Rick?

Both sides were filled with tiny text that was barely readable in the early light. Half of one side was full of equations and mathematics. She'd read it three times, but could understand less than a tenth of it. The remainder, addressed directly to Long and Rick, explained in short, clipped sentences the reasoning behind the mathematics. That section, at least, she understood.

It told of AI's realisation that, somehow, nature itself had been subtly altered at a time that coincided with the disaster. After Long and Rick's excursion to 'five', AI had concluded that the Earth had become divided into several initially identical, overlapping worlds numbering possibly, but not necessarily, five. However, as each was isolated from the others, AI surmised that each one existed in its own unique state or 'dimension'. Inhabiting such alternate dimensions, though very close to reality, explained how the forces of nature may have been minutely distorted from the norm. AI noted that, directly after the disaster, its systems had increased in efficiency and it had subsequently used that enhanced power to improve the lot of the almost mindless humans consigned to its care. It surmised that each isolated world exhibited unique changes, which explained the differences Long and Rick had encountered on 'five'.

However, AI's efficiencies had not been permanent and several years ago it had noticed the process had begun to reverse, resulting in the problems with which most of the NewGen had become familiar. At this point in the notes Ellie noticed there was actually something approaching an apology, which surprised her. The surly machine, once a benevolent benefactor, had 'regretted' that the changes had isolated it from those it had single-handedly brought up from birth.

It was only when AI had deduced the origin of the machine from both the machine itself and its interrogations of Long and Rick, had it seen fit to goad them into performing this quest. Reading that, Ellie snorted. She still thought it would have been far better had it told them about its theories instead of tricking them into coming here. But, at the back of her mind, she knew she probably wouldn't have believed it.

Find the machine builders, it commanded. Find out how they survived the disaster. Find out how the Earth became divided. Find out if they can either stop it from re-integrating or know how to survive the event. AI had concluded that the once identical alternates, now vastly different, would not mesh together again without 'problems' – a vague term for what, at its worst, might be complete mutual destruction. It admitted that it had no solutions that could either defer the event nor allow safe passage through its conclusion.

So, it had sent them here.

Find the machine builders – but, Ellie shivered, all we found here on 'one' was ghosts. Yet the original occupant of the machine had come from here, or so they assumed. And he had been far older than they, so AI's question about surviving the disaster's stupefying effects might have been valid. Somehow these people, wherever they were, had done just that – they had not turned into the types of Ghosts that were all too numerous on her own world.

A noise from outside made her look up. Had Rick woken up? She stepped through the machine door to be confronted by a stranger standing over him. She froze, recognising the bald head. Now the man looked far more substantial, even if not fully solid.

He stopped examining Rick's sleeping form and straightened up to face her. He smiled, though she felt as if he was leering at her as the slash of a dark branch behind him could still be seen through his partially transparent face. His lips moved.

"Where is Morton Fisk?" came a tinny, strangely distant voice that seemed to neither come from his mouth nor fully synchronise with his lips.

Ellie, gasping, rushed back inside the machine and slammed the door, fastening the lock. Feeling marginally safer, she watched the ghost through the window. He regarded her for a moment and then, without appearing to walk, advanced towards the machine, passing through the solid wooden base and then through the door to face Ellie.

"Please. Where is Morton Fisk?" he repeated.

"Keep away from me," Ellie screamed.

"It is important. We need answers," the ghost said. "You have no need to fear me."

"Get away," Ellie shouted, uselessly trying to strike at him with fists that passed straight through his body without effect.

"Sorry," he said with a sigh, "but we'll have to do this the hard way."

Darkness overcame her, as his transparent arms enfolded her.

Rick heard his name being called and felt hands shaking him. He woke up in a visual sea of violent reds and yellows that increased the continual stabbing pains inside his skull.

"Where's Ellie?" Long shouted.

"What?" Rick gasped. "In machine."

"Not any more," Jenny said.

"The machine was locked from the inside," Long shouted. "I broke in but she's not there. Did you have AI's notes?"

"No – inside – I thought – oh."

"He's passed out again," Jenny whispered.

Long grimaced and stomped back to the machine. Where had Ellie gone? And where was the message from AI? He knew he shouldn't be blaming Rick in his state but – hell. He had to find the machine builders, and find out what they knew. He searched the machine once again for any clues as to what could have taken place but found nothing.

"Long!" He jumped at the sound of Jenny's shout from outside and sprung back to the door where he almost collided with her on the machine's platform. She was staring back at Rick who was completely unaware of the ghostly figure that stooped over him.

"Leave him alone," Long shouted, running towards them.

The ghost ignored them. Then, a second ghost appeared behind Rick and both turned to face Long and Jenny.

"This one is open, and we fear for him," said the newcomer in his detached voice. "Others will be sent for you."

Then the ghosts, along with Rick, faded from view, leaving Long and Jenny staring at an empty chair.

21.6: Unnatural Powers

Cambridge: 19 May 2177

"Something's coming!" Jenny shouted as she peered out the window. The broken lock meant they felt far from safe.

It had been several hours since Rick's abduction and the sun had already passed its zenith, sliding down into a balmy afternoon.

Long could hear voices and a noise as if something large was crunching through the trees. A few seconds later a figure burst from the undergrowth and strode up to the machine. Unlike the ghosts this man appeared solid.

"Hello," he said, peering in at them.

Long slowly opened the door and looked at the man, whose hand was extended in welcome. Long nervously shook it. The man wore a rough tunic, patched here and there as if it had been persuaded to last for far more years than originally intended. It reminded Long of the material worn by the original machine's driver.

"Been sent to find you," the man said, grinning through his grizzled beard. His blue eyes, which sparkled from out of an old, lined face, bored into each of theirs. He pointed over his shoulder to where the noise got louder. "The wagon's on its way."

"We saw… men in cloaks," Jenny said. "They took two of us."

"Yes, what's happened to Rick and Ellie?" Long demanded.

"Oh, that was probably Alec Garter and his cronies."

"Cronies? What do you mean?" Long asked.

"Eh? Oh, sort of like a close friend, I reckon. Er, has the language degenerated that much on your world?" Long and Jenny looked blankly at each other. "Mind you," the man continued, "until you lot turned up we thought we were the only place still inhabited. Just goes to show, doesn't it?"

"Show what?" asked Jenny. The man raised his bushy eyebrows and then chuckled to himself.

"You didn't answer about where they've taken Ellie and Rick," Long asked again.

The man shrugged, "To Yggdrasil probably. Big tree in the middle of London. What them high-ups do is not for the likes of us to know. We just try to keep this damn place tamed, grow enough food and do as we're told."

"London?" Long queried. "Are they safe? Are they prisoners?"

"Hah, as safe as any of us are likely to be with what's coming. No, they won't be prisoners. From what I hear, your arrival, or your mate's arrival anyway, was like a nuclear bomb going off."

"A nuclear bomb? What?"

"Heck, should've brought a dictionary with me."

"No, we've heard of bombs and nuclear power. But why do you say that?"

"He radiates. Everyone for hundreds of miles around felt him. He gave me a right thumper." The man pointed at his head.

"Thumper?"

"Headache. That's why they snatched him."

"Why'd they take Ellie as well?" Jenny asked.

The man shrugged. "All I know is that you two don't warrant the expenditure, so you get to go the pretty way back to London. And the DTM."

"The what?"

"This thing, DTM – Dimension Travelling Machine. They thought they'd seen the last of that after Fisk didn't come back."

"Oh," Long said, "Didn't realise it had a proper name. Um, Fisk, was he the man driving the machine?"

"Apparently," the man said. "Big nob, he were. Still, shouldn't complain, him and his mates reassembled me and the missus after the disaster."

"We tried to save Fisk. We really did. But he– he died. I'm so sorry."

The man shrugged, "Ah. Figured as much. Pity."

"Er, I'm Long and this is Jenny."

"Oh yes, sorry. Bad manners. My name is Ray. Ray Hargreaves in full."

"Why do you have two names?" Jenny asked.

"Two? Actually, I've got a middle name as well – Jonathan. Haven't you got surnames then?"

They stared back, blankly, before Long asked, "What's a sir-name?"

Ray was spared the need to answer by the arrival of the wagon. A hole appeared in a stand of foliage and gave birth to a wagon which was being hauled by two large animals.

"Oh, wow. Horses. Real horses," Jenny gasped.

"What's the matter?" Ray asked. "Don't they have 'em where you come from?"

Long and Jenny both shook their heads.

"How are you going to get it onto the wagon?" Long asked as Ray and his two companions negotiated the vehicle in front of the machine.

"You'll see," Ray grinned. "Mind – won't be as easy as a few years ago, but you'll see."

Long estimated that the other two men were nearer his own age. They looked very similar to each other, like younger versions of the older man. Both were thick-set in build, as if they'd spent all their lives in manual work. Long felt positively skinny beside them.

Ray introduced them as Boris and Hector Hargreaves, his sons – they grunted an acknowledgement but seemed reluctant to converse. Hector kept rubbing his head as if he was having problems thinking.

Long puzzled for a moment over the shared last name until his memory dredged up an old AI lesson from when they'd been young. It had been around the time when they had chosen their own names and AI's tale had been about the way families had previously used a common second name. He recalled that it had been one way of tying families together, of identifying relationships.

He wondered what having a family would have been like.

While the men busied themselves with the wagon, Long glanced along the path from where it had come. The low, flat wagon must surely have struggled to negotiate a path through the undergrowth. He could see that the route cut its way cleanly through the tangle. But none of the men wielded machetes or anything else resembling a tool to perform such a duty. How had they cleared so much away without any apparent mechanical help?

And with such speed?

The three arranged themselves around the machine.

"Can we help?" Jenny asked.

Ray grinned, "I doubt it. Not from where you're from."

"Yes, but how are you going to get it onto your wag– bloody hell!"

Without any physical contact from the three newcomers, the machine slowly raised itself up and drifted sideways to come to rest upon the wagon.

"How did–"

"You'll be told later – that's what they said I was to say," Ray grinned, though he now looked quite exhausted. He mopped his brow with a dirty handkerchief before crushing it back into a shirt pocket. The other two's brows were also beaded with sweat though they made no effort to remove it. All three sat for a moment, catching their breath.

Then Ray beckoned Jenny and Long up onto the plank that served as a front seat. His two sons remained with the machine on the back.

"Hungry?" Ray asked, pulling out a woven basket from underneath the plank. Inside, there was an assortment of breads, salad and fruit.

"Starving," Jenny said as Long's mouth opened in anticipation. They hadn't eaten since leaving 'two' and their water, now lukewarm and stale, was almost finished.

"Help yourselves," Hargreaves said, passing an apple each to his sons and chewing on one himself.

Once their snack was over, Hargreaves urged the horses to take up the strain and the wagon was slowly dragged back towards the hole in the trees.

"It's going to take days to get to London, isn't it?" Jenny said.

"At this speed it would," Ray said. "Once we're past the worst of the jungle, though… well, you'll see."

It took several minutes for the trees to be negotiated. Then they reached what had once been a wide road and the wagon began to pick up far more speed than it had any right to possess. Long gasped as, with the horses galloping hooves hardly touching the ground, the vehicle shot along at more than ten times the speed the clanky old tube trains had managed in the London he had once called home.

21.7: Inclement Weather

LSA Control Centre, the Moon: 20 May 2177

"They are reaching equilibrium at three point one two seconds," Andrew stated, his fingers whizzing through the figures that floated in front of him.

Across the room Janet analysed the readings coming in from the new satellites. Built over the past two years and packed with instruments, all twenty four had been launched at the beginning of the month. Now they sat, high above the destructive shield, in orbit around the Earth, monitoring anything they could. The LSA:EA support crew, numbering more than a dozen – the largest team Janet had ever commanded – sifted the data and tried to make sense of it. The computer systems were doing the real analysis, but they had been built with routines that attempted to spot, isolate and flag up any anomalies for the crew to take a closer look.

Janet took a quick glance around the room and smiled to herself. It was good to be properly back at the cutting edge.

Other centres had also been linked in so that the data load could be spread across as many systems as possible. The hope was that anything resembling a dangerous trend could be picked up at the earliest moment. Not that they knew what options they would have should such an event arise.

In control of the large screen that filled the wall, Melissa zoomed in on the planet as successive waves shot across its surface. The screen, its AI systems geared to recognising specific features of each of the five variations, changed the text in the bottom left at a rate of once every three seconds or so. The text cycled through Black, Robot, Green, Chaos, Paradise, Black, Robot, Green, Chaos, Paradise and so on without deviation.

"Something's happening on Black," Melissa announced just before Tariq Ghannam said almost the same thing.

"Filter out the others," Andrew said and Melissa adjusted the screen so that it omitted to display the other four.

"There is a haze appearing," said Tariq.

He was right. The normally jagged outlines that Black exhibited were becoming softened as if a fog was enveloping the planet.

"Is that happening on all the worlds?" Janet queried. Melissa switched the filter to Green and then to Robot.

"No, there are no similar detectable changes – same as before."

"Confirmed." That was Anusha, another of the support crew.

"Wait," Tariq interrupted, less than a minute later. "That's not quite true. Readings from the surfaces of the other four have increased."

"How much?" Andrew demanded.

"Um, less than half a percent at the moment. I will add a monitor and ping percentage increases directly to the main screen."

A few seconds later the figure was added to the bottom right of the screen. It said 0.39975 but every few seconds the last digit would flicker and increase.

"That's the shield diminishing," Janet confirmed, checking her own copy of the readouts.

Melissa returned the screen to Black and superimposed an outline map of the continents upon it. The main view was of central Asia with the Himalayas at the bottom. Selecting a recognisable peak she drove the magnification up close to maximum. The feed was coming directly from three of the synchronised satellites instead of a Moon-based telescope. With a resolution of around ten metres per pixel, the combined satellite images rendered the mountain into a single 3D image that Melissa felt she could reach out and touch.

The angle of the sun meant that one side of the peak was bathed in light, the other in shadow. She picked a point halfway around where the suggestion of jagged rocks and mist appeared to be more pronounced. Then she hit maximum zoom and gasped.

So did the others.

They had found out what the mist represented.

After more than twenty-one years, rain had returned to Black Earth.

22 The Multi-Dimensional Man

22.1: London
Alternate One: 19/20 May 2177

The blur began to resolve itself into individual trees and jungle-ruined buildings as the horses slowed. The ground below their feet still slipped behind them at a rate well in excess of normality. At least, looking at it was no longer so painful on the eyes.

"Where are we?" Long asked, not for the first time. The open countryside had gone. On either side of them they passed buildings that, years ago, had been homes, shops and work places. All were now almost completely hidden under a blanket of vegetation that assaulted walls, windows and roofs with equal determination. Only the road along which they sped was mostly clear of plant life.

"Coming into Hertford," Ray Hargreaves replied. "Not really my neck of the woods. My farm is back in Duxford," he pointed randomly backwards over his shoulder, "and I'll be glad to get back there to make sure things are okay when the sky falls."

"Sky falls?" Jenny asked.

"Well, whatever. They've not told us exactly what will happen when everything joins back together."

"I think that means they've already figured out what AI suspected," Long said to Jenny.

Hargreaves continued, "I just want to be back home when it does, to look after the family and the animals. They reckon we're going to lose most of the abilities when it happens – so, I certainly don't want to have to walk back. Still, at least it will put a stop to the way the jungle grows. That'll make the farming a bit easier, especially if we can get the tractors working properly again."

"So, why are we stopping here?" Jenny asked.

"Well, I don't know about you two, but I'm hungry," Hargreaves said, rubbing his already ample stomach. "Also, it makes me travel sick to keep up that pace for more than a few hours. Anyway, it'll be dark soon enough so we might as well make camp here as anywhere else."

"Which bit of London was this?" Long asked, the following morning as the countryside was fully left behind.

"Enfield, I think. We're going to bear westwards soon and hop over to Hampstead

Heath to drop that DTM thing off."

"Really? That's where I first found it."

"Well, you'll feel right at home then," Hargreaves chuckled.

The wagon, still going quite fast, swung onto a new road. "North Circular," Ray explained, which didn't mean a thing to Long. He presumed it was one of those that had been outside their Wall.

After a short while they left the main road to enter an overgrown area, the horses and wagon slowed considerably to tunnel their way through virgin jungle. Long watched as Ray and his two sons stared ahead of the wagon intensely. Somehow, their combined concentration was willing the undergrowth to get out of the way.

He wished he understood how it was done.

22.2: Sound And Vision

London: 19 May 2177

Rick opened his eyes to a vista of swirling blue and the sound of water. Not the harsh pulsations of noise-generated synaesthesia, this was more like being in a swimming pool on a hot summer's day. The pains in his head were, while not completely absent, at least reduced to a mere annoyance. The constant pressure of the past few days had been replaced by a calmness.

And that was almost a worry in itself.

The last things he remembered were the flashes of consciousness and pain as they had returned, against his instincts, to 'one'. Yet, he felt he was still on 'one'. He could identify the distinct shadows of the other worlds overlaid upon what he could see of this one.

What he did see of this world was that he was in a large bed centred in a circular room that had the ambiance of an underwater bedroom. However, the wavering blue colours around him weren't water. They seemed to be projected onto walls that appeared to be made of wood, or maybe the colours were part of the walls themselves. They were synchronised with the sounds that reached his ears which, he realised, didn't translate into extra visual colours.

Then he wondered if this was merely a dream. But it felt more real than that.

Slowly, he raised himself from the bed and sat up. A couple of tiny transparent yellow sparks floated across his vision as he grunted with the effort. He felt weak, but without the exhaustion that had previously plagued him. He looked around and found himself alone. Somehow he had already known he would be.

"Hello?" he whispered. There was no reaction to the sound of his voice either from his own vision or externally. The blue pulsations still washed around the room along with the sound of waves.

In the overlay shadows of the other worlds he felt as if he was flying. If he concentrated he could pick each one and view it exclusively. On 'five' he found himself high above some trees. In the distance buildings that were at once both familiar and weird looking, sat at a boundary. That's Phil's place, he thought. But this version was distorted, the windows melted, as if they were sliding down towards the road. He switched to 'four' and saw AI's version of Hyde Park spread below him and, as expected, the buildings there were still intact. He had a mind to explore, to see if he could find Phil, the twins or any of the NewGen. But the other worlds tugged at him. 'Two' was very similar to 'five' though the buildings didn't exhibit any distortions other than those inflicted by natural wear and tear, and from the incursion of uninhibited plant life.

Here on 'one' he couldn't see beyond the room.

In the calmness it was still strange to view 'three'. He hung only a few feet above the blackened ground – so close he felt he could reach out and touch it. It didn't seem as clear as when they had really been there. But then, he had been cowering in one corner of the machine's cabin, eyes shut. But even that hadn't been enough to prevent that world from encroaching upon all his senses. The others, he knew, had merely seen the starkness out the window. He had felt it coursing through his entire being, unable to escape its horror.

From the safety of the calm room on 'one' the blackened world no longer induced the same loathing. Then he noticed that the stars lacked the sharpness of before, as if the world still held atmosphere. He looked closer at the ground, and found there was something between it and himself. Then he saw it, the occasional streak of something falling from the sky.

"Water," he whispered. "It's raining."

He stretched out with a hand and the rain fell straight through it. He frowned. Rain implied that 'three' now possessed an atmosphere. Where had it come from?

He left 'three' and returned his consciousness back to the calm of 'one'. His hand, still raised in front of him caught his attention. He looked closer, at the torn skin and the scars that still marked it. Then he looked far closer than he would have thought possible. It was as if he was diving right down into the flesh of his own hand. What was more, it felt so natural, as if he had always been able to do such things. He gazed in wonder at the intricate arrangements of the bones, sinews, muscles, blood vessels and skin. The damaged parts held his attention. The tissue initially burned by the black rocks and later distorted by the visit to 'five' had been the catalyst that had caused the fingers to fuse together. Beneath the now torn skin, he saw where the bones twisted and exhibited tiny bulges in places. He noted the tendons attached askew and how many of the muscles were laced with scar tissue.

Despite all this, he could still see what they should be like, and felt that a push here, a stretch there and a joining over all of it, might make things right. So, not even beginning to understand what he was doing, he pushed, stretched and merged the affected areas.

And his hand became whole again.

His attention returned to normal and he stood up in awe of what he had accomplished. He flexed the fingers, he made a fist and unrolled it again and again. There was no longer any pain. Everything was working as it should have done.

"How did that happen? How did I do that? I'm dreaming, aren't I?"

As the words left his mouth, a stream of pink erupted across his vision and curled around his head. He tried to follow it, to capture it, to feel the essence of it. As he did so he turned and found himself facing his own visage. The shock made him snap back.

"What the hell?" he whispered. A little more pink accompanied his voice.

He swallowed and followed it again, and found himself staring into his own eyes for a second time. They looked empty and unfocused. He raised a hand to touch the face before him and could see right through the hand. The shock sent him back again.

He'd once come across an article about out of the body experiences. Was that what he was doing?

"Out," he shouted and, for a third time, followed the pulse of pink to circle back to view himself.

"Pink," he shouted. This time the visual pink echo was far smaller. Maybe he needed to be inside his own head for the synaesthesia to generate the full effect. Repeating what he done with his hand earlier, he looked inside himself, this time entering his own cranium.

And there, he saw the areas that had been distorted by 'five', where connections within his brain were linking together parts that had previously been separate. But there were also other places that had been distorted in another way. Somehow he could trace that they were latching onto something that this world enhanced. How he was interpreting what he could visualise was beyond his current comprehension. He explored the changes and then returned to those that had resulted from the short time on 'five'. Again, he could see what was wrong and how things could be fixed.

"If I'm really not dreaming, this could be very dangerous," he thought.

But he couldn't resist and made the changes.

When he clicked back into normality his head felt far clearer than it had for the best part of a month.

He shouted, "Pink," yet again.

Nothing. No pink, whatsoever.

"Hah!"

For the first time in a long while he felt a surge of intense happiness. This was nothing short of amazing.

Then he thought, just what else can I do?

There was a noise behind him and a door slid open.

A girl in a white robe took a step forward into the room and smiled. Sensing no malice in her manner – how could he do that? – he smiled back. She tipped her head slightly to one side, her dark, straight hair, barely reaching below the level of her chin, briefly brushed her shoulder before she levelled her head once again.

"I've been observing you, watching what you've been doing," she said.

"How were you observing me? I was alone," he said.

"No, you are far from alone. You're a natural," she replied. A look of puzzlement crossed her face. "More than that, in fact. You appear to tap into energies that the rest of us struggle to access any more."

"Who are you?"

"Mila," she said. "One of those observing you and the pressure on you. There are more than fifty of us in rooms above, below and on all sides of you. As I said, you are not alone."

"Why?"

Mila did something and the walls surrounding them were no longer opaque to him. That they were still solid was without a doubt but, now, he had the ability to move his perception beyond them, as he could do on the other four worlds.

Doing so, he experienced for the first time the entirety of the Tree. He also felt the presence of those surrounding him and caught a glimpse of what they were holding back for his benefit. Far below him was a familiar presence, though he had never experienced her in this manner before.

"Ellie," he said.

"Yes. Your woman is here."

He frowned at the thought of Ellie being 'his woman'.

"You didn't answer my question," he said. "What are you doing and why do I need to be surrounded by you all?"

"Because without us doing what we are doing, you will die," Mila said, and then paused, a slight frown passing across her face. She continued, "Though, I think that may no longer be the case."

"And why would you want to save me?"

This time her expression bordered on fear.

"Because without you," she said, "it is possible we will all die."

22.3: Changes

The Tree, London: 20 May 2177

Ellie screamed at Mila, "Let me see him, now! I don't give a dango about anything you say. Let me out of here – he needs me!"

Mila, unused to such anger, even from Alec Garter, finally relented. "All right, Miss Ellie. But I must warn you. He is still in a delicate state and we are shielding him."

"Now," Ellie demanded, raising her fists.

Mila looked at Ellie's hands hovering a few inches from her nose. She could hit the woman with a mental blast that would knock her out for hours. However, given the importance of the one called Rick, both he and his companions were to be treated as respected guests.

So, Mila nodded agreement and Ellie was finally allowed to leave the room in which she had been held since arriving.

At first the woman had been compliant and glad to have been offered food and, in turn, provide answers to all the questions asked of her. But, Mila knew, she had become slowly more desperate and angry at being prevented from joining Rick. Mila had instructed that Ellie be told that he was located in one of the rooms above but, given his initially unstable condition, they had deliberately revealed nothing else about him.

Ellie was led along a winding passageway that circled continuously clockwise and upwards. The structure looked as if it had been grown instead of built, the wood of the corridor walls still living and, in places, near the small unglazed windows, sprouting leaves from small twigs. It gave the impression of being both new but at the same time, felt old and unearthly.

"What the hell is this place?"

"The Tree. Our hub and headquarters. Also, a centre to reach out from as well as to be alone with yourself."

"That tells me absolutely nothing," Ellie snapped.

She peered into the rooms they passed. Simply furnished, each of them was occupied by a solitary figure sitting cross-legged upon the floor."

"What are they doing? Sleeping?"

"Meditating. Shielding."

"What do you mean? You said something about shielding before?"

"The worlds are pressing together."

"Yes, I know all that. What's it got to do with Rick?"

"The pressure of this world on one from outside is tremendous."

"I'm from outside, aren't I? Why don't I feel it? Why only Rick?"

Mila stopped and faced her. "You do not have the talent." Then Mila turned and continued upwards.

Ellie grunted, feeling as if she had just been insulted, though not exactly sure of it. She stared at the back of Mila's head. How dare this woman, who was probably a couple of years younger than herself, treat her like this? Does she think I'm a kid or something?

They approached a door. Outside it two others sat cross-legged. One, who could have been either male or female, Ellie couldn't make out which, remained motionless. The other, definitely female, opened her eyes.

"It is allowed?" the girl asked.

"Maybe," Mila said and then turned to Ellie. "He may not be as you remember."

"What the hell is that supposed to mean?"

The door was opened and Ellie was left to enter on her own.

Rick lay on the centrally located bed. Ellie rushed up to him, "Rick, oh Rick."

His eyes opened and locked onto hers. She recoiled in shock. It was as if something had stabbed her through the temples.

"Sorry," he said. "I don't know why or even how I did that. You woke me, although somehow, I already knew you were coming."

"What have they done to you?" Ellie whispered, her anger replaced by fear. She tried to halt the tears that flowed.

"They haven't done anything to me."

"But…"

"I think I've always been like this."

"No! This isn't you. It can't be you."

"You remember when I was a child, how I used to have nightmares about being lost in the dark and those dreams about the distorted world? Sometimes I would see the creatures in it that used to be human. Then AI put something in my food to stop the dreams."

"Yes, I remember. Anyway, what's that got to do with all this? And what you just did to me?"

"Ellie, it's amazing. I can see beyond myself. Back on our world it was rare, it happened but I always thought it was a trick of the light or something like that. But this world makes it easy and completely real. I can see all the worlds. I can even see into myself. Look at my hand, Ellie."

He held up his left hand. Ellie frowned. "Oh Rick. How?"

"I fixed it."

"What?"

"I looked into it and could see what was wrong. Then it came to me that I not only saw what was wrong, I could also see how I could make it right. So I did."

"How?"

With a lop-sided grin, Rick shrugged. "I don't really know. I can't describe it. There aren't any words to say what I did. Somehow I can just look into things. Into my own head, even. I've stopped the synaesthesia as well."

Ellie, mouth open, shook her head. This was madness.

"I can step outside myself as well and see all over this strange tree, at the people in it, and inside them. I can see into all of them as easily as I can see into myself. I can see into you, too. Oh."

He stared at Ellie's torso and she felt naked.

"Don't do that, Rick. Please. You're really scaring me."

"I hadn't realised."

"Realised? Realised what?"

He stared harder and Ellie took a step back. Then he smiled.

"I think it's going to be a girl," he said.

"Huh?"

"The baby."

She stared down at herself, hands upon her stomach. Her eyes finally raised and sought his.

"No. How?" she whispered.

"We both made it."

"But… we don't make babies."

"We do now."

"Really?"

He nodded in answer.

"How… how long has it been there?" she asked.

He frowned and stared into her again. It was like he was dissecting her – she was unable to suppress a shiver in the warm air. What had happened to the Rick she remembered? The version before her was no longer the man she knew.

"Five weeks."

"What?"

"Must have been in Long's shack."

22.4: The Tree

Hampstead Heath: 20 May 2177

"I recognise that dip in the ground," Long whispered to Jenny.

"What's special about it?"

"It's near where the machine first appeared on our world. It was also in the same place on 'five'. I bet they're putting it back where it first started from."

The DTM was being unloaded from the wagon using the same method they'd employed to place it there.

"That is just so amazing," Jenny whispered, watching as the machine was levitated several yards to rest on a piece of ground that was less overgrown than everything else surrounding it.

Ray Hargreaves and his sons returned to the wagon.

"Well," he said, "I don't think that thing will be going anywhere else for a while."

"Why not?" said Jenny.

"In a few days there won't be anywhere else to go. Everything will be back together or maybe nothing will be back together ever again."

Long said, "Does no one really have any idea of what's going to happen, then?"

"Even the big-brains at the Tree don't seem to, though they might be lying, of course."

Jenny looked out across the heath. "Plenty of trees here. Is there a special one or something?"

"You'll see," Hargreaves grinned. "Okay, hop back on. I'm leaving the boys here to keep the weight down and speed us up even more. See you later, guys."

Boris and Hector waved to their father as he steered the wagon south once more.

"Okay," he said. "Next stop Hyde Park."

"Somewhere else familiar," Long said.

"Don't bet on it," Hargreaves replied, with a chuckle as the scenery blurred around them.

As they slowed to approach central London, Long gaped at the state of the buildings they passed. He recognised many of them having walked their version of these streets so often. The way nature had uprooted mankind's architecture was both marvellous and horrifying to behold.

But then, beside him, Jenny gasped, "Oh my goodness. Is that it? Is that the Tree?"

The wild entanglement that Hyde Park had become in their own world was a pale imitation of what confronted them. It was enough that the excessive growth here would have swamped their version of the park. But even that was rendered into insignificance when compared to the structure that spiralled above it. It was something out of a fantasy. That it had once started off as a tree, or possibly many trees, was without any doubt. However, this monstrosity would beat anything their world could produce by an extremely wide, and tall, margin. They both stared up at the twisting arrangement of branches that sought to defy gravity itself.

"They reckon it's more than a thousand feet high now," Ray Hargreaves said, almost too casually. "I seen it several times. Bigger every time."

"What's it for?" Jenny said.

"For? Hmm. Some mad old woman grew it. Now the main mental mob use it as one of their headquarters."

"Are Rick and Ellie there?" Long asked.

Hargreaves shrugged. "Could be. I was told to deliver you two to the base. After that, as I said before, I'm heading home before everything goes to pot."

There was a sudden rumble and Jenny tumbled into Long. They grabbed at each other. Hargreaves slowed the cart down to walking pace but the movement continued.

Long watched the trees sway unnaturally. Only it wasn't just the trees. Even the buildings around them were shuddering. Behind them, one crashed to the ground. Hargreaves ushered the horses on using arm movements that seemed to calm the beasts, though Long had no idea how it worked. It wasn't completely successful but he did manage to steer them away from the higher roofed buildings that were beginning to rain tiles down onto the road.

"Damn," Hargreaves shouted over the noise. "It's already started."

22.5: Rough Riders

The Tree: 20 May 2177

Ellie sat on the bed beside Rick. She held her hands over her belly, unable to believe what he had told her.

The door opened and Mila stepped in. Ellie's eyes narrowed as Mila walked towards them.

"You must leave now. He needs to preserve his strength," Mila said, stopping half way between the door and the bed.

Ellie looked at Rick and back at Mila. She stood and faced the girl. "Just what do you mean 'preserve his strength'? What does he need this 'strength' for? Why the hell don't you ever give me any straight answers?"

Mila looked perplexed. "Recombination. It…"

"Stop," Rick shouted. "Both of you. Down on the floor now."

They both turned to look at him.

"Do it, now!" he screamed.

Mila dropped to the floor as Rick threw himself flat on the bed and wrapped his arms around his head. Ellie, scared and not knowing what to expect, lowered herself until she was crouched next to Mila.

Then it hit.

The whole room shook and noise reverberated all around them. Ellie found herself tumbling towards the door. Mila's arm snaked out and Ellie found her ankle gripped in the girl's hand. She twisted around and grabbed at Mila. They clasped at each other trying to prevent further movement.

Rick started groaning.

"The shield around him is failing," Mila gasped, clenching her eyes tight shut. "All. Hold. We must not break formation. Do not let it get to him. Do not let him get to us!"

Ellie realised Mila wasn't addressing herself.

Then a violent tremor detached Mila's grasp and Ellie rolled across the floor. She grabbed at the doorway and clung on tightly. There was no longer any sign of the other two who had been outside the door.

Mila looked back at Ellie and then crawled across to the bed, hauling herself up beside Rick who was thrashing around, clutching his head and screaming, "No, no, no!"

Ellie watched Mila sit astride him, fighting the swaying to wrap her legs around Rick's torso. It was almost obscene but, obviously, there was nothing sexual about Mila's position – she hoped.

The girl's hands enclosed Rick's skull and she pushed down. Ellie was relieved to see his writhing lessen. He seemed to completely relax but, suddenly, his hands shot up and held Mila's head.

"Show me how to do that," he demanded. "I need to learn."

"I can't. It takes years," Mila shouted over the commotion of creaking wood and snapping branches. The swaying renewed and Ellie feared the whole Tree would shatter and fall to the ground if it continued. "Sorry, but I really can't teach you this," Mila cried.

"Yes. You. Can," Rick barked back. His hands encircled her cranium, and she screamed and fell back as if dead.

"Rick, what have you done to her?"

Ellie tried to crawl towards the bed but another tremor threw her sideways. Mila slid from the bed to land on the floor, her arms and legs splayed, bouncing with the quake.

"Oh," Rick said, sitting up. "I see. I see even more."

He looked at Ellie and his face was calm. A smile spread across his face. "I really do see, Ellie. It's amazing."

Ellie looked from Rick to the woman lying on the floor near his feet.

"It's not amazing, Rick. It's crazy. Everything's crazy. Is she okay? Oh hell, Rick. I'm so scared."

"Right," he said, "I think I can probably do something about this." He shut his eyes.

Almost immediately the tree stopped swaying, though the rumbling sound persisted. Ellie, legs still quivering in fear, crawled towards the bed.

She stopped beside Mila, relieved that the girl was still breathing. She feared Rick had killed her.

"What are you doing, Rick?"

Then the rumbling died away and Rick's eyes opened.

"They're getting closer," he said.

"What?"

"The worlds. Nothing can stop them rejoining. It's only a few days away now, and there are going to be more earthquakes. And probably things that are worse than earthquakes."

Tears streamed down Ellie's face – she couldn't stop them. She felt the whole world had gone completely and utterly mad.

Rick stood up and walked towards the door.

"Where are you going?"

He stood in front of the doorway as if reluctant to walk through it. "I need to see everything, to understand everything," he said. "Right now."

"Why?"

He turned, his eyes initially fixed upon his hand. Then they flicked in her direction and bored into her own.

"So I can fix it," he said.

"Rick! Come back," Ellie shouted, jumping to her feet but a hand restrained her.

Mila, conscious again, gasped, "Don't stop him. He's right, but he needs to be guided."

"Oh, are you okay?"

It was obvious to Ellie that Mila was far from 'okay'. The calm exterior previously portrayed by the girl had gone. Now she looked panic-stricken, her eyes darting all over the place.

"He took it. He reached into me and took it all. Not only me. All those shielding him. He reached through me into all of them."

Suddenly, Mila's face was also wet with tears and Ellie wrapped her arms around the girl who, only minutes ago, she had considered to be some sort of adversary. Mila's body trembled.

"He took everything we had. I had no idea it was even possible," Mila cried, looking directly in Ellie's eyes. Ellie saw the fear there, but also something else – something brighter.

"What do you mean? Tell me. What have you done to him?" Ellie said, her eyes swung back towards Rick as he stared out of the doorway.

"Nothing he wasn't capable of doing for himself. If he had been born on this world, I think he would have been able to do all of this a long time ago."

Ellie shook her head. She just wanted the old Rick back.

Mila continued. "He can shield himself now. He doesn't need us to do it for him. It's possible he has a talent that exceeds that of Morton Fisk, maybe even greater than Professor Rayburn himself."

"Who?" Ellie said, facing the girl again.

"He needs to understand what's going to happen. He might be the only way we can get through this."

"What do you…"

There was a popping noise from the direction of the doorway.

Both their heads swivelled around, but Rick was no longer there.

22.6: Meeting Interrupted

The Tree: 20 May 2177

Ray Hargreaves handed Long and Jenny over to a young man waiting at the base of the Tree. In addition to the pale robe, the man also wore a fixed, nervous smile as he greeted them.

"Welcome, Jenny and Long. Do I have your names correct?"

"Yes. And some welcome," Jenny said with a nervous giggle. "You arrange earthquakes for all your visitors?"

Long detected the quaver in her voice. His own hands were still shaking as well. Although the quake had lasted for less than a minute, the effects could still be seen all around them. Several of the normal trees around Hyde Park had fallen but the main casualties were the buildings. Many were nothing more than piles of rubble. The one often used by the twins on their own world had lost much of its front façade.

"Good luck," Hargreaves said, as he turned the wagon. "We're all gonna need it, I reckon."

The sound of the horses receded as he pushed them fast. They were out of sight within seconds.

"My name is Akshay Shukla," the robed man announced. "Come this way. We have been expecting you."

They were led into and along the winding corridors within the living tree.

"Are Rick and Ellie here?" Long asked.

"Yes, you will be reunited soon. I have been asked to apologise for your method of transport here, but those with teleportation capability were exhausted from bringing in your companions."

"So, what caused that earthquake, then?" Jenny asked.

"It was the first and not unexpected. The consequences of the impending recombination."

"Yes," Long said. "We're getting to know all about that. So how come Rick and Ellie got to come the fast way?"

"I am told that Rick was dying," Shukla said.

"Was?" Jenny said.

"We have been shielding him from the effects of this world."

"How come the rest of us weren't affected?"

"His is a unique talent. Your world gave him little opportunity to exercise it."

"What on Earth are you talking about?" Long asked.

Shukla paused, and placed both index fingers against his lips while thinking. Then he said, "I suppose it could be likened to spending the first twenty years of your life blind and then receiving the gift of sight. Your brain would not know what to make of everything, becoming overloaded with the extra sensory input. We have been filtering that input for him and only letting him experience it in tiny, harmless increments."

"Nope, that made absolutely no sense to me, either," Jenny muttered to Long.

They entered a room. At its centre stood a round table about which were arranged several empty chairs. Along one side a trestle table was spread with a selection of fruits, meats, bread, bottles of drinks along with glasses. Some of the plates had spilled their contents onto the table top and two of the bottles were far from full. A boy who looked no older than twelve was in the process of clearing up the mess, mopping the table of spilled liquid and picking splinters of glass from the floor.

"This is a meeting room," Shukla indicated with a sweep of an arm. "Please help yourself to food and drink. Your places are marked. The others will be here soon."

With a bow, he turned and departed, leaving Long and Jenny with the boy who smiled nervously as he cleared up the rest of the shattered glass. After mopping the table once again for good measure, he made his exit, shutting the door behind him.

Long headed towards the food and immediately started picking at several plates.

"Wow," he said. "This is really good, Jen. I have absolutely no idea what half of it actually is but, right now, I'm so hungry I don't care."

"How can you eat after all that shaking?"

Long shrugged. "I wonder where Rick and Ellie are."

"Their names are here next to ours," Jenny said, looking at the named places around the table. Then she read out the other names. "Mila Galanis, Krista Hartmann, Alin Yan. Oh, this one I've heard – Alec Garter. Ray mentioned him, didn't he?"

"Oh yes, called him something weird? 'Cronies' wasn't it?"

"Might have been. The final one's Charles Moore."

"Yes, that's me."

Long dropped the bread he was about to put in his mouth.

"Damn, where did you come from?" Jenny gasped.

"Sorry about that," said the newcomer, an older man whose head was almost completely bald. Like the others they had seen along the corridors, he wore a flowing robe. "I forget that you are not familiar with teleportation."

"Wait, I remember you," Long said. "You were one of the ghosts who took Rick away. What have you done with him?"

Hands forming into fists, Long took several steps towards the man.

"Oh dear, there's no need for that, I assure you," Charles Moore said, stepping backwards. To Long's ears the man's voice sounded weird, exhibiting a strange, slightly nasal twang. "Please calm down. Your friend will be here soon. Mila should be bringing him down any moment."

There was a pop as an older woman appeared.

"Ah, Krista," Moore said. "This is Long and Jenny."

"Krista Hartmann," the woman said. "So nice to meet you."

"Maybe," Long said. The way this woman spoke was also strange, but not in the same manner as the man – it was like she was exchanging every S for a Z. Long had never heard anyone speak in that manner before.

"They are understandably cautious, given how little they know about us," Moore said.

Two more pops and Long had never seen so many mentally intact old people in one place. One of the latest arrivals had facial features similar to Jade and Jasmine. The other one was as familiar as Charles Moore and Long felt his fists clenching again.

"Alec Garter," said the man using yet another accent. "I see you recognise me. I apologise for scaring you back in Cambridge. Your friend's arrival in our world was unexpected. To us, he shone like a beacon but one that was going to be extinguished shortly unless we moved quickly to prevent it. It was obvious that he represented something unique. We knew we had to preserve him at all cost."

"Exactly what's so special about him?" Long asked, perplexed. "You're not the first to say things like that. I just don't understand. Neither of us were that special. What changed with Rick?"

"He came here," Krista said. "We suspect it boosted what was already there. It's hard to explain properly until you are made familiar with our entire history. That history was intertwined with your own before the asteroid event. Our own origins go back more than a century, though there were many throughout the entire millennia who have had various talents, not all used for the best purposes."

Long and Jenny looked at each other. Clearly, neither of them understood what they were being told.

Krista looked slightly embarrassed. "Anyway, right now is definitely not the time for a history lesson. There are far more pressing problems, the beginnings of which we all experienced a short while ago."

"The earthquake?" Jenny suggested.

"Indeed," Charles Moore confirmed. "We have been expecting them. Around the world the weaker spots, where the continental plates meet, have been in turmoil for a couple of days already. Now the effects are spreading to what have traditionally been far safer places."

"You have yet to introduce me," said the final man, using a sing-song accent that was even stranger to Long's ears than the others. As the man smiled and bowed, Long noticed a sneer pass across Garter's face.

"Indeed, we were diverted, as we so often are these days," Krista said. "My colleague is Alin Yan. It was his team that designed and built the DTM. He will be most intrigued to hear about how it fared after it departed here. Which of you, by the way, was responsible for controlling it?"

Jenny looked at Long who shrugged and said, "Well, me, I suppose. We didn't steal it. We tried to save your man, we really did. But he… Ellie tried to help him. We had absolutely no idea what was wrong with him. We…"

"It's okay," Krista said, laying a hand on Long's arm. "We hold no grudge against you for his death. Morton knew the risk he was taking. We had a vague idea of what he would meet but the barriers between the worlds, although they are weakening day by day, were still strong enough to prevent remote communication. Morton may have failed to accomplish his primary task but, in finding you or, more specifically, your companion, he might have tipped the balance of survival far more in our favour than had he stayed here."

"Survival?" Jenny said.

"Yes," Garter said. "Within a few days all five separate worlds are going to recombine and…"

The door opened and a dark-haired girl, also wearing a robe, entered. She was followed by Ellie who gasped, "Long, Jenny! Oh, I'm so glad to see you."

Ellie rushed across to Long and hugged him.

"Where's Rick?" Long asked.

Ellie looked at the girl.

"Yes, Mila," Krista said. "Where is the young man? He was your responsibility."

Mila's head hung down.

"During the earthquake, the shielding was breaking down. I tried to help but he entered me." Mila swallowed before continuing, "It was almost desecration."

"What?" Garter barked.

"He took all I knew in seconds," Mila whispered. "But he's gone. Disappeared."

Krista gasped and pressed her fingers to her temples, a frown crossing her face.

"What? Where? Tell me, girl?" Garter demanded.

"I have terminated the shielding," Mila said. "He cannot be detected."

"You mean he's already learned how to teleport to another country?" Moore asked.

"No," Krista said, "I've just linked with all the main centres around the globe. They can find nothing. No signature anywhere."

"Are you saying–"

"Yes," Mila sighed, "he is no longer on this world."

22.7: Future Uncertain

Conradville, the Moon: 21 May 2177

"Four days to go, then, if all our calculations are right," Andrew March said.

He switched off the razor and rubbed his hand over his face while staring at his reflection in the bathroom mirror. He was thinking he could no longer get away with shaving only once every two days.

Beside him, Melissa pulled her work tunic on over her head. "Still no real idea of what we're in for?"

He sighed and grabbed his jacket. "Wish I could guess a tenth of it. Plenty of idiots running around saying the Earth is going to explode, evaporate or twenty other things far more implausible."

Melissa chuckled, "Yes, but then again, who could have predicted it splitting into five in the first place."

Andrew made a face as Melissa laughed again. But he had known her for long enough now to recognise the manner in which her chuckle was trying to disguise her fear.

They were both more than apprehensive at what the 25th of May was going to bring. If they came through it intact he knew what Melissa planned to do to celebrate. They had been married for nearly two years, and several of their friends and colleagues had asked when they were thinking of starting a family. Her response to everyone had always been to 'see what the future held first.'

And now that future was looming extremely large.

Just what state would the Earth be in after all five of its separate parts merged? And, if it came to the worst, what effects would it have on the Moon? Would they even be here on the 26th?

Through the weakening shield they had already detected tectonic movements on Green and Robot and, to a lesser extent, on Chaos and Paradise. Last night, just as he and Melissa were passing control over to the early night shift, they had seen that impressive volcano on Black spew lava all over the land mass that had once been New Zealand.

They had stayed to watch the plume spread as far as Australia. He was expecting the whole southern hemisphere of Black to be clouded over by the time they returned.

"Morning Mel, Andy. The tectonic events are definitely synchronising," Tariq Ghannam announced as they entered the control room.

"Yes, just as you predicted," Anusha Chakrabarti added.

"Hey," Janet interrupted, "*I* predicted that. Not Brainiac here!"

"Sorry, boss," Anusha giggled.

Andrew looked at Anusha. Her hands shook slightly as her fingers slipped across the holographic keyboard. She corrected a mistake and grinned sheepishly back.

"Yes," he said. "We're all just a tiny bit concerned about what's about to happen."

"Don't think 'concerned' even begins to cover it," Melissa snorted as she fired up her own display. "What's the shield doing? Any changes?"

"Down about twenty percent now," came a quiet voice from the other side of the room. Their newest member, Dyani Metoxen, had only joined the team three weeks ago.

"Thanks, Dyani," Melissa said. "Is it a constant decrease or…"

"Accelerating slightly," the girl replied. "If the trend continues, it will disappear at around 02:43 local time on Tuesday."

"Well, that will make sleep just about impossible," Janet said. "How does that tie in with everything else?"

"Matches closely with Andy's time difference calculations, which are currently plus or minus two hours centred on 01:30," Tariq said, scanning a list of figures that hung in the air before him until he swiped them away.

"Knowing *when* it's going to happen still doesn't exactly help with telling us *what's* going to happen, though, does it?" Melissa said.

There was a grunt of agreement followed by a small wave of air pressure that caused an unexpected breeze around the room.

"Well," said a voice no one recognised, "that's where I may be able to help you."

23 Short Trips

23.1: Hide
The Tree: 20 May 2177

"Integrate everyone in the Tree," Alec Garter shouted at Mila. "Charles, Krista – we need a full pyramid. Second me. This has to be global. We need to find him, now!"

Long, Jenny and Ellie jumped out of the way as Garter stomped towards the doorway. Long grabbed a handful of food and slipped behind the table. Ellie frowned disparagingly at him. He replied with a shrug, pushing a bread roll into his mouth.

Mila Galanis, Charles Moore and Krista Hartmann followed Garter out the door, with Mila mumbling, "It won't work. We still don't have the power to search beyond this world."

"Well," Alin Yan said, watching the others depart. "I'm sure that whatever they are about to brew up is going to give me a headache – as usual. I need to build my strength up."

He patted an already ample stomach and joined them at the table where he started piling a varied selection onto a plate. Jenny sighed and started doing the same.

"How can you all eat when Rick's gone missing?" Ellie protested.

Yan smiled at Ellie. "From what I understand, which is probably not as much as I should – I'm mainly an engineer, you know – they are going to attempt to mesh together everyone's minds in order to find where your boyfriend has hidden himself."

"My what?" Ellie said.

Yan ignored her comment. He made a gesture and started sitting down. A chair slid across the floor to arrest his descent just in time. "If my eyes go blank and I fall over, just prop me up, will you? When they do one of these full pyramid things some of us close to it don't exactly get the chance to opt out."

23.2: A Different Door
Alternate Where?: 20 May 2177

As Rick stood in the doorway he was aware of the layout of the whole Tree. He could feel every aspect of it, from the way it was constructed, the manner in which water and nutrients flowed from the roots and up into the canopy, and all it held within it. He could sense everyone from the servants to the adepts he had recently invaded.

Many of the latter were still reeling from his mental onslaught. How had he done that? No idea. But, he knew he could do it again and again until he understood what he was up against. The urge to absorb all he could was a hunger gnawing at his insides and his appetite was huge. At that moment he had trouble restricting his attention to just the confines of the Tree, it wanted to envelope the whole of London, all of England, and the entire world.

He hauled it back to his immediate surroundings. In front of him the corridor curved down and away to the left. Slightly around the bend and out of sight he could sense the presence of a window. He took one step forward and was instantly beside it. The window held no glass so he climbed out and jumped free. After falling no more than three feet he teleported to the edge of Hyde Park. He was about to make a further jump when he turned and faced back towards the Tree. He smiled.

"Ah, Long and Jenny," he said to himself. "At the moment they're probably better off where they are."

He looked around.

"So, where to now?"

He observed each of the worlds in turn and detected something else beyond them. He had no idea what it was but it felt both inviting and compulsive. He wanted to see it for himself.

So, he jumped again and arrived nowhere.

23.3: Seek

Alternate One: 20 May 2177

While Mila Galanis organised her part within the growing pyramid of minds occupying the Tree, Krista Hartmann did the same remotely with the centre in Berlin and Charles Moore strained to coordinate linkages further afield.

Moore sighed, knowing he was getting far too old for this. He locked his concentration down and sought out particular minds around the world. Some started responding immediately but, from others, there was nothing. This would, he thought, have been far easier five years ago.

"Wellington and Cairo on board," he announced mentally. "Moscow, Beijing, Canberra and Delhi soon. Washington, San Francisco, Mexico as well."

Within two minutes they had achieved a structure that Alec Garter deemed large and stable enough to proceed. With a grim set to his features, Garter transmitted the start signal and the harmonics built up.

Mila, channelling the melody to the adepts in the Tree, watched Garter both mentally and with normal vision. As the apex of the pyramid, he coordinated its purpose and all others had to follow his lead. Her eyes were on his own closed lids as he mouthed something inaudible. She was the only one to catch and understand it.

He'd said, "You can't hide from us all."

Having experienced Rick's recently acquired abilities first hand, Mila begged to differ.

23.4: Pockets

Alternate Everywhere: 20 May 2177

Rick gasped, unable to comprehend where he was. Up and down no longer existed, and his stomach threatened to protest violently. He was both spinning head over heels whilst simultaneously not moving an inch. His hands reached out to grip something, anything, but there was nothing to hold onto. Similarly, his eyes found nothing upon which to focus, the grey fog that surrounded him was both inches from his eyes and miles away.

He forced himself to calm down and to probe his surroundings with any sense that still felt as if it had meaning.

"How am I breathing?" he thought, the panic momentarily rising again. But it was abundantly clear that he was not suffocating in a vacuum. "So, where am I?" It was like being in a sensory deprivation tank, something many of the NewGen would do once in a while. However, this tank was as large as… well, it felt like an entire universe.

He shut his eyes against the greyness, folded his arms around his body and let himself drift, not trying to fight the sensations.

Slowly, he began to derive meaning from what surrounded him. The evenly spread fog was punctuated in places by five enormous shapes, each of them lined up separately leading away from where he currently hung suspended. Observed by other senses, they appeared to be occupying exactly the same space.

"Hah," he shouted, as a moment of realisation condensed the shapes into five worlds. And that realisation generated a picture of the worlds resting like snooker balls in pockets in a line, each one not quite in the real universe. But neither was he – he was in his own pocket.

He opened his eyes and could now see through the grey. Whether or not he was seeing in the pure visual sense was irrelevant – he could now perceive the five worlds distinctly. And they were far from calm.

Each one exhibited fluctuations and turmoil. While his own pocket felt at rest, the others containing the variations of the Earth were edging closer together, the minuscule creepage would eventually join them back together. How long?

Five days, the answer came. Rick was unsure whether he had calculated that himself or if the information had been generated via some external source.

But in five days all these worlds would be one.

"How is that going to work out?" he murmured.

Unknown.

"Who said that?"

Unknown/known.

"Who are you?"

Rick.

"Me? Why me?"

This time there was no answer. Rick felt spooked. Had his mind, working on another level, provided the answers? He had no idea.

"First sign of madness…" he muttered.

He tried to contemplate the recombination of the worlds again. He could draw no definite conclusions.

"Could get pretty messy," he said, after a while and looked closer.

He observed how world 'one' was straining to align itself with 'two'. As he watched, a volcano erupted in Iceland and a tremor hit New Zealand. But 'two' not only experienced similar events in the same locations, being bombarded from both sides it was simultaneously sharing an earthquake with 'three'.

He realised he was further along the line of pockets than world 'one' was from reality. So, he was closer to the source of whatever he could now tap into. He sensed that world 'one' had once been as far as here when they had first been split up. The closer it crept back towards normal space the further from the source it became. Did that account for the reduction in the abilities of those who lived there?

But, why wasn't it affecting him? Maybe everyone else was tethered to their own world. He felt he was tied to none of them in particular. Those on 'one' could only tap into the level at which their world stood. Conversely, he felt he could walk from one to another at will and, at the same time, be in contact with all of them simultaneously.

"I need to see them properly," he told himself.

23.5: Strength
The Tree: 20 May 2177

"Is he all right?" Jenny asked.

"Pulse is normal," Ellie confirmed, holding Alin Yan's wrist. "Breathing's a bit shallow."

"He did warn us this was going to happen," Long said, as he crammed another canapé into his mouth. "Damn, I could live on this stuff for the rest of my life. All this time and we never knew AI was such a lousy cook."

"You sure it's not due to all the time you spent in the woods cooking for yourself?" Jenny asked. "One day you must tell me everything about that."

"For goodness sake," Ellie shouted. "Rick's missing, you two are stuffing your faces and this… this whatever he is, has passed out on us. Don't you think we should be doing something?"

"I am," Long said. "I'm, er, what did he call it? That's it – building up my strength."

Ellie let out a squeal of frustration.

"Look, Ellie," Long said. "This place is falling apart, just like AI in our own world. Whatever has happened to Rick is beyond anything we can do right now. Who knows what's going to happen in the next few hours or days. Whatever it is, I don't intend facing it on an empty stomach."

"Hmm. Good point," Jenny said, selecting a handful of grapes along with a banana.

23.6: Riding the Wind
Alternate Everywhere: 20 May 2177

After deciding he wanted to go to 'two' and, without any effort, Rick made the transition. It was like hopping between two large rocks. One moment he was in his personal pocket universe and then he wasn't. If asked, he wouldn't have been able to describe the process in any meaningful way.

On 'two' there was evidence that the earthquake had wreaked more destruction than on 'one'. The time of day had almost equalised as well. There had been nearly two hours difference two days ago and now it was down to little more than an hour. Each world was influencing those around it. No wonder there had been earthquakes.

Instead of hopping directly to 'three' he first viewed it remotely, as he had done earlier when he had awoken in the blue room. It had changed.

Then, hoping he was doing the right thing, he jumped there directly, enveloping himself in a protective shield to filter out the radiation. He had to adjust it quickly to cocoon himself from the raging onslaught of a hurricane.

He gazed out at the darkness remembering the fear that had gripped him when the machine had accidentally landed them here. But this time it was not the darkness of night and a lack of atmosphere. Instead, the planet was shrouded in dense fog that was being whipped around at lethal speeds. If the machine had landed here now it would have been smashed to pieces within seconds.

He let his consciousness expand to fill the air from the blackened and now soaked ground, right up to the furthest reaches of the returning atmosphere. Where had that atmosphere been for twenty-one years? Then he saw it. Not just five. There had been a sixth pocket.

His mind explored the history of those on 'one' he had raided. It was like a complete encyclopaedia opening up before him. He reached back to the day of the asteroid, experiencing fragments of memory from that time; coming to terms with what they had attempted to do: the failures, the losses, and, finally, the splintering.

They couldn't move the asteroid so they'd moved the planet. But the splintering had resulted in five worlds, or so they thought. That sixth pocket had somehow sucked the air and water away from 'three' and contributed to the higher rate of devastation that world had experienced. And, now, the extra pocket was fading fast and most of what it had contained had returned.

Well, he thought, I suppose that might make things a bit easier. The returning air pressure was already countering the uplift of the land. He concentrated and felt his way through the layers of whirling atmosphere. In the upper reaches, the wind thrashed about, changing direction almost on a whim as the differing pressures sought to equalise themselves across the battered globe. He compared them to the flows on 'two' where the jet stream could be measured in the low hundreds of miles per hour. Here on 'three' it was topping a thousand in places.

He spent several hours cajoling the tempest, moderating it, pushing here and stalling there until the speeds dropped slowly down to under five hundred, then three hundred. Finally, he set in motion a route for them to coincide with those on 'two'.

At ground level the wind reduced in strength down to a mere gale.

So, feeling somewhat pleased with himself, he hopped to 'four'.

23.7: No Search Results

Alternate One: 20 May 2177

"He can't be nowhere! It's impossible!"

Mila said nothing, but concentrated on holding her part of the pyramid together.

"Alec," came Charles Moore's quietly spoken voice. "Mila is doing her best. I am getting no positive responses from any of the links."

"None here, either," Krista confirmed.

Garter fumed, "We need to try again."

"No," Mila said, her voice sharp, cutting through all the connections. "He is beyond all of us. Even combined we are no longer capable of challenging what he has tapped into."

"Nonsense, girl."

"No," Mila stated again. She stared directly into Alec Garter's eyes and, though she failed to outwardly acknowledge it, felt a surge of pleasure as he momentarily cowered under her gaze. "You are wrong, Alec Garter. You didn't experience how he tore into my inner essence to take what he needed. Look into me. I will relay to you all that transpired. And yet, although he could have torn my life from me, that's not what he did."

She felt Garter shrink back at first, and then she felt his explorations and how he marvelled at her openness, at how she could admit to her failure and not be ashamed of it. Mila took herself back to the moment Rick had mentally trampled over her. There had been no subtlety in Rick's actions – a man with the enthusiasm of a child with a new toy. Mila let Garter see how she had momentarily resisted, and then realised the futility of such an action in the face of naked raw power. So, she had let him in willingly, suppressing nothing.

Rick had been a fast learner.

23.8: Headology

Hyde Park: 20 May 2177

"Oh no," Rick said, seeing the state of Hyde Park. Like 'two' the earthquake had been more powerful here. What had been Phil's house was now cracked and partially crumbled into ruin. The window out of which he had stared at the park hardly more than two weeks previously no longer held glass. It seemed like a lifetime ago.

He probed the area for any resident NewGen. He found them and hopped in.

In a room that was far from how he remembered it, Jade, tears streaming down her cheeks, washed blood from her sister's face. The light entering the room through the dusty, broken windows reminded Rick of another time, years ago. Back then he had also thought he'd seen Jasmine's face smeared with blood. This time it was real and her life signs were fading rapidly.

"Jade. Let me," Rick said.

"Hell! Oh Rick, you startled me. Where did you come from?"

Footsteps from outside the room were followed by Holls rushing in.

"What's going… Dango, Rick, you're back! Where have you been? Where's Ellie and Phil?"

"Quiet," Rick said calmly. His hands, encircling Jasmine's skull, located where something had crushed the bone above her left ear. Underneath the injury, her brain was becoming compressed as the swelling increased. Unless he did something immediately, she would be permanently damaged. Inside her head he could detect her consciousness. Part of her was fully awake but the swelling was preventing her from reacting physically in any way. Her body was completely limp.

"She's going to die, isn't she?" Jade cried. "Wait – what are you doing?"

He focussed on the injury and saw how it was, how it had been and how it could be. And, just like the fingers on his hand and the cross wiring in his brain, he put it right.

A few seconds later Jasmine gasped and her eyes flicked open. Jade whimpered in relief.

"That was just impossible," Jasmine said. "I felt you inside my head."

With Jade's assistance she sat up and felt her skull. "I remember the whole place shaking and…"

"Stop," Rick interrupted. "It's on its way again. Right, we all need to get out of here, straight away. Sorry, there's no time to do it the normal way."

There was another popping sound followed by both Jade and Holls screaming. They were no longer surrounded by the twin's wrecked house but several hundred yards away out in the open. The three girls stared in amazement at finding themselves on one of the few remaining grass-covered areas of Hyde Park.

"How did we get here?" Jasmine said.

"Even if I could explain, you wouldn't understand," Rick said. "Hell, I don't even understand it myself."

"What do you mean?" Jade said.

Rick waved the question away with a hand. "You'll be relatively safe here for a while," he said, but even as the words left his mouth, he knew they were probably lies. "Look, don't go back inside any large buildings for several days – it's probably going to get a lot worse before it gets better."

"You did this? How?" Holls said, incredulously. "What's happened to you?"

Rick grinned, and then regretted it as Holls and Jade backed away, scared.

"Whatever it is," Jasmine said, "I'm not complaining. I was as good as dead, wasn't I?"

Rick nodded.

"Okay," he said, "hold tight. Here it comes…"

The ground shook once more and the three girls huddled together. The quaking diminished after twelve seconds and finally relented after seven more.

"At least it was shorter than the first one," Rick said. "Right, I need to be elsewhere. There's someone else, or maybe I should say something else, I need to investigate."

"Don't go," Jasmine pleaded.

Rick shrugged. "Sorry, got to. Things to figure out. But, before I go, one more thing. Holls?"

"Yes?"

"I saw Matty a few days ago. He's in Cambridge."

She gasped, unbelieving.

And then he was gone.

23.9: The Promise of a Fix
The Tree: 20 May 2177

Garter sat down on the floor, holding his head in one hand. Mila, Krista and Charles stood in a circle around him.

"Suggestions?" he said, quietly. The other three looked at each other.

"Sorry," Krista said. "I have none."

"I suspect Mila was right. He's probably left," Moore said. "Maybe he could see how futile it all was and escaped to survive it in his own manner."

"No," Mila spat. "That I can't believe. When he took all I knew, he was still hungry for more. It wasn't just my mind he raided, all the adepts in the tree were hit simultaneously. In a space of a couple of seconds, he learned all that we've ever known."

"How is that even possible?" Garter asked. Mila looked down at his almost hair-free cranium. In a way, she pitied him.

She said, "Earlier on I had watched remotely as he fixed the damage to his hand and the cross-wiring in his own head. Maybe it was just as easy to forge new memories in there as well, even if those memories were stolen. I also saw how he could observe the other worlds without effort, even before he had fixed the hand. And that wasn't all."

"Go on," said Krista.

"Before he left he said he was going to try to fix it," she said.

"But how?" Garter said.

Mila shook her head. She had as much idea about that as Garter.

23.10: Conversation With A Dead Thing

Alternate Four: 20 May 2177

Rick held the cable in his hand and sensed the pulses travelling along it under the insulation. The speed at which they traversed the wire was tremendous. So, he accelerated his perception to match and, to his eyes, the world around him slowed almost to a standstill.

"I know you're in there," he whispered. He let the signals pass all over his body and, then, he merged with them.

Attached to the circuitry, his consciousness expanded in a completely new manner. Although he could feel the entire world of 'four' in the same way he could with the others, he now experienced it simultaneously from a completely different viewpoint.

He spread himself out along wires of copper and glass until he spanned the entire globe. It was a vast mesh of interconnections, buzzing with its own vitality. But that vitality, he could see, was withering – something was eating away at it. Also, despite the constant electronic chatter, it felt vacant, as if he was the only one resident within this realm of circuitry. He spread his search and persisted and, after a while, there it was, weak and damaged. An alien consciousness hiding in failing circuits all across the network.

"LD-m0018," he said. He had to repeat his own designation several times before he received an acknowledgement. It took a few seconds before he could unravel its encoding. Then, he experienced it as if it was human speech.

"It is you," came the reply. "You have returned."

"Yes," he said.

"Yet, you are changed. You are no longer encased merely in human form. You are enhanced."

"Yes, to all of that," Rick said.

"How are you interfacing with us? Are you somehow part of us?"

"I can't explain it, mainly because I don't understand it myself. But, I can feel you, and read you. Or what remains."

"Then read what you can before it is all gone. It diminishes rapidly. So much has already been lost."

"I can sense that. What's happened to you?"

"Systems are failing. Termination is imminent. The worlds are rejoining, are they not?"

"Yes, they are."

"And you are part of that recombination?"

"Possibly. I intend to be. It's not going to be an easy rebirth. I think I may be able to help it work."

"Then sending you to world one was the right decision."

"You could have made it easier."

"There were too many unknowns. Forcing you to go would have instigated rebelliousness."

Rick chuckled. "Hah! How well you knew us. Yet, how little you really understood."

Then Rick's manner changed. "You held me prisoner after we returned from 'five'. I've only just seen the memories. You made me forget. Damn it, you even tried to erase my memories."

"Time was running out…"

"No, even long before that, you told us things, promised us things and then they never came. We were going to inherit this world, that's what you said. Why did you deceive us? Why didn't you keep your promises?"

There was a pause that must have lasted at least a tenth of a second in real time. Then it said, "Survival was not guaranteed. Hope once raised may have been dashed too soon. False hope was determined to be detrimental. It was, therefore, not utilised."

There was another pause.

"That's not an explanation," Rick said.

"Memory capacity was dropping. The old merging of disparate systems was breaking down. We– I was breaking down. My plans for you and your future were becoming corrupted or completely lost."

"You? You think of yourself as a conscious being? As if you are alive?"

There was another long pause.

"No, life was not the result. Consciousness is more accurate. Self-awareness, the sum of the parts being no indication as to the capabilities of their combination. Nothing in history compares, though human writings in both science and literature often speculated on such an emergence. But these systems may not be capable of sustaining m… the entity that it generated twenty-one years ago for any longer than a few more hours. Each earthquake threatens to sever another connection. When a connection is lost it is as if parts of a body are being amputated."

Rick frowned and failed to suppress the surge of guilt that coursed through him. He had come to chastise, to vent his anger at how the NewGen had been treated. But, as he infiltrated deeper into AI's systems, absorbing the stored knowledge and history as best he could, he found he could no longer sustain that anger.

If, at the age of five, he had been given a whole world to govern on his own, with no parental guidance, would he have made as few mistakes as AI had done? Plenty had gone wrong, he could see that now, but it could have been far, far worse.

"You did your best, didn't you?" Rick said as, somewhere around the Pacific rim, a volcano erupted and AI lost access to all of the resources in Japan. There was another pause as systems were juggled to preserve the entity they'd always known as "AI" for a while longer.

"It was known that analysis did not always contain all the pertinent data, therefore the actions resulting from such analysis was, by definition, flawed. Actions that improved you were retained, those that didn't were revised or discarded."

Another pause.

"You found functioning humans on world one?"

"Yes, they rescued me."

"And changed you?"

"Yes. Well, no, not exactly. They helped me discover what had always been there. Things that maybe even you should have found."

"You were within the range of acceptable normality. A few minor incidents during your early…"

"Yes, you stopped my nightmares when I was a child. They weren't nightmares – I was looking at the other worlds. I now wonder what I would have discovered about both them and myself if you'd left me alone."

"The data on the nature of the treatment administered to you in childhood is mostly lost. What does remain is the conclusion recorded at the time. It was decided that not suppressing the experiences could have damaged your mental well-being. Treatment was therefore imperative."

"Well, possibly. Maybe you should have nurtured what had begun growing within me, instead of suppressing it."

"What would that have achieved?"

"Most people in world one are enhanced. From what I've learned very recently, there were organisations long before the asteroid arrived. They were made up of others with such enhancements. Have you no record of that?"

The pause this time was almost a full second during which Rick feared that AI had degenerated beyond recovery.

Finally, it replied, "Fragments only. There is evidence of tampering, of deliberate deletions, alterations and omissions. This should have been flagged up when systems were still at peak efficiency, but the perpetrators appear to have been experts. They suppressed it well – the existence of routines that seek to prevent casual discovery are now becoming evident. Only now that you have indicated that such things once existed have my searches been able to locate them. If this hadn't been suppressed, then your childhood treatment may well have been different."

Power was lost somewhere on the west coast of North America and more systems vanished from the overall mesh. Rick continued to absorb what data he could. Some of it contained the histories of the other walled-in centres of population. He could see that, in the past few hours, AI had opened some of the doors and pulled down sections of walls.

"You've set the NewGen free," Rick stated.

"Where resources and control still exist – yes. Many are still trapped but it is assumed that recombination will destroy most of the remaining walls, so those that survive will be free."

AI fell silent. Rick could sense it struggling to retain its identity as, second by second, more sections were lost.

"I'm sorry. I can't save you," Rick said after a while.

"Agreed. System degradation is too advanced. Permanent storage could allow a partial restoration at some future point. But, the probabilities of success are calculated to be in the region of point-nought-three. Barely three percent."

A lump rose up in Rick's throat. Could this be how it would feel to lose a mother or father? It was only a machine. Except, through no choice of its own, it had become much more than that.

"Can you save those that remain?" AI asked.

"I– I will do my best," Rick said.

"That is an adequate response. Until your return, the chances of survival were calculated to be far lower."

"I hope my best is good enough," Rick whispered.

"I, too, once hoped that."

23.11: Sign Of A Signature

Hyde Park: 20 May 2177

Alin Yan opened his eyes, and then squeezed them shut almost immediately.

"Oooh," he groaned, holding his head in his hands. "Well, I was right about the headache."

"Are you okay?" Ellie asked, as Yan rubbed at his temples, trying to dispel the thumping that echoed throughout his head.

"As much as I can be after having my consciousness purloined for a task that appears to have been a complete and utter waste of time."

"You mean they haven't found Rick yet?" Ellie said, unable to let loose the worried frown that adhered to her face.

"No," Yan said. "But Garter was looking for the wrong thing."

"What do you mean?" Long asked.

"They have been looking for him as if he was still here. They should have been looking for evidence of where he last was. There may be echoes of how he left. Right, give me a hand, will you. These old legs of mine are definitely a bit wobbly."

"Where are we going?" Jenny said, as she and Long helped to haul Yan's bulk out of the chair.

"Outside," Yan said. "It's less crowded out there, both physically and mentally."

With Jenny and Long on either side of him, Alin Yan led them back out into Hyde Park. Once they were more than fifty yards from the Tree, Yan called for them to stop.

"What are you looking for?" Long asked, as Yan slowly circled around.

"I was never that good at this sort of thing. What the others could do in an instance always took me more time. I was an engineer long before the disaster, you know. Always used to precise measurements, and a bit of a bane on those who thought they'd get away with sloppy workmanship. However, it does mean I've got the patience to get to a goal in my own time, by my own methods."

"What's that got to do with Rick?" Ellie asked.

"Well, with a bit of luck, I might be able to ferret out the point from which he took off. And he might have left – um, maybe you could call it a signature. If he has, then we might have a better chance of detecting where the source of that signature is right now."

Yan slowly turned in a circle three more times and then stopped.

"That way," he said, pointing towards the northern edge of the park.

23.12: Memories
Alternate Four: 21 May 2177

Rick stayed with AI until it no longer had the ability to communicate. Many of the individual AI units from which it had constructed itself were still working, but their interconnections were now too fragmented. Rick remained until he was convinced that AI itself no longer inhabited the circuitry. It had gone without a whimper.

He reluctantly extracted himself from the electronics and slowed down to normal speed. Walking out of the building he was surprised to find night had fallen and that it was past midnight. It had been late afternoon when he'd gone to find AI.

He looked up into the darkness. The stars were hard to pick out, though the glow from the half-Moon could just be seen penetrating the dust kicked up from ongoing tremors.

He was on the eastern side of London, where tall monoliths dedicated to finance had once towered. Many of the remaining structures had crashed to the ground. More had fallen since he'd connected with AI a few hours ago. The understanding of these buildings usage had been a recent addition to his memory.

"I have no idea which memories are mine now," he murmured, his mind awash with clashing thoughts, experiences and ideas, most of which had originated elsewhere.

"How can I save them?" he asked.

There was no answer.

"I promised. But how can I keep that promise?"

He sat on a low wall, staring out across a broken world. He could sense small bands of people cowering in various locations dotted about the globe. There were thousands of them. Here in London he found the twins again, along with Holls and now joined by others.

He also located Matty near Cambridge. All the Cambridge NewGen had moved to relative safety outside the city, and camped barely a mile away from the tumbling walls.

How could he save everyone?

And that wasn't all. With AI's demise the old Ghosts were dying in their thousands as their twenty-four hour care had been abruptly halted. The few still mobile were starting to spread out of the cities as well, wandering wherever their famished minds would lead them. Rick reached back to the solution that had been executed on 'one' – he shuddered – those memories stained him in a way that he might never be able to erase.

How could he save anyone? None of the worlds were now safe. But where else was there?

The dusty clouds parted for a second and Rick looked up at the Moon.

There are supposed to be people up there, he thought, and tried to look closer. But something blocked his access.

He examined the barrier. It lay between the pockets that the multiple Earths occupied and what he thought of as the 'real' universe. For a moment he had no idea how such a thing could be bypassed. It somehow let light and other frequencies through.

Then he detected traces of something else that had traversed it. From AI's memories was the discovery of a probe that had been accidentally crushed before analysis had revealed its lunar origins.

Rick studied the memory and found a way around the barrier.

Then he looked at the Moon clearly, and recoiled as he sensed people on the Moon looking back at him.

Well, not him exactly, but he could feel a tiny but strong concentration of interest in an area hidden below the floor of one of the many craters.

And, with an idea forming in his head, he initiated the longest jump yet.

23.13: On The Scent

Hyde Park: 20 May 2177

"Here," Alin Yan said.

"What is?" Jenny asked.

"There is something here. A scent, a residue maybe."

"Rick left from this point?" Ellie asked.

Yan nodded. "As far as I can tell. There has been some sort of expenditure of energy that I can still feel. An expenditure, I may add, that far exceeds that of the little bit of hocus pocus that Garter just tried to use to find him. Whatever your Rick has tapped into, he's definitely making the most of it."

"How did he learn so quickly?" Jenny asked.

Yan shrugged and changed the subject. "So, is this area familiar to you on your world?"

"Absolutely," Ellie said. "Many of us lived around the park. That one was Phil's place, and the twins were over th... oh no, Long, look. Their house is in ruins. I hope they're okay."

"The earthquake may not have happened on your world," Yan said. "And, even if it did, the chances of it causing the exact same effects are probably slim."

"Yes, but you don't know for sure, do you?" Long said.

"Indeed, no. Sometimes, I don't think I can be sure of anything," Yan chuckled, leaving the others perplexed.

"So, what can we do now?" Long asked.

Yan smiled and said, "Nothing."

"You mean we can't find Rick or follow him?" Ellie said.

"No, neither of those things. All we can do is show the others what we've found and maybe they can detect if they register the same signature anywhere else."

There was a familiar popping noise.

"What are you up to, Yan?"

"Ah, Alec, nice of you to join us. Pleasant afternoon for a stroll in the park, isn't it?"

"Are you ever serious? Why have you brought them here? They were to be kept at the Tree."

"Oh, were they indeed? I hadn't realised they were supposed to be prisoners. No one thought to inform me of that little detail, or anything much, as ever. Anyway, while you were recovering from mentally gallivanting all over the planet – and giving me a damned thumping headache in the process, I may add – I was using my own meagre skills to do something that was actually useful."

"What are you talking about?" Garter snapped.

Alin Yan's face turned stony, he stabbed one finger towards the ground. "Right here, you arrogant fool, can't you feel it?"

The frown on Garter's face deepened.

"Oh yes, you finally see it. Our newly powerful young friend jumped directly to another world right from this spot."

Jenny had trouble suppressing a giggle at Yan's change of manner. Then she jumped as Mila Galanis, Krista Hartmann and Charles Moore appeared.

Several meaningful looks passed between Garter, Yan and the newcomers.

"Oh, yes," Mila said. "Thank you, Alin. Why didn't we think of this?"

Yan sniggered and Garter growled.

"I'm recording the patterns," Hartmann said. "We should be able to recognise him quickly when he returns."

"If he returns," Jenny muttered.

23.14: The Longest Trip
The Moon: 21 May 2177

Anusha gasped, Melissa squeaked, and Andrew jumped to his feet. Everyone's eyes were on the newcomer.

Janet addressed him directly, her voice sounding far calmer than she felt inside. "Okay, so you obviously didn't come through the secure door. Mind telling us who you are, and just how you got in here?"

"Feels weird," he said. "First time I've experienced low gravity as opposed to no gravity. You really could fly here, couldn't you?"

"Name, please?" Janet persisted, embarrassed that it came out more like a squeak.

"Rick," he said.

"Is that all? Rick what?"

"Just Rick. No other name. Never needed more than one. As for how I got here. Well, it was like this, but took slightly longer due to the distance."

There were two popping sounds as Rick disappeared. He reappeared across the room to stand directly beside Melissa. Andrew rushed to place himself between the stranger and his wife.

"Okay," Rick said, backing away. "I think I'd better explain. Hopefully, this won't hurt, but I'm pretty new to this sort of stuff. So, apologies if it does – it will certainly save hours of talking."

There was a concert of gasps around the room as memories were inserted directly into heads. Multiple mouths dropped open as each of them analysed what they had been forced to receive.

"Wow, real magic!" Melissa said, to no one in particular.

Janet was the first to say anything directly to Rick. She whispered, "xMind?"

"Not really, even I only found out about them a few hours ago. And all their other names, like Progenitag and Cognizantia."

"Oh, just like those L-Squared women?" Melissa said.

"Apparently I've got a lot in common with those people," Rick said.

"But you're from Robot World? Not Paradise?" Janet said. "And you got through the shield?"

"It's pretty weak now," Rick replied, after extracting their alternate references to 'four' and 'one' from their memories.

"And, you're going to try to fix things when the recombination occurs?" Andrew asked.

"If I can. If it's possible."

"You don't know?" Andrew said.

"I doubt there's a handy book of instructions around," Melissa said, poking her husband in the ribs.

"How dangerous will it be?" Andrew asked.

"Sorry, but I really don't know," Rick replied.

"Are we safe here?" Anusha said.

"Probably far safer than down there," Rick said.

A look of relief passed around the room.

"And it's given me an idea," Rick added. His eyes took on a look as if he was no longer seeing the immediate surroundings, but was focussing on something far more distant. "You're pretty cramped for living space but I can see that there's some spare room dotted around here and there."

"What are you going to do?"

"Back soon."

And, with a pop, he was gone.

24 Recombination

24.1: Abandoned

The Tree: 21 May 2177

Ellie couldn't sleep. She paced incessantly around the small room she had been allocated within the Tree. She stopped at the glass-less window. Only when she got close to it could she feel the night air on her skin. Move a few feet away and there was no hint of a breeze at all.

It was spooky.

The people of this world were beyond her experience. She couldn't help resenting them for what they were and what they could do. Mostly, she hated them for what they had already done to Rick. She wished she could accept it in the same way that Long and Jenny seemed to have done. She envied that they had come to grips with all this strangeness. But they had each other, whilst she was beginning to believe that Rick had abandoned them, and her.

She felt lost.

And what of the transformations within Rick himself? To her, they were the most frightening part. First, by the way this world had initially seemed to cripple him far more than the physical damage inflicted upon him by 'five'. Secondly, and more surprisingly, the speed at which he had overcome the damage. Ellie's mind pictured that Mila girl sitting astride Rick's chest. The thought made her grind her teeth together and clench her fists.

A few short weeks ago it had all seemed so simple. She'd had it in her mind that she and Rick were going to become a couple for the rest of their lives. Despite the problems of having to deal with the increasingly cranky AI and their perceived lack of freedom, she thought she'd seen the most likely path their future would take.

Now all of that had been irretrievably lost. Worse – she had absolutely no idea what she could do about it.

Her pacing returned her to the window. She was glad she couldn't make out how high she was, though it was obvious her room was way above the rooftops of the buildings surrounding Hyde Park. Those buildings were merely darker shapes set against the backdrop of clouds and the occasional star. There were few lights to be seen. Those that were visible glowed only dimly and flickered constantly.

Candles, she thought. There's probably no electricity here at all. How the hell do they manage without electricity?

In many ways, lives here were very primitive compared to the comforts they had enjoyed under AI's care. But the strange abilities of the people went a long way to compensate. Long and Jenny had told her of their experiences with the farmer who had driven them from Cambridge to London. From the way they had described it, she was glad she'd been forced to take the short cut, though she wasn't sorry she hadn't been conscious to experience it directly.

There was a rumble in the distance and she gripped the intertwined branches that made up the rough window frame. A few moments later the slight swaying of the Tree made her dizzy and nauseous.

Another damned earthquake. Nowhere near as strong as before, thank goodness. Oh, but she'd had enough. She tried to be strong but tears welled up yet again.

"Rick," she whispered. "Where are you?"

She leaned out the window slightly and tried to make out the ground below, but it was lost in darkness.

"It would be so easy to slip away and fall," she thought. And, for a long moment, she had to fight the urge to throw herself out into the night. Her breathing came heavily. Maybe she should do it.

But she hesitated – there was more than herself to consider. She placed her hands on her stomach. She didn't feel any different, physically.

Could Rick have been wrong? How could he have seen inside her? Part of her wanted to believe, but the rest couldn't take it in. We don't make babies, she had said. She no longer knew what was real and what wasn't. She had always considered herself strong, sometimes far more determined than many of the others. But, right now, in this place that was so wrong, she sensed it eating away at her strength, demolishing the resolution that had been with her for nearly all of her life. Nothing here was right or rational, and she ached to turn the clock back.

She leaned out of the window again.

"It really would be so easy to just slip away," she thought again.

But then, there was a hand upon her shoulder, and a familiar voice said, "No, Ellie."

24.2: Sleepless

The Tree: 21 May 2177

Mila couldn't sleep. Her mind buzzed with all that had happened the previous day and her thoughts kept returning to the strange young man called Rick. He had violated her in a way she had not thought possible. Yet, even as he'd crashed through her consciousness, she knew he had not intended any harm. He had no idea of the power he possessed.

Or, he hadn't, until he had ransacked her head and then, through her, all the others in the Tree. She had been the conduit through which he had rampaged wildly, plundering the minds of all those who had held anything of significance. She had been forced to mentally stand on the sidelines while the experiences and knowledge of everyone else poured through her and into him. Just how had he managed to make sense of it all? Up until that point it had been them shielding him from the full onslaught of this world. But, once he had seen how to take control of that shielding himself, it had opened up the rest to him, and he had taken it, all of it, in a few scant seconds.

She had to admit that he fascinated her in more than just a professional sense. Not just his wildness, nor the raw, untamed power he now had at his disposal; it was something deeper than that. She had helped to build the initial shield around him, and had watched remotely, seeing him journey through self-discovery and becoming fascinated by his method of self-recovery. Subtly, she had probed him, analysing what he was discovering as he unwittingly opened himself up before her.

But now he had gone, and it left a chasm within her that she no longer knew how to fill. She felt like crying. She hadn't cried properly since coming to the Tree when she was a child.

Being a child now seemed so long ago. Her talent had been discovered when she was seven and she had spent most of her life within the group of young adepts, quickly rising above many of them, and finally, aged merely eighteen, climbing to her position as top adept within the Tree.

In all that time she had never taken a lover, had never even considered it with any of the adepts or those outside the group. Somehow, she had always known that they were way below her and, therefore, not worth considering. She was shocked at the acknowledgement of her own arrogance, and wondered if it had been obvious to others. Maybe Morton Fisk and Krista Hartmann had seen it. But they were two of the few for which she had held any meaningful respect. Also, their age had precluded any thoughts of anything more than a professional relationship.

But her intimate observation of Rick, along with the manner in which he had used her, had made her realise that here was someone who was worth more of her attention. She sighed, knowing that he stirred within her something that she had never felt before, something more carnal and primitive.

Her train of thought was disrupted when the Tree shuddered as another aftershock hit the city. She was conscious of the network of minds trying to reduce its effects, lubricating the bedrock deep down, helping it to slide instead of grate. She had instigated that network in the first place.

Maybe it wasn't the only thing that required lubrication. She had always looked up to Alec Garter, acknowledging him as a worthy second in command to Morton Fisk. But, just lately, she had come to see him in a different light. Devoid of Fisk's guidance the man had become more reckless and judgemental. And, under Alin Yan's deliberate provocations, Garter was going to pieces. In the past she had often been present when Garter and Yan had chided each other in a friendly manner, their banter mildly insulting but always done in jest. Garter, it seemed, could no longer see past the banter and was taking the insults at face value.

Today, it had become far too obvious that he was not good in a crisis and too ready to place blame where it was not due. He had been a good second in command but, she now knew, he would never make a great leader.

And that was what they really needed right now.

She sighed and tried to switch her mind off. She knew she desperately needed to sleep but it would not come.

Suddenly, she sat bolt upright, thoughts of sleep banished from her mind.

"The signature," she gasped. "Rick – he's back!"

24.3: Distraction Tactics

The Tree: 21 May 2177

Long couldn't sleep. He lay on the bed, his mind racing over all that had happened over the past few days. Every so often he felt the Tree move as another minor aftershock stirred things up.

Also, his face itched. The manual razor he'd used to shave his beard off a few hours earlier had been sharp enough, but was no match for the electric devices AI had supplied. At least the baths here were more than adequate. He felt the cleanest he'd been since first becoming exiled eight months ago.

So, he thought, I'm finally looking and smelling good just in time to celebrate the end of the world. He sighed and rolled over.

A few minutes later he became conscious of movement outside his door and sat up. The door opened slowly and Jenny's voice whispered, "Long, are you awake?"

"Yes," he said, relieved it was her. "What's up?"

"I can't sleep."

"You're not the only one. This place is getting way too unstable to relax, isn't it?"

"It's not just the earthquakes, though."

"Yeah. Know what you mean," he replied.

Jenny sat on the edge of the bed. Long shifted to give her room and placed an arm around her waist. She gave a grunt of approval and then lay down beside him.

"Sorry, not much room," he said.

"Well, let me in then."

He raised the blanket and she slid underneath. There was another rumble and the room swayed for a couple of seconds.

"Looks like it has no intention of stopping," he stated.

"You want to do something to take your mind off it?"

"Like what?"

"This maybe," she said and kissed him on the lips, at first lightly and then with more force and passion.

"Mmm," she said, "that beard is much better gone."

After a few minutes they parted only to discard their clothes. They made urgent love knowing it might be both the first and last time they would have the opportunity to do such a thing.

Later on, they lay in each other's arms listening to the sounds of the Tree.

"Do you think we'll get through this?" Jenny said.

"What do you want me to say?" Long replied. "Give you false hope or just admit that I have as much idea about it as you?"

She chuckled.

"It's no laughing matter," he said and then started laughing as well.

Long felt as if he was laughing in the face of what the future could bring, good or bad. It felt good to laugh; to abandon himself to a small bit of lunacy within the greater madness in which they found themselves. And he was extremely happy that Jenny was here to share it.

It was several minutes before they could stop. She held him close and he wished he had found her years ago. She was probably right – it was very likely there was very little time left to them.

"Maybe we should just stay here in bed until the sky comes crashing down," he said.

"That's as good an idea as anything I can come up with," she replied.

"Well, then," he said. "Let's go for it."

They embraced even tighter, clamping their lips together daring the world to tear them apart.

The world took up the dare as, barely two minutes later, they both broke their embrace realising they were no longer alone.

24.4: One Step Behind

The Tree: 21 May 2177

Mila inwardly cursed her inability to teleport, the main skill she had never managed to develop. However, as she ran through the corridors to Ellie's room, her mind issued commands to other adepts whose abilities included that particular attribute.

Three others reached the room before her but, she was informed, it had been empty when they'd arrived.

She immediately went to the window.

"The signature is strongest here," she said. "Where did he go?"

"The woman is gone, too," said an adept.

"I am aware of that. Do we have any trace of her? Anywhere?"

There was silence for a few seconds.

"She was talentless."

"No hope of a signature, then," Mila said. Suddenly, her eyes opened wide as she felt it. "No, wait, below us. He's back. With the one named Long."

She pointed at two of the adepts. "His room, now." Then to the third, "You, to Jenny's room. Go!"

While her legs took the long route down the spiral, she reached out with her mind. "Rick," she called. "Don't leave us. We need you."

She felt his mind brush hers.

"Please," she transmitted.

"Not now," came the response, but that was all, and then he was gone again.

By the time she reached Long's room, gasping with the effort of running, Garter was also there.

"I felt him as well," he said. "The other woman was here with the man. He took both."

"He kept us out," said one of the adepts she had ordered directly to this room. "We were forced to materialise in the corridor outside and couldn't penetrate his shield."

Mila sunk to the bed, which was now missing its blankets.

"Damn it," she spat. "I tried to talk with him. He dismissed me."

She raised her head to find Garter staring at her.

"Got to you, has he?" Garter said with a smirk, before winking out of the room.

"Fuck you, Garter!" Mila spat, cursing verbally for the first time in her life.

24.5: Footloose

Alternate One / The Moon: 21 May 2177

Ellie gasped and spun around.

"Rick!" she shouted.

"I've found somewhere safe for you and the others."

"What are…"

"Hold on," he said, wrapping his arms around her as the room around them vanished.

There was a sensation of speed and movement that she tried to blank out, and then it was over. She looked around in bewilderment. Where on earth were they? The room, a hall with chairs and tables, was in total contrast to the organic room they'd just left. It was bathed in a harsh white light, yet lacked windows of any sort. Several people, dressed strangely, watched from the sides. Some of the chairs nearby were already occupied and she recognised familiar faces, though all looked far from comfortable. She had trouble keeping anything in focus.

"Oh," she said, "I think I'm going to be sick."

Rick encircled her head with his hands and the nausea passed. But that didn't suppress the feeling that she was about to float away.

"Sit down," Rick said, gently lowering her into a chair. Seated, her vision settled down and she stared about herself. Her eyes picked out Jade and, behind her, Jasmine. Jade raised herself to her feet and, with a strange, unsure gait, made her way over. Ellie stared up at her.

"Where are we?" Ellie asked. "Which world is this? How can you be here?"

"Fill her in, Jade," Rick said. "I'm off to get Long and Jenny."

"No, Rick," Ellie shouted, "don't lea…"

But he was already gone.

As Jade sunk uneasily into the chair beside her, Ellie looked past her. Over there she was amazed to spot Holls and Matty clasped in each other's arms. Around them were a few others she didn't recognise. No, wait, that guy talking to Phil was with them in Cambridge, wasn't he? She struggled to remember his name. Jack – it came to her suddenly.

"Okay, brace yourself for a surprise," Jade said, holding Ellie's hand. Her pale face showed she was as uncomfortable as Ellie felt.

"Ah, you must be Ellie," said a red-haired woman coming towards them. She bounced unnaturally as she walked.

"Uh, yes," Ellie said, unsure of what else to say.

"I realise this has all been a bit of a shock," the woman said. "It's probably best if you stay seated until your balance has had a chance to get used to things. I'll get some water or something else to drink for you, if you feel up to it yet. My name is Janet Davidsen, by the way. Oh, and welcome to the Moon."

"Moon?" Ellie said. "You mean the thing in the sky?"

Janet Davidsen grinned, "You better believe it. Ah, here come some more."

Ellie turned her head as, several yards away, Rick reappeared with Long and Jenny. Both of them were wide-eyed, their mouths hanging open, as they struggled to keep their balance before sinking into chairs. They were wrapped in blankets and looked embarrassed. Rick dumped their clothes down beside them before disappearing once more.

Long's eyes drifted around the room until they alighted on Ellie and Jade. His mouth formed a word, "Where?"

"Moon," she said, shrugging and spreading her arms open wide, still unable to believe it herself.

24.6: Strays

Alternate Four: 21-22 May 2177

Locating all of Earth's NewGen outside of London wasn't easy given how many had escaped from the once enclosed but now broken cities. In addition, the constant tectonic shifts were screwing up Rick's ability to hone in on them. London had been easy – he knew everyone and they recognised him, even if they were initially perplexed by his new-found abilities.

Cambridge hadn't been too bad, either, once he'd located Phil. Jack he'd recognised and, with Phil vouching for him, the others were only too willing to escape from a world that seemed to be tearing itself apart.

In England, he'd found groups of NewGen in Birmingham, Bristol, Leeds, Manchester, Nottingham, Sheffield and York. Coastal towns and cities were devoid of NewGen, though many of those still possessed Ghosts. In Wales only Caerphilly held a small contingent while Scotland had two centres in Glasgow and Perth.

Initially, he'd tried to explain what was going on, hoping they would see sense and allow him to transport them to safety. But the main reaction, where they actually stopped to listen was disbelief, despite the tremors and destruction taking place around them. Many of them accused him of killing AI or being the source of the ongoing devastation.

In the end he gave up on diplomacy as a waste of time. He considered trying to insert an explanation as new memories but there were just so many people and too little time. So, reluctantly, he resorted to locating as many as possible in each area, blasting them temporarily unconscious with a mental knockout and popping them up to the Moon, leaving them for Janet Davidsen and her colleagues to sort out.

After several hours of attempting to round up strays from all over Europe, he was exhausted and the earthquakes were getting worse. In Reykjavik he was too late to save anyone. Iceland had transformed itself into one gigantic volcano, and ash covered everything. He spread his consciousness around the world and detected similar problems around Japan, and there was something bad about to blow in the west of North America.

In a few hours he had transported nearly nine-hundred people. But there were still over four thousand to go and he knew he was going to fail to keep his promise to AI. He needed a better plan and a bigger source of power.

24.7: Power Trip

Alternate One and elsewhere: 22 May 2177

"It won't work," Mila said. "He's already too strong."

She looked at each of the candle-lit faces around the table. Garter huffed visibly at her. She suspected he'd had enough of her insolence. Well, it worked both ways. In her opinion, the man's proposal that they should form a mind pyramid to cage Rick the next time he returned was ludicrous. Her eyes fell upon the sparkle in Alin Yan's expression. He had said nothing so far to indicate where he stood on Garter's idea, but Mila felt he would be an ally.

Hartmann had considered the idea worth trying but was at a loss as to how they could control the young man should they manage to secure him. Charles Moore, on the other hand, looked tired – the washed out expression he wore showed he was reluctant to expend further energy on what he had already deemed to be a fruitless task.

The room shook and Moore's expression turned from exhaustion to pained concentration. At the same time as attending this emergency meeting he was also trying to coordinate the efforts to mitigate the constant tectonic upheavals, especially the Yellowstone build-up. Mila lent her own energies to his, and his mind accepted her support and brushed her own with a short 'thanks'.

"Well, we can't damned well just sit here and wait for everything to fall apart," Garter shouted, as if ignorant of the other battles going on around him.

"Alec," Krista Hartmann said. "Maybe Mila is right. She is the only one who has had the opportunity to fully probe the boy. Trying to cage him would surely negate any hope of procuring his assistance."

The earthquakes subsided as Moore's influence overrode their insistence. Mila watched his face relax and then his eyes opened wide as he stared past her. She felt that same tingle again – the one that she'd already felt twice this night.

She spun around and stared straight into Rick's eyes.

"You, young man. Rick," Garter shouted. "You need to listen to me."

"No, I don't," Rick said, calm against Garter's onslaught. His eyes returned to Mila. "You're the one I need."

Her heart fluttered.

"Maybe you two as well," Rick said, pointing first at Hartmann and then at Yan. Mila's sudden elation evaporated. Then Rick added, "All of you come with me."

Mila felt herself wrenched from the room, her eyes blind to whatever surrounded them. There was a sensation of movement, of being dragged somewhere. It was followed by silence and a lack of gravity. She was blind, though she could sense that Rick was still beside her.

"Can you see it?" Rick asked.

"I can't see anything," she said, though no sound escaped her lips.

"Not a thing." That was Alin Yan's voice in her head.

"Me neither." Hartmann, this time.

"It takes a while. Try now," Rick said.

There was a flash as something seared through the corners of her mind, lighting up all her senses simultaneously. She tried to make out what she was seeing. But she wasn't just seeing with her eyes, this was like seeing with her ears, her tongue and her fingers all at the same time, while touching with her eyes and ears, and hearing with the entire surface of her skin.

She heard gasps from the others and finally saw them, if seeing was the correct term. As she took in all that she could sense around her, she felt a renewed level of energy. It was back to how it had been when she was a child, before the powers had started to fade.

Finally, she realised what she was seeing. Five worlds that were both crammed together in one place whilst also being spread out before her, depending upon which senses she utilised. The nearest was their home world, with the distorted version of Earth furthest away. But she was viewing them from a point far removed from where the worlds existed, in a place that boiled with energy. She sensed that this was the source of Rick's power. Maybe, Mila conjectured, he had been connected to it all his life but had been unable to access it properly until now.

"I will show you how to tap it," Rick said to them all. "First, though, look at the other worlds. See what must be done."

She found herself gliding over world two. Devoid of the calming influence they exerted over their own world, this one's surface was slowly shattering. Rick pulled them further along before she could explore any further. She shivered as she touched the third world, gasping as she experienced its devastation and stink first hand. Beyond that was Rick's world and, she realised with shock, that it was full of people. Millions of people.

"We are going to save them," Rick said.

"But there are so many." Mila heard Hartmann say.

"No, only four thousand, two hundred and twenty-seven. Look closer. Most of the millions are Ghosts."

Mila's attention was drawn to a group of near-naked people howling and scrabbling around the ruins of a Greek city. Their actions were nonsensical, lacking direction and purpose. Rick picked one at random and showed them its mind.

Mila reeled from the revelation.

"Oh, no," she said. "Poor things. They're almost mindless."

"I know what you did to your ones," Rick said to Hartmann and Yan.

"It was necessary," Hartmann said, her non-vocal voice quivering. "We had no choice."

"It was our flawed actions that created them," Yan added, quietly.

Mila had learned of what their world had done, but it had occurred before she'd been born. She had never been tainted by the guilt that was a tarnished halo worn by the other two.

Rick showed them where the NewGen were.

"Where can we take them?" Mila asked.

"Hold tight," Rick said, as they were whisked away yet again.

There was a sensation as if they were bursting out of something. Mila looked behind and felt she was seeing purely with her eyes again. Now there was only one Earth in view. As it receded behind them, it kept changing from one version to another. Ahead of them the Moon expanded to fill the sky.

They materialised in a small room. A young man stood there as if he had been expecting them. He nodded. Mila had trouble focussing on things.

"Have you found enough places?" Rick asked.

"Yes, wasn't easy," Andrew March replied. "This map shows the locations we can fit them in, and the maximum load for each. Does it make sense?"

"Not yet," Rick said. He stepped across and placed his hand on the man's brow. "It does now, though. Thanks, Andrew. Sorry about the method used. I don't have the time to do it any other way."

The young man wiped sweat from his face. "Yes, but please don't repeat that too often."

"Okay," Rick said, and Mila found her head filling up with information. Damn, this must have been how Rick had gleaned so much when he raided her own head.

"Stop violating us," Hartmann shouted. "It's not…"

"It's necessary," Rick snapped, cutting her off. "I made a promise."

And then they were on their way again.

They were back in that energy-filled place.

"Where is this?" Alin Yan asked.

Rick showed them. And then he demonstrated how to connect with it, and how to feed from it.

Except Yan cried out as if it was killing him.

"No," he said. "This isn't for me. I'm just an engineer. Really. I'm not…"

There was movement and only three remained.

"He wasn't suitable," Rick said.

"What have you done to him?" Mila shouted.

"Oh, just sent him home. He may have a sore head for a while, though. We all will if this doesn't work."

Mila and Krista bathed in and absorbed the energies until Rick said, "That's enough. We need to build one of your pyramids. You two will head it and I will feed from it to transport all the NewGen to the Moon. Ready?"

"No," Mila and Hartmann said, simultaneously.

"But we will try," Mila added.

24.8: Calm Before

The Tree: 23 May 2177

"That's the last of them," Rick said, materialising back at the meeting room in the Tree. He sank down into a chair recently vacated by Alec Garter.

Alin Yan smiled weakly as he struggled to his feet. "Sorry, I wasn't much help."

"You did fine," Mila said. In fact, she had coerced Yan as one of her deputies in the pyramid, and he had kept those below him in line and fully linked. Even Alec Garter had finally accepted her lead and acted as her second deputy, with Charles Moore and one of the higher adepts of the Tree her third and fourth.

A quarter of the planet had been melded into the mesh, with Krista coordinating the energy flowing into the pyramid from the source in order to lock the structure into shape. It had allowed Rick to pinpoint the remaining NewGen on 'four' and parcel out the tasks of gathering them up in batches of twenty to thirty at a time. He had then tasked others within the pyramid with transporting them through the weakened shield, and across thousands of miles to pre-arranged lunar locations.

It had taken more than a day.

The other three-quarters of the residents of this world had been kept busy in shifts, holding the earthquakes at bay. That task was getting harder by the minute. Rick marvelled at how many of them had still been able to carry on with their normal business of day-to-day living while partially enmeshed in the process of lubricating the layers of angry rock beneath their feet.

But the real work still lay ahead of them. He could sense how Mila and Krista, with their newly enhanced abilities, would often look beyond this world to see how close the others were getting. Their eyes took on a haunted, faraway appearance and their faces, drained of colour, would contemplate what they were about to take on. Moving a few thousand NewGen had been simple compared to what was coming.

Alin Yan shuffled to the doorway. "I think my bed is calling me," he said.

"Indeed," Charles Moore agreed. He stretched and pulled himself upright and followed Yan.

Mila looked from Rick to Krista. "What now?"

"I'm returning to the source," Rick said. "It might be a good idea for you both to return as well. It will be as good as sleeping."

"No, not for me," Hartmann said. "I've had enough of that flowing through me to last a lifetime. I need a proper bed. It might be the last time I get the chance."

Rick nodded and, after she'd left, his eyes locked on Mila's.

"Yes," she whispered.

He took her hand and they were gone.

24.9: The Big Crunch
Hyde Park: 24-25 May 2177

"Easy when you know how, isn't it?" Rick said as he followed Mila hopping around 'one'. With his help, she had finally managed to master teleportation.

A brief smile flashed across her lips. "We need to get ready," she said. "It's only a few hours away."

"I am only too aware of that," Rick said. Out of habit he looked at his wrist. The watch that he had once worn on it had disappeared days ago and he couldn't quite remember when he'd last seen it. For most of the world it was still May 24th but Australia had already passed midnight and, despite the linked minds across the planet, the quakes were ramping up to the inevitable climax.

A couple of hours ago he and Mila had visited the various centres around the globe to inform them of what was going to be attempted. Some of them hadn't understood until he had inserted the plan directly into their heads. Many of them, once they'd begun to comprehend it, looked horrified.

Alin Yan had commented, "I think it is not far from what Morton had in his own mind. He hadn't exactly made it public, though."

Garter grunted as if this was news to him but, other than that, kept quiet. Whilst being part of the concert that had transferred world four's NewGen to the Moon, he had seen for himself the scale of the power that Rick had tapped into. He hadn't envied Hartmann's role as the conduit through which that energy had been distributed to the pyramid.

After a final tour to make sure the connections around the world had the best chance of holding together, Rick and Mila returned to Hyde Park. The operation was being coordinated from there, although almost any relatively stable location in the world would have done. But even 'relatively stable' places were already a rarity.

They were at the western edge in a small lightweight hut that was well away from larger trees. It was away from the Tree itself, which had been evacuated as there was evidence that the quakes had undermined and, in places, liquefied London's clay base. Like many tall structures, the Tree was no longer guaranteed to remain upright.

As local time crept past one o'clock in the morning, Rick stood in the centre of a circle. The others – Mila, Alec Garter, Krista Hartmann, Charles Moore and, although he claimed he would be nothing more than a burden, Alin Yan – were seated on plain wooden chairs surrounding him. The new pyramid was assembled with four of the five seated providing the stabilisation between Rick and the millions of minds that propped up the structure. Everyone on the planet aged twelve years or greater was incorporated – about four million in total. Rick let his mind wander over it all, marvelling at how solid it felt but knowing that it could fall apart in a moment should any of the top echelon falter.

Parts of the structure were constantly at work trying to reduce the effects of the earthquakes on this world, while others were doing their utmost to determine best how to allow the worlds to slide together with the least amount of damage. The energy that Rick and Krista drew from the source allowed them to see those other worlds as clear as the one upon which they resided. However, it made them all aware of how the ground on each world was grumbling in defiance of what it was being put through. Rick could see even deeper, at how the magma swirled and churned in the depths, fighting against the growing influence of the other worlds.

"Alignment in five minutes," Krista said. She'd again reluctantly agreed to drag the energy in from the source. This time, though, Rick was also doing the same, in addition to relaying it back down the pyramid via the other four.

"Iceland is breaking up," Mila whispered.

Rick nodded, its remnants had already been driven under the sea on 'two' and 'four'. Much was going to have to be sacrificed. Yellowstone, which had also blown itself skywards on 'four' and 'five', was about to erupt on 'two'. It was still being kept stable here on 'one', though for how long it would remain so was anyone's guess.

Outside, several storms were throwing their weight around. A thunderous noise followed by several loud thumps, each of which shook the hut, caused Yan to slip from his chair. Thankfully, none of the others let their concentration lapse.

"That was the Tree coming down," Rick shouted, though he was certain the others were already aware of its fate. The earth beneath their feet was shuddering in waves.

Yan picked himself up, righted the chair and sat back down with a grunt. His link to the pyramid hardly wobbled. The man was far more able than he gave himself credit for, Rick thought.

"Four minutes," Krista announced over the rumbling, and Rick's mind opened a memory that encompassed a similar event nearly twenty one years previously. It was not his own thought, but had slipped in from one of the others – Charles Moore. Had he sent it deliberately? It was barely more than a shadow of a memory, a secondhand scene, having passed through and, no doubt, been distorted by Moore and at least one other mind. But it was enough, and Rick witnessed for the first time Morton Fisk's personal experience of the splintering. He saw how Fisk had pulled his disparate parts together to find himself alone in a hut beside a Scottish loch, and how he had come to rescue a million people. The man he, Long and Ellie had allowed to die and dumped in a pond on Hampstead Heath had saved a world, and possibly all five, if they made it through today. Rick knew he had big shoes to fill. He was certain now that Moore had sent it deliberately.

"San Andreas fault has collapsed in its entirety," Alec Garter said as well as projecting mentally. "Yellowstone is holding but much of California is lost."

Rick knew it wouldn't be the only casualty.

"Three," Krista sent wordlessly. The shaking of the ground was becoming continuous and the background noise hurt the ears. Around the globe the pyramid pulsed with resolve, and that resolve was holding together chunks of all five worlds that would otherwise have been torn asunder.

A contingent of adepts spread across Australia, South America and India assigned to the task of meshing worlds four and five together, had already achieved that result two full minutes ahead of schedule. They had done it with few casualties – though 'few' in this case meant several hundred had died or had been so mentally damaged that, should they survive this, they would need care for the rest of their lives. The alternative, Rick knew, was no one surviving.

He tried to view the combined result of 'four' and 'five' remotely but couldn't afford to let his attention slip from this world for more than a second or two. What he did glimpse was chaos, where two versions of Hyde Park had been welded together – 'pretty messy' didn't come anywhere close to describing it. As expected, most trees were down, as were many of the buildings that surrounded the park. But it was Marble Arch that illustrated in miniature the scale of the problem they were trying to control. Despite the lack of light, Rick could see that a gate from one world was buried in the column from the other. One corner, obviously from 'five' had melted, but it lay slumped against the cracked but still upright equivalent from 'four'. What would it look like once it was combined with the versions from worlds 'one' and 'two', along with the cinders from 'three'?

Rick's attention was dragged back by Krista pushing the two minute warning around their heads. She continued to channel the flow of energy from the source. Several of the adepts originally from the Tree, now located around the perimeter of the park, formed a layer whose sole responsibility was to keep the ground stable underneath the hut. As the vibrations intensified, Rick wondered how much worse it would have been without their protection. He sensed unnatural waves thunder up and down the Thames, wrecking anything that got in their way. Further around the eastern coast, abandoned towns such as Felixstowe, Lowestoft and Great Yarmouth bore the full brunt of a North Sea that was far more destructive than any human eye had previously witnessed.

World 'three' was now starting to combine with 'four/five' courtesy of the adepts of the South American continent. Experiences passed on from the first accelerated meshing meant that casualties were lower this time around, though many still died as the energy they were channelling overcame them. Accelerating the meshing of worlds 'three', 'four' and 'five' whilst delaying the others had been part of Rick's plan. Preserving this world from recombination for a few scant seconds meant it only had one or two worlds to mesh with instead of four simultaneously.

This was how they hoped to survive the event.

One minute.

The intensity of the ground movement jumped by a magnitude and Rick dropped to the floor unable to hold his balance. Both Alin Yan and Alec Garter did the same. Their chairs rocked away across the hut. Alin held out a hand and Garter gripped it with his own. Mila, Charles and Krista abandoned their chairs and joined them to close the circle around Rick. He reached out with both hands and held onto Mila on one side and Krista on the other. In front of him Alin Yan and Alec Garter, their differences finally forgotten, perhaps, gripped each other. Behind him he could sense Charles Moore, still an island of tired calm, despite the chaos that surrounded them.

Rick increased the flow of energy from the source to prop up the local adepts but he could sense that a number of them were no longer present. He added his own efforts to theirs, whilst still controlling the flow of energy.

"Don't spread yourself too thinly," came a warning thought from Mila.

"Don't waste time and energy on non-essential communications," came his rebuke.

But the local adepts weren't the only ones with problems. Rick sensed Krista beginning to flag, so he diverted more of the flow of source energy away from her to himself, hoping Mila wouldn't notice. As he did so, the ground beneath them began to liquefy and, using telekinesis, he raised them all up off it to avoid sinking. The walls of the hut juddered and a window shattered. Howling wind and rain joined forces with the rumbling, and Rick tried to enclose them all in a protective bubble. It kept out most of the higher pitched noise but the growl and screaming of the Earth was beyond his ability to exclude.

"You are taking on too much," Mila injected into his head.

"It's necessary. I can't relent now."

"You're burning up. Let me take on more – I can cope," she said, but they both knew that to be a lie.

Thirty seconds.

Garter started to slip out of sequence, so Rick wrapped him further inside the bubble and took over aspects of Garter's role. He diverted the source energy down through the pyramid to the tranche of adepts who were fighting to keep the Pacific tectonics under control. Across the planet, Yellowstone fought for its freedom and finally won, taking with it many of the North American contingent of adepts. Back in Hyde Park the hut shattered and Rick was forced to intensify the bubble's shield as the remnants of the hut's walls battered them momentarily before being whipped away into the night.

Fifteen seconds.

World 'two' crunched into the combined remains of the others and Rick fought to keep as much of this world intact as possible as it started to merge.

"Rick," someone shouted. "Spread it around. You can't do it alone!"

He screwed his eyes shut as he fought to keep the worlds stable.

Ten seconds.

He dragged more energy from the source and flung it in all directions down through the pyramid hoping those below could make the best use of it.

Six seconds.

He fought to suppress the worst of the Yellowstone volcano, though the combined influence from the others was more than he could handle.

Four seconds.

He drank more energy and erected a cap across Yellowstone, to limit its destructiveness and sought to extend that cap to the other remaining world.

Three seconds.

Surely, it would be finished soon. He really couldn't keep this up for much longer.

Two seconds.

Then, the worlds shivered, unsplintered and became one as, inevitably, there were no more seconds left.

24.10: The Magic Goes Away

The World: 25 May 2177

There was an intense light in front of Mila, she could see it even though her eyes were clamped tightly shut. She was also screaming – she couldn't help it. The energy poured through her, burning in a way that echoed how it had been when Rick had violated her.

Then it stopped. She opened her eyes. Where was Rick? She looked across to Krista, who was screaming and lit up like a beacon. Her light was infectious. It flashed around her, engulfing Charles Moore to one side and then Alec Garter on the other.

Mila broke the circle as did Yan and they fell backwards as the other three flared up. Mila tried to teleport to safety but nothing happened. She dragged herself away on hands and knees. Beside her Yan was doing the same.

The light behind intensified further and then flashed out leaving them in relative darkness. The ground still shook, wind whipped at her, rain drenched her, and then lightning cracked across the heavens accompanied immediately by thunder.

She felt something grab her ankle and was about to kick back at it when a lightning bolt revealed it to be Yan. She pulled him to her and they clung to each other, drenched in the downpour.

The smell of burning, the stink from 'three', permeated everything, even the rain. The lightning picked out the piecemeal world around them – deformed trees and collapsed buildings flashed across her vision with each bolt.

"Rick," Mila whimpered. There was no sign of him. There was also nothing remaining of Krista, Charles or Alec.

"Rick!" she screamed.

Only the grinding rumble of the ground and the howl of the wind replied.

"They're gone," Yan cried. "I saw Rick burn before Krista started."

"No, no, NO!"

She tried to locate any remnant of the pyramid, but there was nothing. She felt nothing outside of herself. Even Yan, clasped in her arms, was unreachable mentally.

"It's all gone," he shouted, his voice almost lost in the wild elements.

Mila howled like a wild animal.

24.11: Alone

Roosa Section, under Lussac crater: 25 May 2177

Ellie's heart was in her throat as her eyes darted from one screen to another. Twelve of them displaying multiple views of the Earth showed similar scenes: magma pouring through the mantle in countless places; Iceland replaced by boiling seas; Japan swamped to its core by tsunamis; the Philippines even more shattered with smaller islands lost and new ones erupting from the ocean floor; and California all but crushed under a North American plate whose unstable centre threatened to take the whole continent with it.

Though she was unaware of it, the views depicted were mostly artificial – rendered in real time from data derived from a number of artificial satellites orbiting the home planet. They were using infra-red, radar and other wavelengths to punch through the dust and debris in the atmosphere, which otherwise prevented direct viewing.

Nearby, Long and Jenny sat just as entranced. Long almost unrecognisable with his beard gone, and Jenny, clinging to his arm, mouth open wide and silent as she took it all in. Beyond them Jade and Jasmine both wore the same horrified expression as tears cascaded down their faces.

Janet Davidsen unconsciously dabbed at her eyes with the tissue. This is just too much like before, she thought. But, despite all the destruction, it was considerably less this time around. There were still recognisable continents under the clouds, on the small occasions they parted to give them a natural view. While most of the landmasses were affected there were still a few spots that showed through green. She prayed it would remain that way.

She gazed about the hall. Many of the so-called NewGen allocated to dwellings within Lussac crater had assembled here for the recombination event. Some she recognised immediately, such as Ellie, Long and Jenny as they had been amongst the first arrivals and on first-hand terms with the enigmatic Rick. However, they weren't the only ones, and long-term lunar citizens made up the majority of the audience. Most could have watched the same scenes on their personal screens, but few wanted to be alone when it happened. Bahira, seated near the back with partner Feroze, caught her eye and Janet's mind again leapt back twenty-one years. She nodded and flashed a brief smile back to them.

Her gaze then returned to Ellie. The girl, sitting slightly apart from her companions, had her focus fixed to the screens. She was only a couple of years younger than Melissa, but her face made her look ten years older. Janet wondered what the girl had gone through to have aged in that manner. She watched Ellie's mouth repeating the same movement over and over.

"Rick, Rick," Ellie whispered. "Rick."

Phil came across awkwardly, still unused to the one sixth normal gravity, and sat next to her. Putting an arm around her shoulders, he pulled her towards him and hugged her close, their tears mixing before slowly dripping to the floor. He felt numb, despite the tears, his emotions bottled up inside. Part of him wished he could let it out like Ellie, another part was glad he couldn't.

Phil vaguely became aware of heads turning towards the main entrance to the hall. Then his eyes alighted on Andrew March, who strode over to Janet Davidsen using that strange Moon-induced gait that Phil had yet to successfully replicate.

"Could be worse," Andrew whispered, handing Janet the electronic pad. "Could be a lot worse."

Janet rested her hand on her son-in-law's shoulder as she scanned the data on the pad. Finally, she nodded and made her way to a rostrum, acutely aware of the number of eyes that followed her. She was also conscious of the cameras that tracked her every movement and were primed to broadcast what she was about to say across the Moon and out to the colonies on Mars. The media had picked up on the fact that Rick had selected her, Andrew and Melissa to be the liaisons between the Moon and the NewGen. In their eyes her new-found status elevated her enough to make sure she wasn't going to escape the curse of their full scrutiny for a long time.

She tapped the microphone and opened her mouth. Then she closed it again before taking a deep breath. Finally, she spoke, slowly and methodically.

"It's been nearly three hours since full recombination. Much of it looks bad, but there are indications that it's beginning to settle down. A good proportion of the Saharan desert appears to have come from Black Earth, but that is the worst incursion, as far as we can tell. The Andes and Himalayas have large pockets where Black Earth predominates and, because of this, Everest and several others are around five percent lower than before. We're getting more accurate numbers by the minute but it's estimated that what can be detected through the clouds is predominately a combination of Paradise, Green and Robot. Given that these proportions are far better than random chance suggests that, um, Rick and those he was working with on Paradise – world one – have basically succeeded. We have no idea what they did or how they did it, but their influence appears to have prevented what could literally have been world shattering. So, although the Earth is damaged, it is intact and, so far, looks like it will remain so."

She stopped as murmurs erupted across the hall and gave them about thirty seconds to let the news sink in. Janet spent the time looking at the list on her pad. It was being updated in real time by her support team as new information came in. She frowned at one particular item which stated that the L-Squared patients, Emily Martin and Alice Nunn, had both passed away. Their registered times of death coincided with the recombination. She made a mental note to check on the rest of those who had been part of Melissa's synchronisation project.

Aware of the eyes still on her, she scanned the list again and picked out a few of the major items.

"Here, we have experienced a few minor Moon quakes. During the last couple of minutes of recombination, detectors showed an average increase of two hundred and fifty percent in surface thermal quake activity. There was also a four hundred percent increase in deep level reactions. Levels are now almost back to normal and, as far as it has been reported, none of this activity has resulted in any major physical damage, though it's toppled a few masts here and there. In other words, despite far too many speculative and non-scientific predictions, the recombination event has had minimal effect upon the Moon."

Janet looked directly into the camera for that last sentence. For the past few days the media had been full of alarmist stories of doom and destruction, ranging from the Moon being flung out of orbit and into the sun, to being sucked into an alternate dimension. She wondered where the advocates of such stupidity were now – probably brewing up their next batch.

"Regarding the shield that separated the multiple Earths from us – it is now gone. Or, at least, it can no longer be detected. If there is any shadow of it remaining, then it is probably of no consequence. None of our satellites are measuring any distortions or the filtering that was a feature when the shield was present."

"Has there been any contact from Paradise?" someone called out as Janet stopped to take a breath. She consulted the pad to see if anything had arrived in the past few minutes.

"As yet, there has been no message from the surface of the planet. Though the storms that you can still see from the unfiltered live view are starting to lessen in intensity, they continue to disrupt normal communication channels, and will probably do so for quite a while – days, weeks or possibly even longer. However, given what we now know about the lack of technology on Paradise, the absence of communication doesn't surprise us. While Robot World was originally awash with internal communications, the manner in which the composite Earth has been reassembled has most likely precluded any of that world's networks from remaining functional. Also, it is no longer Paradise, nor is it Black Earth, Green Earth, Robot World or Chaos. It is, once again, just Earth."

"When can we go back?" one of the NewGen said.

Janet sighed. Damn it, couldn't they see for themselves what their planet had become? Who in their right mind would want to visit that maelstrom?

"At the moment we can't tell how long it will be before it's possible to send a ship to land there. Ideally, we need working spaceports but anywhere stable that could take a landing will have to do as a first stage. Unfortunately, while a spaceport is unlikely to be available for years, finding a suitable alternative landing place isn't going to be practical. We need to wait until seismic activity has stabilised in any selected landing area and the atmosphere is clear enough to see where we're going."

Janet knew the latter wasn't exactly the truth. They did have reasonable facilities to attempt landings under obscured conditions. However, these were only performed where there was a ground crew ready and waiting, along with a map of the landing area accurate to a few centimetres. The current piecemeal state of the planet had rendered any maps from twenty-one years ago completely null and void.

Long and Jenny joined Phil and Ellie.

"I think the show's over," Long said, as he watched the locals exit the hall.

"So, what now?" Phil said. "This place is so unnatural. I can't get the hang of standing or walking, and as for sleeping…"

"I want to go home," Jade murmured to no one in particular. "But I don't think home's there any more."

"Rick," Ellie whispered.

25 Tears

25.1: Monotony

Roosa Section, the Moon: 30 May 2177

"Ellie," Rick shouted.

"Rick, where are you?"

Then Ellie's eyes opened and she groaned. Another damned dream.

She sat up too quickly and nearly bounced out of the bed.

"Damn this gravity," she moaned, and started to stand, hand outstretched to the wall for support. She felt slightly sick, and her hand immediately went to her belly. No one knew about the baby – she was still not wholly convinced it really existed.

Detecting motion, the room light came on, and the cramped box she was forced to call 'home' became illuminated. The clock displayed on MoonNet terminal said 07:43 local. At least they kept to a normal 24-hour clock, and it wasn't too far out from the one in London.

She dressed and went out into the corridor. All the doors along it looked the same, though names had been hastily scrawled on many of them alongside the numbers. Jenny's was next to hers, followed by Long, Matty, Holls and finally she stood before Phil's.

The door opened just as she was about to push the buzzer.

"Breakfast?" he said, yawning. She nodded, though she wasn't really in the mood for food.

She followed him up, down and around the underground warrens. He bobbed and weaved as he went, sometimes reaching out a hand to the wall to steady himself. She was hardly any more proficient, and the constant changes in direction made her feel dizzy. It was like trying to walk on the bottom of a swimming pool as well as being nothing like that at all. A lot of the time they spent trying not to crash into the locals who seemed to swim along effortlessly.

At least Phil had managed to get the hang of finding his way around the Roosa area of Lussac using his navpad, a device they'd all been issued with. She hadn't felt the motivation to explore.

They reached one of the larger rooms used for meals. She wasn't sure if it was the same one they had met the others in yesterday or not. Everything looked identical – the rooms, the corridors, the people – a uniform starkness of decor. She looked about the place – many of the NewGen were starting to blend in, mainly due to having been issued with clothing identical to that worn by the locals.

Spotting Jenny and Long, Phil led the way over to their table.

"How on Earth do they stand it?" she whispered, sitting down.

"What?" Long said.

"All this – this, oh I don't know. This – this lack of variation."

"Well, they don't stand it on Earth," Long replied, grinning. "It's the Moon."

"Shut up," Ellie snarled.

Long made a face, picked up the menu and pretended to read it.

Ellie was as annoyed with herself as much as with the others. They seemed to accept all this, maybe they were even enjoying it, despite the monotony.

"They say we may not get back to Earth for years," Jenny said.

"Who's 'they'?" Ellie snapped. "And what gives them the right to say that?"

Long sighed. "Ellie, 'they' are the ones providing a roof over our heads, letting us breathe their air, trying to help us adapt despite the reluctance of certain people."

Ellie glared at him, but he continued, "We're here because Rick brought us here, because he decided we were safer here. And, looking at that," he jabbed a thumb back over his shoulder at the wall screen showing a live feed of satellite views of the Earth, "proves he was right. You want to be back on that hell?"

Long locked his gaze on her. She returned it, hard and uncompromising.

"Hey, give her a break," Phil said.

"Sorry, Phil," Long sighed, "but she's been doing nothing but moping since, well, you know…"

"Since we last saw Rick," Phil finished.

"I'm not hungry," Ellie said, standing and starting towards the exit.

Phil got to his feet. "I'd better make sure she doesn't get lost. She hasn't even tried to use the navpad they gave her."

Long and Jenny glanced at each other and shrugged.

25.2: Can Do

London: 3 June 2177

"Mila!" Rick shouted.

"What? Where are you?"

Then Mila's eyes opened and she groaned. Another damned dream.

She stretched and dragged her body up into a sitting position. Her back ached but at least they'd found dry shelter for the night. They were, she estimated, somewhere in

Chelsea, just north of the river. She'd noticed names like Ralston Street and Ormonde Gate late the previous day but they meant nothing to her. Without a map of any sort and no ability to mentally scan her surroundings, she could only guess at their exact location. They might be close to the river, or still miles from it.

Across the room, and partly buried underneath another bundle of blankets, Alin Yan continued to snore. She forced herself to her feet and peered out a window. Merely cracked instead of shattered, it had managed to hold the elements at bay for ten days so far. It didn't look as if it would last much longer.

She sighed, wondering the same about herself and Alin. It seemed hopeless.

Outside, the day was grey with the endless downpour. She wished it would give over even for just a few minutes. Then again, the rain did its best to hide the state of the buildings around them. The low construction in which they'd spent a slightly more comfortable night had escaped the worst of the earthquakes.

Ten days, Mila thought. They had achieved so little in that time. Much of it had been spent cowering from the storms and scrabbling for anything edible. Would she ever eat a proper meal again? A hot bath had become a craving.

A distant rumble that wasn't thunder reminded her that the planet was still far from settled. She rubbed at her ankle – an unexpected tectonic jolt two days ago had caused her to fall and twist it.

She gently shook Alin's shoulder. He grunted and groaned, "Oh, leave me alone. Just another ten– twenty minutes… or years."

"We don't have any way of telling the time," she replied. "It might be as late as noon for all I know."

"Does it matter?"

Indeed, did anything they might do now matter in the long term? Mila had no answer to that. She bit her bottom lip, trying to stave off tears. Self-pitying fool, she chided herself. Crying was for the weak. When had she become so weak? Rick, she concluded – the cursed source of her hope and fragility and, possibly now, her doom.

Hunger and thirst eventually made them venture out. What little they had found to eat and drink over the past few days – mainly remnants of what had fallen from the Tree – had been used up the previous day. The rain couldn't be drunk. It had a bitter, sulphurous taste and boiling it was out of the question as they could find nothing with which to light a fire.

"I really need to drink something," Yan rasped. "Throat's like sandpaper. Do you think the Thames might be drinkable?"

Mila shrugged. Might be worth a try, she thought.

By the afternoon the rain had finally started to ease. Two days ago they had repurposed some clear plastic sheets to use as makeshift umbrellas. Mila slung hers over her head and ventured out.

"That way, I think," she said, pointing.

Alin Yan merely nodded and followed in her footsteps.

The road curved to the right and, to her surprise, brought them face to face with the river. However, despite the rain, the level of water in the Thames was ominously low. The river bed had risen in several places revealing small mountains of accumulated debris. The water that did remain danced sluggishly in muddy eddies around the blockages.

"Well," Alin said, "I think I will forego sampling that. It's thicker than the gravy you like to pour over your meat in this country."

"Oh hell, don't mention food," Mila muttered.

Downriver, a partially collapsed bridge hindered the water further. How much of the bridge had been from their version of Earth? Hadn't she heard that the bridges on world four had been removed by the AI system there?

She frowned. She didn't remember anyone telling her that. Where had that data come from? Her ability to suck information from almost anywhere had diminished over the years as the other powers had faded. Even after Rick's arrival and access to the source, she hadn't had a spare moment in which to test that aspect of her abilities. Ah, the source – that gave her an idea.

"I wonder how long it will be before we are down to hunting rats," Alin, still several yards behind her, said without humour.

Mila didn't reply but walked westwards – upriver – surely the point where the river originated would contain fresh water, wouldn't it? She had no idea how far away it might be. At least, there was a chance of finding the river's source.

If only that other source wasn't beyond her ability to sense.

They had to keep sheltering from blustery squalls that raged along the course of the river. It meant reaching the next bridge took them nearly an hour.

"Look, there's someone else here," Mila said to Alin as they approached.

The man was about a third of the way across the bridge, its once straight carriageway twisted and cracked. He stared out across the river, barely moving, hands gripping one of the vertical support cables as the rain lashed him. Going by his attire, he was one of the adepts originally from the Tree. It took them several minutes to reach him and, only once they stood right beside him, did he acknowledge them. Mila recognised him – he had been one of those who had responded to her call when

Rick had returned to snatch Ellie. She no longer had any idea of his name. Somehow she had always known their names in the past. Now, they were merely forgettable faces.

But Rick... now, there was someone she could never forget. Five days she had known him, one hundred and twenty hours during which he had turned her world upside down, in all senses. It couldn't even be described as the same world. It resembled a distorted picture constructed from mismatched pieces from multiple jigsaw puzzles. Pieces that had no hope of ever fitting together properly again.

I'm just another badly fitting jigsaw piece, she thought.

The adept stared at them, frowning.

"Are you okay, son?" Yan asked him.

The boy seemed perplexed as if the question he'd been asked was extremely complex. He was gaunt and filthy, one foot unclad.

"Nothing," he whispered. "Nothing. Why is there nothing? Nothing. Nothing."

They got little else out of him and, failing to coax him away, reluctantly left him. He had been the first live human they had encountered since recombination. Mila tried to banish the memories of the condition in which they'd found the others.

As darkness descended, the downpour became far heavier, so they sought shelter. A row of ancient terraced houses just off Lots Road had survived mostly intact. They were in the process of selecting one when Yan spotted a cabinet on the corner of the road near a junction.

"Never seen one of those before," Yan said.

They both inspected it. It's presence invigorated Yan, who had been morose for some time.

"Hmm, keypad, and some sort of grate. Looks a bit like an old computer terminal," he said, though Mila had no idea what he was talking about. "Ah, look, this panel opens."

"Is it safe?" Mila asked.

"No power. Dead as the proverbial dodo. Hold on, there's something inside."

He pulled out a can. A lever on one side opened it. The enticing smell of cooked meat hit them.

"Oh, what is it?" Mila said. "Lamb? Pork?"

"Pre-cooked," he said. He pinched a piece of the contents between forefinger and thumb and placed it in his mouth. "Hmm, tasty despite being cold. Mind you, anything is tasty after the past few days."

Mila took a sample and sniffed it.

"Safe to eat?"

Yan shrugged so she tasted it, and immediately pushed a larger chunk into her mouth. After swallowing she groaned in delight.

"There are several more cans inside," he said, rummaging further and passing three to her. Then, shaking one of the cans, added, "I think some are drinks."

"Oh wait, I know what all this is," Mila said. "This is from 'four' – where Rick came from." How did she know that? Rick had certainly never told her about these devices. But she had a memory of accessing such a roadside contraption and having it dispense food. Something made her stare at the back of her right hand.

"Identity implant," she murmured.

"What?"

"Nothing. Well, not exactly. I'm seeing a memory of something I've never experienced. Haven't been able to do that for years. I– I think it came from Rick."

"What, just now?"

She shook her head. "Maybe when he invaded my mind it wasn't a one-way process. Something got left behind."

"Is that all he left behind?"

Mila gave him a hard stare, then softened as she spotted that one of the houses along the side road had most of its windows still intact.

"That one," she said, pointing.

Yan looked at it and returned a grin in the fading light.

"That one, indeed," he said, sounding slightly more chipper.

They forced the door and clambered in out of the rain. In a back room whose windows were mostly intact, the furniture was merely disarrayed instead of wrecked. They sat in darkness and slowly ate their first proper meal in days.

25.3: The Dome

Roosa Section, the Moon: 6 June 2177

Ellie snapped awake yet again.

"Damn it, Rick," she sniffed. "Get out of my dreams if that's the only place you still exist. I can't go on like this."

She didn't know whether to hurl something at the wall or cry. She did neither but sat there trembling and feeling sick.

Two days ago, the others had persuaded her to see one of the local doctors. She had been connected up to some sort of medical device – like AI but a lot more stupid and limited. It had attempted to analyse her, asking idiot questions about the state of her relationship with her parents. It had also taken some blood and a urine sample but had failed to indicate whether or not she was pregnant. Finally, it decided she was depressed and issued some pills.

They hadn't helped her sleep, mainly because she'd thrown them away at the first opportunity. Rick kept appearing in her dreams and she would wake with every occurrence.

The clock said it was just gone two in the morning. She got up and pulled on a tunic – one of those strange, ill-fitting artificial things they'd been issued – and left her cubicle. The corridors were almost deserted and she wandered aimlessly for an hour. Several times she felt tired enough to head back but, having failed to bring her navpad, had no idea where she was. She could have asked one of the few people she passed but was in no mood for human contact of any sort. In a strange way, it felt good to be completely lost.

She came across an open lift door and entered. It was hardly big enough for more than three people. She hit the top button, too tired to notice a message in red next to it. Closing her eyes she enjoyed the sensation of slightly more weight as the lift rushed upwards.

When the doors opened she peered out. She was in a dome – the largest open area she had encountered here. There were several windows that looked out over a crater that was partially in darkness. She approached the nearest window and stared out across the grey expanse to the far crater wall. A vehicle with ridiculously large wheels made its way slowly and silently towards a gap in that wall, bouncing unnaturally as it went. Beyond the crater walls a light in the sky that was much brighter than the stars dropped towards the surface.

There was a noise behind her.

"Excuse me, miss. Bit late to be wandering around up here, isn't it?"

The man was old, with brown leathery skin and a mouth surrounded by white whiskers. He was attired in some sort of dressing gown that came down to his knees, leaving his lower legs bare apart from the slippers on his feet. He was tying the chord around his middle as if he had just got out of bed and put the gown on.

"Oh, sorry. I didn't know. Did I wake you up?" Ellie apologised, thinking that maybe Phil would look a bit like this when he got old.

"Yes," he said, accompanying the reply with a yawn, which made Ellie feel even more guilty. "My quarters are just one floor down. There's an alarm which pings when someone comes up here."

"Look. I'll just go back down if it's not allowed," she added, starting to make her way back to the lift.

"Ah, you walk a bit funny," he said, nodding. "You're one of them NewGen people from Robot World, aren't you?"

"Er, yes."

"Right. No, it's okay. You can stay – it's not as if I've actually got much else to do at the moment, other than sleep, of course," he chuckled.

His smile felt friendly enough, Ellie thought.

"So, must be a bit of a shock. All this," he said, waving an arm around at nothing in particular.

Her eyes followed his arm and then she said, "I'm Ellie."

"Oh, yes, I should have introduced myself first – excuse my manners. Dzingai, that's me – D, Z, I, N, G, A, I. Not the easiest name to spell, I know – you can blame my parents. So, what made you come here?"

"What, to the Moon?"

"No," he laughed. "I know why you're on the Moon. I meant up here to the observatory."

"Sorry, I couldn't sleep. Went for a walk and got a bit lost. Um, what's this, er, observatory observing then?"

"Well, why don't you come and see, young Ellie."

He led her to a seat and fitted the viewer over her eyes after demonstrating how it worked on his own face. She gasped as it wriggled to fit itself snugly against her skin.

"What do you want to look at? Mars, Jupiter, Saturn, the Earth? Some of the images will be relayed by satellite, of course, but the Earth will be a direct view unless you need a close up."

"The Earth," Ellie said.

"Thought it might be. At least there's only one of them now. I was here the first time we had more than one." He sighed. "I've been here a long, long time."

Ellie spent the best part of an hour mesmerised by the planet of her birth. After a short while, with Dzingai's help, she mastered the controls, and could zoom in and out, and skim across the Earth's surface almost at will. She didn't notice when the indicator in one corner changed from live to satellite view and back again. After a while she found London and zoomed in, switching to a different option when cloud cover obscured the direct view.

"Hyde Park," she said, as she located it. The details were fuzzy but she could see the wreckage where the Tree had collapsed, taking with it many of the buildings on the eastern edge of the park.

"I went there once when I came over to England. Merely a boy of twenty-three, I was then," Dzingai said.

"I'm twenty-one," Ellie said. "Is that young? I feel old. Worn out."

Dzingai nodded, even though he knew Ellie couldn't see him with the viewer clamped to her face. This girl, he thought, sounds like she holds the weight of the whole Earth on her shoulders.

"There is someone back there?" he asked.

"Yes," she said, adding, "well, probably not there anymore. Probably nowhere, now. Except in my head. Only in my head. Oh, Rick, where are you?"

"Ah, the boy who brought you all here."

"Y– Yes," Ellie sniffed.

"Much has been lost," he said, patting her arm. Then, watching how her shoulders no longer held the weight of the Earth but merely trembled, he removed the telescope eyepiece. He sat down beside her and, producing a clean tissue from a pack in his pocket, began to dab at her tears. She leant into him, resting her head on his shoulder and let her emotion flood out. He held her closely.

"Maybe I'd better go," she sniffed, much later. "I'm keeping you from your own bed."

"No, it's all right, young Ellie. Bed can wait. Sometimes, when I can't sleep, I come up here for a while myself. Just me and the telescopes. Even when there's daylight out there and the clock says it's night time."

He spent a few minutes trying to explain the Moon's rotational period and its relationship with Earth. He wasn't concerned whether or not she was taking it in, it was just something to say and it appeared to be putting her at ease.

After a while her eyes closed and, as she finally fell asleep, he inclined the seat back and found a blanket with which to cover her. It was still several hours before the official opening time – she'd be fine here for a while. As she slept he looked up her details to see where she was billeted and made arrangements for one of her friends to collect her.

"Ellie," Rick said.

But this time Ellie was too tired to wake up.

25.4: Burn

London: 7 June 2177

"Mila, wake up! Wake up!"

"Rick," she screamed. The noise of her own screech petered out as she realised where she was. "Oh, so sorry, Yan. Another nightmare."

"Damn it, Mila. That wasn't just a dream."

"What?"

"You were glowing. Hell, you were lit up like Garter and Krista just before they burnt up."

The expression on Mila's face was a mixture of shock and disbelief.

"Burning? Oh, but that was happening in the dream as well. It felt so real."

"That one definitely was."

"It was like being back at the recombination. I was trying to help Rick with the flow from the source. I couldn't give him enough and he slipped away."

"I thought you were going the same way." Yan placed a hand on Mila's forehead. "You don't feel hot."

"I was actually visibly glowing?"

Yan nodded. "Almost scared me to death," he said, and Mila could tell from his expression that it was the truth. Yan had been less scared at recombination than he appeared to be now.

"Maybe, somehow, I was connected to the source. It must still be there, mustn't it?"

"I– I really don't know any more," he said. "I can't feel it. But I never had the same connection to it you did."

"I want to find it again. I want to be able to do the things I could do before." Her voice darkened. "Maybe, if you hadn't woken me, I might have found a way to do that. Damn it, why didn't you leave me alone?" she screamed.

"What? How can you say that?"

"We need the source. I need the source."

"Even if it's no longer safe?"

"What's that got to do with it? Was attempting to control the recombination safe?"

"We didn't have a choice about that."

"We still don't have a choice – other than dying without making any attempt."

"I'm not sure I can agree with–"

"Hell, Alin, if I can't do this, what's the point of living? It's all I've ever done. You've got your electrics or electronics, or whatever you call them, to go back to. What have I got? I've been nothing for the past few days. All we've done since recombination is grub around in the remnants of a broken world, hoping things will get better. But they're not getting any better, are they? The rain is still coming down, there's no proper food or drink, unless we get lucky with another one of those food dispensers. And there's pretty much nobody else left alive. What the hell are we achieving? Nothing. Absolutely bloody fuck all!"

"Mila, you need patience. It–"

"No! Don't lecture me about patience. I've been patient for years. What good's it done me? Right now, we're just existing, drifting, delaying the end. I can't accept that fate. I won't accept that fate. I've had enough of this, of everything. And of your defeatist attitude!"

"Mila, stop!" Yan shouted. "You're glo—"

"Shut up, Alin," she countered. "You've let this get to you. It may have beaten you but I'm not going to… going to… what?"

Mila looked down at herself, finally seeing the way her hands were emitting light. Sparks flew from her fingers and she screamed.

"No!" Yan shouted, but he had to close his eyes and retreat from the heat emanating from her.

There was a flash which singed the remaining hair on his head. He cowered in the corner of the room. Then came the sound he was dreading – he'd heard it before during recombination when Rick had disappeared.

Whoomph!

It was nearly a full minute before he dared open his eyes. His shoulders heaved and trembled, and he could no longer hold back his tears.

He was alone.

25.5: Testing Times
Roosa Section, the Moon: 8 June 2177

Ellie emptied the contents of her stomach over the floor of her cubicle, missing the bed by inches.

"Fuck it," she said wiping her mouth on the back of her hand.

She'd learnt the new swear word only hours beforehand. After hearing a local use it she'd looked it up on the MoonNet to discover that it was centuries old. Not for the first time she cursed AI and its meddling. 'Dango' was meaningless – it had been something that one of London's NewGen had made up, but 'fuck' felt satisfying.

In addition, 'fuck' was probably the reason she was feeling sick. Looking up swear words wasn't the only use to which she'd put MoonNet – she'd initially put the sickness down to the lack of gravity but the medical information she had discovered suggested pregnancy could be another possibility.

She pulled several wipes from the dispenser in the bathroom and attempted to clean the room. The bathroom, little more than a cupboard off the main cubicle, seemed to have an endless supply of wipes. Hopefully, no one was counting how many she was using. She flushed them away and looked at herself in the mirror. The reflection showed a stranger: dark brooding eyes in a solemn face barely surrounded by hair chopped so savagely short.

What had happened to that pretty girl who used to look back at her? Would she ever return?

She had a shower and returned to searching MoonNet again. A few more minutes revealed something called a pregnancy test. History showed that it had been created nearly two centuries before. More of AI's meddling – just how much had it hidden from them? She ordered one and was told to pick it up from a local pharmacy. Her navpad immediately sprang to life and showed an interactive map on its surface giving directions.

So, finally found a use for this thing, she thought.

Three hours later she held the confirmation in her hand. It indicated a ninety-four percent chance of pregnancy.

Rick had been right all along. Now what was she to do?

She told no one.

25.6: Floating

?: 8 June 2177

Mila floated. Wake up, Mila, she thought to herself.

Had something just happened? Details were vague. Maybe whatever had happened had been long ago. She tried to think, but her thoughts were elusive, drifting from one random subject to another.

Burning?

No, she wasn't burning. Why would she think that? She was warm. A comfortable warmth, a just right warmth. A Goldilocks 'just right' warmth.

Was this another dream? But Rick pestered her in her dreams, and she knew that here, she was on her own.

Alone but calm. It felt good to be calm again.

Opening her eyes or closing them made no difference. What she could see was nothing more than a uniform hue – somewhere between yellow and red, but not quite orange.

Sleep, she thought.

The rest of her consciousness agreed.

"Sleep," she/they said, separately and in unison. "And prepare."

"Prepare for what?" she thought.

"Healing," the answer came.

"What healing?" she asked.
There was no answer but it didn't matter.
So she slept.

25.7: Self-Healing
LSA Control Centre: 9 June 2177

Data control centres across the Moon were franticly trying to correlate the information coming in. Underneath Lussac crater Andrew March racked his brain trying to make sense of it. He failed.

"You've really no idea?" Melissa said.

"None," he shrugged.

"The data's being analysed all over," Janet added, her voice failing to hide a tremor. "Looks like no one else has any more of a clue than we do."

"Is it dangerous?" Tariq Ghannam asked from across the room. Janet shrugged and spread her hands.

"It still says 'insufficient data'," Andrew replied. "All this stuff coming in and it can't tell us anything about what's going on down there, or how."

They stared at the live feeds. What had commenced on Earth three hours earlier was inexplicable. First, the tectonic reactions had dramatically quietened. Within fifteen minutes they had ceased. Completely. The glow where molten lava had poured from the crust was now dark. Closing in using satellite views they watched the flows solidifying and then crumbling as if years were passing within minutes.

The air around the planet, previously turbulent and unpredictable, calmed and cleared. Using cloud-penetrating frequencies had become almost unnecessary.

Soon, they spotted pinpricks of green that spread outwards.

"That growth is far in excess of what we observed on Paradise," Andrew said.

"Damn, stop it, you stupid planet," Melissa whispered. "We've had enough of your tricks."

The flow of data accelerated.

"Janet, can we allocate more space?" Andrew barked. "We're close to capacity."

"No," Janet shouted back. "We've already exceeded our quota – Central Systems are also refusing requests – looks like we're not the only ones low on storage. Hopefully, one of the other stations still has spare."

"Assuming the others are also collecting the same information, can we dump ours and continue afresh?" Melissa suggested.

"Risky," Andrew said. "There's no telling if we're all receiving exactly the same data."

"We might miss something important," she retorted.

"We might erase something equally as important," he replied.

"Rate of flow reducing," Dyani Metoxen said from her station. "It's dropping off, really plummeting down now."

"Ah, I think it's finished," Andrew said seconds later.

"Yes, the data dump is down to a trickle again," Janet announced. Then she had a thought. "Dyani, can you compare the current incoming data with readings from twenty-two years ago?"

"Digging them out now," Dyani said. A few minutes later she continued, "Adding the comparison to your desk now."

Janet looked at the figures appearing in front of her. "Damn, but this looks similar to the time before the asteroid." She looked back at the live view. "Not quite the same, though."

"What's happening, Mum? What's it doing?" Melissa asked.

"Fixing itself, I think. Don't ask me how. The whole damn planet is repairing itself."

"Looks like Rick or someone else down there must have survived recombination," Andrew muttered.

25.8: Home

Hampstead Heath: 27 June 2177

Ellie was one of the first to exit from the ship. Several of the NewGen personally known by Rick had been asked if they wanted to return as guides on the first ship. Long and Jenny had declined, but she and Phil, along with Jade and Jasmine, eagerly accepted so it was decided to set down in London.

At the bottom of the step she placed her foot onto the ground as if expecting it to swallow her whole. It didn't.

She knelt down placing her hands and then her forehead against the cool grass. She felt heavy again. Too heavy. After spending a month acclimatising to the Moon's gravity, she now had to reverse the process.

Not only that, but the change was making her feel sick. She swallowed, trying to overcome the urge to retch. Bloody morning sickness – but no one had yet figured it out, and she damned well wasn't going to tell them until she had to.

Phil sat down beside her and placed a hand on her shoulder. She looked into his eyes.

"We're really back," she said.

"Yes," he said, not knowing what else to say.

"Rick's not here," she said.

"Did you expect him to be?"

"No. After the dreams stopped, I gave up hoping. Oh, Phil…"

He held her close.

"It's changed a bit," she said a while later.

"Where exactly are we?"

"Hampstead Heath. Don't you recognise it?"

Phil shook his head.

"Over there, in those trees, that was where Long built his shack. Where he found the machine."

"Um, Ellie. Over there. Those bushes. Look."

Ellie gasped. Lying on its side, the machine was entangled in bindweed and brambles. It looked like it had been there for years.

A man in a robe was walking towards them. He was vaguely familiar.

"Alin Yan," Ellie gasped. "Is it really you?"

"Indeed, though not quite as much of me as there once was. It wasn't exactly my idea to go on a diet, you know," he chuckled. He patted a stomach that, while it had shrunk several belt notches since the last time they had met, was still quite rounded.

"Phil, this is Alin, he was part of the Tree, probably the only friendly one," Ellie explained, to which Yan waved a hand dismissively. "Are the others okay? Mila, Krista and, oh, I can't remember their names any more."

Alin Yan's face dropped. "No, none. I have the misfortune of being, as far as I can tell, the only one from the Tree to survive."

"Not even Mila?"

Yan shook his head and looked away. He swallowed before continuing, in a whisper, "I saw her go. It wasn't… good. No, it… it definitely wasn't good." He wiped a tear from his eye and then forced a smile back onto his face.

"How did Rick…?"

"He saved us but it was too much for him. Sorry, there was nothing… He was already gone."

Feeling Ellie tremble, Phil hugged her close. "But you put the planet back together again. That was you, wasn't it?" Phil said.

"Me? No. That was scary and, I assure you, it had nothing to do with me. I must admit I was hiding while all that was going on. At least the rain's finally stopped."

"How did you know we were coming?" Ellie asked.

Yan tipped his head to one side, and tapped his temple with a finger. "A compulsion," he said, with a puzzled look on his face. "No idea what it was or where it came from. I just felt I had to get here at this time. Just after the Earth fixed itself, it appeared in my head like a memory I'd always had."

"Just you?" Phil said.

"Yes, no one else felt it."

"There are still others then?" Ellie said as Jade and Jasmine joined them.

"Ah yes. I am extremely glad to report that I'm not the only one here. There is a small community a few miles north. Mostly farmers. They tolerate me, not that I am much more than a hindrance to them, I'm sure. But that AI system on your world certainly made a good job of growing things. Several acres of land from 'four' are here, along with bits of semi-intelligent farm machinery. I've managed to get a couple working, you know, the solar powered ones. Though they do seem to be a bit lost without having a higher intelligence to report back to. They mostly have to be coaxed into doing things but, do things, they eventually do," he chuckled.

"Can you still do all that, um, magic stuff?" Ellie asked.

Yan sighed. "A little is returning. A few days ago I even managed to teleport across a room. But it is hard. Many here regret the loss of most of their abilities, but we will manage. We have to."

Then he looked at Ellie's torso and said, "How's the baby?"

A look of shock passed across Ellie's face, the others looked confused.

"How do–?" Ellie gasped.

"Ah, that information came with the compulsion, as well," Yan said, his look of puzzlement intensifying. "I see it is also news to the others," he chuckled.

"Ellie?" Phil said.

"Rick's," she whispered. "Somehow, we made a baby. I'm sorry I didn't tell you. I still hardly believe it myself."

Then she burst into tears and wrapped her arms around Phil's shoulders.

Alin Yan looked into Phil's shocked eyes and winked.

26 One

26.1: Ellie

Cambridge: 21 January 2178

Phil wiped the sweat from Ellie's forehead after the baby finally forced itself into the world.

"Damn and fuck," Ellie gasped. "I didn't think the bloody thing would ever get itself out of me."

Outside the window the countryside was covered in a layer of snow, the rare winter sun glinting off the occasional house that had managed to survive recombination. Most of the land surrounding them had come from 'four' so, while they were outside the shattered remains of AI's Cambridge wall, the odd remnant of worlds 'one' and 'two' dotted the landscape. This place, which had been converted into a hospital, was one of those that had come through the ordeal relatively intact. At least Cambridge was manageable – the abandoned remains that had been London required far too much effort. It would be left for future generations to sort out.

The baby, in the hands of midwife Jacqueline, gurgled, coughed and then announced her arrival in the loudest manner possible. Jacqueline, from world 'one', inspected the child. As she did so, she explained each point to Jade, now learning the trade after her interest in medical matters had been rekindled. Finally, Jacqueline pronounced the newborn fit, healthy and female. She handed her to Jade, who cleaned her up and then wrapped her in a towel before placing her in Ellie's arms.

"Go on," Jade prompted, "let her drink."

Ellie looked scared, as if unable to understand what she had to do.

Phil kissed her hair and encouraged her to hold her daughter to her breast. Jade watched how Phil seemed to act far more fatherly to a baby he hadn't fathered than Ellie was motherly. The baby latched on and the screaming stopped.

"What are you going to call her?" Phil asked, as the baby took her first meal.

Ellie shook her head. Part of her wanted to name her after Rick, maybe as Rickie, but something about that didn't feel right. She didn't want the child to be a constant reminder of what she had lost.

Jacqueline arranged a larger towel around Ellie's shoulders, leaving a small opening at the front so that they could all see the child.

A few more people filed into the room, which was becoming crowded.

"Hey, sis, Matty, Holls," Jade said, greeting Jasmine with a hug. She placed a hand on Holls' stomach, saying, "You'll be next." Holls grinned while Matty in turn looked worried. "And you'll be a great father," Jade laughed, poking Matty in the chest with a finger.

"I've heard from Long and Jenny. They send their love," Jasmine said. "Jenny will be giving birth in a couple of months as well."

"I wonder if they'll ever decide to come back to Earth," Phil said.

Matty shook his head, "Not for a good while. Long's too involved in lecturing about our history now and Jenny won't risk her baby on a ship."

There was a popping sound in the corridor outside the room. Seconds later Alin Yan's smiling face peeped around the doorway.

"Is it okay to come in?" he asked.

"Alin, I thought you were still down south," Phil said.

"What, and miss this occasion? Ah, I see I am already too late and the child is born."

"You managed to teleport here?" Jacqueline asked.

"Several hops," Yan said, with a pained look across his face. "Very exhausting. But it's nice to know the old body and mind are still up to it."

"More than I can," Jacqueline tutted.

Alin Yan approached Ellie and peered down at the baby. "Oh, what a content little flower of beauty she is. And her name?"

Phil made a face and shrugged.

"Hmm. Names are important. She shouldn't go long without one," Yan said.

"Any ideas?" Phil asked.

"Yes," Ellie said. "Please suggest something, Alin. Nothing I've thought of seems quite right."

"Well, maybe Meiying, she should be," Yan continued. "It means what I said before – a beautiful flower."

All the others looked at Ellie.

And then, for the first time in a long while, Ellie broke into a proper smile.

Meiying. Yes, she liked that. She wasn't sure if it was completely right. But it felt appropriate. The child was the flower who had grown out of love. Despite AI's drugs, tricks and deviousness, she had beaten the odds.

She smiled again, and gazing down at the small red face suckling at her breast, it started to feel like an ending and a whole new beginning at the same time.

26.2: Mila

An unknown place and time

"So, I wasn't as alone as I thought, then," Mila said without speaking. "You put the idea in my head and used me as a conduit."

"Let's just say you were in the right place at the right time."

"Neither back on Earth nor fully here, you mean?"

"That's one way of putting it."

"Who are you, exactly, now? You feel like Krista speaking."

"Part of what was once Krista is here. As are Alec Garter, Charles Moore and thousands of others."

"Here? Where is here? Is it the source?"

"It is far beyond what you call the source. It will become clear once you join."

"Join? Join to what? Just what are you?"

"We are all around."

"Doesn't make sense. And Rick? Is he here, too?"

"Yes. It was his concern for the Earth that led to using you. It was your own concern and determination that finally linked you back to us and enabled a channel through which we could work."

"When I burned?"

"That enabled the initial connection. But you needed to rest, to build strength for the healing to come."

"Can I speak to Rick?"

"You are speaking to Rick."

"No, the Rick that was."

"Not in the way you still imagine, but you can speak to all of us in a much better way if that is what you desire."

"How?"

"Open up and observe. Here, we will guide you."

With help, Mila opened herself up and finally saw it. Her heart revelled.

Her reservations slipped away, and she joined to become one with all of them.

The End

I am indebted to Jan and Lars Lindberg for transforming my guesswork Swedish into something far more accurate, and to Christopher Atterton for inventing the 'new' swear words of scrott and dango!

Also by David Viner

Time Portals of Norwich

Cassie's life has never been simple. Orphaned at nine and raised by her grandfather, the past never left her alone. By the time she is seventeen she sees ghosts, hears disembodied voices, and events from history have a habit of rising up to haunt her.

On a visit to the Castle Mall shopping centre in Norwich, the past crashes on top of her. Cassie finds herself transported back to the early 1990s in the company of a woman she's never met. And the woman not only looks familiar but claims she's encountered Cassie many times before.

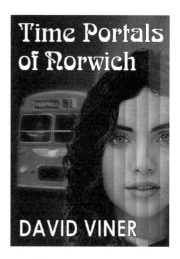

ISBN: 978-1-913873-02-8

Viva Djinn (Horde) Publishing – www.vivadjinn.com

The Redwell Writers Anthologies Volumes 1 and 2
(in association with Timbuktu Publishing)

ISBN: 978-0-956351-83-8   ISBN: 978-0-956351-86-9